Shadowman

By

Matthew F. Winn

Printed in the United States of America

Other Books by Matthew F. Winn

The Sandman
Bring Me a Dream
Circle of Friends
Every Picture Tells a Story
Stealing Rembrandt
Chasing Shadows in the Dark
The Legacy

Coming soon

Jack Kerouac Can Kiss My Ass
King of Hearts
Driven
Bokeh

Cover photography by the author
See more photographic works at www.splashofsunset.com
Published by Artist's Point Press

For

Angela and Maddie for their dedicated work in getting my head back on straight!

Preface

Port Oneida
1850's

Shadowman

Having spent several lifetimes wandering this earth there has been one constant that has remained true, life is complete and utter chaos from the first breath to the last. Every creature enters this world the same, ripped from the comfort of their mother's womb where they are immediately thrust into unrelenting chaos for the remainder of their lives. Existence is not about escaping that chaos, it is about adapting to the bedlam until we finally depart this world, hopefully on good terms.

To die is to escape this world's earthly manacles of pain, despair, and drudgery where we are rewarded for our obedience. In nearly every documented religion when a human's physical form expires, they move on to another realm where their afterlives are blessed with milk, honey, and other assorted remunerations. Mere mortals are promised an unseen kingdom bequeathed to us by our Gods in tomes forged of simple ink and parchment. These texts are filled with ancient legends and stories which have been passed from mouth to ear over a multitude of generations. Ah, but faith, faith is the key to unlocking those promises held within the bound pages. Promises which allow us passage through the pearly gates of Heaven, into the mead halls of Valhalla or on to the Happy Hunting Grounds. Sadly, faith is something I have extraordinarily little of.

I gazed across the expanse of forest that lay before me and stood resolute as if I were the only person on the planet. Like an insurmountable army the pines stood stalwart against the winds, majestically challenging the skies. I was quite possibly the first human to join their ranks. Sure, there had certainly been natives inhabiting this land at some point in history, but they were nomadic tribes that simply foraged and moved on. I would the first civilized man to call this place home. For many it was too desolate, too isolated, but for me that is precisely what made it perfect.

Even shrouded within this dense forest of pine I could hear Michi Gami calling out my name, beckoning me to her golden sands. It was such a contradiction for me, the water, especially the big expanse of this great lake. I was terrified of water, and yet, the beauty and serenity of her depths were like a comforting blanket.

I followed the sounds of the lake through the thick trees, stopping every so often to clear a trail by chopping down smaller trees and saplings and setting them aside for later use. I used my knife to fashion a toothpick from one of the saplings and dug a troublesome piece of meat from between my canine and first incisor. Raw meat is always so sinewy and hard to chew up completely but does provide a certain amount of nutrients not found in cooked meat. That was the last my raw meat, everything else was salted and dried which would sustain me through the winter.

Daylight shone down through the trees casting a heavenly glow upon the dew laden needles of pine. The tiny droplets sparkled like diamonds held up to a lantern's glow. This invading light told me I was nearing an opening in the trees that would lead to a meadow or possibly even the beach. The sounds of the water reaching my ears was no longer a gentle lapping of the shore but a slapping of the sands with wetted hands. It would not be much longer before I ran out of timber land. I cleared a half dozen or so more saplings and broke free from the forest's grasp.

Clumps of dune grass undulated in the winds blowing up the sandy crag. A few dozen paces found me perched on a ledge of sand overlooking the coast. I stood on the ledge watching the intricate dance of the great waters. White caps rolled from as far away as my eye could see, crisscrossing the small bay.

Even though the trees had barely started their colorful process of ushering in winter, it was still apparent that the brutal season was fast approaching. I would need shelter much sooner than I would be able to build something sturdy and proper. All of the signs in nature predicted it would be a rough season indeed and I was destined to have to ride it out until the next spring. Squirrels were busy storing up nuts while black bears had all but abandoned any vegetarian semblance of their diet for pure meat. I ran across several deer carcasses as I was clear cutting the woods which sent me to my pack to check how many cartridges I had left for my Sharps rifle. Less than a dozen was all that remained. I would have to make my shots count that is for sure. Not that they would be of any use against the beast who was the principal danger to my existence.

I spent the better part of that first week after escaping Toledo cutting saplings and dragging them off to the side before moving deep into the forest where the thickest boughs resided. Using grape vines I found near the shore I fashioned a crude shovel to dig the pit I would need for shelter and also fashioned a crude travois to drag my dead horse and meager belongings into my new home. I had not known her for long and rode her much too hard. My mind drifted to an old friend from another life and I wondered what had ever happened to her. Not being a big fan of horsemeat, I hadn't decided whether or not to smoke the meat or just bury the critter.

I took a break from my labors and wedged myself comfortably between two mammoth pines and stared at the blue skies allowing my mind to drift away. After several moments I reached into my jacket pocket and pulled out a notebook fashioned from scrap parchments held together by waxed twine. I pulled out one of my prized pencils, all the way from London, England and honed the point with my knife. I started to put down my thoughts which were a jumbled mess as was the norm.

I was not certain if the order of events should be kept strictly in a chronological order, or in order of what I deemed most important. But I was most assured that if my story were to ever be told I would locked away as a lunatic or worse, end my days at the end of a hangman's rope dangling there alive, kicking and thrashing until the end of days for the amusement of the kingdom. And the tragedy of either outcome caused me to shudder to my marrow as I was learning day by incredulous day that one simply endured immortality, they did not live it.

Toledo Strip
1850's

Chapter One

"But I swear, I did not kill those little children. I did not, I swear it," Robert Marigold pleaded with the court, eyeing each juror with his face filled with remorse. Chills ran up his spine when all twelve faces stared back at him with contempt. They were not buying his line of poppycock no matter if it were the truth or not.

The prosecutor turned and smiled at the jury. He had already ascertained where their hearts and minds were, they could recognize a load of shite, especially when they were waist deep in it. He was a decent looking man, clean, broad shoulders with deep blue eyes and he knew how to use his looks with female jurors. He exuded a friendly warmth, yet still projected his anger and repulsion over the gruesome facts of this case. His emotions were purely genuine.

Robert Marigold, or Goldy as he was called in certain circles sat nervously in the polished maple witness box. His court appointed barrister had advised him not to speak, that it would achieve nothing but harm to his case. But Robert insisted on telling his side of the story. Trouble was that his side was merely his word against the facts of the case and there was no way to corroborate anything he related to the court which was quickly pointed out to the jury by the prosecuting attorney.

His face was not nearly as comely as his adversary's and he would never appeal to the ladies of the jury. He was a rugged man, latticed with scars on his face, hands and arms, badges of honor for a hardworking man. Surely there were at least a couple jurors sympathetic to the plight of the laborer who toiled the better part of his life away making an honest wage.

The scars he bore deep down were the ones the jury would never see, yet they were the ones that maybe one or two of the twelve might be sympathetic to. His throat tightened as the memory of his lost jewels pounded their way out of the darkness and into the light. He tried to stave them off with a crooked grin that came across as more of a snide sneer.

Even though he had bathed that morning his nervousness brought on a sweat which oiled his black hair until it fell in greasy, snake-like strands over his shoulders. His masculine scent rose up from his armpits, the astringent odor stinging his nose. He hoped the gentle breeze from an opened window did not send it in the juror's direction.

He scanned the jury box for a sympathetic face and did not spy a single one. He did, however, catch sight of a painful memory. Her long flowing ebony hair and deep chestnut eyes called to him from a place so far away from where he sat. Maybe when all this was over, he would be able to join her. Though he doubted they were destined for the same place.

"Mr. Marigold, you claim that you did not kill these children, and yet, their corpses were all found in your possession. Is that not the case?"

He glanced over at his attorney who sat with condescension painted on his face, shaking his head from side to side as if it were on a greased pivot.

"No, they were not technically in my possession at the time of my arrest," he claimed.

"So, are you calling the police liars? It says here in the report," he shook several sheaves of paper in front of the jury box, spittle formed at the corners of his mouth for emphasis. "Five mutilated corpses were found in a warehouse on Water Street where you were employed. They were found in a duffel bag with your name stenciled on it. Is that not the case?" the prosecutor asked.

"Yes."

"Yes, to which question, Mr. Marigold?"

"All of them."

"So, you admit these corpses were found in your duffel bag?"

"I have never denied that fact."

"Now that this truth has been authenticated, the police also found three more mutilated corpses of children in your living quarters across the Maumee in Mendota. Is that also true?"

"Yes, sir it is," Goldy responded while running a stubby finger over his thick, black eyebrow.

The prosecutor's tone betrayed the fact he was a little more than flustered by Marigold's testimony.

"And two more children's corpses were found at your mother's residence on Wabash above the canal. Is that also correct Mr. Marigold?"

"Yes, sir, that is also true."

"If all three of these facts are true Mr. Marigold, then why on God's green earth have you pled not guilty to these crimes? Or are you amusing yourself by wasting the court's time?"

"I can assure you, sir, that I am getting absolutely no amusement from this charade you call a court proceeding. I pled not guilty because I am not guilty of killing those children, merely possessing their corpses which is not the crime for which I was charged. You have no evidence that I committed murder because I did not commit such heinous acts. Therefore, I must insist you declare a mistrial and set me free at once," Marigold slammed his open hands on the burnished banister separating him from the magistrate while staring directly into the judge's eyes.

The courtroom exploded in chaos. Several townsmen bolted to their feet and approached the witness box, no doubt fathers of the deceased. Several bailiffs moved in to keep the peace.

"I will have order," the judge bellowed from the bench. "And you, sir, Mister Marigold. I and I alone decide whether there has been a mistrial. You will refrain from such outbursts or I will have you shackled and gagged. Do I make myself clear?"

Marigold decided this was neither the time nor the place for this battle and simply nodded in agreement. He eased back into his seat, wiped his sweaty brow with a dirty coverall sleeve and put a crooked grin on his face. He glanced at the weasel to his left who was shaking his head back and forth while making clicking noises with his tongue. That would be a murder Goldy was willing to go to prison for.

The prosecutor, William Breckenridge, adjusted his neck wear and went over his notes while dabbing his forehead with a cloth. He took several minutes to compose himself which lent an uncomfortable atmosphere to the courtroom. Murmurs started to circulate through the pews, but the judge quickly quashed them with a furrowed glance.

"On with it would you please, Mister Breckenridge."

"Yes, your Honor, I am sorry, I lost my place in the uproar. I believe I have found where I left off."

"Very well, proceed."

"Yes, thank you your Honor. Mister Marigold," he started, turning his attention back to the defendant. "So, we have established that in all three locations where the corpses were located were locations where you not only frequented but also resided, is that correct?"

"Yes."

"But you still claim you did not murder these children?"

"I did not harm nary a hair on any of their little heads."

"So, if I may be so bold, why did you have them in your possession?"

"Just came to be that way I suppose."

"Do you know who murdered these children?"

"I believe so. But I do not believe for one minute that they were murdered, not in the true sense of the word anyway."

"What is the name of the person who murdered these children and then gave you the bodies to hide?"

"Wouldn't matter if I told you his name and I weren't hiding no corpses."

"Who and where is this person whom you claim has murdered these children?" the prosecutor demanded.

"Don't know, he weren't no person, least not a person in the traditional sense. He might be sitting there right next to you and you would never know it if he didn't want you to," Marigold sneered.

This line of questioning, more deliberately, the responses to the questions had Breckenridge flustered once more. He knew the witness was just running in circles and would not admit to the crimes. However, by the looks on the faces of several of the jurors he was doing a surprisingly good job of instilling reasonable doubt. William needed to corral this killer into confessing to the crimes or risk a hung jury.

"Do you not see the absurdity in your own answers, sir?"

"Of course I do, it was quite the absurd situation. And still is, I might add," he said, flashing his best smile for the jury and waving to an empty seat at the prosecutor's table which drew a stifled chuckle from more than one of the members.

"So, you still declare that you did not murder these poor children."

"No, sir. Like I said, I harmed nary a hair on the littles ones' heads."

"And you weren't hiding the bodies for someone?"

"No, sir. If I were hiding them you would not have found them, at least not in my belongings or in my house. They would have been anchored to the river bottom somewhere on the Maumee."

"Then why on God's green earth, Mister Marigold, did you have possession of these children's' corpses?"

Robert "Goldy" Marigold paused for dramatic effect. He knew how the judge; the prosecutor and the jury were going to react to his response. He was already knee deep in the manure pile, he might as well dive in headfirst. The executioner was already measuring him for a length of rope no matter what the truth may be. He was ready to swing; it was his time. What little pleasures he had left on this earth, watching the womenfolk in the gallery swoon and faint would be one of them.

Goldy sneered and slowly turned to face the jury head on, "Because I was eatin' 'em." He burst into a round of raucous laughter for several long minutes before regaining his composure. He stared down the jury, many of whom he recognized as loyal customers of his soup cart, "And you have been eatin' 'em too."

Chapter Two

An intruding thought of Robert Marigold melded into the swirling mass of guilt roiling about in my gullet and I had to stop for a moment and take a long drink of water to settle my stomach. I struggled back to my feet and continued to dig even though my arms were leaden. Luckily, the soil of this place was mostly sand so digging was not as difficult as it would have been in hard packed earth. Subconsciously I had dug a pit deep enough so it would also serve nicely as my grave should things suddenly turn sour. Once the pit was dug, I began to tunnel into the sandy loam until I had shaped a very nice den for myself that would serve as both a wind break and to keep the snow off me.

I located my fire pit at the far edge of the cavern to discourage any curious predators and to keep the smoke out of my quarters while still being able to provide enough warmth to keep me from freezing to death. If that were even possible. I had only been in this place for less than a month and already the solitude was harder than I expected. I had been living amongst the shadows for the past decade, but I still had Goldy whenever I needed his company. It is one thing to not interact or converse with others but the absolute lack of any sounds of civilization reminded me just how truly alone I am. But this is how it must be. I have chosen this life over my only other option. I simply refused to kill again no matter the circumstances.

I knew my den still had much more work before it would be complete but for now, I needed a respite from my labors. It was nearing sunset and earlier in the day I had found a place overlooking the coast that should prove to be a fantastic view for sunsets. I gathered an armload of saplings I had already fashioned into torches using vines and pine tar. I did not relish walking back in the dark of night from this place I named Pyramid Point due to the sand dune formation overlooking the lake. It was at least an hour's walk so by the time I would make it back to my den it would be well past dark. The sapling torches would guide my way through the darkness should my reckoning skills be rusty, or the skies cloud up and obscure Orion's belt.

A gentle breeze blew through the pine tops casting an eerie whisper throughout the forest. Occasionally I would spook a creature who would then dart off in a panic not realizing that I was much more panicked than they were. Step by step I breathed in the air as if every breath were the last to fill my lungs.

At least with life there is some certainty of death. If you crush your skull or you pierce your heart you will surely leave this world and pass unto the next whatever that may be. If you managed to spend enough days upright until you were too feeble to even walk you had comfort in the knowledge that it would soon be over.

My life had become imbued with the mystery of the unknown. If I became too comfortable in my immortality and let my guard down, began to embrace what my life had become, would then something as preposterous as a simple butterfly flitting on the end of my nose prove to be my demise? Were all of my days already accounted for and the minute I used them up would I simply cease to exist? These are the things I pondered while stumbling through the darkening forest all alone with nothing but my own morbid thoughts to entertain me.

I was surrounded by critters, whitetail deer, opossums, porcupines, skunks, and raccoons, and not a single one was much of a conversationalist. Now the chipmunks and the little red squirrels on the other hand, they would talk a person's ear off if one would let them. Occasionally the wind would die out completely and the denizens of the woods would all take a break, it was then I swore I could hear her taunting chant echoing in my skull. A shiver ran up my spine. I would much rather run into an angry black bear than meet that child face to face ever again.

Shadowman, Shadowman,
When the sun comes up,
Your eyes won't shine,
When the sun goes down,
Your soul is mine!

Shadowman, Shadowman
You cannot run,
Nor can you hide,
For I am everywhere,
Even way down deep inside!

I shuddered at the thought and tried to block her wicked incantations from burrowing into my brain. The evil little creature who had bestowed this curse upon me. In an effort to shake her from my mind I let my thoughts drift back to Goldy and wondered what had become of him. He was never really a friend in the true sense of the word, merely an acquaintance who had gotten caught up in my tribulations. But I honestly did care about his well-being just the same.

Goldy was a jagged man who played the dunderhead rather well, though he harbored an intelligence he let very few bear witness to. Once tragedy touched him, he became much more jagged and a lot less in control. And though he never spoke it, I am certain as anything he harbors a great deal of resentment toward me because I was the cause of all his tribulations.

It was wrong of me to run out on poor Marigold like I did, but I was left with no other option. I cannot remember how many children there were, six, seven, or maybe even a dozen. I had already consumed and cleansed their souls which made me vulnerable and we had yet to properly inter the bodies. I sensed, the men coming long before they arrived and was able to steal away in the darkness. And though it was at Goldy's insistence, the guilt still gnawed at me daily. That was more than six months ago, and it was the last I saw of Robert Marigold. I did see that he was lucky enough to evade the constabulary, but he left some very damning evidence behind.

I was, I am, terrified of what is becoming of me, and even more terrified of being locked in a cell. Can you imagine that, because I have many times over? What would it mean for an immortal man to be locked in a prison cell? When the jailors all got old and time marched on eventually someone would notice that I was still the same, day after day, year after year, decade after decade, unchanged by the advancement of time. But is that what would truly happen?

Although more than a hundred years have passed, I am but a novice to these things. This was my first and only attempt at immortality. I had never been dead and yet undead until this malady I have been so rudely afflicted with. Maybe I will eventually start to rot away. Like a dog, but in reverse. Instead of one year equaling seven, maybe seven years equaled only one.

And those times when my thoughts drifted from the calamity of being trapped in a cell they ventured into even blacker territory. Because surely, I would be given the death penalty and not simply life behind bars. And if they swung me from a rope's end, what would happen? Would my neck simply break forcing me to live out all eternity with my head flipping and flopping around on a broken neck like a busted wagon wheel on its axle?

Would they be dissatisfied when I failed to succumb to the hangman's noose and then put me in front of a firing squad? Burn me at the stake when that did not work? And when my charred corpse continued to walk amongst them would they then guillotine me, my charred head rolling around in a wicker basket staring at the sky for all time? And what would become of my body, would it wander aimless, forever searching for my head? And the pain of it all, how much would I be able to endure without going mad. Or even more mad than I had already become. A man has far too much time to think when he lives in solitude.

I was once considered ruggedly handsome, now, just rugged. I have learned over time that while I do heal faster than most, even from catastrophic injuries, I do not effectively regenerate destroyed tissue. The nubbin that used to be my left thumb has been regenerating for more than fifty years now. And my right pinky I not much more than a bump after fifteen. My arm functions almost normally after having Goldy break and set it more than a dozen times, it still tingles a lot, but it functions. And there is nothing like having a musket ball drop out of your backside decades after being shot through the heart. Yes, I heal, I survive, but I ache all over.

Before I knew it, my legs had carried me through the forest and into the open field as my mind contemplated the darkest corners of my being. I spied a deer trail leading up to the dunes edge from where I stood, a golden sliver weaving, snake-like through the dune grass. Outside of the forest's protection the breeze was more noticeable. The sun was dipping and so was the temperature. It was a fair bit cooler, even trailing on the edge of cold now that I had moved into the open meadow. And again, my thoughts took a morbid turn as they tended to do. If I were dead, truly dead, why then did I feel the cold of winter and the heat of the sun and know the difference? Why do I fear the chill of winter? It cannot kill me as I have already learned.

As I crested the top of the pyramid of sand I gazed out across the open waters while trying to catch my breath which begged the question, why did I even need to breathe if I were truly dead? Why did my organs continue to function? My heart pumped blood, my lungs filled with oxygen and my liver produced bile. I have also learned that I cannot bleed to death. I cut myself deep across my femoral artery, a mishap cutting firewood. The blood flowed like a mountain stream until I passed out. I awoke an indeterminate amount of time later, the wound had begun to heal, and I was none the worse for wear.

It was hard to find solace in the beauty surrounding me in my current frame of mind. This happened to me from time to time, the melancholy, the self-loathing, it was all a part of being dead I supposed. The sun was giving a gentle kiss to the water as the horizon transitioned from blue to blazing orange. From where I stood high above the water I looked down on white winged gulls as they swooped across the sky. I reveled as one folded its wings tight to its body turning itself into a harpoon and launched straight downward into the blue waters. A few moments later it reappeared, bobbing effortlessly on the surface while snacking on a scaled morsel. Cicadas and crickets serenaded me as I sat in the cool sands trying to forget my dilemma for just the briefest pause. The wind sang to me as well, not a song of hope but a song of despair.

Shadowman, Shadowman
Why do you cry?
Shadowman, Shadowman,
When will you die?
Shadowman, Shadowman,
You will never be free,
Shadowman, Shadowman,
You should not have played with me.

I shuddered and pulled my jacket tight around my neck. It had to be my imagination playing tricks on me, there was no way she could have found me here in this desolation. But the trick is on her, I came here, to this deserted place for a specific reason. Maybe I cannot die, but I will surely no longer satiate her hunger no matter the agony it will bestow upon me.

Chapter Three

Robert Marigold rolled over in his sleep and bolted upright, suddenly wide awake. He cringed at the excruciating pain stabbing at his innards. His sweet dreams of pretty girls and shiny baubles dissipated like smoke on the wind. He was still in jail, chained to the cold stone wall. His ribs, face, internal organs, they all ached from the last beating and the beating before that. He had deduced that eating children was frowned upon in these parts. He smiled and gave a soft chuckle which immediately wracked his body with pain and his brain with regret.

"Things could be worse, eh Goldy?" he commented to the darkness.

He pulled himself up to where the window of his cell overlooked the Maumee River. The bastards had boarded up the window so that only tiny slivers of light crept into his concrete cubicle. He drank of what little sunlight bathed his lips as he sucked at the fresh air through cracks in the boards. The dank, stale air of his dungeon was choking the life out of him. His memory was not serving him well and he was unsure of what day it was or even how long he had been down in this dungeon. He cursed the Shadowman and then quickly recanted. His dilemma was not the Shadowman's fault, it was but his own. How far he had fallen in such a short amount of time.

Robert tried to remember the end of his trial. Had he been found guilty? Had he been sentenced? These things he did not know. He did remember the beatings though. A man, most likely a grieving father, broke through a gauntlet of police and tackled him shackles and all. On the ground a few of the police officers decided to get a few licks in while attempting to subdue the aggressor. Billy clubs, fists and boots all found their mark on his ribcage and head. He remembered smiling up at them with a sneer foamed with blood just as the police chief put an end to the fracas. One thing was for certain, Robert Marigold was certainly destined for the history books. *Feral Cannibal's reign of terror has come to an end,* the headlines had read.

Several minutes after regaining consciousness Goldy's eyes adjusted to the darkness of his cell and he caught notice of a tray of food slid under a slit in the bottom of his iron door. Food was using the term very loosely. A half pint of water, a small loaf of unleavened bread and two pieces of dried meat, no doubt horse or jackass from the taste. His jaw and teeth were still too sore to chew so he tore apart the bread and dipped it into the water and let it dissolve in his mouth. The taste was so horrendous he felt the baker should be in the cell next to him. He laughed until he coughed up a mouthful of bloody phlegm and spat it in the corner.

The golden shafts of light creeping in between the boarded-up window were getting darker by the minute and his tomb grew colder by the same rate. Night was coming soon. Was this his first night in this cell? Or only his first night being aware of it? He heard footfalls in the corridor outside of his cell but could not see any shadows moving about through the slat in the solid iron door.

"Shadowman, might that be you? Here to rescue me?" he called out to the darkness. "Let me get a peek of your hideous mug."

He strained his ears against the silence but did not hear the disturbance again. His mind was playing tricks on him as the darkness wove a cocoon around him while shadows danced across the black surface of the stone walls.

Moldy Goldy,
Alone in a cell,
Moldy Goldy,
Is going to hell.

"Who's there," he cried out, snapping back awake after nodding off briefly.

Once again there was nothing but pure silence and looming darkness. Struggling through the pain he pulled himself up to the boarded-up window. A miniscule flicker of yellow light crossed his path and then disappeared. A distance coach, too far away to even hear the horse's clip-clop on the cobblestone. He felt more alone than he had ever felt in his life, and yet, so afraid that he was not truly alone.

Moldy Goldy,
Have no fear.
Moldy Goldy,
You will not die in here.

"Who is out there," Robert called out. The voice was louder this time. Closer. But he also thought it might have been coming from inside of his own head. "Damn, Goldy, you've only been in this place for a short time and you're already a stark raving lunatic."

He pulled the little scrap of blanket he had been given up around his neck and huddled into the cold, damp corner. His mind was playing tricks on him, which is all this was. Maybe he had suffered some brain damage in the melee.

He recalled the Shadowman and how they had come to be what he considered to be friends. It was a symbiotic relationship, Shadowman made the messes and he cleaned them up. Although, he didn't clean them up in the manner in which it was described to him. No, times were tough, and food was scarce. His back had seen many a better day and hard labor was not anything he could perform any longer. He was much too ignorant for a thinking man's job, or so he chose to accept. Sure, he wasn't moron stupid, but numbers and letters just seemed to get away from him at times. Truth be told, he was lazy, mentally, not physically. After losing the only things he held dear life was more of a chore than a blessing.

He harkened back to his first taste of human flesh and how it repulsed him so. A chunk of arm flesh skewered in the fire to medium rare. He barely swallowed two bites before he was regurgitating into the mop bucket. He put the idea away for a few days but then the hunger began to gnaw at him again, so he tried a steak cut from the thigh cooked to well done with a nice char on the outside. Goldy was able to choke down three bites before nausea overwhelmed him. He knew that it could not be the meat itself, but the thought of consuming human flesh that sickened him.

Several more days passed, and he had sustained himself on a few rotten potatoes and apples picked up by gleaning nearby fields and orchards. While not appetizing to the eye, they sustained his life for another pitiful day. What an existence he had been forced to bear. Dragging himself through the streets and back alleys in the wee hours between dusk and dawn away from any other living soul.

On the third attempt to dine on the flesh of innocent's he gathered his half rotten produce, onion, potatoes, carrots, and some dried beans. He then cubed up the tender cheeks of a cherubic little boy of about six years old. He sautéed the flesh with some lard he had managed to scrape off a spatula at the local inn when the cook was distracted. He added some garlic he had squirreled away with the onion and found himself wishing he had some mushrooms. The aroma was a bit sourer than he would have liked, probably due to the body being several days old. After everything was rendered, he rid the pan of the tallow, added some water and the vegetables, and brought it to a boil before simmering for another hour. The entire time his stomach protested in anger.

He dipped a wooden spoon into the roiling pot, let it fill with broth and blew the steam from the surface until cool enough to taste. *Not bad. Needs salt.* He grabbed a chunk of salt from a shelf and whacked a few pieces off with his knife. He stirred the pot for a minute or two and then tasted the mixture again. *Perfect.*

This bowl of stew hit the spot and stayed there. No more cramps, nausea, or vomiting. And the psychological aspect was no longer haunting him. This was just simply stew and nothing more. But Robert Marigold didn't notice something at first, he craved more as soon as his bowl was empty even though his stomach was full. He ate another bowl even though he knew he didn't have the room. Even after that serving, he still wanted more but his stomach was so tight not even a drop of water would fit. He sniffed at the concoction and salivated before shoving his bowl away from himself.

That was the first night he had slept well in such a very long time. And when he awakened, his back felt better, not good, but well enough to walk without so much of a limp. However, by the end of that day, he was exhausted and in severe pain once again. That night he made some more stew, this time with bigger chunks of flesh. And once again, the morning brought him better spirits.

Robert Marigold was ecstatic over this new development. No longer did he have to toil under the moonless sky until his back was so tender it brought tears to his eyes just to breathe. All he had to do was consume the flesh the Shadowman had left behind, take the bones to the grist mill and feed the innards to the pigs with the bone meal and there would be no evidence to implicate him.

But then the Shadowman stopped coming and all the meat went rancid leaving Goldy broken, flat broke and hungry again. Was then that he remembered the orphanage across the river. No one would miss an orphan, or two, would they? A haunting voice ripped him back from his reverie and back into the world of pain. He knew that the Shadowman would never approve of his murdering children, there was reason for what he did, a divine calling. He did not murder children, he rescued them.

"My God, what have I done?" Goldy cried out in the darkness.

Moldy Goldy,
How on earth will you eat?
Moldy Goldy,
No more little, tiny feet.
Moldy Goldy,
How on earth will you sleep?
Moldy Goldy,
With so many secrets to keep.

Tiny shadows danced in the torchlight beneath his prison door. Two little bare feet reflected off the damp stone. She was there. She had found him. No longer did he fear the unknown because no matter what the warden or jailer did to him it would be humane compared to what her plans for him were. He hunkered into the corner and closed his eyes as tightly as he could. He could hear her humming her wicked little rhymes. He slowly opened one eye and strained at the darkness. She was lying flat on her belly peering under the cell door. Robert Marigold wet himself the moment their eyes met.

Chapter Four

Dawn brought a frosty chill to the air; autumn was not far off. I drug myself out of my sandy cave and stretched my aching muscles to the rising sun. I breathed out heavily, spewing a plume of vapor into the air. Definitely getting closer to autumn. The carpet of pine needles was covered with a cold dew, so I kicked the layers around, turning them over. I was not ready for my boots yet this morning as my feet were still tender from yesterday's hiking.

Shafts of sunlight beamed through the trees in a golden starburst. I looked at the flesh on my arm, I had grown even paler from the shorter sunlit hours and lack of nutrition. But that was the plan was it not? To see just how long it would take. I scratched another notch in a large oak that served as the marker to my underground dwelling. I had only been in this place for ten days so far, but it seemed like a lifetime ago that I was holed up in a back room in the Toledo strip. Once again, I thought of Robert Marigold and how I had abandoned him like I had done everyone else who had been unfortunate enough to make my acquaintance. He wasn't a bad man, at least not until he met me.

I lit a small fire, just enough to warm up some wash water and then make coffee. I was gathering up twigs, sticks and pine needles for kindling when I saw them, and my heart stopped. Small footprints in the frost covering the forest floor. She had been here during the night. She had found me.

Get a grip on yourself man, it was just an animal. What kind of animal walks through the forest on two legs?

I felt an unbridled fear creeping back into my very soul. How could she have possibly found me out here in this utter desolation so quickly? I did not see any evidence of a companion which was odd. How would she have gotten here; she was but a mere child? Ah, but she was so much more than that and I knew it. Still, after seeing what she was capable of I continued to make excuses and try to reason with the illogical. What she was, who she was, it was not possible, and yet it was my reality. I heard the sizzle of my coffee hitting the coals and took the pot off the fire. I reached into my spice bag, pulled out a precious cinnamon stick and put it into the bottom of my tin cup. I then used and old cheese cloth to strain the coffee into the tin cup where the aroma tantalized me as it whispered up to my nose.

Shadowman, Shadowman,
Why do you run?
Shadowman, Shadowman,
Are you not having fun?

I shivered as the chant echoed in my brain. It was nothing audible, but it resonated inside of my head just the same. Was this my own mind playing tricks on me or had she burrowed her way into my brain like a parasitic worm? *No, I am not having fun,* I barked at the phantom voice. And then the irony hit me, and I laughed out loud.

One time in my miserable life, many decades, maybe even centuries ago, I was an evil man through and through. I committed every heinous act that the Bible and man himself decried. I had broken every commandment God had laid out. Theft, adultery, blasphemy, hell, even murder if need be. And then she came along, and my world grew ever darker.

Eventually my heart had become pure as it is now. Circumstances delivered me from evil, but not from her. I found myself with a conscience and was quite aware of what was right and what was wrong, something that had been as unfamiliar to me as a foreign language. And while I choose to do right, she defiantly fights against me, trying to corrupt me. Her hunger becomes my hunger, an insatiable hunger that will not be denied. For as long as I can remember I have done her bidding but no more. Not after the children.

I finished my coffee and went about my morning chore of cleaning up camp before returning to work on my underground haven. I continued to dig at the sand, burrowing deeper and further out away from the entrance. I had to stop quite often and drag a buck skin filled with loose sand back out of the hole. I had been spreading the sand around the forest but after this morning, I began dumping the sand just outside of the hole. I spread the sand around creating a lawn around my den entrance. What I was really creating was a detection device. Footprints left in the sand overnight would alert me to the critters who were visiting me as I slumbered. I would know soon enough if she were just in my head or if she had truly found me.

Chapter Five

Moldy Goldy,
Wake up sleepy head.
Moldy Goldy,
Someone might think you are dead.

Robert Marigold bolted upright from his slumber. Again, not knowing how long he had slept or even if it were day or night. This was cruel and inhumane punishment to leave him alone in this desolate place. It just weren't right. He noticed a new tray under the door and scampered to retrieve it. It must have been there a while; the coffee was nearly ice cold. He picked at the insides of the hard-crusted bread, put a piece of jerked meat in his mouth and savored each morsel as if it were a freshly grilled steak. His meal was too soon finished, and his stomach protested in earnest.

He sipped at the insipid liquid not certain he wanted to drink it. Being wide awake trapped in this cell alone would surely drive him to the brink of madness. The young girl's voice echoing in his head wasn't making things any easier. After a small taste he deduced that the coffee was so watered down that it surely didn't have very much caffeine, so he guzzled it down for the sake of the water alone.

How many days had he been in this dungeon? He had started using his shackles to scratch stick numbers in the rock surface but then he had slept so long he wasn't sure if one day had passed into the next. He gave up on the endeavor and decided it would be more torturous to know how many days had passed than not. It was the lack of human contact that was driving him mad. Sure, Goldy really hated people and was quite content spending his days alone. But that was on his terms, this was not. He ran his fingers over the scratches, eight as far as he could tell. At least eight days and nights in this hell hole without seeing the sun, feeling the wind, or hearing another voice other than those living inside his head.

Down in the darkness, Robert Marigold had no way of knowing what the dire truth of his situation was. If he had known, he surely wouldn't be calmly sleeping away his days and nights but would be clawing at the walls and floor until his fingers bled.

There was only one living soul who knew he was being housed in a section of the prison that had been deemed unsafe and was slotted for demolition because it had been built too close to the river and over the years flooding had eroded the base of the walls. It could collapse in on him with the next flood or he could be blown to smithereens along with the building. The only reason it had not been demolished was the lack of funding.

He also didn't know that the one lonely soul who made sure he was being fed was an eighty-seven-year-old prison trustee who happened to be an idiot with an IQ of less than fifty. He was a deaf mute with no one to tell of Goldy being down there in the tombs. Even if he did find a way to communicate, no one would have believed him. His name was Smith, not because that is what his parents named him but because the courts had. He had no way of communicating his name, so they gave him a simple one. A simple name for a simple man.

Smith may have been stupid, unable to communicate and unable to free himself from his own bonds, but he did know a man had to eat. He squirreled what he could from his own dinner and leftovers on trays when no one was looking. Before lights out he crept down to the tombs. He was also smart enough to know that the man behind the iron door had to be a very bad man or he would not have been put here so he kept his distance. He made sure the man never knew he was there.

Smith didn't like the little girl who followed him, she didn't belong there, and she looked at him funny.

There was one other living soul who knew Goldy was there, the man who put him there. The warden was convinced that Robert Marigold had starved to death by now and had all but forgotten all about locking him away in solitary confinement, alone in a wing all his own. Poor Robert had no wife, no kids, his mother, and his father were dead, there was no one looking for him. The only person who knew he even existed was the Shadowman, and he himself was long gone by now.

Distant thunder rumbled the ground beneath his feet and soon the patter of rain joined the symphony. Goldy didn't mind. At least the familiar sounds were a reminder that he was truly still alive and not trapped in an endless nightmare; trapped in purgatory for eternity. He drifted off to sleep because it was the only thing he could do.

Chapter Six

Smith tucked some dried meat, a handful of stale peanuts and half a loaf of peasant's bread inside of his clothes. He wasn't feeling very well so he decided to take the man his supper early so he could go back and lay down. He was shuffling along a dark, unused corridor when the little girl appeared in front of him. Although she smiled at him, he knew it wasn't a friendly smile because of her eyes. They were not the friendly, curious eyes of a child. They were wicked, all-knowing eyes that frightened Smith to the very depth of his bones.

Don't you want to play with me?

Smith paused for a moment and then shook his head. She hooked her delicate index finger and beckoned him forward. His smoky blue eyes hazed over with cataracts scanned the little girl up and down. She looked peculiar to him, alive but dead, but not like a ghost in the stories his brother would tell him as a child. He gave her a crooked smile and mimicked her beckoning gesture. Playing with the little girl couldn't possibly hurt anything could it?

She was a pretty girl dressed in a pretty yellow dress with ribbons and bows just like his sister's dolly. The one he ripped the head off by accident and got into trouble. He got the switch that day, and then the belt when his father got home. Out of natural human instinct he had fought back which angered his father, a big brutish man. He dragged Little Bastard, what Smith thought his real name was, out to the wood pile and beat him mercilessly with an ax handle all the while his little sister laughed and mocked him. That was the night he killed them all. He carried bales of straw into the house and put them all around the living room. Then he doused them all with kerosene, lit them on fire and went outside to watch the pretty flames.

He could hear their screams as the fire engulfed the house. He was still standing there with the kerosene can in his hand and his sister's headless doll at his feet when the sheriff arrived. The man had felt bad arresting Smith but as he said, he had no other choice. Besides, he might be better off in prison. And honestly, he was. No one beat him in prison.

You are not going to rip my head off too are you?

The little girl's voice echoed in his head, but her lips never moved. He furrowed his brow and took two steps closer. Fear ebbed over him as he realized she looked a lot like his little sister and was wearing the same dress as his sister's dolly. This confused Smith. Was this the ghost of his sister come back to haunt him from the grave?' If so, why did she wait so long?

Moses, do I really look like your sister?

He shook his head. Moses? Was that his real name? Yes, yes it was. He could remember the soft nightingale voice that used to sing him to sleep when he was just a young boy. He wasn't stupid then. Tears glistened his eyes as a long-repressed memory slid to the surface and his mother's face was as clear as it had ever been. He closed his eyes and he swore he could smell the sweet scent of his mother's lilac perfume as she held him close to her bosom, her long brown locks cascading down over his face.

She loved you didn't she Moses?

Suddenly he felt fearful once more. This little girl knew too many things about him. This was not natural, it wasn't right. And then a memory came flooding back to him and gripped his heart in an icy grasp. His father, drunk as usual, had come home early and caught the two of them playing together in the yard. This his father had strictly forbidden. They were not to leave the house when he was not home. His father commenced to beating his mother with a belt, something Moses had borne witness to time and time again. This was one time too many and he began clawing and hitting his father trying to get him to stop. The man grabbed his son and punched him in the side of his head as he would have a grown man. Moses fell to the earth in a lump of battered flesh, never to be the same again.

You failed her, Moses. You should have fought harder. It's your fault she is gone.

Tears streamed down his face as the memory of watching his mother being beaten to death right in front of him enveloped his very existence. His salty memories ran in rivulets into the valleys age had carved into his haggard face. Jagged lines formed from too many jagged years. The little girl was right, it was all his fault. He had not fought hard enough. He dropped to his knees and began sobbing.

Do not cry Moses, I can make it all better.

Fear still had an icy grip on him, but her voice was so soothing, so comforting he just wanted to melt into her. He paused, what an odd thought. For him to melt into her. And even odder yet, his thoughts were coherent, unscrambled. They were not the jumbled thoughts of a man whose brain had been damaged by an oafish thug when he was but a small child.

Moses Roses,
Your mommy misses you.
Moses Roses,
Is your love for me true?
Moses Roses,
Will you bloom for me?

Moses Roses,
As one we could be.

Every fiber of his being told him no, but Moses reached out his arms to the little girl. His chest still heaved with the pain of true sorrow. She was close enough to see now and although her face appeared happy and innocent, he suspected that was the furthest thing from the truth. Maybe it was just that prison life had taught him to trust no one. Her sweet, cherubic smile should have made him feel warm, but instead, he was like a blizzard inside. A chill set upon him that he could not shake. He was freezing from the inside out.

And then suddenly there was a warmth. An all-encompassing glow that surrounded his heart. The little girl in the yellow dress reached out and put her tiny hands on each of his cheeks and kissed him lightly on the forehead like his mother used to do. The sweet scent of lilacs permeated the air and suddenly he felt light, lighter than he had ever felt in his life. All his bad memories seemed to be erasing one by one, leaving only those golden moments he had been able to share with his mother. Memories he had forgotten, or more truthfully, had been beaten out of his brain, rushed in to fill the void the bad memories left behind. He felt warm, in a cocoon surrounded by warm water. Floating. He closed his eyes and hummed a lullaby from when he was an infant, and then it was his mother's voice he heard singing softly in his ear.

One by one the pleasant memories faded and the memories that remained grew bigger, more detailed and crisper. But as his memories faded, the little girl became more detailed as well. She was no longer a mere shadow, an anomaly on his brain, she was real. He could feel her touch. It was an angel's touch. Soft, gentle, full of love.

Moses's eyes bolted open. Blackness had suddenly seized his heart. He felt a pain in his chest, like a hand gripping his pumping organ and squeezing as hard as it could. His mother's melodic intonation had been replaced by his father's angry, frothy voice and the sick dull thud of his fist pounding against the side of his tiny skull. Crack. Crack. Crack. The delicate bones gave way with each blow. He looked into the little girl's eyes and realized that his father was not truly pure evil as he had once thought; she was.

Moses Roses,
You came out to play.
Moses Roses,
I will consume you this day.

Chapter Seven

I felt a peculiar sensation wash over me as morning caressed the earth. It was nothing tangible I could put my finger on, I just felt off. I lit a candle and gathered up my bedroll. I was surprised to see how much I had accomplished over the past several days. My den was shaping up very nicely and was so far back from the entrance now that morning's light did not reach me. But there was still much work to be done.

I dragged my bedroll out into the sun where it could air out from the musty air of the sandy cavern. Although I had dug my pit a dozen feet down or so, it was still not deep enough for my tastes. But now that the cavern was deep, it was also susceptible to cave-ins so it would require a good amount of structural support. As I cut and dragged small timbers to the area, I stopped to ponder whether or not I should have just built myself a small cabin. In honesty, that would have taken me months where this will take me but a few weeks. Not to mention, out of sight, out of mind.

Rejuvenated from a restful slumber I put coffee on to boil and began working on clearing the pit out a little more before shoring up what I had already constructed. I was dumping my third load of sand from the tunnel and spreading it as I had done the days before when I noticed them. Footprints. Tiny footprints in the sand.

I knelt to inspect the footprints more closely. They had to have been left quite recently as the top layer of dew dampened sand had been pulled away from the dryer sand beneath. Had she been standing there the entire time I was cocooned beneath the earth?

I sipped at my coffee while my mind drifted. How many people has this little girl tormented? Killed? No, I am the one responsible for the killing. I am the one who did her bidding, I am the one who has abandoned everyone I have ever considered a friend. It is I who has chosen to live the rest of my days in utter isolation. The good Lord has given me the gift of freewill and I have squandered it for the sake of my own ego.

If she is watching me, what is her motivation? Why has she not come to me in my dreams as she had done in the past? Is she toying with me like a cat does with a frightened little mouse? At what point will she clutch my throat with her fangs until she suffocates the life out of me, leaving my lifeless body in a heap by someone's doorstep?

My coffee had gotten cold, yet I sipped the lifeless liquid without so much as an afterthought. The forest was quiet, unusually quiet. Was she out there in the endless tangle of trees watching me right that very minute? I could feel the eyes, her eyes, from the hollow of every tree piercing through to my soul.

I went about my business putting every thought of her out of my mind. I was no longer the person she needed me to be, and I was not about to revert to who I once was. Ironically, it was she who had changed me. Her intrusion into my life put me on a path that led me to my savior, my angel of sorts. And that pumped my cold, black heart with vibrancy and a lust for life I had never possessed. And it was she who doomed me to an everlasting life which I have grown to tolerate and even at times embrace.

As evening began to set in and my chores were coming to an end, I had time to reflect on the day. I realized I was getting hungrier as each day passed and it was getting increasingly harder to tolerate the gnawing pangs. I had to feed, but I refused to. I would not capitulate to her desires any longer and come what may. I brushed the sand clean around the entrance to my sanctuary as I slid inside for the night.

Chapter Eight

Robert Marigold leaned against the cold, dank stone blinking his eyes at the ever-present darkness. His body had healed enough that it no longer screamed at him to rest. He no longer needed the recuperating powers of sleep, so he sat there in the darkness, alone with his thoughts. Alone with the demons who haunted his past, present and undoubtedly his future.

A crash of distant thunder reverberated through the thick night air. Winter was fast approaching and with it so were the gales of November. First one raindrop, then another slapped against the wooden planks that shuttered his window. His hunger had grown ferocious and just like Pavlov's dog his mouth salivated. It must be time for his feeding he thought to himself. Without a timepiece he had no way of telling time other than his own body which seemed to be playing tricks on him as no one slid a tray beneath his door.

The knot in his stomach grew in size and intensity as the hours passed. The rain had intensified as well and was pounding the earth beyond his walls. Streaks of lightning illuminated the night sky enough that through the cracks Robert could see night had fallen. He tried counting to keep track of the time but soon tired of that game, so he tried singing songs. That worked for a while until his throat became so parched, he was forced to quit.

He had sung five songs which he estimated were three minutes long so what felt like an eternity was probably less than fifteen minutes. The solitude was going to drive him mad. The rhythmic raindrops were plopping in a pool that had formed outside his cell window. Goldy recalled a story he had read a year or two back that precisely fit his predicament, something by Poe if his memory served him. Plop, plop, plop, constant and unyielding for hour upon hour. Joining in the concerto was his stomach, plop, plop, plop, grumble, grumble.

He found himself staring at the miniscule beam of light that wiggled its way under his door waiting for something to break the ray. And then it just disappeared. That was when true fear set its fangs into Robert Marigold. They had forsaken him. The light was a torch or oil lamp that had simply run out of fuel and could no longer illuminate the night. He wasn't having difficulty with time; they had quit feeding him.

When the shafts of light brought on by lightning flashing through his boarded windows transformed from pitch black to a dreary gray panic set in. No one had fed him throughout the night and as he had suspected they had either forgotten about him or had decided upon a death sentence. He suspected the former were true as the warden's five-year-old nephew was among the bits and pieces strewn about the city.

He jerked at his chains and shackles until his wrists and ankles were bloodied and raw. Robert had also come to the realization that the more he labored the sooner he would starve to death. And as his thirst began to nag at him, he understood he had a much bigger problem than lack of food. Lack of water would kill him much more quickly than the lack of nutrition. He spent the next several minutes trying to get himself turned around but could only manage to stick his tongue against the cold stone in a spot on his left and another on his right. There was moisture on the stone but not nearly enough to slake his thirst.

Thunder boomed and the clouds dumped even more rain. He sagged in desperation and loosed a laugh against the darkness. Irony was such a fickle mistress. Marigold recalled a passage from a writing he had been fond of, Rime of the Ancient Mariner.

Water, water, everywhere,
And all the boards did shrink;

Water, water, everywhere,
Nor any drop to drink.

A few more cracks of lightning and the deluge resumed, turning day into night, as if Robert could even be certain that is what occurred. He felt slow trickles of moisture dripping down the walls onto his shoulders. He tried desperately to crane his neck to sip at the elixir but was thwarted on every attempt. The mounting frustration was worse than the hunger and thirst themselves.

At some point Robert passed out and slept most of the day away. His subterranean tomb had altered his body's biological clock and transformed him into a nocturnal creature. The sky still rumbled around him and the rains pummeled the earth as he struggled to find ways to entertain himself in an effort to forget his intensifying thirst and ravenous hunger. What had it been, two, three maybe even four days since his last morsels of bread and tepid coffee?

Moldy Goldy,
Alone in a hole.
Moldy Goldy,
Poor desperate soul.
Moldy Goldy,
No one hungrier than thee.
Moldy Goldy,
Would you even eat me?

"Shut up! Shut up you little devil," Robert Marigold screamed, pounding the sides of his head with his palms. The chains of his shackles rattled with each strike.

How on earth did that little girl get down here into the dungeon where he sat condemned? Was she real, or had she simply taken up residence within his own imagination? His heart raced as he strained to hear the darkness.

Where is he Robert?

"Where is who?"

You know who.

"I've lost my marbles that I have. There's no one here, Goldy, you're just hearing things."

Suddenly an aroma permeated his cell. It was an all too familiar aroma. The sweet, salty scent of bacon wafted through the air causing his stomach to lodge a violent protest.

How long has it been Robert, you must be famished?

Although it was pitch black in his cell, he knew she was there, peeking under the door at him. He could almost see the whites of her eyes glowing in the darkness. And that wicked little sneer she creased across her mouth.

"Ignore it, Goldy. This is not real. You're going mad."

Mad with hunger maybe.

The smell of bacon was growing stronger causing his stomach to protest more loudly. It felt as though someone had punched him hard in the gut when he was not prepared. He began salivating as nausea crept in. His hunger gnawed away at his sanity piece by tiny piece. Maybe he had died, and this was his hell. Or was it all just some nightmare he would wake up from soon?

Where is he Goldy?

"Where is who!" he bellowed at the darkness, once again rapping his fists against the side of his head.

But Goldy knew. He knew exactly what the little girl wanted to know but he wasn't going to tell her. He made a promise, one he would keep to his grave because he was far more devoted to the Shadowman than he was scared of her.

"Do you think I'm scared of you?" he called out to the darkness. "You're nothing to be afraid of. If you were so powerful you would know where he was and wouldn't need to be bothering with me. You found me, why can't you find him?"

The driving need for water and food was making it hard for him to concentrate. He was on the very brink of blurting out every secret he had ever locked away. But he could not betray his one friend left on this earth. Would not betray him.

"And look around you little girl, what could you possibly do to me that would be any worse than the predicament I already find myself in?" The lack of response from the little girl was further complicating things in Goldy's brain. Was she even there or was he just arguing with himself?

Moses lay on the cold damp floor outside of a jail cell door. His head was foggy, yet clear as a bell at the same time. He was quite aware of the fact that he was dead from a heart attack, yet he was also still very much alive. He could see the little girl in the yellow dress standing over him as clear as day. He could even feel his heart beating inside his chest. But his brain screamed at him that this was not possible. He remembered dying. But if he died, how could he remember?

Moses Roses,
How do you feel?
Moses Roses,
You are Goldy's last meal.

The little girl smiled then reached down and grasped Moses by the throat. A searing pain enveloped him as she ripped it free from his neck. The pain was excruciating eliciting a scream from way down inside that escaped as nothing more than a whoosh of air from his purloined windpipe. But he was dead, how could he possibly feel pain? And then the acrid smoke from his own broiling flesh wisped in tendrils up his nostrils. He was smelling his own cooked flesh and yet his belly grumbled as if it were a choice cut of steak fresh off the hot iron.

Moses held his hand to his face and then centered his open palm over the little girl's face to block out her wicked little grin. Her sneer was still reflecting at him. His hand was translucent, like a soft shadow on the ground. He moved his hand away and her image moved sharply back into focus.

Moses Roses,
Can you still see me?
Moses Roses,
From death I've set you free.

Moses slapped the stone wall out of frustration. No sound reverberated from the flesh of his hand slapping the cold, hard surface. Tentacles of fear clutched him, he was dead, and yet so very much alive. He realized he had never really ever heard the little girl. Her voice had always been in his head, there were no footsteps when she walked and no reverberations of laughter when she giggled. She was a ghost, and now, so was he.

Moses started to cry. He didn't want to be a lonely old ghost trapped in this prison forever. He spent more than seventy years of his life behind these walls, each one wishing he wasn't there. Each morning when the sun hit his face, he was consumed by a depression brought on by the knowledge he had to endure one more day in hell. Now, he would spend an eternity in hell with no escape.

Moses Roses,
No, being a ghost is not your curse.
Moses Roses,
Your fate is far, far worse.

Robert strained at the darkness. Although his cell was as silent as it could be, he sensed a presence. Someone, or something, was just outside his cell door. He couldn't hear it talk, walk or even breathe, but he knew it was there just the same. It was then that the bacon smell increased to the point he was certain this was not just a vivid dream. He was wide awake and there was no denying there was charred meat in the room with him. It was just too tangible.

Moldy Goldy,
I've brought you a treat.
Moldy Goldy,
Do you dare to eat?

A little girl in a yellow dress appeared in the cell in front of him. She was bathed in an ethereal glow and her presence seemed to cause the iron door to hum and vibrate which translated into the rock wall he was leaning against. Robert Marigold shook his head violently side to side trying to shake this mental apparition from his brain. He knew she wasn't real. He knew this was a figment of his imagination brought on by the extreme solitude, hunger, and insatiable thirst he had been suffering. She smiled an awkward smile and outstretched her hand in what seemed a peace offering.

A bolt of lightning cracked across the sky and Robert jumped. It was close, very close. May have even been a direct strike on the prison grounds. The little girl smiled at him from out of her glowing blanket which caused him to stir with fear. Was she taking credit for that lightning? Was this a warning to him? She laid something on the ground just within his reach and her light slowly faded like a stick match whose flame has eaten away all the wood. Just a little flicker and poof, he was thrust back into his ebony abyss.

Chapter Nine

I was jarred awake from a deep slumber unable to discern reality from my nightmares. This brought a chuckle from deep within as my life no longer resembled anything close to reality. My very existence was a living nightmare. I recalled there was thunder and lightning in my dream, so I crawled forward out of my den and into the black night. Instantly I was surrounded by a million stars, something that does not generally occur on a stormy night.

A foreboding sense of sadness washed over me, and I sensed fear, yet it was not I who was afraid. I scanned the night sky for a familiar star and found Orion the Hunter. From there I scanned all four points and found no cloud cover whatsoever. No storm was approaching, and the night air was much too cool for there to have been any lightning from the heat of summer. I found it hard to fathom that my dream had been so palpable that the echoes of rumbling had awakened me. Once again, an ominous cape enveloped my being and tears slid from the corners of my eyes as I shuddered.

And then a face appeared in my vision, not in my brain, not in my thoughts, but right in front of me. It flashed but for a brief moment in time the breadth of a spider's silk, so I didn't recognize the face and yet, I knew who it was just the same. Robert Marigold, and he was in trouble. I knew exactly why he was in trouble too and who he was in trouble with. Seems my little nemesis had found him, and if she hadn't already, she would soon find me as well because I was certain Goldy would reveal my whereabouts if enough pressure was applied. And if I knew one thing about that little demon, she knew how to apply the pressure that much he was certain of. Ironically, Goldy would surely hold his tongue for as long as he possibly could, not out of respect for me, but respect for what I had become and the seemingly divine calling that had been bestowed upon me.

Oh sure, at first, I told him all of the tales of my past, and yes, they were not only to regale him but to instill a certain amount of fear as well. Fear breeds a particular amount of loyalty if seasoned properly. I never let him know that day after day I felt my heart changing. I felt my conscience growing. No longer was I the bitter, angry, ruthless killer I was in more than a century passed. I was not the blood thirsty wolf destined to be alpha by tearing out the throat from every last rival. That man died the moment this man was born in that ramshackle barn so long ago.

How was I to know that the series of events I had set into motion so many decades ago when I cared nothing about death would instill such a lust for life within me? Robert Marigold was neither stupid nor naïve, just very crude around the edges. He was also smart enough to notice as time passed in our relationship that I was not undergoing certain changes. I did not gain weight from overindulgence, my hair did not thin, my skin did not wrinkle, and my mind remained as sharp as the day he met me. All the while Goldy's own body slowly betrayed him a little more each day.

I think it was this fact about me that scared him the most. Not my tales of brutality against my enemies or my propensity to discard women when I was finished with them. No, Robert Marigold understood very well that a man who felt he could not die, whether true or not, was an extremely dangerous man indeed. A man who had nothing to lose also had no boundaries.

I stood in the cool night air contemplating my next move, or if there should even be any. If the authorities had caught Goldy I might be able to free him, but it would prove very difficult and he would probably be slain in any escape attempt. And if she had found him, there was nothing I could do to prevent his demise. I crawled back through the tunnel and curled up under my blankets and prayed to whomever would listen that Robert Marigold would be able to take my secrets to his grave. I drifted off to sleep not sure if I was enjoying my newfound morality.

Chapter Ten

Robert Marigold knew there was a morsel of sustenance on the floor between his legs. He could not see it, nor could he smell it any longer, but he knew it was there just the same. A wicked offering from an equally wicked temptress. He contemplated all of the possible tricks she might be trying to corral him into and came back to the same conclusion, what harm could eating a little piece of meat cause. It would not make him feel obliged to reveal secrets to the little miscreant.

He reached out for it in the darkness but withdrew his hand at the last moment and kicked it away, out of the reach of his chains. A thunderclap resounded off the walls and the rains began to pound the earth once more. And once more, a yellow glow began to materialize outside of his cell door.

Moses was still lying on the cold, stone floor when the little girl reappeared. He had taken off his shoes and was wiggling his toes in the air. He could barely see them, but he knew they were right there in front of him. Was he slowly dying, fading away with each passing moment?

Moses Roses,
Fading away.
Moses Roses,
Is gone the next day.

Moses clawed at his head trying to get the little girl's voice out of his brain. Slowly he began to realize that one of the side effects of dying was that he was no longer stupid. He was no longer a wounded animal whose brain had been damaged beyond repair. Moses tried something he had not tried in a very long time, speech.

"Why?" his dry, scratchy throat echoed hollow in the darkness as nothing more than a hiss of air.

Why not?

Once more the little girl in the yellow dress hovered over Moses and ripped his left foot free from his body. The pain was excruciating, and he screamed a scream of both pain and the pent-up frustration of not being able to speak for decades. It resonated through the stale air as nothing more than a guttural blast. And then he remembered, she had already stolen his voice. She just smiled at him and faded away. The sardonicism was not lost on this iniquitous child.

Goldy was abruptly yanked from a nightmare filled with screams. How long had he been asleep? Had it been a few minutes, a mere hour or had another day already passed? He was disturbed at how realistic the scream had been, as if it had been just outside of his door and not deep within his own subconscious. From just a tiny spark an ember began to glow and the little girl in yellow appeared from out of nowhere. He did the math in his head, he had always been a little frightened of what the Shadowman could do to him, and the Shadowman was deeply frightened of what this little girl could do to him which left Robert terrified of what havoc this innocent looking little girl could wreak.

She placed something between his legs, smiled and backed away. The aroma of freshly cooked meat was delectable and impossible to ignore any longer. He fumbled around in the darkness until he laid hands on something warm, something wet. Without another thought Robert Marigold brought the chunk of flesh to his mouth and tore into it with his teeth. Ravenous he attacked poor Moses with a vengeance, ripping and tearing the flesh and swallowing it with no more than two or three grindings from his molars. Juices ran down his chin which he lapped at with his tongue.

At one-point Goldy paused long enough to notice that there was something odd about the meat. Not that it was human flesh, he knew that and didn't rightly care. There was something else different about it, something intangible. He laughed aloud which startled him. Perhaps he was supping on a court jester because his dinner tasted funny. He soon realized that he was becoming a bit giddy, almost euphoric.

Under any other circumstances he would have welcome the feeling of invincibility, of floating amongst the clouds. But not chained to a prison wall, forgotten and the only visitor was a cheeky little ghost.

"Get a hold of yourself, Goldy, none of this is real. You're hallucinating."

Moldy Goldy,
You have broken the seal.
Moldy Goldy,
No, this is so very real.

Once more she stood before him, illuminating the room with an unnatural glow. He glanced down at what he had been eating, what he now held in his hands and dropped the object in sheer terror. He had been dining on the Shadowman.

Chapter Eleven

Because of my evening jaunt I woke up much later than usual. The tweetuh, tweetuh, tweetuh call of a cardinal drifted through the sand corridor into my sleep chamber. Before letting it annoy me, I made the observation that his song was so much more pleasant than a rooster's. I tidied up my bedroom and drug it out with me to shake out the sand. There was still so much to do before the winter winds blew in on icy breath.

I put water on to boil for some good, strong coffee and went to work digging a second pit. I needed a storage pit for my meager supplies as hoisting them up into a tree was getting to be quite tiresome day in and day out. I took stock and realized I was running low on several staples that would require me to venture out into the world of the living, coffee being a main culprit. I could do with running out of just about anything as I could grow or scavenge most of what I needed. But coffee, coffee would never grow in this snowy region the thought of which made me yearn for the Blue Mountains of Jamaica. Although, the sandy soil might be good for grapes one day and I was almost as fond of wine as I was the java bean.

I did pack a few pounds of tea, but I had yet to punish my palate that severely. I had but a pound or so of coffee left so I opted for my first cup of the bitter beverage in this northern frontier. It was bitter and astringent at first sip which I quickly spat out onto the forest carpet. I had no sugar as it was both heavy and took up a lot of space and since I had brought no flour as well was not necessary. I did however have a small pouch of cinnamon, so I added a stick of the curled bark to the brewing pot.

The cinnamon took the bitter edge off the tea and I was able to semi-enjoy a cup. I wandered the perimeter of my growing campsite and inspected its boundaries. Reaching the outer edge on the western side I was once again confronted with evidence of a nightly intruder. I traced my index finger lightly around the indentation in the sand. Another footprint, definitely human and definitely that of a small child. If she had found me, why was she just taunting me so? And then I recalled her propensity for playing mind-twisting games.

I followed the footprints as far as I could but lost the trail in the dense underbrush. I scanned my surroundings and used deductive reasoning to anticipate her direction of travel. Maybe I could pick up her trail if she had to cross a sandy patch. I got my bearings straight and headed west up a large sloping incline. I was out of breath and sweating by the time I reached the crest and gladly welcomed the breeze off the water as the forest had given way to an open, sandy expanse. The shore was only a few hundred yards below me and since I had no intent of climbing back up that dune I decided to stay put and enjoy a snack of apples and walnuts with just a pinch of cinnamon.

I alternated between bites of the apple and a perfectly roasted walnut meat rolled in spice. It was a delectable repast which allowed me just a brief respite from my tribulations. I sat on the crest of that hill for what seemed eons without a single thought but of the gulls swooping and diving on the beach below. I could see lightning off in the distance and the clouds were taking on a dark tone. The clouds hanging over the horizon had blackened, and I could see sheets of rain dotting the landscape beyond the two islands. The storm would be upon me very soon.

I was gathering up my things for the trek back to camp when I spied something very disturbing. A vessel rounded the smaller of the two islands and continued through a passage between the two land masses where it turned west into a sheltered cove of the smaller of the two islands. From the direction the ship had been coming I assumed it was either from Green Bay or maybe even as far south as Milwaukee. This was very disconcerting as I had thought I had found a bastion away from civilization. The trend had been for civilization to move westward, not up here in the far north.

A beacon shone through the growing darkness, something I had not seen before. There must be a lighthouse on the island which meant this was not as desolate a place as I had been led to believe. And though I had seen a few night fires burning here or there I assumed it was just Indians on their way across the bay. The overall lack of movement around the island left me thinking it was mostly deserted. I was wrong.

All the way back to the camp I contemplated leaving this place, running away before civilization could find me. Maybe leave the northern territories all together, or maybe even forge further north if I could make it across the straits. How was I to be a hermit if everyone continued to encroach upon my solitude? But this was a growing land and I knew I would soon run out of places to hide. I would have headed west but from the tales I had been told it was a hot, miserable, dusty place blocked by mountains and hostile natives. And I had no desire to live out eternity as a pincushion filled with arrows.

I decided I would ride out the storm, head down to the beach after and monitor these interlopers. Perhaps they would only stay on the island long enough for the storm to pass and push north to Canada. Or continue on east through the Erie Canal and I was fretting over nothing. Perhaps.

The winds ahead of the storm made landfall on my way back to camp. Pine boughs swayed until smaller ones snapped and fell all around me. By the time I had made it back to safety my face was a crisscross of welts, not that I could see in any reflective surface, but I could feel them with my fingertips. As I was crawling into my safe harbor, I noticed two sets of tiny footprints in the sand.

Chapter Twelve

It had been at least a day, maybe two since Robert had been visited by the apparition. She had left him several more pieces of flesh which he devoured eagerly despite the warnings his brain was sending him. He couldn't help himself. his hunger became an all-consuming boil that would not be ignored. Guilt also ate away at him with each bite, the Shadowman had been his friend, his one and only true friend left in this world and to partake of his flesh seemed downright blasphemous.

He felt his body going through changes as well. He felt hollow, empty, even more so than usual. But there was also this certain aspect of his psyche that seemed peculiar to him. The storm still raged outside, and the winds had loosened one of the shutter boards enough that he could now see outside, or at least enough to be able to determine day from night. But it was also enough to let the rains in.

The high winds were driving the rain into cracks left by the loosened boards and Robert felt the cold water pooling up along his legs and soaking into his prison pajamas. His predicament was getting better by the moment bringing a sardonic crease to his face. He pulled at his shackles to reposition himself and that was when he noticed something that terrified him to his core. In the new found light of his cell he could see the shackles but could barely see his wrists. He could see the backside of the shackle through where his wrist should be.

Apprehensively he poked his finger just above the shackle's edge. He felt the touch to both his wrist and his finger but saw neither make contact with each other. A bolt of lightning exploded from the black clouds, illuminating his cell as if it were broad daylight. He was starting to fade, just like the Shadowman.

At first, Goldy was somewhat giddy. By eating the Shadowman he had consumed his powers as well. He was becoming immortal! That is when the full weight of his true dilemma began to take shape for him. Immortal, yet chained to a wall where no one knew where he was. He was already on the brink of madness after just a week or so of solitary confinement, what would a lifetime, no, a thousand lifetimes be like?

"How could she possibly make it any worse, eh Goldy?" he said aloud just to hear his own voice. "You are a wicked, wicked little girl."

Chapter Thirteen

It had been two days of solid rain before the weather broke enough for me to climb outside and stretch my legs. While my deep, sandy den may be very suitable to keep out the snow, it was not much of a deterrent for the rains. I spread my bedroll out over some low hanging pine boughs and checked my matches before lighting a small fire under my wet gear. Fortunately, I only lost three matches to the rain.

I was sipping at some putrid cinnamon laced tea when thoughts of Robert Marigold wrapped around my brain and I found myself consumed with guilt. I should have never abandoned him as I had, but I had run out of options. He didn't seem to mind at the time, but I'm quite sure he regrets it now as he is likely in prison, dangling at the end of a hangman's noose or worse.

I was heading back into my den when I noticed two tiny handprints at the edge of the hole inside of the thatched cover. She had been peering down inside, maybe waiting for me to come out where she would have the element of surprise. Or perhaps she was gathering her nerve to come in and attack me while I slept. Either way, I didn't like it one damned bit. It was becoming more and more apparent that my showdown with her was nearing its apex.

I lost her trail as she entered the forest heading west. I felt dejected but then noticed the hoar frost hanging in the trees at the edge of the meadow. Maybe this patch of rain would eventually turn into snow and then I would surely be able to track her comings and goings. I breathed a plume of vapor out into the cool morning air as if I could tell the temperature simply by my own breath. It was not an exact science, but it would do. The little imp would not be able to toy with me forever.

Chapter Fourteen

By his best estimations it had been nearly a week since Robert Marigold had partaken of what he believed to be the flesh of the Shadowman. His body had been changing rapidly from day to day. He felt a renewed strength, yet also weakened to his very core. The girl had yet to visit him during this time, he wished he could say the same for Mother Nature. The storms continued to batter the walls of his cell while the waters rose until they had covered the tops of his thighs.

By the third day he was beginning to understand the gravity of the situation. The combination of dehydration and the temperature falling to extreme lows at night should have killed him quite easily, and yet day after day, morning after morning he had awakened. The torturous irony of being surround by water, even immersed in it, but unable to drink it gnawed at his brain. He didn't dare partake of the parasite infested water lest he suffer a bout of crippling dysentery. He was certain this was all due to her pure wickedness.

By the fourth day it was very apparent he was deluding himself by thinking this was anything but catastrophic. The rains continued day and night until the banks of the Maumee River had washed away buildings and streets while flooding the entire city. The prison had not escaped the weather's wrath. Although he could not see what was happening in the world outside, he could deduce from the sounds his situation was rapidly deteriorating. The prison had essentially become an island and was being evacuated by boat. Guards and prisoners alike were fleeing like the rats they were, abandoning him to die. Little did the bastards know what they were condemning him to was far worse than death.

By the end of the fifth day even the most subtle of ambient sound disappeared leaving him feeling utterly alone in the world. And still the rains pounded the earth and the waters continued to rise. It was at this point Goldy started contemplating his condition. Was he truly immortal or just harder to kill? If he were immortal why then did he feel hunger, pain, cold and the need to sleep? An immortal being would not be bothered with such trivialities.

And there was this little, nagging question he had every time he glanced down at his shackles and saw that he was becoming more and more transparent as the days passed by. Would he become an invisible man, or simply fade away into nothingness? His situation was nearly impossible to ponder and even harder yet to fathom for a man with no drink and no friends. Hell, Goldy would have settled for an enemy, even the little girl in the yellow dress at this point.

Robert was contemplating the pros and cons of immortality when he felt the first shudder. It wasn't much at first, just a small tremor in the walls. Cracks began to appear in the mortar which let in even more water which of course caused the cracks to expand. He remembered asking the little girl how much worse could she make it, even she couldn't be this cruel could she?

Moldy Goldy,
Things sure do look grim.
Moldy Goldy,
It is your choice, sink or swim.

As her words trailed off in his crowded mind, he heard a deafening crack and felt the earth violently shift. Water began pouring in all around him through a six-inch break in the wall. The water rose as high as his neck and Robert once again contemplated his situation. Was him being immortal just a fantasy his deprived body and broken mind had dreamt up?

Once the water rose above his head would he simply drown and die? He and the Lord had never been on speaking terms but Goldy said a few prayers just in case. If for nothing more than to ease his own corroded thoughts.

There was another loud crack and a large portion of the wall he was chained to detached from the main building. Ever so slowly the wall began to sink into the mud and fall away from the building. He felt himself both floating and sinking into the depths of the river. Robert's wall came to rest at the bottom of the river, him still chained to it staring upward into the black, murky depths.

On the bright side, several breaths later and Robert had not drowned. On the darker side, if one could believe it possible, things got even worse. Every breath of water he drew into his lungs wracked his body with excruciating pain from which there was no escape. It might have driven him to the brink of madness had he not gone over that ledge a long time ago.

Where is he Goldy, I know you know where he is hiding.

Robert tried to speak but his mouth flooded with water and the only sound to escape was garbled gibberish. His situation would be laughable had it not been a reality. He pulled hard at his chains to no avail, he was as stuck as stuck could get. The water surrounding him was darker than it had been in his cell, yet he could still see a small, orange bead hovering above him. But it was raining, cloudy, so there was no possibility the sun was shining. And then the bead moved closer. It was her.

Moldy Goldy,
Nevermore, doth the Raven did say.
Moldy Goldy,
And then he flew away.

Chapter Fifteen

I awoke shivering with my bedroll tossed to the side. Sand was kicked about, and I knew I must have had some bad dreams during the night. As my slumber eroded, I recalled a dream about Robert Marigold, nothing specific mind you, just that he had been at the center of my nightmare. I offered a short prayer for his safety.

I opted for coffee as the unpalatable tea would not suffice on a bitter morning such as today. No, I needed the bold, bitter taste of burnt coffee. I burned myself three times trying to pick the pot off from the fire. It was already a delicate procedure but even further complicated when one could barely see their own hand. I had lost even more density in the night and that was somewhat worrisome as well as relieving. Either way, I was one step closer to anonymity which would allow me the freedom to roam, spy and gather supplies.

I found my hunger to be considerably more argumentative with me this morning. Not my belly hunger, which was always a nag that a little warm coffee and a few chunks of jerky seemed to settle down. No, it was the other hunger gnawing at me to my very core. Like a headache you knew was coming on, it was almost there but not quite. It was warning me this was going to get much worse and there was only one solution, one which I refused to succumb to. I would not succumb to that hunger ever again, thus I had removed all temptation.

I checked the camp for signs of my intruder and sighed in relief when I found no evidence. Maybe I was just imagining things and my visitor was an animal with human-like paw prints. I made my way through the forest to the western shore. I needed to check on the ship moored at the island since the storm had passed. Hopefully, they were going to pull anchor and head out for their ultimate destination, much further to the east would be preferable.

I collected a few bunches of wild grapes and a small sack of late-blooming woodland strawberries for the excursion. The morning had a pleasant chill about it that was just right for my old bones. The sky was clear, and the sun was already starting to get quite warm. I hoped we were heading into second summer. And then I thought of the little girl and my plan to track her. A warm spell would not suit my needs no matter how pleasant it was.

As if on cue once I exited the protection of the forest the winds were considerably stronger and tiny white flakes floated through the morning air. I held my translucent hand out and captured a larger flake which appeared to be suspended in midair before it melted in my palm and disappeared. This certainly would be a neat parlor trick under different circumstances. I realized the winds were strong gales when I crested the large dune and peered down on the whitecaps surrounding the islands. Just as I was afraid, that ship was not going anywhere any time soon.

I pulled out my spyglass and focused on the boat. From this distance people were just specks on the shore, like insects scurrying about. They were dismantling the ship and carrying pieces ashore. I had heard of this practice on the rivers, but I wasn't aware of any instances on the big waters. The river rats, a nickname of river lumberman, would live on their floating logs as they meandered downstream to the mill. The company would construct a large floating raft that served as a company store selling staples and providing the men with dry clothing. This wanigan would be deconstructed at the end of the float and sold for lumber. It appeared to me that this might be what was happening with this ship.

The more I watched the more I realized that they were not simply selling this lumber, they were constructing an edifice with it. They must have sailed from Milwaukee, Green Bay or even as far as Chicago with the intent of setting up a trading post, lumber mill, or both on the island. There were piles and piles of cut timber being hewn into firewood and stacked on the western shore.

I began to rethink my present condition. I may not be completely invisible yet, but the dark of night may prove me to become nothing more than a mere shadow. I would be able to move stealthily through the forest and would certainly go unseen on moonless nights. I had never been one to shy away from pilfering when necessary, and now seemed like as good a time as any. I was in dire need of certain supplies I did not have with me. I left Toledo in such a hurry that I failed to procure enough ammunition to last a winter and I needed warmer gear than I had first anticipated. I found myself needing them day by day as the weather turned. Raiding the island under the cover of darkness seemed to be the only logical choice. Besides, I was almost out of coffee and that would simply be unacceptable.

While devising a plan of attack I soon felt dejected, I would certainly need a boat to get across the large bay to the island which would also negate any element of surprise. Even though the expanse was not too great, and it was sheltered for most of the way there would also be open water to have to deal with. If the weather were to turn on me, I could be in severe trouble. But I was immortal right? I had no reason to fear drowning or exposure to the elements other than the sheer discomfort of the experience. All I would really require would be a crude raft easily constructed from pine logs and wild grape vines.

I decided to put my idle time to good use and pulled out my writing pad and pencil. It wasn't so much that I was writing my thoughts and activities down into a tale as an author might craft a story in hopes of selling a book. No, I chose to document my yarn because it was a way for me to accept all of this as being real. Or then again, maybe I was trying to convince myself that my entire life has been nothing but a work of fiction.

I am afraid I misspoke earlier in my tale as I am not truly immortal because I am very much dead. But I am very much alive as well. Not in the sense of being undead as portrayed in a penny dreadful, novels and native folklore. No, I am dead as dead can be and yet so very much alive. I require food and water for sustenance, not blood like the fabled vampyre. I need air to breathe lest I suffocate which I have found to be quite painful when testing that theory. And my memories are so very vivid, although there are so many of them now, they tend to get jumbled.

I think more than a hundred years has passed since meeting my destiny face to face and my tribulations began, although it seems like only yesterday that I sipped a bitter brew with a charming old hag. Yet here I am, appearing as a man still in his late thirties. And at the risk of being cliché, once upon a time I had a heart blacker than the night itself and not a shred of a conscience to speak of. I believe maybe at this juncture I should venture back and explain what events have brought me to this very precipice in life.

Northern Territories Mid 1700's

Chapter Sixteen

I had been in these God forsaken parts for more than I cared to admit, and I was getting desperate to return to my old life of luxury. Or at least as much luxury as one could find in a wilderness frontier. I had run afoul of both the colonists and the British through similar dealings of playing one off the other to maximize my profits. And of course, the French had never been fond of me, and I not of them in the least, so I was a man without a country so to speak. With a hangman's noose chasing me and a looming war in the eastern colonies I decided it was best to cut my losses and head for the northern territories where the natives were far more civilized than the interlopers.

My horse, Helga, was weary of the trail so I headed for a small settlement nestled along the big lake in a tranquil looking bay. She was a well-defined Narragansett Pacer, deep chestnut with an attitude of fire. She had an hourglass of white painted on her snout, so she rightfully felt she was the one in charge of how we spent our time. She gaited down the path with her head held high like a princess set out to greet the masses. For the life of me I could not remember where we made each other's acquaintance, but she didn't complain, nor had she ever tried to return to whence she came.

I set up camp on the shore for the night once I spotted several night fires dotting the landscape. These were much too small to be wildfires which meant they were campfires and I had found civilization. This also meant I might find supplies I desperately needed but it also necessitated my keeping to the shadows and limiting my interactions with the townsfolk. I laughed at the thought of this desolate place as being civilized.

In the morning I ambled down along the lake so my horse could get a much-needed drink. I had also hoped for a quick bath, but the sand was black silt and smelled as if a hundred dead souls had washed up on the beach so I didn't brave making it down to the water's edge. Although the lake loomed out in front of me as big as an ocean it was still just a lake with many swampy inlets. The warmer waters of the bay served as a perfect breeding ground for algae which lent the waters a greenish hue and spiked the air with decay.

"You behave yourself, Helga" I said as I tied up my mare and wandered around town letting my nose search out my breakfast.

I only had maps of the general region and most of the names of this area were in French. And although I saw there were a lot of British folks as well as colonists and quite a few natives most of the people were speaking French. My map called this place *La Baie Verte* whatever the hell that meant. The French never cared for me, so I never cared to learn their language. It didn't take long to realize this was a fur trapper's town so I kept my guard up and my head down as they could be a dangerous lot and usually well-armed.

Even though I had altered my appearance with some self-inflicted scars and grew a flea ridden beard I was still very wary of being recognized. And with a trail of bodies a mile long I would prefer not to end my days on the short end of a noose. I felt it best to keep my distance from others for as long as I possibly could.

I found a little inn that served biscuits and a local thimbleberry jam with strong tea. I preferred coffee but it was proving difficult to find this far west. With my belly full I decided to meander around town hoping to catch a conversation or two that would lead me to some prospects as my coin purse was in dire straits. Slopping through these muddy streets was wearing thin after just a few short blocks of slipping and sliding about. I would never talk ill of the cobblestone streets of Charleston ever again. It seemed I was worlds away from my home, a home to which I could never return.

The town was a mixture of both old and new dwellings and businesses. It had the typical establishments, a blacksmith, a livery stable, a granary and the two I was looking for, a sheriff and a saloon. I stopped by the sheriff's office and discreetly perused the wanted posters. There were only three and they were petty crimes so no real bounty to speak of, especially not enough to risk injury over. Some of these men appeared to be rather large, Nordic looking men whom I had no desire to tangle with over a coin or two. I was, however, quite pleased to see that I was not among those wanted in this territory. My exploits had not preceded me which was always a good thing.

The small town of a dozen buildings or so thinned out as I neared the water. It was then I spied where the fires had been burning, there was a fort at the river mouth that seemed to be a trading post of sorts. There were not many soldiers, but they were French and one Frenchman, especially a soldier, was plenty enough for me to want to avoid the place. I doubled back to the saloon which was at the furthest end of the sloppy boulevard, as far away from the Jesuit monument as possible I assumed.

I ordered a bottle of whiskey and sat in a far corner by myself where I could blend into the shadows and absorb the conversations around me. The place had a stench about it that was neither man nor beast but an unbearable combination of the two. A lake so large you cannot see the other side and yet none of these men had bathed in weeks. I kept my whiskey glass close to my nose in an effort to ward off the odiferous spirits.

A thick Cockney accent floated to my ears. "Those damned Frenchman have got to go."

"Quiet, they would have your head if they heard you speaking of such things," another Brit whispered.

Ah so there was some tension in this little slice of paradise, I could deal with tension, I could profit from it as well. I listened to their grumblings for the better part of an hour before deciding I needed to know these men much better.

"Gentlemen, I seemed to have purchased far more whiskey than I can possibly consume by myself, would you care to share a bottle?" I asked as I sidled up to their table.

Even in the dimly lit tavern with its flickering torchlight I could see the wariness lining their face as they looked back at me. I walked to the bar and grabbed two more glasses, set them down on the table next to mine and filled my own glass with two fingers of whiskey. I touched the bottle mouth to one of the other glasses and smiled at the men who relented their skepticism and eagerly motioned me to fill their glasses as well. One of the men held up his blackjack to the bartender, ordering another round of beer.

"Where are you from, friend?"

"Back east," I replied.

"Of course, you are from back east, everyone in this place who ain't an Indian is from back east, except for the Frenchies and you don't sound like one of those bastard sons. Though you do kind of smell like one."

"Kind of looks like one though, don't he," the smaller of the two men laughed showing a mouthful of blackened teeth. I resisted the urge to shove my dagger between his ribs for the insult.

"I'm Josiah and this here is Obediah, but we just call him OB for short. What's your name?"

I paused to think this one through. I had yet to reveal my new persona more from the lack of human contact than anything else. Now was as good a time as any to shed my past life and start anew I supposed. "I'm Thaddeus Morgan, pleased to make your acquaintance. You can call me Thad for short," I said.

"You new to these parts?" OB asked while taking a drink from his mug, his ham sized hand making the glassware appear to be a mere child's toy.

"One might say that. I've been here in the northern territories going on three years I suppose."

"You here looking for work or just passing through?" Josiah put his two cents worth in rubbing his fingers through his greasy black hair and inspecting his fingers for what I could only imagine was lice.

"I prefer to keep moving, I am more of a wanderer, but I suppose I could take some time to refill my coin purse. You fellas know of anything an able body could do around these parts?"

"You good with a knife?" the big man asked in a tone that had me questioning his motives for the line of inquiry.

I thought about this for a moment and pondered the possibility of a trap. "I suppose one could say that," I said.

"Trading post could always use a good skinner."

"You mean out there by that fort I saw on the edge of town?"

"One in the same."

"Lot of French soldiers wandering about from what I could see. Not too fond of Frenchies."

"Oh, don't pay them no never mind. They have been around here so long they're pretty near locals. They're just here to protect the traders."

"They're still soldiers and they're still French," I said under my breath.

I poured another round of whiskey while Josiah went up to the bar to refill our beer. I suspiciously eyed the crowd, most of whom were engaged in quiet conversation themselves. It seemed no one trusted anyone which was my position as well. Josiah returned with the beer and sat back down.

"Might be more prudent to find a friendlier place to converse. Where are you staying?" Josiah asked.

"No place in particular. I've got a bedroll on my horse and it looks like it will be a clear night."

"We've got a camp set up down on the Fox River, you're more than welcome to join us. Safety in numbers are words to live by around here."

"What is there to worry about around here other than wild animals?"

"Indians," OB interjected after downing his whiskey and eyeballing the glass to make sure he didn't leave a drop behind.

"Indians? I have not heard of any attacks. I thought they were pretty peaceful around these parts."

"They are, and they mostly fight amongst themselves. Tribes from the east have started pushing in on Sioux and Fox territories and it can get ugly at times," Josiah said.

"I don't think I would ever be mistaken for a Sioux warrior or an Ojibwa for that matter."

"But you are a Brit just like us," OB added. "Damned Frenchies have them turned against us Brits, even those of us who ain't soldiers."

"We should probably save this conversation for a more suitable time and location," I said when I realized we were drawing some unwanted attention.

The two men nodded, and Josiah handed me a scrap of paper with a crude map drawn on it. I folded it and slipped it into the pocket of my jacket and grabbed my trifold from the table.

"We can introduce you to Lieutenant Gagnon at the fort in the morning. That is, if you're interested in some work."

"I look forward to it. Now I must tend to some errands before the sun goes down. Maybe I will see you by the fire later this evening," I said and made my leave.

The sun was high in sky when I left the dark tavern which left me temporarily blinded. I ambled down the street slowly keeping my eyes on my boot tips until they adjusted to the brightness. The whiskey and beer were starting to hit me a little harder than expected so I went and got Helga, took her to the livery and took a nap while she was fed and tended to by the stable boy.

After leaving the livery I stopped at the mercantile for some coffee and decided to splurge for some back-strap jerky as well. I sprung for a hot bath at the hotel and learned of numerous wounds and sores all over my body once I hit the hot water. While I was soaking, I took out the map Josiah had given me out of my jacket and studied it until I had committed it to memory. Shouldn't be too hard to find their encampment. When I was folding the paper back up, I noticed something familiar and turned the paper over. Although it was mostly obscured and barely recognizable, I could tell it was a scrap piece from the bottom of an old wanted poster. What little print was left on the scrap of paper it was enough for me to know it was my name on the bottom of the page.

Chapter Seventeen

Helga and I made our way through the small town and away from the French fort back out into the wilderness. The night was moonless and there were few if any clouds in the sky leaving me shrouded under a blanket of stars. A shooting star streaked across the night sky and I stopped to wonder, was that a star or some type of vessel hurling through space. I wondered if man would ever learn how to leave this place and join God in the heavens, without dying first of course.

"What do you think, Helga, with a running start could you jump that high?" I smiled and we continued on our way with a disinterested snort.

Coyotes were yipping off in the distance and by their echoes it became apparent they were circling a kill. I heard a musket blast and the yipping stopped for a while but then started back up again until another shot scared them away. It was bound to be a very long night for that hunting party who must have been camped on a kill of their own.

I could hear the rushing of water ahead of me and knew I must be close to the river even though I could not see it in the black of night. The air grew a little cooler as I neared the water, so I slowed down. I had not had a chance to scout the landscape in the daylight making me leery about getting too close to the water's edge. Helga was not much of a swimmer and I was even worse which fueled my apprehension. I wondered if Helga was affected by the optical illusion of the water as I was. We slowly moved forward while the water flowed towards us at about the same speed making it appear as if we were standing still at times. I was so preoccupied with this illusion I nearly missed the balanced rock marker leading to the encampment.

I ambled slowly up the worn trail hoping to get a head count before exposing myself to potential danger. I dismounted and had Helga hold fast while I scouted the trail in the diminished light. Having been in a similar circumstance more than once in my lifetime my hackles were already up. About fifty yards from the camp I found what I expected to be there, several bear traps set along the trail hoping to catch my horse and break her leg. Any doubts I may have had about these men disappeared.

I hitched Helga to a tree and made my way into the forest where I could flank the encampment. Their fire was rather small but did provide me with enough light to make out their faces. There were only two bed rolls laid out and after watching the pair for over an hour I felt safe to assume it was just the two of them I would have to contend with. I was looking forward to the looks on their faces when I rode into camp on my horse.

I made my way back to Helga, pulled a bottle of whiskey from the saddlebag, took two long swallows, and poured another over my head. I rubbed some more whiskey into my beard and prepared to play the part of just another drunken trail rider. We set off for the camp with me draped over my horse's neck.

"Evening Thaddeus," Josiah said, helping me down from my horse. The look on Obediah's face almost made be bust out into laughter.

"Evening and thank you. Guess I had one too many at the saloon. That reminds me, brought you guys a bottle too," I said, pulling the whiskey out of my saddlebag and handing it to them. They eagerly downed a swallow or two before reluctantly handing the bottle back to my outstretched hand.

I took a long pull from the bottle but kept my tongue in place, so I never actually swallowed any of the amber nectar. I would be needing my wits about me as the night progressed, of that I was certain. In the dim glow of the campfire they never knew the difference and I was quite the thespian when the need arose. I set about clearing a place for my bedroll as far from Josiah and as close to OB as I could which set well with them. I had the luxury of anticipating what they were up to, while they on the other hand had no clue what I was about to do to them.

"Tell me about this Frenchie at the fort," I slurred.

"Not much to tell. He basically oversees the protection of the traders and skims a little off the top for himself. He charges a fee to work the docks and tannery. Not much, but enough to make him a nice spot of coin as well as a few enemies."

"What if I don't feel like paying?"

"Then you don't work, plain and simple," OB interjected. His tone led me to believe that these two were getting a cut as well.

"What's your story, Obediah? You're a pretty big man, looks like you haven't shied away from hard work. Are you an absconder?"

I saw immediately that I had touched a nerve with that inquiry. He started to get up and I instantly moved my hand to the tomahawk at my side. I had spent a good portion of my life either fighting with or fighting against the Seminoles and had plenty of run ins with the Iroquois nations as well so I was no stranger to hand to hand combat, though I did not relish the thought of tangling with this dark behemoth.

"Easy OB, the man didn't mean no harm, it was a simple question," Josiah said, putting a hand on the big man's shoulder.

"I apologize if I offended you, OB. It is just we all seem to have some skeleton or another in our past that we would like to forget. I kind of like to know who I am bunking with and whether or not I might get involved with the law on account of guilt by association."

"I'm a free man if that's what you're asking."

"Oh, it's fine by me either way, just like to know what to expect is all," I said with smug grin as I passed the bottle around.

Josiah declined my offer and said, "No thank you, it's been a long day and we have plenty to do tomorrow."

"Suit yourself," I said and took a long pull off the bottle. When the two of them bedded down I quietly spit the whiskey out onto the ground.

I stirred the fire and threw a few more logs on before slipping into my wool blankets. I tipped my hat down over my eyes just far enough that I could still see shadows moving in the darkness. I pulled my tomahawk out and held it close to my chest.

I had just dozed off a little when I heard the slightest crunch of dirt beneath a bare foot. I strained my eyes to the side and saw a large, dark foot to the left side of me. In one swift motion I lashed out with the tomahawk and took the three biggest toes off the big man's foot. Before he could react, I spun the blade and swung and upward arc into his groin. He dropped the rock that had been intended for my skull and grabbed his bleeding crotch. My next swing cleaved his skull.

As I had suspected, in seeing this Josiah rushed to his horse to flee. Anticipating this I had loosened the saddle straps when he wasn't paying attention and he found himself with a face full of dirt. I landed a punch across his temple that stunned him. By the time he came back around I had him tied with his hands behind his back. I walked over to my horse and rummaged through the saddlebag until I found what I was after. I gave Helga a handful of molasses oats and a kiss on her snout.

"Sorry about your friend, but it looks like he bit off more than he could chew."

"It was his idea, not mine, I swear," Josiah pleaded.

"I'm not inclined to believe that. The way I see it, you were the brains and he was the brawn of your outfit. I do use the term brains loosely."

"No sir, it was all OB's idea."

"Where did you pick up that poster of me?"

"I don't rightly remember. We been carrying it with us for a while."

"It wasn't at the sheriff's or the fort?"

"No, we picked it up back east, before we headed out here."

"Did you tell the Lieutenant at the fort about me?"

"No sir, that scoundrel would keep any bounty we brought him."

"We have a real dilemma on our hands here. I can't trust you enough to let you go and I wouldn't know what to do with you once I've killed you."

"You can trust me, mister. I'll ride the hell out of here tonight and never look back."

"Where is the rest of the poster, the part with my face on it?"

Josiah eyed the black sock in my hand as I hefted it up and down. He could only imagine what was in the bottom of the sock and wasn't in any hurry to find out.

"In Obediah's bag, there behind that rock," he pointed with a nod of his head.

I rummaged through the dead man's belongings until I found what I was looking for. I unfolded the yellowed parchment and read over the long list of offenses that were attributed to my good name. The drawing was a decent likeness of my old self but resembled me a lot less since my self-inflicted alterations. The broken nose seemed to be the deal breaker. Still, the damned picture had my eyes and there wasn't much I could do about that. I walked over to Josiah and held the poster up beside his face. There were a lot of similarities.

"This just might work, especially if I take Frenchy a bottle of whiskey to drink aforehand," I said.

"What might work?" Josiah asked nervously just about the time he figured out what I was talking about which was just about the same time my sock full of knikkers struck him in the mouth.

Josiah leaned forward and spit a mouthful of blood and broken teeth out into the sand. As he was bent over, I swung hard again into the back of his head and then swinging in a figure eight pattern swung upwards into his face driving him back upright. The next two blows were across the left and right sides of his lower jaw, breaking the bone and taking out several more teeth. I landed several more blows making sure not to hit his nose as it was one feature that resembled mine the most, before I mangled mine with a smithy's hammer of course.

He fell over into the dirt and rolled over to face me. "Please, mister, don't kill me," he said between labored breaths.

"Sorry, friend, I'm going to have to kill you, how else am I going to get the bounty."

"But I don't have a bounty on my head."

"Why sure you do, just look at this long list. Murder, thieving, and wow, both sodomy and buggery, you really know how to entertain yourself."

"I didn't do none of those things."

"Ah, but I did and now, you are me."

"But I ain't you and no one is going to believe that I am," Josiah said, suddenly brazen.

"I aim to rectify that situation," I said, swinging hard with the sock and connecting with his mouth once more.

Josiah struggled and squirmed and tried to dodge the blows as I rained fury down upon him. The beating tore a hole in my sock and my knikkers went scattering about the ground with the last blow. The wounded man was almost fifty yards away by the time I got to Helga and got her unhitched. I bore down on him hard and fast, pulling up at the last second so my horse could plant her front hooves to the back of the man's skull. It made me a bit unnerved the way she seemed to enjoy our little romps into violence. It was one of the reasons I never turned my back on her.

The kick to the man's head cracked his skull which meant I had to work fast. There was one thing I learned over the years, once a man is dead, he no longer bruises or swells up and I needed Josiah to be nearly unrecognizable. I made sure to limit my blows to his cheek bones and jaw to keep him alive for as long as possible. His cries of pain had diminished into guttural moans that were more instinctive than anything Josiah was aware of. I felt a tinge of pity for the man when I made eye contact with him but not enough pity to want to change places.

No, I needed to get the hangman's noose from around my neck for good and work to keep it away from Thaddeus Morgan's.

I was exhausted so I rolled Josiah onto his back where he could choke to death on his own blood and then slipped back under my blankets. It was still six hours until daylight and I would need a good night's sleep before heading for the fort in the morning.

Chapter Eighteen

"State your business," an eager young guard with a single stripe ordered with a thick French accent as I approached the gate. He eyed the two corpses draped over the saddles of two horses trailing behind me and gripped his musket firmly.

"I wish to speak with Lieutenant Gagnon," I said.

"Are you a trapper or a trader?"

"Neither."

"Then what is your business with the Lieutenant?" he shouted.

Before I could answer a disheveled man appeared on the parapet with him. It did not appear as though he had been to bed the night prior. "Why all the shouting?" he said, tapping the young soldier on his shoulder while putting a finger to his lip. "I would tell you to come back at eight if you are looking for work, but that does not appear be the case," he nodded at the horses behind me.

"No sir, these two men are wanted by the law. One is an absconder and the other a murderer among other, more dastardly deeds."

"What would you like me to do with them? I do not have a jail here."

"But I was told you do have a cemetery."

"That we do. Then it is safe to assume those men are deceased?"

"Yes, unfortunately, I have cheated the hangman out of his wage."

"I have no authority to pay you for capturing these outlaws."

"I have an idea how we can work something out," I said.

He took off his hat and smoothed his greasy, black hair back with his large hand which he then waved to someone unseen inside the fort who then opened the gate. Helga and I strolled in like we owned the place and I dismounted near the water trough. Although I was undaunted on the façade, I was a bundle of nerves inside. If I miscalculated this situation even a little bit, I would surely face a firing squad, or worse.

He reached a hand out to me as I passed through the gate into the fort proper. I offered mine and when he paused, I saw it was still coated with a menagerie of blood, so I washed it off in the horse trough and dried them on Helga's saddle blanket. He shook my hand firmly and offered me as warm a smile as a man on a three-day drunk could muster. I assumed it was only three days as that was about as much beard stubble that was covering his face.

"You're a Brit?" he asked, but it echoed as more of a statement of fact rather than that of a question.

"In a roundabout way I supposed. But not a loyalist and not by choice. I was merely born on the island and made my way here to this new, growing land."

"Hmmm, don't recognize either of them," the lieutenant said, lifting each man by their hair to give their faces the once over. "You did this to them?"

"It was either that or they would do the same to me."

He motioned a hand to the young soldier who enlisted help in lifting the men off their horses and onto a wagon. I smiled when the inexperience pup rolled Obediah over and got a glimpse of his brains oozing out of the cleft I made in his skull and immediately ran for the bushes.

"Pretty good with a tomahawk I see," Gagnon said as he looked over the big man's wounds.

"I've had some experience with the Indians."

"Fighting for or against?"

"Both one might say."

"Ah, a man of opportunity."

"Again, one might say."

"An absconder you say. What proof do you have of this?"

"I believe it is apparent."

"Meaning?"

"Meaning, he's an African and he attacked me when I questioned whether or not he was a free man. A free man would have been insulted enough to give me a beating, but not try to kill me," I said.

"Understandable conclusion to come to. You said you had a plan, care to enlighten me?"

I walked over and grabbed my whiskey bottle from Helga's saddlebag. The lieutenant seeing this quickly grabbed two pewter glasses from a table on the courtyard. He blew into them and then handed them to me. I poured us a generous portion, his more so than mine, and put the bottle on a nearby table.

"I was thinking you could compensate me for half the reward and then turn them in yourself for the full amount. I'll throw in their horses to sweeten the deal."

"But I have no way of getting these corpses to the proper authorities back east to collect the reward."

"Surely, a man of your reputation can simply send a courier with a letter stating the fact that you paid out the reward and need reimbursed."

"One third and you keep one of the horses," Lieutenant Gagnon offered, realizing he was dealing with a shrewd negotiator.

"Fair enough I suppose, it's not like I'm going to get a better deal elsewhere," I said.

We drank a couple more whiskeys and talked about the particulars of the town and the lay of the land so to speak. After four drinks Gagnon's face began to take on a glow that told me his hangover was done and he was on his way to being drunk again. I guess that was all there was to do in this part of the country for some. He was feeling good enough that he didn't realize I had slowed down on the whiskey after the first one. I wanted just enough to take the edge off the morning and nothing more.

While pouring him another whiskey I took the time to absorb my surroundings. The fort was nothing of the sort, it was more of a small stockade with palisades running to the water's edge. It appeared when erecting the eastern palisade, the builders misjudged the high water mark as two thirds of the log wall was knee deep in water. The roughhewn timbers were covered in vibrant green moss and algae residue. More than one pair of breeches had been hung to dry in the sun telling me that these men were no strangers to mucking around in the swamps.

"So, mister, hmmm I guess I never got your name," Gagnon said with a tilted eye.

"Thaddeus Morgan," I offered.

"Phillipe Gagnon, at your service," he tipped his head and bowed in mockery. "I am the commandant of this magnificent outpost."

I laughed. "And the finest I have ever had the pleasure of visiting."

"What brings you to this God forsaken land Mister Morgan?"

"Just following my horse's lead my good sir. She knows where she wants to go and so far, I have not veered too far off course."

"Seems like a mighty fine way to live one's life. What do you do for work, besides killing absconders and fighting with Indians of course?"

"I tend to lay my hands on whatever can fill my coin purse. I've trapped, hunted, both man and beast, soldiered myself a time or two and even gambled though I'm not very good at that."

"You strike me as a man with quite the vocabulary. Do you know any Ojibwa or Sioux?"

"A little of both I presume, enough to get me killed in either."

He laughed. "If we were to, let's say, enter into an arrangement, is your being a Brit going to be a problem? I mean working with a Frenchman?"

"As I said earlier, I am loyal to myself and my coin purse and not much after that. If you plan to fill my coffers, then I am loyal to you until you decide that is no longer the arrangement."

"That is an answer I can live with. I am in need of a man of your talents."

"Tongue or tomahawk?"

"Possibly both but hopefully the former most of all."

"And what makes you so certain I will prove useful?"

"Because you are either more stupid or more courageous than anyone I have ever run across. Maybe a little of both," he said with a scowl.

"Excuse me?" I responded, taken aback, and caught off guard by the lieutenant's sudden change in disposition.

I realized that several of the soldiers had taken up position with rifles that would afford each of them a shot at me without endangering either of them or their commandant. It had become glaringly apparent that I had over played my hand.

"You see, this is why I do not gamble," I said, resting my hand on my weapon.

"Relax, they are only precautionary. I was not sure how you would react when you realized your charade had been unveiled. While very clever, there was a fatal flaw in your plan. You should not have gotten greedy and brought in the big man as well. Even with his face obliterated he is unmistakable. Now, armed with that knowledge I naturally deduced the other man with him must be Josiah as they were inseparable. A quick check of the tattoo on Josiah's neck and I knew you were being less than truthful," Lieutenant Gagnon said with a smirk.

I started to stand but the riflemen raised his musket into a shooting position, and I thought better of it. "So, where do we go from here," I asked, with a slight tremor in my voice.

"That all depends on you I suppose. And do not worry, you will still get your one third of the reward. I never liked those two vermin anyway and who will be the wiser. Besides, the reward is offered by the Brits so why not take their money. As for you, I think I can put your talents to good use."

"I'm afraid to ask."

"Nothing too dangerous, just make alliances between tribes to the west and north of us."

"Sounds a little too easy," I said, unable to mask my cynicism.

"To make them friends and allies you will have to convince them to make peace with the Ojibwa."

"What purpose will this alliance serve? It doesn't appear they are hostile towards the colonists or the French."

"As I am sure you are already aware, we have not been getting along very well with the British so the more allies we have the better."

"Are the Indians going to prove to be trustworthy allies?"

"No less trustworthy than yourself I suppose," he said with a smile. "For a bunch of savages, they are remarkably noble to their word."

"It sounds as though you are anticipating a war. Aren't we just a little too far to the northwest to be caught up in anything like that?" I asked.

"Who knows how a thing like this might play out? There could be a treaty signed tomorrow that brings peace and makes the damned British our allies. But a thing like this could escalate as well."

"True, there is certainly a lot of unrest in the colonies, one of the reasons I chose to head west where things were more provincial."

"Also, an alliance with the Winnebago or possibly the Ho Chunk might prove useful against the Fox who have been nothing but trouble to the fur traders on the Mississippi."

"I was told this was Sioux country?"

"It is further to the west; they are being encroached by other tribes and have been pushed further and further to the west. The more the colonists push eastern tribes west the more those tribes threaten the existing tribes. This is all good for us though."

"Yes, I suppose it is. If the tribes were to ever unite into one force, they could drive us colonists east to the sea and slaughter the lot of us. Aren't you afraid of that outcome if you bring these tribes together?"

The Lieutenant pondered this while pouring himself another whiskey. He dismissed the guards, shouted some orders in French and sat back down as the soldiers scattered about to do his bidding.

"I am a shrewd war tactician Mr. Morgan, I have that angle already covered. We will use them mostly as scouts and frontline fodder which will thin their ranks considerably. Then, once the war is over and we are victorious we will disperse them back to their respective territories and then either kill them, starve them or finagle them into starting a war amongst each other."

"And just what is it that you need from me?" I asked, tracing the long scar on my cheek.

"You strike me as a shrewd man yourself, so I feel pretty safe in assuming that you know more than one their many dialects and languages."

"That I do, as well as German, Dutch and enough French to get me by."

"I simply need you to meet with the leaders of each nation and offer them my terms."

"They will not enter into this agreement easily and trinkets may not be enough."

"I didn't think they would be. Land, you will offer them land," he said, handing me a hand drawn map.

I looked over the map which included what I could tell was the Ohio River valley as well as other parts east. This did not appear to be land the French were able to give.

"Isn't most of this British claimed land?"

"Yes, and that is the beauty of it. They help us defeat the British and then the land is ours to give them."

"And if you lose?"

"If we lose, they will all be dead anyway, so I won't be bound by any promises you make. See my scout, he has a packet of information you might find useful."

"Seems you were already prepared for this."

"I told you I am a shrewd tactician. One of my scouts who just happens to be British spotted you a few days out from here and reported back to me. Your reputation precedes you and you are not as anonymous as you think. And as fates would allow, you came to me, I didn't have to go to all the trouble of having you arrested and flogged until you agreed to my terms."

I shot him a look of disdain which he responded to with a smug grin that I wanted nothing more than to wipe it from his face. The more I got to know this Frenchman the less and less I liked him and the less I felt I could tolerate the French. I met with Gagnon's scout who provided me with a satchel of maps of the area and notes on the various tribal leaders one of whom was a young Ottawa warrior that he did not have much information on. He was encamped in the Northwest Territory so it looked as though I would be heading back to the land of big water.

Chapter Nineteen

Helga had grown bored of the mundane scenery and was getting a tad bit ornery as we wandered through the scrub grasses surrounding the swampland. She paused to drink from a stream which was taking her much longer than usual. She was a hard rider and preferred to tear up the ground over this slow, methodic pace. But we were in no hurry and my back was still tender from dragging Obediah through the cemetery.

The slow pace left me plenty of time to ponder Lieutenant Gagnon and his offer. I was certain whether successful or not I would surely see a hangman's noose when this was all over. He was too quick with his tongue about his plans for the Indians and I am certain he held them in a much higher regard than he held me. Besides, he was French so he could not be trusted any more than I could trust a Brit. I also deduced he was intelligent enough to know that I would be well aware of his imminent betrayal.

By the second day in the New France wilderness I had already talked Helga's ear off, and she was doing her best to ignore me. It had been weeks since it had rained, and the land was becoming parched which caused me to be mesmerized by the clip clop of her hooves on the hard earth. The sun was blazing and I knew Helga needed some fresh water as did I, and since we were already south into the Illinois Territory I headed for the wide river I knew cut a swath through this untamed land.

The further east I travelled the angrier the sky became, and it was becoming apparent I was in for a night of rough weather. Having passed this way once or twice before in years past, I was aware of a series of canyons littered with sandstone caves along the Illinois River where I would be able to seek shelter from the impending storm. Local tribes used these caves for tribal council, peace negotiations and temporary shelters under just such conditions as I found myself currently in. Hopefully, I wouldn't stumble across a war party in a frenzy. I scouted the area for a bit and found there were no tracks around the area so there was nothing to be concerned about for the time being. I dismounted and let my horse drink her fill before heading into the canyons for the night.

The trail snaked parallel to a stream through sandstone cliffs rising higher and higher as we traversed deeper into the intertwined canyons. There were dozens of canyons, many of which I had never been in, so I hoped I was taking the right trail and that my memory wasn't leading me down a dead end. The melodious sounds of water rushing over rocks sang to me, so I dismounted my horse, not wanting to make the mistake of misjudging the direction of water flow in the diminishing light. I had no desire to plunge to my death over a canyon waterfall.

As I feared the trail dead ended into a horseshoe of striated sandstone with a stream of water plunging nearly one hundred feet over the cliff. Even in the dim light I could see the variations in the colors adorning the walls as if a painter had stroked his brush across the rock before changing shades and repeating the process over and over with a different shade each time. It was nature's artistry at its finest.

I walked Helga around the cliffs until we came to an intersecting trail. We followed that trail, having to ford the stream more than a few times, until we came to another dead end. Here the stream spilled out of the moss-covered canyon walls like a silver tongue. The waterfall was no more than five or six feet high, so I scrambled up the stone face to get a better view. To my chagrin the canyon walls narrowed to a point where only the water could make it through so there was no shortcut in our future.

After several miles of sheer sandstone walls reaching hundreds of feet in places and several more dead ends, I found the place I was looking for just as the rains let loose from the heavens. The cavern, if one could call it that, was fifty feet deep to the back wall which tapered down and a hundred feet tall at the opening. We would be well sheltered from the impending rains.

"Looks like we found this place just in time old girl," I said, leading Helga under the sandstone canopy and out of the storm. I didn't worry about hitching her while I went about setting up camp as she was not one to wander too far off and wouldn't go out in a thunderstorm.

Before bedding down, I checked the high-water mark to make sure I wouldn't be drowned in the middle of the night by a flash flood which were common in these canyons. There was already plenty of dry firewood in the back of the small grotto as was the custom, leave it as you found it and be thoughtful of the next man. There were a couple of bladders filled with fresh water hanging on the back wall as well. Enough for coffee so I put a pot on to boil. Although it was getting dark in the canyon it was still quite early in the afternoon.

Against her wishes and ten minutes of arguing about it I walked Helga out into the rain so we could both rinse the trail off. I used a stiff brush to lather her up and wash away weeks' worth of sweat and grime. I am not all that sensitive, but the poor girl was getting rather pungent, even more so than myself. I got a fire going well enough to dry my clothes, so I waded down into the stream, which had now grown into a river, as far as I dared. Water and I were still not on speaking terms after my ordeal in the Caribbean some years back. I did not miss the ocean one iota, but I was missing pineapples, coconuts, and beautiful island women.

As it was early, and I was not tired enough to sleep I lit several of the torches affixed to the walls of the small cave so I could study the communications left behind from previous visitors. I recognized many of the symbols and drawings from tribes I had encountered over the years. Most were from the area, the Illinois, Ho Chunk and Shawnee but also their enemies, the Winnebago to the north and the Mohawk which were from quite a distance to the east. I was none too pleased to know that the Mohawk knew of this place, this was a long way from their stomping grounds, and I was certain they had not visited this place with the best of intentions. They were not a people I wanted to run into in the broad daylight let alone in a cave at night by myself.

I felt a little more at ease after some more scouting of the area. I concluded this must be a neutral place where fighting was not the norm as I had found no evidence of combat or bloodshed neither recent nor old. Helga seemed to be relaxed so I joined her by setting down on a log near the fire. I had snared a rabbit earlier in the day and set about roasting it over the fire.

Lightning streaked across the sky and thunder rumbled through the canyon. Rather than being ominous, it was almost peaceful in its cacophony. I felt safer with the storm raging. Most animals were smart enough to hunker down in severe weather and even men sought shelter so I might be able to enjoy a good night's sleep for a change. No coyotes yipping or wolves howling or twigs snapping every few minutes.

I threw some more wood on the fire, made certain Helga was securely tied to a tree that served as a hitching post and slid beneath my skins. The rhythmic sounds of the water flowing over the rocks and under branches was quite therapeutic. The tinny sound of the water rushing across small pebbles in the stream was accompanied by the deeper tones of the water flowing under hollowed logs. Before long I was asleep without a care in the world.

Chapter Twenty

I laid motionless, enjoying the warmth of my blankets while listening to the screech of a distant jay and the constant drumming of a woodpecker not much farther off than the blue bird. The rain had stopped, and the world was coming back from the dead as if no storm had ever happened. I sat up and tossed some small sticks on the ashen coals and blew a few strong breaths. As soon as they burst into flames, I arranged four larger pieces as a rest for my coffee pot which I had prepared the night before.

I poured some cold water into the boiling coffee and let the grounds settle before pouring the elixir into my cup. I was blowing the steam off the cup and taking a sip when I heard Helga snort. It sounded peculiar so I glanced over to the hitching tree and she was not there. She snorted again and thumped a hoof on the ground to get my attention from about fifty yards away. At first, I thought she had gotten loose and wandered off but then I realized that she had been tied off to a tree branch. My heart went cold as my hackles went up and I sensed a presence in the grotto with me.

I slowly turned my head around to see three pairs of eyes peering at me from out of the darkness. With as little movement as possible I reached for my bag still unsure of what it was, I was seeing. I had quite possibly chosen to spend the night with a family of black bear who were now hungry for breakfast.

A single word broke the silence, "Gaawiin."

I halted my movement as I could hear a bow string being drawn taught. I recognized the word as a command in a northern language, Ottawa, Ojibwa, maybe even Potawatomie, but definitely not from around here. Just my luck, I made camp with a war party on the prowl or on the retreat, either way they were dangerous.

"Who are you and what brings you to these lands?" a raspy voice asked out of the darkness in English.

"I might ask the same of you," I responded.

"A swift tongue may not be your best option," she said.

"I do apologize, but I have heard that word before much further north. Ojibwa, Potawatomie? Definitely from the Anishinaabe people."

"Your ears hear well. I think you know enough already."

"As long as you are not Mohawk, I can breathe a little easier," I said, and someone grunted from the shadows alerting me to the fact there was at least one male in the group.

"Ha, those flesh eaters, I'd rather starve to death. Is that coffee I smell?"

"Yes, I only have one cup but you're more than welcome to share," I said, refilling my cup and handing it into the shadows of the grotto.

"Thank you. My progenies prefer that nasty tea the British drink," she said.

"I hate tea myself, so I ration my coffee."

"You sound British, but you also sound French?"

"I'm a little of both I suppose with a few measures of Dutch and Indian as well."

"It is good to be all things and one thing at the same time. You still have not answered my question."

"And you still haven't answered mine," I said with a smug grin I was certain she could see even in the diminished light.

"It seems we are at an impasse. Maybe my next question will clear things up for you."

I stared into the dark shadows hoping to catch a glimpse of who I was conversing with. But to no avail, she could see me plain as day and I was as blind as a bat.

"Are you prepared to die today?" she asked, her voice no longer jovial.

"In this violent, unpredictable world in which we live, I wake each morning prepared to die that day. But I would prefer not to," I responded.

I took my cup from her and refilled it with a couple more sips of coffee while contemplating my options which appeared to be dead center between slim and none. If she were traveling with only two warriors, they would undoubtedly be very skilled. In a fair fight, where I could see my aggressors I might stand a fighting chance, but as blind as I was I did not stand a snowball's chance in hell of making it out of that grotto alive without negotiating properly.

"I am on a mission given to me by a French commandant at Fort La Baye further west."

"I know of that fort and of that soldier. I do not like him very much. He is friendly with the Fox and Dakotas, we are not. What is this mission you speak of?"

"He sent me north to speak with a young warrior, the leader of the Potawatomie."

"What will you speak about?"

"Fighting with France against the British."

"It is not wise to meddle in other people's squabbles."

"I agree wholeheartedly. However, I do not have any other option."

She said something to the other two in a language I not only didn't understand but didn't recognize either. I sensed they relaxed a little and were no longer aiming a drawn bow at me. She handed me back the coffee cup and from the noises she was making I determined she was gathering her things.

"Thank you for the coffee, it was much welcomed after being forced to drink the putrid drink of the British for so long."

"You are more than welcome."

"So, what are your plans once you meet this young warrior?"

"I hadn't really thought that far ahead. I imagine I would talk with this warrior and let him know what the French were offering."

"Do you know this man well enough to sit down and have a talk with him?"

"Never met him."

"What makes you think he will even speak with you?"

"You are speaking with me, aren't you? I have a way of warming up to people."

She laughed long and hard before she said, "This warrior might be warming you up instead."

I looked back at her with confusion painted on my face.

"If this is the same man, I am thinking of he likes to use fire to loosen tongues and coax the truth from people."

"I will remember to speak the truth at all times then and relieve him of the need to use such harsh methods."

I heard some more rustling from within the darkness. I moved back away as the light flickered and danced revealing that she was exiting from the shadows. When she finally made her way into the daylight, I was more confused than I had ever been in my life. She stood before me, not much taller than my waist and no more than eight years old, yet eyes milky white from age. The skin of her face was smooth and taught like a baby's bottom, but her hands were wrinkled and jagged with arthritis. She was a contradiction before my eyes. She giggled at my first impression and it echoed like a little girl at play.

I scanned over her wardrobe which itself was a contradiction. It held no particular tribal or clan style, but instead represented many tribes I knew of and many that I didn't. From a belt around her midsection dangled dozens of human scalps, again representing many different nations by their complexions and adornments. There were Europeans, and a few what I assumed to be Africans as well. I shuddered. How did such a slight little girl manage to send that many souls to hell?

Around her waist was a belt that Noah himself would have been envious of. Encircling her waist were the shriveled feet of birds, mammals, reptiles, a complete menagerie of denizens of the earth. Interspersed with the hooves and talons were several sets of baby's feet, human baby feet of all shades. At second glance they revealed themselves to be merely the feet of some unidentifiable animal. I shuddered.

And then she smiled at me a jagged smile with a mouth filled with teeth like that of a shark. Several strips of fresh meat dangled from between her teeth. She was neither man, nor beast, she was both at the same time. Never in my life had I experienced a fear as deeply as this one.

She made a motion with her hand and giggled. Her companions slid out of the shadows and into the light of the day and my fear increased tenfold. They stood before me pale like ghost warriors but without the aid of ashen paint. Their eyes were wild and staring and seemed to peer right through me. She smiled, and they smiled. She frowned and they frowned.

For lack of anything else to say I asked, "Can they see or are they blind?"

"They see what I want them to see," she replied.

"Do they speak?"

"They say what I want them to say," she said.

She said something in a language I did not understand, and they repeated it as best they could without tongues. Two angry red nubbins of flesh vibrated as they grunted their mimic.

"Did you cut out their tongues?"

She shrugged. "I was hungry, and they talked too much."

"Are they dead?"

"When I want them to be. And when I want, they are also very much alive."

I wanted to run to Helga and ride out of that canyon as fast as her legs could take us but somehow, I knew that was not an option. The two man-creatures turned their gaze upon me, but I was certain she was the one looking me over. I had heard tales of a creature the north eastern tribes called a Wendigo, but that was all just folklore to scare children with.

I am not a wendigo, but you are wrong, they are not just imaginary creations to scare children.

I heard the little girl's voice in my head just as plain as if she had spoken the words into my ear. A sense of dread washed over me like tides in a monsoon. I feared my life was about to change forever.

"I am none of the legends you have heard of from the tribes you have had the pleasure of visiting, and yet, I am all of those legends and more combined."

Although terrified, I was also intrigued and had a thousand and one questions. "Are you human?"

"I like to believe so, at least part of me is."

"So then are you a ghost?"

"I am neither alive, nor dead and yet I am both at the same time."

"Do you always speak in riddles?"

"Do you always ask such obvious questions?"

"What do you want from me?"

"I have this, shall we call it a gift, of finding the darkest souls living among the rest of humanity."

"Are you insinuating that I have a dark soul?"

"As black as the night itself."

"I think your magic has failed you child, or old woman whichever may be the case," I said.

For some reason, her comment had struck a nerve with me. I may have done some shady things in my life, but I was still an honorable man, at least to a degree. Although I must admit to myself that I had forsaken God on more than one occasion.

"My perception never fails me. You on the other hand, you have failed the dark gift you have been given."

"Failed it? How?"

"You fail to embrace it. A dark soul is a powerful tool to be used wisely, for both good and evil. A dark soul does not mean that you are not an honorable man," she said, her voice dripping with sarcasm.

"Can you read my thoughts?"

"Until I get bored with them," she said with a sneer. "In a sense, but in truth, you tell me your thoughts, I do not go looking for them. I do not read them, you read them to me."

"Why on earth would I do that?"

"You do no such thing, your soul does it for you. Just as I am drawn to dark souls, dark souls are also drawn to me."

"Woman, you speak nonsensical like an insubordinate child. I am finished with this conversation and will be moving on. If I have to kill them, I will," I said, realizing the two braves had taken up an offensive posture had been staring me down with their weapons at the ready.

"If you kill them you will just have to take their place. But you are worth far more to me than that."

"Your sorcery does not scare or intimidate me in the least. I've seen better parlor tricks than your little mind reading gag and these two who you have entranced on the islands in the Caribbean. Call it voodoo, obeah, whichever you choose, it scares me not."

You certainly did enjoy being a pirate, didn't you? Other than that dastardly run in with the French I imagine. Can you still feel the burning of the water as it filled your lungs? Can you still hear the screams of the women and children you murdered to save yourself?

I shivered as my chest tightened and my throat began to close. I was thrust back into the memories of my past as if they were occurring at that precise moment. I heard the roar of the cannons and felt the timbers beneath my feet groan and crack from the onslaught. I could hear the tearing of the sheets as grape shot tore through my vessel's masts.

My stomach roiled as the smell of burning flesh invaded my nostrils mixed with the pungent vapors of smoldering pitch. Searing heat surrounded me as did the anguished screams of dying men. And the pigs were much worse than the men. They let loose the most terrifying squeals as the ship floundered and tossed them into the sea, squeals so loud they even drowned out the cries of my own child begging me not to leave her behind.

I could feel shackles being fastened around my wrists and ankles and then the stinging of the cat o'nine across my back. My friends were dying all around me and these French bastards were putting the whip to me. They demanded information I would not part with, so my wife and child parted with their heads.

"Scuttle her," I heard a French officer cry out as they abandoned my vessel for theirs, leaving me lashed helpless to the mast. As they broke away from my vessel, they fired a deadly salvo into her broadside. I laughed an ironic laugh, a sea captain who could not swim.

The yardarm gave into the assault with an eerie crack that split the night. The mast toppled and the ship capsized, pulling me down into the briny depths. I felt the burning of my lungs as I tried not to breathe in the deadly seawater. At that moment I sought out a Lord, any lord who would save my retched soul.

The woman released her grip on my mind, "Have you ever seen that parlor trick before?" she asked.

I was gasping for breath and could not answer. How had this woman invaded my mind in such a manner? How had she brought back memories so vivid that I almost didn't even recognize them as my own? If I had not feared her before, I truly feared her now. I wanted to touch my skin, but I feared it would be coated with briny sea water.

I looked over at the two human statues guarding her and said, "Please, I do not want to be like them."

"These two? No, these two had souls of pure light and would do me no good other than nourishment and pack mules. No, to sustain me I need a dark soul, a soul such as yours."

"What will you do with my soul?" my voice quivered as I asked. I suddenly felt like a small child, helpless and terrified.

"I will take nothing from your soul, it is what your soul will provide to me. You strike me as a man of ambition, a man who wants everything possible out of life. Is this not true?"

I found myself very leery about answering any more of her questions. I felt as though each were a trap set to ensnare and enslave me as she had done with her companions. For the briefest butterfly flutter of time my mind drifted to Helga and a thought of escape.

You will never make it to your horse before their arrows bring you down. And they will not aim to kill.

Again, the woman, child, never uttered a single word out loud but her voice echoed in my head just the same. I was trapped inside of a nightmare of which there was no awakening.

"So, you plan to kill me then?" I found the courage to ask.

She let loose a laugh that was both the laughter of a child coupled with the cackle of an old hag and entirely sinister. Shivers ran across my skin as though a cold wind had just blown through the cave. Goosebumps were visible on my forearms.

"Quite the contrary my dear Thaddeus Morgan, or should I call you Elijah Blackwood, the famed pirate, scourge of the Caribbean?"

"Elijah will do in this closed company. And I was a privateer, not a pirate."

"Call it what you will. I have known of you for a long time and fate has put you right in my lap and I intend to make good use of your many talents."

"And if I do not agree?" I asked, trying to ignore the fear coursing through my veins. The entire time we conversed her two companions stared me down with calculating looks which I knew were actually her scrutinizing my every word, thought and twitch.

"If you do not agree then that will be your loss and we will both go our separate ways. But even if half of your legend is true then you will be regretting that choice for the few short years you have left on this earth."

"Few short years? I am still a fairly young, virile man what do you mean by few short years?"

"Can we agree on something? That I am wise beyond my years however many they may be?"

I nodded, "You appear to be."

"And that I know things I could not possibly know?"

"Yes."

"You are ill Mr. Morgan-Blackwood."

"Sick? How? I feel perfectly fine."

"And you are perfectly fine, for now. But you have a malignancy festering inside of you. It is growing without your knowledge and eventually it will consume you."

I thought about her words and what they meant. At first thought I was filled with a sense of dread, of impending doom. But then I came to the realization that I had already lived my entire life prepared to die at a moment's notice. And while I did not wish to die, I would welcome death just the same.

"If what you are saying is true then I must start living my life as each day is my last which would mean I do not have any time to spare for your nonsense."

"Oh, dear Elijah, but you will not go gently into the darkness. You will start to slowly rot away, piece by miserable piece until the sickness consumes you. This will impart months, maybe years of agony upon your life. Are you prepared for that?"

Once more I paused to think about this woman child. Was what she spoke the truth? Or was this the shapeshifting trickster Loki I had encountered? Although far from Viking lands, it was not out of the question for a god to travel long distances. What in the hell was I thinking, the gods were not real, they were myths, stories spun by storytellers with an insatiable appetite for an audience?

No dear Elijah, I am not Loki, although I did meet him once and he is very real. Her cackle echoed in my brain.

"Assuming what you say is true, just what is it you want, and just what is it you are offering me?" I asked, sensing I had no other choice than to play along with her little game.

She waved a wrinkled, arthritic hand and her two warriors dismissed themselves to go lead Helga to water. I watched them carefully as they tended to my longtime companion. For some reason I had visions of them tearing into her flesh with their teeth like rabid beasts. But they were gentle and caring to my horse, so I relaxed. I still had the sense I was treading through a nightmare and would awaken from this all to a good laugh with Helga.

"I am offering you life, pure and simple."

"There is no such thing as pure and simple and I feel safe to assume even less so where your offer is concerned. Exactly what is it you demand in return?"

"The same from you. I give you life so that you give me life as well."

"And how would I accomplish this?"

"I know you are a wise man, a man of the world so to speak so I know you sense there is more to me than meets the eye."

"That is putting it mildly as what meets the eye isn't clearly observed."

"Would it make it easier for you to believe if I told you I am a god?"

"Or maybe a demon working in consort with Satan himself to steal my soul and condemn me to hell."

"Dear Elijah, I'm afraid you condemned yourself to hell a long, long time ago. I offer you an alternative to the eternal misery. I offer you immortality, which will in fact cheat the devil out of his due."

Chapter Twenty-One

Beset with the urge to run, to escape, I wandered away from the grotto. My new acquaintance allowed me to walk through the canyon to be with my thoughts, albeit she sent one of her companions to tag along. He followed far enough behind that soon I had forgotten all about his being there. I contemplated what she had said even though I found I was hard pressed to believe a word of it. Her stories were those of legends and untruths. How could she possibly know I would grow ill? I found myself wishing I had Helga to talk to rather than this mute creature who had become my second shadow.

The longer I walked the more outrageous I found this whole situation to be. I had permitted this roguish old woman get into my head with her lies and half-truths. I laughed to myself as I gathered my thoughts and decided to head back to camp. It was time for me to forget the old woman and go about my business.

When I turned around my traveling companion was standing on the trail blocking my way. His eyes were no longer lost in a distant stare, but rather staring right into my soul. I was preparing myself for battle when I lost control of my senses and my mind drifted away from me. I was no longer on a trail in the hills of the Illinois Territory, I was in a small cabin surrounded by snow.

I could see my face as clear as a reflection in a crystal pool, but it wasn't my face either. My face was gaunt and distorted, lips blackened and eyes hollow. I only knew it was my own reflection because of the self-inflicted wounds to my face. The slash across my cheek to my chin and the flattened nose that curved to the right at an odd angle. I deduced this must be the older version of me, the sickly me. I tore myself away from the image and turned away from the ashen warrior. This was nothing more than a mere trick and I was being a fool led around by an old hag. I had heard tales of Europeans who purported to be able to manipulate men's minds through suggestive thought, maybe she was a gypsy from the east.

Shall I dance a gypsy dance for you?

I turned away but still, without even facing him I saw his hollow gaze haunting my every thought. I clamped my eyes shut and still, there he was. And there I was, a broken man only half there. My face was distorted in pain and my eyes black as the night. A wound opened in my chest, black blood oozing down my sides into piles of bandages. I could see my heart pulsating, beat by beat as it struggled to keep me alive.

In the center of this human stew was a large black mass resembling a potato with tentacles reaching into my every organ. Was this the sickness the diminutive oracle had warned me about? Gazing further down I saw my body ended at the waist and silhouettes were cutting even more of me away. Piece by piece I had been excised from my own body and was too frail to even struggle let alone fight back.

I was in some sort of chamber with seats set high above and dozens of eager faces peering down into my gaping chest while a man dressed in white cut slices out of this blackened globule attached to my innards. I wanted them to stop staring, I wanted them to leave but I had no voice. I was held fast to the table and unable to move. I realized I did not feel any pain. Was I dead?

Elijah, Dear Elijah,
See what becomes of you.
Elijah, Dear Elijah,
They will cut you clean in two.

Her voice taunted me from beyond my own brain. I could feel her wiggling through me like worms on a decaying corpse. I spun around to face her, but she wasn't there. I was exasperated and exhausted.

Once more the warrior caught my gaze and once more, I was transported to a different world. But this was not my world, this was his world. I saw him with dozens of other warriors facing off against an unseen foe. Men with bows drawn and others with long war clubs adorning spikes up the shaft and large stones tied to the ends. A dozen men sat on painted ponies with lances at the ready. I recognized the dress as that of the Iroquois nation, more specifically, the feared and loathed Mohawk.

And then I saw their enemy, a lone little girl standing at the edge of the forest in a pretty yellow dress the color of daffodils. The horsemen split up and flanked the girl while the archers took up a rear position. The warriors held their clubs high as they readied their charge. And yet, she stood there, defiant against all odds.

I scanned the warrior's eyes and saw a fear I had never seen before. Even when my cutlass was arcing through the air toward an enemy's throat, I did not see this depth of fear. This was not a fear of life and death of the flesh, this was a fear that cut through to the soul. I felt a chill encapsulate me and struggled to pull away from his gaze, but I was held fast.

The clubmen charged the little girl, letting loose an eerie war whoop in unison. The archers let their arrows fly and the clubmen fell. The horsemen charged full speed, turned, and charged the archers with lances low impaling the bowman one by one. The horses screamed, threw their riders, and dashed off into the forest. Somehow this little girl had dispatched more than fifty warriors without lifting an eyebrow.

The horsemen gathered their composure and began to run, but instead of running away, they ran straight for her. They dropped to their knees in front of her and it seemed they were awaiting instructions. Each of the twelve men turned to face each other, locking eyes with their hands at their sides. The little girl fidgeted and rocked back and forth from the balls to the heels of her feet for several minutes. It was as if time were suspended and the world had come to a standstill.

And then she turned to seemingly face me and smiled a wicked little smile. I saw that this little girl had the same teeth as the old hag and the same wrinkled, arthritic hands. I then realized that she was indeed the old hag. But her eyes were not milky with cataract and age, they were vibrant, almost flaming red. She turned her gaze back to the kneeling warriors, all of whom were looking back at her. She raised her hands to the heavens in what I felt was more of a dramatic effect then out of necessity.

What ensued was the most horrific thing I have ever witnessed. The warriors all turned to each other and attacked one another with their teeth. Chaos ensued as a dozen men grappled with each other's blood-soaked bodies. They were both fighting to feed and fighting to not be fed upon. The air was split by the god-awful sounds of gnashing and gnawing of teeth and guttural screams of men who had been robbed of their humanity by some unseen force.

When all was said and done there were two men writhing on the ground, still alive. That was when I recognized who they were, they were her two bodyguards. She floated over to them and buried her face in their pulsating fountain of life spewing from their necks. At first, I thought she was drinking their blood, but then realized she was actually healing their wounds. She stood above them and I watched in horror as she drained the very life force from them. She was consuming their very souls.

The warrior, or was it she, released their grip on my mind. Although his stare was once again distant and aloof, I thought I spied a certain measure of sorrow behind the mask. I knew then that I did not have an option, my fate had been sealed a long time ago. As if reading my mind the brave spun on his moccasin clad heels and started leading me down the trail back to the grotto where the rest of my life awaited me whether I wanted to embrace it or not.

Chapter Twenty-Two

After what proved to be a dreadfully long, quiet night we packed up and left the grotto on foot the next morning. Helga followed along beside us carrying our packs. I didn't feel it would be very chivalrous to ride while the old woman-child walked, and she declined my invitation to let her ride. Truth be told, Helga was the one who truly declined as she wanted no part of this crone.

The two men were not much for conversation, so our little troupe ambled along mile after mile in silence. I found it odd how hushed the forest had become. Not one single jay screeched in protest of our encroachment, not one single squirrel foraged through the underbrush and not one single chipmunk let us know who was king of the forest. Even Helga kept her snorts to a minimum and straggled back so far at times I had to stop and wait for her to catch up.

I began to rethink my role in this entourage and was seriously considering lighting out at the very first opportunity. Helga was showing a true disdain of this situation and she had proven her judge of character correct on many occasions. I was formalizing a plan in my head when I was made aware of just how fruitless escape would prove to be.

Elijah, Dear Elijah,
When will you begin to see?
Elijah, Dear Elijah,
You have no choice but to play with me.

I heard the old woman's voice taunting me as we made our way through the forest, and although it had the sing song lyric of a child's playground rhyme it had the tone of a raspy old crone. What on God's green earth was this creature? She was neither old, nor young, alive, nor dead. She was living within the gray matter of my skull like a parasite devouring my every thought.

"No, you are not in hell, nor purgatory," she said seemingly even before I had thought the thought.

"Then have I gone completely mad?"

"On the contrary, you're as sane as ever. Have you considered my offer?"

"What offer might that be?"

"Immortality."

I glanced over at the two guardians walking beside me, their vacant stares and blank expressions haunted me even in the daylight. I wondered if they had even so much as a coherent thought that was their own. Were they cognizant of their plight? Or was it even a plight at all? Maybe they were volunteers, and this was a great honor for them. Either way, it was not something I relished to spend eternity as my role.

"If it comes at a price such as theirs, I think not."

"These two? They are not being rewarded, they are being punished. I leave them with just enough humanity to remember who they were and what they had done to offend me."

"How long must they endure this?"

"For as long as I have to endure what angered me in the first place."

"And if I anger you in any way?"

"That would not bode well for you I am afraid. Now, enough of this nonsense, I am hungry," she said and angled off the trail toward a majestic oak reaching into the sky to cradle the sun.

The two men disappeared into the ebon forest as I helped the woman spread out her furs and blankets. She scooted up against the tree for support and took a long pull from her water bag. I pulled a few sticks of jerked rabbit from my pocket and offered her a piece which she gladly accepted. The men returned about a half an hour later bringing gifts of apples and rabbits they had already skinned and cleaned. They built a small fire and set out roasting sticks of rabbit meat. My belly grumbled at the aroma.

The apples were petite and were rather sour. The old woman must have seen the look on my face and offered me a pouch filled with a strange brown powder. I followed her lead and dipped a slice of my apple into the powder and touched it to my tongue. At first it burned and tingled but then a flavor coated my tongue and made the apple taste delectable.

"Woman, what is this strange substance?"

"It is from the bark of a tree far, far from here. Across the great waters."

"How did you come to possess such an exotic spice?"

"I cannot remember actually. I sometimes acquire things and then forget about them. I am a collector of sorts," she said without looking up from the bag she was rummaging through.

The two men worked at cooking the rabbit and a few handfuls of wild rice they had managed to forage. An odd aroma caught my attention and I watched them closely as they prepared lunch.

"That smell is from a root also found across the great water. It is very finicky, not enough and you won't taste it, too much and it will ruin the flavor."

"You sure are filled with mysteries aren't you, old woman?"

"Not to me, to me these things are as old and common as life itself."

"Ah yes, and you continue to speak in riddles and conundrums. Tell me woman, what is it you truly desire from me?" I asked, taking a seat opposite her.

The woman rummaged through her bags and pulled out a small leather pouch. Upon further scrutiny I saw the leather was tanned and sported several long, black hairs.

She looked up, caught my gaze, and said, "oyhótsaˀ."

I looked at her bewildered, it was a dialect or language I had yet to hear. She reached out and touched me on my chin but then made a gesture of my chin being much bigger.

"Was an Oneida, I did not like him."

"Obviously."

She dumped the contents of the bag out into a small wooden cup shook it a few times and dumped it onto a tanned piece of leather which resembled a human scalp. I was expecting to see bones or runes of some sort as was the practice of seers I had had the misfortune to run across from time to time. But I could have never been prepared for the dozen or so dried, withered eyeballs that rolled haphazardly out onto the leather mat.

After my initial shock I looked over the tableau once more. Two of the eyeballs were not dried and withered, they were very much alive and vibrant with color. They glistened with tears and seemed to stare straight into my very soul. For a reason unbeknownst to me I was blanketed with sorrow and tears glistened my own eyes. I glanced over at one of the warriors tending the rabbit.

"No, Elijah, they are not his eyes, he still has his," she let her words trail off. "For now."

"This must be some kind of trick."

"No trick, but maybe just a smidgen of magic," she said with a snaggletooth grin.

"What is the purpose of this?"

"To see the road before us of course."

I let myself wander through my memories and recalled with horror all of the places I had been recently. In each of them there had been a sightless child with blackened scars for eyes begging for something to eat, a few coins. The contempt shown in my eyes.

She shrugged, "There is sometimes a high price for immortality. One must sacrifice something."

"Their sacrifice or yours?"

"Surely you do not expect me to sacrifice my eyes, I am the one offering the gift."

"But they are just children."

"Children tend to observe more of their surroundings. Adults tend to see only what they wish to see."

It was then that I realized the horror of these children's plight. Not only were they blind, unable to see and care for themselves, but she had made them immortal as well. It was high time I bid this woman adieu. I began to gather my things.

"You are wrong Elijah, I do not enslave them for eternity. It was a gift for another they received. A sick sibling, or parent. They prayed to me and I entered into an agreement with them, just as I have done with you."

"You wait just a damned minute, I never agreed to anything with you," I said, standing up. The two warriors stood up as well.

"Oh, but you did dear Elijah. Do you recall partaking of my flesh?"

"I did no such thing."

"Ah, but dear Elijah, you are the apple of my eye."

"What? You are mad woman. You cannot feed me some foreign spice and claim it was your flesh. Do you take me for a fool? I am not so easily swayed by your trickery as others."

"I assure you, no trickery is afoot."

Suddenly I felt strange, as if the earth had disappeared beneath my feet and I was floating. Was I ascending to Heaven as spoke about in the great book? Truly I could not be, as I never once believed in such nonsense and believed them only to be words meant to enslave men. But here I was, walking in an ethereal plane of existence. I could see the old woman watching me as bewilderment enveloped me.

I felt euphoric, warm, yet cool, hungry, yet sated, dead and yet so alive, passion burned all around me engulfing my very soul. I could feel myself changing and wondered if this was what a caterpillar felt while in the cocoon. I started to laugh, little chuckles at first, but then big, deep belly laughs that echoed across the countryside. It was then I began to ponder, had I become a god? Is that what she meant by becoming immortal? Was I to live on the mount of Olympus with Zeus and Apollo?

Then all at once I came crashing back to earth and was consumed with a hunger unlike anything I had ever experienced before in my existence.

"No dear Elijah, you are not a god and you do not belong on Olympus."

Once again, the old woman had read my very thoughts. Maybe this was all a dream, a nightmare from which I had revealed my thoughts without realizing it.

"No dear Elijah, you are not asleep, you are very much awake. In fact, I have awakened your soul and it is its' hunger you are experiencing."

Chapter Twenty-Three

I was up before the dawn, pacing about like a madman in the moonlight. Both body and mind were under siege from unseen forces. I was experiencing extreme anxiety without reason as to why. And no matter what I tried I could not get Helga to come near me which tormented me even further. I needed someone to talk to and she had always been the perfect listening ear.

I cannot possibly convey into words the internal agony I was feeling. If I had to describe it in a word it would have to be hollow, empty, I had become a shadow of a man. The hunger burning inside me like none I have ever known. But it was not a hunger of the belly, something a good slug of warm water could abate. No, this was a hunger which I could not begin to reason with.

"What in God's name is happening to me?" I cried out to the darkness.

"God is not responsible for your plight. You and you alone have brought this upon yourself," her voice whispered on the black wind.

Shadowman, Shadowman,
We are now one.
Shadowman, Shadowman,
We've only just begun

"What have you done to me?" I screamed out in desperation as I writhed on the cold earth trembling with cold whilst sweating with fever. In a brief moment of respite my thoughts wrapped around the idea I had somehow contracted influenza, or worse.

"No, you are not ill from fever. You have neither the fever nor the pox. You have the hunger," she said while standing above me.

"The hunger? But I do not crave food, in fact, I believe I would vomit should I eat."

"Then what is it you are craving?"

"That is precisely the problem, I have no clue what it is that I desire, and it is driving me mad. If it were a grumbling in my belly I would partake of food, if it were a thirst, I would slake it with water or wine. But this, this is something unimaginable."

"I can imagine because it is my hunger you are feeling. Is it knowledge you crave?"

I searched my emotions with her words in mind, "Yes."

"Power?"

"Yes, most definitely, yes."

"Fear?"

I thought long and hard about this and yes, I very much desired to see the fear in my enemy's eyes. I longed for that precise moment when they realized they had lost the battle and I was about to steal their life from them. Yes, this was something I truly missed now more than ever. I wanted to fight, I wanted to kill but most of all, I wanted to be feared above all others. I felt a desire burning in the very pit of my soul, a desire to be God.

"Very good dear Elijah, you are starting to understand just what it is I am offering you."

"What do you get out of it?"

"In short, I get to survive as well."

"And how will my desires help you to survive?"

"We are both parasites, you and I. You will feed from the dark souls of wicked men and I in turn will feed from you."

"When does this pain and discomfort subside?"

"When you feed dear Elijah, when you feed."

"Will I become like them?" I nodded to the two men who simply stared off into the morning sky as if watching birds that were not even there.

"No, you will become an extension of me."

The old woman took hold of the freshest scalp on her belt, held it to her face and breathed in deeply. Somehow this seemed to placate the tremors rushing through my body like lightning.

"It will not satisfy me much longer. We need a fresh soul."

With that she spread her tableau on the ground in front of her and pulled the chin pouch from her pack. Once more she dumped the collection of eyeballs onto the leather mat. This time there were four of them glistening and alive.

"What are you doing old woman?"

"These are my eyes throughout the world. They show me things I need to see."

"And what do they show you right now," I said with skepticism.

She picked up one of the pair, gazed into the wet orbs and dropped them back into the pouch with the dried eyeballs. She then picked up a set with the most vibrant green irises I had ever seen and gazed into them for several minutes. Tingles ran up my spine from the sheer macabre nature of the scene. Slowly her old mouth curled from a spiteful, sour frown into the smile of a child. Once again, I was overcome by the phenomena that was this old woman. I had always thought medicine man and shaman rituals were nothing more than tricks to amaze the weak minded. I now realized just how wrong I had been.

"I have good news dear Elijah, there are dark souls about."

"And these emerald eyes have told you this?"

"Yes, there is a small village north of here. And outside this village there is a small band of highwaymen whom I have no doubt are scoundrels of the worst sort."

"So, I am to be a vigilante then?"

"Of sorts I suppose, but only out of convenience not righteousness. You must know that innocent souls will not do, in fact, they will do you much more harm than good. You must remember to keep your distance from children as they tend to have clean souls."

"But what of you and the children's eyes?"

"I did only take their eyes, besides, they still have their souls as they still have their lives."

"What about these two? Do they still have their souls?"

"In a roundabout way. I have them tucked away for safe keeping. If they serve me well, when the time comes, I will return them and let them pass into the afterlife."

"So, does that mean you believe in the Heaven spoke about in the Bible?"

"Almost as much as I believe in Hell," she nodded with a grin.

Chapter Twenty-Four

Helga still wanted nothing to do with our travelling party, but she had nothing better to do so she followed us at a leisurely, safe distance. Every time I slowed down to let her catch back up, she would snort and match my pace, so I just let her straggle. We came upon a small river with no way across other than to ford the river. I walked back and grabbed Helga's reins against her protest and dropped them just as soon as I had picked them up. My hand was nearly transparent, and I could see the leather straps through my flesh. I turned an astonished glance toward the old woman who simply shrugged and started off across the water.

"Old woman, what is the meaning of this?" I cried out while holding my semitransparent hand up to the sun.

"Wenonah," she responded.

"What in the hell does that mean?"

"That is my name, quit calling me old woman for I am neither old, nor a woman."

She turned to gaze at me, waist deep in the river. Something about her was so much different. Her eyes, they shone in a different light. And suddenly I realized she was right, she was neither old, nor a woman but just a little girl. A frightened little girl.

I was torn between her fear of the water and Helga's fear of us. I tied my horse to a tree lest she get the idea to abscond while we were fording the river. I picked Wenonah up and placed her on the backs of one of the warriors and held her there while we crossed. Once safely on the other side I went back across for Helga.

"Thank you, Elijah, while I do not fear much, water is a true nemesis. One day you will understand."

"Now, explain this," I said, once again showing her my hand.

"In short, you are dying."

"But you said I would be immortal?"

"In a sense, you are. But your immortality is something you must constantly work at. I am immortal as well, but as with you, I must always work at staying alive. We do not retain our corporeal forms if we become too ravenous."

"How long can we survive without feeding?"

"I do not know, and I have had no desire to find out. You will grow to embrace this gift I have bestowed upon you."

"Doesn't seem I have much choice in that matter."

Wenonah simply smiled and shrugged her shoulders. I was struggling to believe this woman and deep down in my heart of hearts I knew this was all just some sort of trick. And yet, my body was wracked with pain and desire whilst fading away into oblivion. Minute by minute I could feel not only my body going through changes but my mind as well. I had rambled through my life to this point with no real motivation or goals other than seeing the sun the next day. But now, I sensed a purpose even though I had no tangible idea what it was.

"Does this intense, gnawing desire ever subside?"

"At times. But it will always remain within you in some capacity. But remember, whatever you are experiencing, for me it is much worse."

"It could truly drive a man insane."

"I never had much use for sanity anyway," she said, laughing until she coughed up phlegm.

"I'm glad you're amused."

"Do you always bellyache this much? I am trying to have a peaceful moment before we continue," she said, picking at something in her jagged teeth.

I sat back down with a grumble and began rummaging through my pack. I ate a piece of hard tack, then a piece of jerky, but then I wanted something sweet, so I scrounged around until I found some wild strawberries. Nothing satisfied me. I found myself seriously contemplating what one of the warriors, or even the old woman would taste like.

"I imagine I would taste similar to shoe leather in my present state. But he might taste better than that fellow from Martinique," she said, nodding to one of the men squatting beside her.

How the hell had she known about Martinique? The longer I was around this creature the less I could tolerate it. She was an enigma wrapped in a mystery.

"What in the devil are you talking about?"

"You were marooned so I can't say that I blame you. And had I been in your shoes I'm sure I would have dined with a bit more voracity than even you."

How on earth could this creature before me know about such things? Only two of us made it off the ship alive before she went down and Henri' was gravely wounded. We made it to the shore of some small reef island near the waters off Martinique, but I did not know that at the time. This island was but a mere grain of sand in the expansive sea. There was no life other than the two of us and an occasional passing bird. Henri' had taken a French musket ball to his abdomen and while the shot would not be fatal under normal circumstance, on an island with no surgeon or medical supplies he was doomed.

The desolate days passed, and I cared for him the best I could, but his life slipped away with each ebbing tide. I had managed to trap a few minnows with my shirt and found a coconut or two but not nearly enough to sustain my life for more than a day or two let alone enough for Henri' to share. Infection had set in and it was but a few hours before I would be saying goodbye to an old colleague.

I could not find a rock large enough to put Henri' out of his misery quickly and I did not have the heart to choke my good friend to death even though he had begged me many times. I was standing knee deep in the water with a piece of conch shell getting ready to draw enough blood to hopefully attract enough sharks to end our despair when an armada of canoes came from the windward side of the island. First two, then three and eventually half a dozen canoes with six men in each came ashore.

In my weakened condition the most I could do to defend myself was to smile at them. I prayed they would end my life mercifully and give me a proper burial. I was still unsure of their intentions even after they had given me a few bites of fruit and fresh water. As they were tending to my minor wounds another canoe rounded the cape with only two oarsmen, a very large man and a small little girl.

The pretty little girl wore a yellow flowered dress and a carefree attitude. She stopped where the men were tending to me and smiled down at me. She bent and kissed me on the forehead before making her way over to where Henri' was dying in the sand. She gazed upon him with eyes that seemed gleeful, not sad as one would think in the presence of death. She whispered something in his ear, he nodded, and she motioned for one of the men.

I watched in horror as the man pulled a large knife from a sheath on his waist and sliced off one of Henri's cheeks. My friend screamed in agony as another slice of the blade removed his calf muscle. Even from where I was, I could sense the fear emanating from him as his life spilled onto the sand. The young girl turned at looked upon me with a sinister gaze, one that I thought I would never forget.

I looked up at Wenonah and said, "That was you?"

"What in the devil are you talking about? What was me?"

"The little girl, on the island, that was you."

"How could that be? That was not that long ago, and I am an old woman now as you can see," she laughed, yet, it was more of a child's giggle.

I pulled my tomahawk from my waistband and stood up over her. "You, you made me eat my best friend."

"I did no such thing. You were hungry, I merely offered you food which you took from me willingly. I did not compel you to do anything."

"He was my friend."

"You were both going to die. I saved your life in exchange for his soul which he also gave willingly."

"What are you talking about?"

"Your friend Henri' agreed to give me his soul if I would spare your life."

"He was dying, delusional, and you took advantage of that."

"Maybe so, but I held up my end of the bargain."

I thought back on a memory I had long suppressed and recalled how succulent the meat was. How it seemed to ebb life back into me with each morsel. And how I partook of it willingly, even knowing where it had come from. A sickening sorrow invaded my soul as I recalled I had done this to myself.

"But how could you have been so far from your homeland?"

"How do you know of my homeland?"

"You speak with an Ojibwe tongue so you must be from the north."

"I also speak French, does that make me from Paris? I am from nowhere and everywhere. I am nobody and everybody."

"Why must you speak in riddles?"

"Why does who I am and where I come from interest you so? You should just be content with the fact I have given you life, not once, but twice."

"What kind of a demon are you?"

"The kind who is well aware of all your deeds and darkest secrets. Do you not recall the Liberty off the coast of Charleston? Are you not a demon for killing women and children?"

How could she possibly have known about that? No one knew about that. Well, no one other than Henri' and the rest of my crew who now resided at the bottom of the Atlantic. We had been given bad information that the Liberty was under sail with ten thousand pounds of English gold. But instead she was merely carrying passengers to the colonies to reunite with their families. Once we boarded her it was plain to see what we had done. Bodies of children were strewn about the deck, fodder from our cannons. Mothers were screaming as they clutched their dying babies. The captain of the vessel damned us to hell and swore we would swing from ropes each and every one of us sealing his and the survivor's fates.

"We had no choice," I said softly.

"You had many choices that night, Elijah. Your soul, although dark as coal still had an ember of goodness burning within it. But what you did that night darkened your soul forever."

"How do you know these things? Are you the devil himself masquerading as a child-like old woman?"

"I can assure you, I am not the devil. Although, I am certain he does look on with great interest."

We must have spent most of the day on the trail when I started seeing a plume of dust rising in the air in front of us. We were moving faster even at our snail's pace and soon met up with a wagon with two old men and an old woman. From their garb I discerned they were of some religious order or another.

We spent the fair part of an hour making our greetings and passing about small talk. Wenonah said something I did not understand, and I swore her two underlings smiled a crooked, sinister smile.

"Why don't we stop for a nibble," Wenonah offered.

The two men agreed and stopped. They felt around their wagon and pulled out a large blanket they laid upon the ground. I found their movements rather odd and began to study them. It was then I realized their eyes were cast with a strangeness as was the woman's. Once I saw this, I realized they were all blind which set rather well with me given my current condition.

"So where are you traveling too," I asked.

"We are headed north to purchase a piece of land that we will then erect a school upon," the oldest of the three said.

"For blind children," the woman added.

"That sounds rather noble."

"Rather than see our affliction as a curse, we chose to see it as an opportunity to help others."

"God certainly has a way of both testing us and then blessing us," the youngest man said.

We spent the better part of an hour sipping tea and eating little sandwiches. The conversation was as bland as the tea and I was getting anxious to move along so I helped them gather up their things and stow them aboard their buckboard.

"Come here, Elijah," the eldest said to me. "I would love to get a look at you," he said with his hand out.

I stood there, unsure of what he meant by the gesture.

"Here, let me feel your face," he laughed.

"You can see me by feeling my face?" I asked.

"Oh, I can see you even better than if I had my eyesight."

I walked over to the man and he laid his hands upon my face. I did not like the way he seemed to be exploring my every nook and cranny. He let loose a troubled sigh.

"You have lived a rough life my son. I hope the road ahead treats you better than the road behind."

"I hope so too father. I hope so too."

"Now you, little one, let me see you," he said to Wenonah.

"How did you know she is small?" I asked.

"Because of where her voice comes from."

Wenonah casually walked over to the buckboard while shooting me an impish smirk. She had the most baleful look upon her face that it frightened even me. She was up to something.

The sightless priest began feeling her face gently at first with a gentle smile upon his face. But then his expression took on a perplexed look and his hands roamed faster and harder across her face. Suddenly he yanked his hands away from Wenonah and screamed. All the color left his face and he slapped the reins as hard as he could. I could still hear his screams even after they had ridden out of my view. Wenonah was still laughing well after the wagon and its dust were out of sight.

"What did you do?" I asked.

"Why, I simply let the poor man see my true appearance."

Chapter Twenty-Five

We bedded down early that evening and my slumber was continuously interrupted by hauntings of my past. I found myself drifting through my memories of that night, a night I wanted to erase from my existence. She was right, I had not been a good man up to that point, but I had not been evil either. Of all the commandments I had broken, they were against well deserving adversaries who were even more dastardly than I.

I saw myself as a young sailor, on my first vessel and voyage. We were not privateers then, we were escorts for the king's tax collectors. But the years of low pay went by and grumblings grew louder. My first captain passed of dysentery and his replacement was a foul beast of a man who drove us hard. Mutiny was not just a grumbling, it was inevitable and somehow I had been chosen to lead the crew in rebellion. It was either that or die by the sword along with the captain.

It was also decided on that voyage to attack and scuttle the tax ship and lay claim to the bounty. I saw my first wanted poster in the New World claiming I was responsible for far more crimes than I was truly guilty of and the severity of these crimes far outweighed the truth. The only thing they left off the poster was buggery, which was added later. From there my life took a turn of which there was no coming back from.

I awoke to the stars twinkling overhead. By the position of the dipper I knew it was several hours before dawn. The aroma of coffee wafting on the night air alerted me to the fact Wenonah had found my stash.

"Are you daft woman, coffee at this wee hour?"

"We have business to attend to."

"What possible business could we have that requires us to be up at this hour?"

With that one of the warriors came over to where I was sitting and hovered over me until I got to my feet. He then led me up a winding deer trail atop an outcropping on the edge of a small crag. He pointed in the distance at a tiny orange spec on the horizon. There was a campfire a few miles away. We descended the trail back to camp where a hot cup of coffee was waiting for me which was the perfect remedy for shaking off the morning's chill. I blew the steam off the cup and took a long sip, perfect, it was even stronger than I usually make it. Bitter drink for a bitter old woman.

I am neither old, nor bitter dear Elijah.

"Damn it, would you stop doing that, please," I said, unnerved by her reading my every thought and even more so by her injecting her own.

"Sometimes I cannot help myself, it amuses me so," she said with a grin and took a drink of her coffee.

The men cooked rabbit they had snared overnight, and we shared a pleasant breakfast without any conversation. I was on my third cup of coffee when my hunger returned with a vengeance. I broke out my tomahawks and began to sharpen them to take my mind off my present condition. While not indicative of any specific tribe my weapons were fashioned after the Indian weapon but still held true to the form of a boarding axe, only smaller in size and easier to wield.

They had a sharp blade on one side and two curved spikes on the opposite. The handles were hardened hickory and the steel heads were affixed to the shafts with rivets and leather thongs. The shafts were encased in leather wrapping designed to allow me grip even when covered in blood or sea water. They were light enough to handle and fight with for an extended battle yet heavy enough to sever a man's limb with one blow. I am well versed in using them, so these two warriors had never been a threat to me, and I think my companion was well aware of this which unnerved me as well. Not once had she shown any fear of me whatsoever.

"So, do you have a plan?" I asked, feeling a sense of urgency as my physical being was fading ever faster and my insatiable hunger growing to an incapacitating point. I was still grasping at the last straws of my sanity as this partnership progressed.

"Plan? Why should I have a plan? You are the warrior, you should be the one to have a plan."

"Woman do not toy with me," I said, picking up on the amusement in her voice.

"You have to remember I am but a child beneath all of this beauty."

I went about my business of packing up my bedroll and fastening my gear to Helga who did not want to stand still for a single moment. As each grain of sand slipped through the hourglass, I expected to awaken to this just having been one long nightmare.

"There are three of them set back off the road out of sight waiting on an unsuspecting traveler I presume."

"And what do we do when we meet up with this trio?" I asked.

"Way lay them before they way lay us, I would imagine."

I nodded in agreement and found myself thinking this young girl as she claimed seemed to be worldly and knowledgeable. I was afraid to think about any one certain thing for too long lest she read my thoughts. But maybe she was reading my every thought including these. Every once in a while, she would sneer at me in a way that left me wondering.

"Let us move, you are just about ready," she said.

"I'm just about ready? What do you mean by that?"

She nodded her head down towards my hands. I gasped when I saw what I was becoming. A shadow, nothing more than a shadow. I could see the ground through my hand. There was no flesh, no bones, just a darkened aura.

"What in the hell is happening to me?"

"What you are seeing is your soul becoming you. If you allow it to continue without feeding it, it will consume your corporeal self and you will never regain your physical form. You will still be alive, but also dead. And do not ask because I do not know."

"Ask what?"

"If your soul will remember."

"What do you mean?"

"If you lose your physical being it may take your thoughts and memories with it. I do not believe a soul has a brain, so it does not have coherent thought. You will be alive, but you will not be aware of it."

I let her words sink in. If what she said was true and I was immortal, I could still die. For being simply a soul wandering aimlessly with no purpose for existence would surely be the same as experiencing death. And maybe even worse. I started feeling a sense of urgency to my plight.

"How long does it take for the separation of soul and body?" I asked.

Again, she shrugged. "I do not know, I have not tested it. But I sense it may be sooner than later with you."

"Then I guess we had better set off to way lay them before they can way lay us."

She smiled and gathered her things which I then packed onto Helga who was being more than consternated. Crickets chirped their eerie songs in the distance, quieting only to allow us to pass before resurrecting their concerto. A few coyotes yipped in the distance, but they were much too far away to be of any concern. The constant clip-clop of Helga's hooves on the hard-packed earth allowed my mind to drift to the point I didn't realize Wenonah had stopped moving.

"Is there a problem?"

"We are getting close and the night is quiet. Your beast is making too much noise and will alert those we seek to surprise."

I nodded and reached into my pack for a leather bundle. I pulled out four squares of thick, soft bear furs and bound each of Helga's hooves with leather thongs. Somehow, she always knew that this meant to keep quiet and kept her snorting at bay.

We drew near enough that I could smell the wood smoke from their fire but no aromas of coffee, tea, or cooking food so it was safe to assume they were still asleep. We made our way into the forest to come up from behind them. I glanced into the pre-dawn sky and determined I had about an hour before the first trappings of daylight would appear.

Once I could hear their sounds of slumber I disrobed, tied Helga to a tree and crept along the shadows. Being scoundrels themselves their horses were also trained to be quiet in the night lest they attract unwanted attention. These men were smart enough to have separated themselves while sleeping so attacking all three at once would be next to impossible. That ruled out a quick, clean attack with little or no fight. I quickly formulated a plan in my head and unsheathed my tomahawks. With one in each hand I attacked.

I cleaved the man closest to me, splitting his skull in two. This awakened the other two who both looked on in astonishment. They saw the carnage I had caused but they could not see me even in the light of the fire which seemed to flicker right through me. I caught the second man in the thigh with my spike and then buried my second weapon in his chest. I was about to cleave the third man's skull when Wenonah cried out for me to stop.

"Do not kill him," she said.

He charged her with his sword drawn so I instinctively cleaved his arm off at the elbow. He dropped to the dirt in agony.

"Why not? I thought that was the whole point of this."

"No, not entirely. While they are men with dark souls, it would be much better for us if they were also blackened with fear."

With that she gazed at her two companions who immediately went into action. They first checked the man I had hit in the chest and dragged him up into a sitting position. Blood cascaded out of the wound around the blade of my tomahawk. I reached to pull it out but one of the caught my wrist and stopped me. I was taken aback. How did he see my wrist, I could barely see my own wrist?

The other one moved over to the third man, dragged him up and against a tree where he bound him tightly around the waist. He continued to slap the squirming man in the face until he got his attention. He held the man's head so that he could see his dying compatriot. Wenonah began chanting or singing or maybe a combination of both. I stood in the darkness overwhelmed and unable to fathom what was taking place.

"Is this some sort of ritual? Is this a song that has to be chanted every time?" I asked.

She smiled and said, "No dear Elijah, I just like the song. My father taught it to me eons ago and I sing it when I am pleased."

She continued to hum and sing while watching her two cronies prepare the highwaymen. I was unsure what to do so I sheathed my weapon and sat down next to her. One man was fading fast and the other was still bewildered but seemed to be grasping what was going on around him. He pleaded with the two men who simply walked away without another word. Wenonah pat my arm and stood up, so I followed suit.

She bent down and hissed into the man's ear, "You are bad men who do very bad things."

"No, we are just traders."

"Traders of stolen goods and innocent souls."

"No, just furs. Look at our packs."

"And a liar too, eh, Ansel?"

The man looked at her bewildered and I could see the fear creeping into his face. The two warriors were positioned next to his dying companion as if awaiting orders from Wenonah. I myself was entranced by the fact this man did not realize I too was standing before him. This could prove useful if it was not so damned agonizing. I swear from this proximity I could smell his very soul. My hunger cried out and I wanted to consume him that very instant.

Shadowman, Shadowman,
In due time.
Shadowman, Shadowman,
Patience will prove sublime.

I backed away from the man hoping it would placate the growing beast inside of me. I tried to do the same to her, get into her head with my words but it had no effect whatsoever. This meddling with my brain was beginning to get quite tiresome. I had half a mind to turn her over my knee.

"The unknown can scare a man to his rotten core. Are you more afraid of dying or of what it is that comes after death, Ansel?" she said as she hovered over the man.

"Neither scares me and you child scare me even less," he spat, his machismo winning out over his better judgement.

"We shall see dear Ansel, we shall see," she said with a smile and then turned to face me. "Dear Elijah, can you feel the power of his dark soul? Can you feel it being fed by his fear?"

"You crazy old woman, who are you talking to, the shadows?" Ansel blurted out.

I did feel a certain surge of energy from his aura, but it was subsiding as he grew bolder.

"Yes, but it wanes," I replied, standing less than two feet from him. Astonishment washed over him at the sound of my voice cracking the night. It was then I felt a powerful surge of energy which made my hunger that much worse. He was terrified.

"So, this is what fear tastes like," I said.

"Do you now see that what you have been fighting against you should have been embracing?" she said.

"I'm starting to get that impression, yes."

"That dear Elijah was only a crumb," she said. "Dear Ansel, this is what will become of you."

Without a word one of the warriors ripped my tomahawk from the dying man's chest and tossed it to me. I caught and sheathed it while the man screamed in pain. The second warrior put his hands into the wound in the man's chest with his hands back to back, palms facing out. He then ripped the man's ribcage open with a wet, sickening sound. The first warrior sunk his teeth into the man's cheek and ripped the flesh away.

Together they began to devour the man who had suddenly come back from the dead and was flailing about while letting loose a deafening scream. Streams of blood were flung from his hands as he tried in vain to defend against the assault. The surge of power I felt as Ansel's fear spun out of control as he witnessed this onslaught was sumptuous. I cannot even begin to describe the adrenaline rush or make someone understand the enormity of my hunger. I would have tried to eat the wind were it possible.

Shadowman, Shadowman,
As black as coal,
Shadowman, Shadowman,
Devour his soul!

I drew my weapon and grabbed him by the hair. I jerked his head backward so I could stare into his eyes. I could feel his fear had reached a feverish pitch. His eyes followed my tomahawk as it reached its apex and started a downward slice. I spun the blade at the last possible second and drove the spiked end into his eyeball clear through to his brain, killing him instantly.

All at once my entire being swelled with the sheer power coursing through my veins. It was like a raisin dried out in the sun suddenly reverting to a grape. This was not a manifestation that I could see with my eyes nor did it seem to cause any reaction from the dead man, but I could sure as hell feel the effects. In an instant I felt virile, vibrant, and indestructible. I felt immortal.

I glanced over at Wenonah who seemed to be lost in the throes of passion. Although her change did not appear to be as dramatic as my own, she did change some physically. I thought she looked a bit younger, perhaps it was a youthful vibrancy returning to her eyes more than anything else. I on the other hand had not only transformed into my own flesh, I felt repaired from all the hard years I had put my body through as well.

It was only a matter of euphoric seconds before it was over, and I was left exhausted. I glanced down at my hands and saw that I had stepped thickly back into my flesh. I was visible once again to the point even the tiniest of scars were evident.

"Ahhh, only a hundred more or so of those and I'll be right as rain," she said.

"Wenonah, why was there not much effect on you?" I asked, stretching my muscles, and trying to tame the electricity running through me.

"I did not take more than I needed. That was more for your benefit than mine. A little spot of training as you will."

The two warriors consumed as much as they could and then dragged the remains into the forest where they buried them beneath piles of deadfall. I watched them walk down to the river and decided I could use some cleaning up as well. Wenonah followed behind.

"Pretty ingenious clean-up crew you have there. I wondered why you had them tagging along with you, they didn't appear to be your protectors," I said.

"I thought it was a clever little trick myself. Keeps me from having to tidy up after myself. Eventually you will need to find something similar."

"I'm not certain I want to be followed around by two brain dead servants," I said.

"These two, they are only like that because I want them to be. I'm not much of a conversationalist and prefer a man who shuts the hell up when I want them to. You may handle things any way you wish."

"Not much of a conversationalist? You haven't stifled yourself since we met," I laughed. "Am I to assume you were only half joking when you made the comment that you needed quite a lot more than just one?"

"Might have been a small exaggeration on my part. But yes, I would need a lot more to be able to return to my former self."

As each minute passed, I felt more and more alive, more and more energized and began to understand just how much power I had absorbed. Suddenly I was overcome by an acute pain emanating from deep with me. The pain induced a fear unlike anything I had ever experienced. Even staring down the blade of an executioner's axe would not have left me with such trepidation. And to add insult to injury she was smiling at me as I writhed in agony. This had been some kind of trick all along. I tried to gather my strength as I was bound to kill her before I took my last breath.

"You will do no such thing, Elijah," Wenonah said after having read my thoughts.

"What have you tricked me into old woman?"

"Oh, dear Elijah, you have not been tricked. But I did fail to mention this aspect of this, shall we say, malady. What you are feeling is the sickness I told you about. It is being eradicated from your body, but in doing so it is also killing you."

"I thought you said I would be immortal?"

"And you will, but you must die first. You cannot possibly be reborn without dying."

The pain continued to grow in intensity to a point where I could not stand it anymore. I felt what a woman might feel being impregnated, germinating a growing creature inside of her. I could feel something growing inside of me as well, something black and sinister. I fell to the ground locked in pain's evil talons. Wenonah stood over me, smiling, as I felt my life ebb from my body. And then, I succumbed to the endless night.

Chapter Twenty-Six

I drifted through space, disembodied, and lost. I did not know if I were alive or dead, but I did know the pain was gone and that was all that mattered to me at the moment. I could feel the warmth of the sun's glow on my face and a thirst that demanded to be slaked. Slowly I opened my eyes and saw a piercing blue sky surrounding me. At least someone had been kind enough to turn my face to the heavens.

As my consciousness slowly returned, I became increasingly aware that my skin was cold, slimy, and itched. I started to speak and could not, I tried to take a breath, but I could not, my airways were blocked. I rolled to my side and began to cough so violently it hurt. And then I saw them. Dozens upon dozens of assorted insects were spewing from my mouth and nostrils. Maggots, worms, beetles, and cockroaches. God, I hate cockroaches!

I would have disrobed had I not already been naked. Disoriented I scanned the area and saw only myself. My belongings were on the ground, but Wenonah and the men were gone. This had all been one crazy nightmare. What the hell had I gotten myself into? I spied Helga standing down by the river, so I put my clothes on and headed down to her.

Bugs. Why all the damned bugs? I guess I should have been grateful there was not a vulture tugging at my eyeballs while coyotes tried to separate me from my ball sack. And where the hell did Wenonah disappear to and what was I supposed to do now?

Shadowman, Shadowman,
You're as dead as dead can be,
Shadowman, Shadowman,
Critters eat the dead you see.

The old bat was not anywhere to be seen and yet here she was tormenting me with my own damned thoughts. I took a quick bath in the river and mounted Helga. I was glad to see that she seemed more receptive to me now that I was back to my old self. Maybe she just did not like Wenonah.

I wandered aimlessly for several days not knowing where I was going or what I was doing. As the days passed, I began showing signs of transparency, once more squashing the idea that this had just been one long nightmare. The more I faded the less Helga tolerated me and I was forced to dismount, or risk being thrown from the saddle.

As I traveled, I began to feel, or sense certain things about certain people who crossed my path. I could distinguish between the good, the bad and everything in between. But I had yet to run across anyone who could whet my appetite and my hunger was growing exponentially as my flesh faded. I had yet to see the blessing of this curse but for a few brief moments of bliss.

One of the most disturbing aspects of this new partnership was having thoughts in my head that I know I did not put there or create on my own. There were times I felt compelled to take certain paths without having a cognizant plan to do so. This was all disconcerting enough, but it was my dreams that haunted me the most. Or I should say, it was in my dreams where Wenonah haunted me the most.

I could never quite recollect what had transpired in my dreams, but I knew she had been there just the same. I had yet to discover whether her motive was to read my thoughts or to implant me with her own. I was, however, aware that her hunger was increasing as was mine. Somehow her hunger was amplified through me. And it was a hunger that would not go unsated.

I found myself thinking about my original motivation for being in this god forsaken part of the world and remembered Lieutenant Gagnon's wishes of a tribal unification resulting in his having more allies against the British. That was when I realized I had travelled into the northern territory, land of the big lakes without having plotted a course or even so much as glanced at a map.

On several occasions I was able to be blessed with some poor soul with the intent of robbing and maybe even killing me crossing my path. After half a dozen or so I realized that Wenonah was indeed onto to something with her speechless entourage. I began to understand just how powerful it was to consume a soul that had no purpose on earth other than to be vermin.

But as I absorbed more and more of these wicked men, I could feel something stirring inside of me. Their souls were squirming about like earthworms underfoot. And as their souls melded with mine, I began to understand, they were becoming a part of me. My darkness was growing with each new piece added to my collection. And it was just that, I was becoming an amalgamation of every person's soul I thieved. It was as though I were a tree growing more limbs and branches with each passing season.

With each new personality added to the mix I could see better, hear better and think so much more clearly. And I became much more adept in the tactics of battle, stealth, and deception. I was no longer myself but a conglomeration of everyone I assimilated with. I was ever changing, ever evolving and the more power I consumed the more I desired. But there were many times when I did not know if these feelings were my own or Wenonah's. Was I but a puppet and she the puppet master?

I had grown quite weary of awakening every morning with a cornucopia of multi-legged carrion spewing from my mouth, so I began sleeping with my shirt over my face. It was then I learned a valuable lesson which I had never contemplated before, my ears were connected to my throat. How utterly mad! So, then I was forced to sleep with wads of cloth in my ears as well. Eventually I had to sleep with every orifice protected from the little buggers. On a positive note, I never had to worry about fishing bait.

For some odd reason I was in a rather jovial mood this morning and was relishing the sunshine on my face when I heard the distant sounds of a wagon and horses coming my way. I scrambled up a small hill overlooking the well-worn path hoping to get a glimpse of them before they got a glimpse of me. It was a supply wagon traveling under the French banner. Four soldiers, a couple of Indian scouts and what appeared to be a child.

As they drew closer, I realized it was none other than Lieutenant Gagnon and a few of his men so I made my way back to Helga and we trotted out to meet them. I shot an accusing glance at the little girl in the pretty yellow dress sitting atop the buckboard once I was close enough to see her. It was the scouts who tipped me off. Even though they had altered their appearance to that of a more regional tribe I knew who they were, which meant I knew who she was as well.

"Fancy meeting you here," I said, offering my hand to the lieutenant.

"Nothing fancy about it. This little tyke led us straight to you. So, does she belong to you?"

"I think the more correct statement would be that I somehow belong to her."

The moment I grabbed Lieutenant Gagnon's hand I felt an incredible surge of energy. It was dark and foreboding, cold as ice and black as a moonless night. The little girl smiled at me and I understood. It took every ounce of my self-control to not slay the man right where he stood and dine on the malevolence of his essence. I sensed he had a disease within him, but very much unlike mine. Mine had been in the very core of my body, his was a disease of the brain. I began to crave that power for my own.

"So how do you two know each other?" he asked in a suspicious tone.

"Elijah saved me once," Wenonah chimed in, her voice oozing with girlish charm.

"Sounds like an interesting story, I'd love to hear it."

"Maybe some other time, when there is whiskey around," I said. "So where are you headed?"

"Figured I'd go north into the lands of the Anishinaabe tribes, speak with an elder or two. Try to gain their favor with some trinkets and other supplies."

"So, you think they might be willing to send their young men to die for a few shiny baubles?"

"No need for the sarcasm Mr. Morgan. They need blankets and medical supplies. Should they prove loyal we may get them gunpowder and muskets as well."

"Sounds like you have this all figured out. And what will you do with these new allies?"

"Hopefully, we can unite a few of these warring tribes and get them to help us drive the British from these lands. I mean, that is our ultimate goal."

"And what is your ultimate goal?"

"I beg your pardon?" the lieutenant asked even though I was certain he knew exactly what I was eluding to.

"What do you stand to gain, personally I mean?"

When I asked this question, I felt a surge of dark energy rush through me. The longer I possessed this macabre ability the more I understood it. I had directed his thoughts to where he pondered the power, he himself would gain through this manipulation of his. And his grandiose dreams of power manifested into dark energy which would eventually become mine. I was quite aware of what Wenonah was up to, I just could not imagine the extent.

"Me? Oh, I stand to gain nothing. Maybe a rank or two with a meager increase in wages but nothing more than that."

Shadowman, Shadowman,
Hatred, fear and lies,

Shadowman, Shadowman,
What we love, most despise.

"I see. Then why go to all this trouble?"

"Why for God and country of course. Because it is the right thing to do."

"I hardly see how sending young men to their deaths is the right thing to do."

"Come now, Mr. Morgan, when did you suddenly develop a conscience? I seem to recall you have no trouble at all sending people to their deaths."

"Deserved people."

"If that is what your conscience needs to believe, so be it."

Every minute I endured in the company of this arrogant man the less I liked him and the more I wanted to dispatch him. The smile on Wenonah's face alerted me to the fact that she was thoroughly enjoying herself.

"Do you have a plan?"

"Yes, I have received information from an envoy who recently returned from speaking with a band of the Potawatomie who are willing to make peace with the Mesquaki, a tribe who has been making a lot of trouble for us as of late. I would love to bring the Fox into our fold."

"And how do you intend to do this?"

"By kissing arse of course. These supplies are not only for our allies but also for a feast in their honor. The leader of the Fox is an arrogant man who relishes a good fight. Maybe we can swoon him into fighting with us, not against us."

"Sounds like a tall order. From what I have heard these two tribes have a lot of bad blood between them."

"That's where you come in. Your little angel here tells me that you are quite adept at negotiating with the locals."

"She told you that did she? Well I am afraid she has been embellishing my oratory talents."

I glanced over at Wenonah who smiled and shrugged. I knew she was up to something and I wished I knew what it was because I was certain it included me doing things, I probably didn't want to be involved in. I found myself backing away from Gagnon every time he leaned in to whisper. I could smell his darkness and it teased a passion in me that I was having a difficult time controlling. He would never know how close he came to losing his head many times that morning.

The lieutenant was rambling on about something I could not possibly care less about and his incessant droning was giving me a throbbing headache. I scanned the faces of the handful of soldiers he had brought with him. Most of them were much too young to have been led too far down Gagnon's darkened path. But there was an old codger who was keeping to himself on the far side of the wagon. I meandered over to where he was sitting and put my hand on his shoulder wanting to learn if I had also been gifted with the same second sight as the warrior who had first shown me the sickness within me.

Immediately I felt a surge of energy and time seemed to cease spinning the clock. I could see this soldier wandering through a bloody battlefield taking joy in smashing the skulls of wounded enemy scattered amongst the already dead. I watched as he cracked the skulls of man after pleading man and then scooped out their brains with his fingers. He appeared to be in bliss as he devoured these men with ravenous enthusiasm. Wounded men scrambled to their feet and tried to run away at the sight of this monster cannibalizing their friends with maniacal gusto. One by one he cut them down with wanton abandon.

As he traversed the battlefield, I could feel an ice-cold wind churning around him, yet by the looks of the surrounding territory it was the height of summer. The fear he induced charged ahead of him like a stallion chasing a mare in heat. Wild eyes stared back at him, terrified he was coming for them next. Blood dripped down his fingers onto the trodden earth and a smile creased his face. I too found myself in a state of bliss as I reveled in his repressed memories. He would do just fine.

What felt like hours were only mere seconds. The man looked up, scowled, and knocked my hand from his shoulder. His eyes sagged with fatigue and his smile had long disappeared. He wore the look of a man whose conscience had finally caught up with him. I know, I carried that very same look about me until Wenonah had come crashing into my life. I wondered if we would be on opposite ends of the stick had she met him before me.

I studied the defeat in his eyes and could only imagine the depth of the demons he was taking to hell with him. A sense of pity for the man washed over me for a brief moment until I recalled his actions and his own lack of sympathy. No, this man deserved to walk through the valley of darkness fearing all evil.

Gagnon and I talked for a couple more hours over a bottle of whiskey while Wenonah looked on. She pretended to stay busy playing with her little girl things, but I knew the old woman residing within her was watching us with a calculating eye. She wanted to know what I was up to about as much as I wanted to know the same about her. The crackling of the fire took my mind away from his babbling giving me a respite from the incessant chatter. I was never one much for tolerance but ever since I gained this acute awareness of each of my senses I was much less accepting of intrusions.

"Who has next watch?" Gagnon called out, interrupting my self-exile.

"Me," a faceless voice grunted half asleep.

It was the seasoned veteran who would be out there all alone in the darkness. My hackles bristles and my hunger echoed deep within me. But how would I explain his death away? Coyotes? Wolves? A rogue band of natives? I laid back and began to formulate my plan of attack.

Shadowman, Shadowman,
Have you learned not a thing?
Shadowman, Shadowman,
It is hatred and fear you must first bring.

Wenonah was right and I knew it. I was being impetuous and about to waste a particularly good meal. I rolled over and glanced in her direction. I thought she was sleeping which really set my nerves on edge. Could she really invade my thoughts as she slept? Then slowly she opened one eye, winked, and wagged a finger at me. I rolled back over and began formulating a new plan until I fell asleep to crickets and snores.

Chapter Twenty-Seven

I was up before the dawn, awakened by the smell of fresh coffee and worms which meant a storm was brewing. Trudging through the mud was bound to put the sour puss in an even more cantankerous mood. *Hatred, fear and lies*. I might not make him fear me, but I sure as hell had a plan that would make the gargantuan hate me to the core.

Lieutenant Gagnon ordered the canopy erected on the buckboard so that he, Wenonah, and her entourage were all safe from the rain. Helga and I had spent many a day travelling in the rain, so it was not much more than a nuisance to us. But to the four soldiers in tow on foot, trudging through the ever-thickening soup of mud was setting their moods afoul. They were bellyaching and grumbling, the big man protesting the loudest. My target was hanging to the rear of the wagon trying to use the buckboard as a shelter.

"I'm going to run back and check the rear flank," I called out over the rain and turned Helga.

We went speeding past the rear of the buckboard and as we neared the men, I veered my horse into the sloppy mud kicked up by the wagon wheels. I made sure to give her a good kick just as we passed so she kicked up clumps of mud and soupy water. I could almost hear the old bastard cursing me over my own laughter. I made sure to stay on patrol a good fifteen minutes before speeding back to the convoy. Just as I passed the man, I urged Helga on and she sprayed him with muddy water once more. She whinnied in such a manner that made me believe she enjoyed my tactical maneuver as much as I did.

I fought the urge for one more pass and suggested we stop for lunch. I spent the next few minutes calming myself down, being aggressive was not part of my game plan. I had to make sure he was not just angry, but hatefully so.

"Whiskey?" the lieutenant offered.

"No thank you, I had better keep a level head, besides, Helga doesn't behave when I've been drinking. No telling where I might wake up," I replied.

Wenonah busied herself by what appeared to be hosting a little tea party. Although she seemed to not be paying attention, I was certain she was aware of my every move. As was Corporal Stick Up His Ass who was storming toward me that very moment. I was up for some fun.

"Just what kind of numbskull are you?"

"I beg your pardon?"

"Just look at my uniform."

"I would agree with you, it would take some kind of a numbskull to get their uniform that muddy, even in this deluge."

I could feel him percolating. Inside he was a jumbled mass of blackness.

"Me? This wasn't my doing, it was your'n fault."

"How on earth could you getting mud all over yourself be my fault?"

"When you rode past me, your horse kicked it up."

"Ah well then, maybe you ought to take that up with my horse. I have no control over who she slings mud at. Maybe she does not like you for some reason or another. But I will warn you, if you do decide to have a word with her be careful, she is a tad bit smarter than you are."

Gagnon felt the tension brewing and put himself between me and the big man before things escalated further. I was glad he broke it up before it came to blows, I was having too much fun tormenting the behemoth. I sat down and pulled some jerky from my pack and began to nibble on it all the while smirking at the skulking hulk. *Do you hate me yet, Corporal?*

Once I was finished with my jerky and a few sips of coffee I positioned myself just right and began cleaning the mud off my boots. The corporal had taken off his uniform, cleaned it as best he could under the circumstances and hung it up to dry. Little did he know it was hung right in the path of my boot cleaning. I almost felt sorry for the oafish giant until I recalled the young men, just boys really, begging for mercy as he stood before them smiling with brains dripping down his fingers. No, he deserved everything I was about to give him and more.

"You are begging to get clobbered," he bellowed as I flung a good-sized clump of mud onto his freshly cleaned uniform which he obviously took pride in keeping clean.

"And just who will be doing the clobbering Abigail?" I asked.

The man stood up with his fists clenched and nostrils flaring. I had a slight inclination that I may have underestimated this brute. I checked my hips to make certain my tomahawks were readily available because I was most assuredly going to need them very soon.

The lieutenant staggered to his feet and said to me, "Listen, you two may not like each other but that is no reason to insult the man."

"I didn't insult him any more than his mother and that prize boar did when they sired him."

That was all the impetus it took to progress the man's severe dislike of me to pure hatred. He stood and readied his charge. I could feel his essence drifting toward me like the aroma of a freshly seared steak. Tantalizing. It was teasing my senses.

Shadowman, Shadowman,
Let him simmer.
Shadowman, Shadowman,
His hatred is but a glimmer.

I kept my weapons sheathed and fended his charge with a graceful sidestep and grabbed him with both hands. I shoved him as he flew passed me, using his weight and momentum against him. He went spilling to the ground into a swill of mud and horse droppings with a splash. We did this dance three more times before I finally placed a hard blow to the back of his ear and took the fight out of him. Wenonah was right, he was angry, but now he would be hating me even more. He was not accustomed to getting a lesson in the art of war. I had best be watching my back until this thing was settled.

Once the dust had settled Lieutenant Gagnon pulled me aside and asked, "Is there some bad blood here I am not aware of?"

"If there was why should you be aware?"

"Listen, I don't need you stirring up trouble, so you are going to steer clear of the corporal and stop egging him on."

I felt a surge of dark energy reaching out from him like tendrils, teasing my every sense. My right-hand rested on my tomahawk and I so very much wanted to cleave his skull right that very moment, but I caught sight of Wenonah's wagging little finger.

"And just who put you in charge of me? You may be able to order your troops around but you sure as hell are not going to bark orders at me. Are we clear?"

"Listen you ungrateful scalawag, I will have you cast in irons right this very minute if you don't start obeying my command."

"This little ragtag group of miscreants? They are the ones who are going to throw me in irons? Did I not just easily handle your biggest man? I could kill each and every one of you without so much as breaking a sweat."

Gagnon tensed up but then thought better of pushing the boundaries. I now had to watch my back with two of them. This was going to be a fun expedition indeed.

The small brigade went about doing chores to prepare camp for nightfall, so I took the opportunity to have a chat with Wenonah.

"You are learning dear Elijah. Would you like some tea?" she asked, pouring a tiny cup of tea from a children's teapot.

"I'd love some. That is just about as much tea as I can stomach. So, what is your main objective here?"

"Don't you mean our objective?"

"Don't play word games with me and just answer my question," I said, feeling quite odd having a very adult conversation with an eight-year-old child.

"If you insist. All business with you isn't it?"

"There is no time for anything else."

"Oh, dear Elijah, all you have is time."

"I'm still not convinced of this immortality you speak of."

"You will be, and very soon I would imagine the way you keep pestering evil men," she said with a grin.

"Would you please stop evading my question?"

"Our main objective is a very simple one indeed. Create chaos amongst those easily angered."

"Does that mean war?"

"A word is just a word. I mean more than just a war. I mean chaos. I mean not only chaotic actions but chaotic emotions as well."

"And then what?"

"We feed of course."

I looked this little girl up and down and for the life of me was having a difficult time believing any of this, let alone all of it. Had I stumbled into the depths of hell itself? She cocked her head and looked at me in a manner I knew she was reading my thoughts again.

"So, tell me, if when I partake of this feeding as you call it, it also feeds you correct?"

"Yes, that is how it works, dear Elijah. I need you and you need me."

"Then who do you feed?"

"Ah you're a wise one indeed. Most do not care, they are simply content when given a gift of this magnitude."

"I am not so certain this is truly a gift. At times it seems to be a curse. And once again you evade my questions."

"It is what you make it, dear Elijah, a gift or a curse, it is purely your choice. And I do not answer your questions because I do not think you want to know the answers."

"I wouldn't ask them if I didn't want to know the answers."

"But you cannot possibly know that without knowing the answers first."

"If you continue to act like a child, I am going to treat you like a child."

She laughed, more of a giggle, before she set her piercing black eyes upon me and said, "Be very careful. What you see before you is not always reality. But to answer your question, yes, I too feed another."

"Who?"

"Why should that be any of your concern? That is a contract between myself and them, not you."

"But that is where you are wrong dear Wenonah, it is of the utmost concern to me. Because in essence I am feeding them as well, so I want to know who I am benefitting."

"You are truly making me second guess my decision about you."

"I apologize for not being the brain-dead lackey you had hoped for."

We both spent the next few minutes brooding over our little spat which left me feeling like a complete idiot. I was being bested by a child. I let our conversation roll around in my head trying to make sense of what had happened to my life. I just could not let it go, I had to know.

"Are you going to tell me?"

"Tell you what?"

"Who it is that you serve?"

"My father and let us just leave it at that."

"And just who is your father? Have I met him?"

"I'm sure you have met him once or twice, but you wouldn't know it if you had."

"Why are you so blasted cryptic?"

"Why are you so blasted inquisitive?"

"Because I like to know what is going on."

"No, you cannot stand not being in control. Dear Elijah, all you have is time so there is no need to rush through life any longer. You have a lifetime, several in fact, to learn the answers. If you solve all of life's riddles this very moment you will then spend eternity being wracked with boredom."

Once again, bested by a child. I resigned myself to knowing that this line of questioning was fruitless and these answers I may learn over time just as she claims. And once again she was right, I was having a difficult time not being in control of my situation.

"As I understand it, your plan is to create chaos, war, between these many different people in the area."

"It will serve us well," she said and nodded.

"And then what?"

"What do you mean?"

"All wars eventually end."

"True."

"And then what will we do?"

"We will simply start another one."

"Another war?"

"Of course. There will always be individuals out there with blackened hearts and souls. We simply seek them out."

"For eternity?"

"Yes, for eternity. Has that not already been happening since the dawn of time? Since the very first spark of humanity lit on this planet?"

"I suppose so. If that is the case, what causes this?"

"Causes what?"

"All this darkness mixed with the light. Why are men destined to fight and kill for all eternity?"

"Simple dear Elijah, they were given free will to do as they please with no one handling the reins but themselves. Most souls choose the path of light and goodness, but others choose the path of least resistance. It is far easier on oneself to be dark and hateful than it is to struggle with keeping the torch of righteousness lit."

Chapter Twenty-Eight

Over the next few days the party was taciturn at best. We rode, marched, rested and ate apart from one another, except for Wenonah and her two companions, but they had proven themselves not much for conversation anyway. Helga and I had a few words over the miles, but those conversations were mostly one sided.

I thought a lot about what Wenonah had to say, or what little she had to say to be exact. Free will. Was it really that easy to explain all the ills of the world? To understand right from wrong. Righteousness from evil. Was it all just simply a choice and did we all have that choice to make regardless of which path we chose? Could a preacher man have chosen any other destiny other than teaching about the Lord?

If we all truly have free will then why do words like fate, kismet and destiny exist? If we are ill-fated then do we have free will or just have to succumb to the will of a higher power regardless if we choose the right path or not? I was never one to wax philosophical, but Wenonah had left me believing my whole life was a lie and would have been much different had I simply chosen a different path at the very onset of my life.

I began to feel strange, not ill, just a little bit short of normal. Maybe it was all the rain or the prolonged travelling, but I needed to rest.

Shadowman, Shadowman,
Do not be dismayed.
Shadowman, Shadowman,
You are starting to fade.

I glanced down at my hand holding Helga's reins, it was true, I was starting to fade away again. I do not believe I could ever get used to this. I distanced myself from the pack hoping to be able to escape scrutiny until nightfall. I watched the sun dipping off into the western sky painting the landscaped with vibrant layers of purples, reds, and oranges. The world seemed so alive while I was feeling so dead.

Being away from the group had a calming effect on both Helga and I. Crickets had started their nightly song and I heard Lieutenant Gagnon call to make camp, so I dismounted and began to make camp myself. I thought it best to stay away from the others until I decided upon a path to follow in this dilemma which my life had become. Free will.

I made a small fire mostly of sticks I gathered in the scrub and bed down about fifty yards away from the others. Helga moved even twenty yards further out and would have gone further had she not been afraid of the dark. I laid there listening to the lieutenant's drunken ramblings for about an hour before I drifted off to sleep.

Disoriented I bolted from my slumber. Even though I could not hear a sound I sensed there was someone out in the grass creeping toward me. My first thought was that it was the big man come to claim his retribution. The more I listened the more I realized whoever they were they were much too quiet to be that lout. I readied myself for battle, doctored up my bedroll and crept out into the darkness.

I found it peculiar that I sensed the men creeping through the woods long before I heard or laid eyes on them. I felt their essence oozing from them like thick primordial sludge. Black shadows crept in front of them as they prepared themselves for their ambush. There were but three of them, so I circled around behind them. They were still quite some distance from my encampment and had separated themselves from one another. By the time they realized my camp was deserted and my bedroll empty it was much too late for them to regroup.

The spike end of my tomahawk went through the first man's eyeball killing him instantly. I was on the move before being able to savor his essence and although I did consume a portion of it, I did not get to enjoy it. I did not have to see the other two men, I simply trailed them by the trail of darkness they left behind them. This was proving to be a rare and useful gift indeed.

The second warrior went down quickly as I yanked his head back and drew my blade across his throat. I sidestepped the arterial spray and stared into the man's waning eyes. I drank in his fear as his life ebbed away and at the very last moment before death, I severed his head from his body with a powerful swing.

The last man bore witness to this and in fear for his life began to run away through the woods. I gave chase but he was much faster than I and before long put a good distance between us. But his essence stopped moving. I am sure he thought he was safe in the darkness cowered behind a large tree or in a fallen stump. I took off my boots and began creeping through the ebony forest following the allure of his scent. I was able to discern the very moment his anger and hatred had turned into fear. They each held a completely different taste, fear being the more delectable of the three. At that very moment he was deathly afraid for his life as well he should have been.

I tracked him to a cluster of dense thickets and waited on the perimeter. I made just enough noise to let him know I was there. I could sense his fear growing with each passing minute, so I allowed him to steep like a British tea until it was bitter and foul. I could feel his breathing and his heartbeat starting to slow, he was about to get his second wind. I readied myself for his pending escape attempt.

My appraisal of the situation was dead on accurate. A few minutes passed and he bolted from the thicket and into the shadows of the forest. I could not see him with my eyes, but I knew exactly where he was just the same, so I let my tomahawk fly. I heard a muffled cry followed by the sounds of him hitting the ground. I hoped I had not killed him as I wanted to prolong his agony and increase his fear.

I took my time walking over to where he lay squirming in pain in the forest floor. With each step I could feel his fear rising so I slowed my pace giving him time to anticipate what I was going to do. My weapon had found its mark in the back of his thigh which was shredded and bleeding profusely. The whites of the man's eyes glowed wide in the darkness. I grabbed him by the cheeks and drew his face close enough to mine he could smell my breath.

But then something strange began to happen. The fear I sensed was starting to subside with each passing moment. He was no longer as tense as when I first walked up on him and was starting to relax which perplexed me.

Shadowman, Shadowman,
You jeopardize his release.
Shadowman, Shadowman,
Kill him now, before he makes peace.

I immediately ripped my weapon from his leg with one hand, drew his face to mine with the other and bit his nose clean off his face. The man screamed in pain and I felt his fear intensify. With that I swung my blade and cleaved his skull. I felt the rapture of his essence flooding my body the instant he passed from this life into wherever it was he was bound for next. Both his hatred and his fears were joined with the memories associated with them as they poured through me. I absorbed everything, even the memories which were gone in a flash. Not gone as in forgotten but gone as in cataloged within my own brain.

I was becoming lupine in the sense that I could recognize fears and hatred like a wolf recognizes a pack member. I could also sense Wenonah was right there with me to absorb a portion of this soul with me. The more of this hatred and fear I consumed the more it consumed me. It became a part of me at the expense of a part of me being compiled away as well.

I had never really been a bad man, I had just done some awfully bad things, or so I had convinced myself. I had always thought there was a shred of decency left within me, that I could be merciful and pure when needed. I fear that is no longer the case. I fear the longer this goes on the darker I will become and the more of me that gets lost along the way. I was already finding it harder and harder to recall my youth and days when I was a helpful, courteous child. I fear that child is buried in an unmarked grave.

It was almost daybreak by the time I made it back to my camp. I should have been exhausted but the opposite held true, I was revitalized and ready to hit the trail. In all honesty I was eager to screw with the big man some more as I was craving the day I would sup on his inner being.

The caravan came up the road and stopped long enough to allow me to stow my belongings. Wenonah gave me a warm smile and handed me an apple for breakfast. I smiled and tipped my hat to the corporal who scowled and cursed me under his breath. Lieutenant Gagnon was obviously still feeling the effects of last night's whiskey as he nearly fell out of his saddle more than once. We were one big, happy family.

The lieutenant found a moment of stability and said, "You should probably try and make peace with Corporal Faust, he makes a far better ally than enemy."

"Faust eh? German?"

"Hessian to be exact."

"Hessian? Don't they tend to side with the British? I thought the Hessians hated you Frenchies," I said.

"Normally yes, but the corporal ran afoul of his own kind, so he chose to ride with me."

"Interesting. Interesting indeed. Can you trust him?"

"With my life in fact, which he has proven to me on more than one occasion. So, I would appreciate it if you would make amends."

"That is assuming I have anything to make amends for. Perhaps it is Corporal Faust who should be making amends," I said and turned away from the lieutenant. The anger seething inside of him painted a broad smile on my face. This was becoming quite entertaining.

We rode alongside of the St. Joseph River heading west for the big lake. In a day or two we should be in the lands of the Potawatomie and the tribal elders we were seeking. The day was perfect for a ride and Helga was taking her time now that she was not as skittish. I eased her over to the lieutenant knowing I had to be civil, at least for a while longer. I could sense his anger the closer I got and gave him a forced smile.

"So, what is your master plan here anyway?" I asked.

"We meet with the elder's son and let him know we would like to broker peace between him and the Fox."

"Is the elder the chief?"

"In a manner of speaking."

"Is the son a chief as well?"

"No but he does have the authority to speak in that capacity as he is the chief's son."

"And you think he will be interested in your offer?"

"Yes, from the information I have been given."

"Reliable?"

"Not as reliable as I would have hoped, but it will have to do."

"And the leader of the Fox, how receptive will he be?"

"That is an unknown. I am certain he knows he will be negotiating from a position of power, so I do not expect much."

"Then why bother?"

"Hopefully, this will be a thawing of ill wills and will lead to more talks."

"So then this is merely a chit chat?"

"Why all the questions? Your role is not as a negotiator, your duties are as a translator and moreover, a sergeant at arms in case things go sour."

"Which is precisely why I ask the questions. I want to know what I am getting myself into."

"You seem to forget that I hold all the cards in our little arrangement. If you would prefer to be swinging from a hangman's noose please, by all means, let me know."

I took a moment to not only let my anger subside but to also assess the lieutenant's hatred toward me. It was beginning to wane the more confident he became in the knowledge he was in charge. I had to liberate him of those thoughts before I was back to square one with him.

I looked him straight in the eye and said, "Do not be daft, sir. And do not overestimate your hand, the best you have is a bluff."

"I think it is you who is doing the bluffing."

"Am I? I dispatched your ace in the hole rather easily did I not? You think your threats scare me, but they do not. I have buried men much more proficient than yourself. Do you really want to continue on this journey haunted by the fear of sleep because I can assure you, I will outlast you there as well," I said in the most menacing of tones.

"Are you threatening me?"

"Not just you, but Corporal Faust and those two whipsnappers you have lagging on your boot heels."

"You are pretty confident for an outnumbered man."

"The way I see it, I have the advantage. You might have held the cards at the fort when I was surrounded by muskets, but out here, you are nothing more than a mere annoyance to me. Make no mistake, I am only here because I want to be here," I said. I was not sure about this immortality thing yet, but it had made me just brazen enough to throw caution to the wind.

Lieutenant Gagnon's face was redder than a child's bottom after a switching. It was apparent he was not accustomed to being challenged in this manner. I knew he wanted nothing more than to test my theory that I could best all of them but was not certain enough to call my bluff. And I stood before him half-heartedly prepared to test my immortality. It was time to test the old crone-child and her nonsensical ramblings. Besides, I had made peace with myself and was ready to die if need be.

Chapter Twenty-Nine

As I had done the previous evening, I distanced myself from the group once night fell. This night however, I took extra measure to ensure I was not well defended and could be vulnerable to a stealthy attack. As the sun dipped and the stars became visible, I took note of something I had not been aware of up until this night. The night was silent. No longer did crickets chirp around me nor did the wolves or coyotes dissent about human presence as if they sensed my darkness. It was unnerving to say the least to have beasts look upon me as less than human.

Nightfall descended upon the plain and even though my mind was racing I laid down to sleep. I had moved Helga further downstream so she would not alert me to intruders. If I was going to see this thing through, I wanted the brunt of it to come as a surprise. I was on the very precipice of sleep when Wenonah imparted her unsolicited wisdom upon me.

Shadowman, Shadowman,
Have you no trust?
Shadowman, Shadowman,
Ashes to ashes and Dust to dust.

The last thing I needed was more of her cloying nursery rhymes. I began to feel agitated, impatient, as if lightning were striking inside my body and I had no way of escaping it. I wanted to run as far as I possibly could. I could feel the darkness growing inside of me as the souls of those I had consumed vied for attention. A sadness crept over me as I realized I could no longer distinguish my own soul from the others. Yes, death would be welcomed.

I cannot say when it was that I fell asleep but when I awoke the moon was high overhead. I felt a presence off in the distance, but it was different, not like when I was near and could sense the lieutenant or the corporal. No, this felt the opposite of their auras, this was light, imbued with innocence. It tasted acrimonious on my tongue. My eyes darted open in time to see the young soldier standing over me with his saber drawn. His hands were trembling, and tears streamed down his face as he thrust the weapon into my body but missed his target. Instinctively I rolled away into a standing position and charged with my own weapon drawn. The young man dropped his weapon and cowered in fear.

Shadowman, Shadowman,
Do not kill this one.
Shadowman, Shadowman,
He flies too close to the sun.

Wenonah's sing song ringing in my ears distracted me just long enough that I did not sense Corporal Faust charging me from the rear. By the time I heard him and turned around it was much too late to defend myself. Searing hot pain shot through me where his knife had pierced my chest. His momentum drove us both to the ground and I struggled to free myself from beneath his weight. Blood was pouring from my chest and I was losing consciousness. I felt the weight of the big man lift off me and then my tomahawk being tugged out of its sheath.

It was then that I began to second guess my irrational behavior. As my life waned from me so did the essence of the souls I had consumed. Maybe I should not have tested this immortality theory and just accepted it as truth. I was beginning to think the repercussions were going to be hard to overcome.

"Not so tough, now are you?" Corporal Faust barked in a thick accent spraying my face with his hatred.

"Doesn't take any courage to attack a man from behind. I knew you were a coward the moment I laid eyes on you," I said.

"You son of a whore," he said, clamping down on my throat with both of his mammoth hands.

When the man touched me, I felt something stir inside of me; fear. I had the same vision I had seen earlier of him devouring the brains of his victims as they lay helpless on the battlefield. In truth, Wenonah had claimed I was immortal, but she never said I had the power to regenerate so if this brute were to scramble my brains with his meaty fingers would I be alive but brainless for all eternity? Would he be able to eat my memories leaving me to stumble this earth forever without any recollection whatsoever of who I was?

My will to survive kicked in and I lashed out at the big man knocking him off balance. I was about to regain my footing when the lieutenant's musket ball found my heart. I was stone cold dead before I hit the earth.

Chapter Thirty

I swirled within a dark quagmire of thoughts drifting through an ethereal plane as a spirit without form or function. A conglomeration of voices, sounds, sights, and sensations bombarded me as I drifted in this sea of purgatory. I eavesdropped on conversations I had never been part of, tasted things I had never eaten and felt the pain of wounds I had never suffered. I felt as though my very being was merely but a dream; a long-forgotten memory that belonged to someone else.

Suddenly I was ripped away from this womb of darkness and thrust headlong into the brightness of excruciating pain. My heart felt as though it were in the grasp of a clenched fist that refused to relinquish its hold. And in fact, the more my heart tried to beat the stronger the grip became. It felt as though my heart refused to be held silent and was forcing itself between the fingers of death's clutches.

My lungs felt scorched, as though I had breathed in the very flames of Hell itself as I struggled to take my first gasp of air. More out of instinct than thought I reached my hand to my chest and probed the hole left by a musket ball. I could feel my heart trying to beat against my intrusive flange. I shoved my finger hard into the hole which forced me to suck in a lungful of fiery air. My heart pulsed harder as it struggled to find its rhythm.

As every minute passed my thoughts snaked and swirled as my mind struggled to untangle. Slowly my own memory started filling in the details. I watched the events that put me in this predicament unfold as pieces of my memory fell back into place. I saw Faust attack and then the lieutenant fire his weapon. The more I thought about being dead the more it made me think about being alive. The more I thought about being alive the more my body struggled to make it happen. I began to focus my energy on what was about to happen rather than what had happened.

I felt the warmth of the sun and slowly opened my eyes. Everything was black at first but slowly began to fill with color. The same with my hearing, at first there was nothing, but slowly the babbling of the stream I lay beside began to serenade me with its fluidity as the wind rustled high atop the pines. I took a long sip of air to fill my lungs which caused me to fall into a coughing fit. Diamonds of light sparkled in my brain as it too began to regain life. My heart seemed to seize as if in defiance but then gave one, hard thump inside my chest and I felt my blood once again coursing through my veins.

And then I laughed. I laughed so hard it gave me the dry heaves. While on my hands and knees trying to suck life back into myself, I realized I had become almost completely transparent. I could still see my clothes and such but as for my skin and bones, they were gone. It was alarming to say the least. To imagine if I had been naked, I wouldn't even know where my own body was. This must be a ramification of death.

Not wanting to accidentally run into some poor trail rider in my condition I abandoned my clothes since I could not find Helga or my pack. I was completely unaware of how long I had been dead, so I assumed they had put days if not weeks between us. Oddly enough, as lost as I was, I could somehow sense Wenonah. Not in the sense I knew where she was, but I knew the direction they had headed.

The trail was lonely and hard without Helga. What kind of bastards steal a man's horse? But was it really stealing once I had been murdered? I'd have to have that discussion with the lieutenant when we crossed paths again. I ran into a couple of unfortunate souls and commandeered their river raft. I justified it to myself in such that stealing a raft was not the same as stealing a man's horse. Besides, I let them live so they owed me.

I drew several odd looks from riders on the bank seeing a raft floating down the river unattended. I could see at first they wanted to stop the raft but then took off back up stream. They were good souls, so I was of the mind that they were making sure no one had fallen off into the river and were in peril. They never knew I was on the raft as naked as naked could be watching their every move. I could really get used to the anonymity of my situation, but it was a tad bit drafty.

My arms were getting weary guiding the raft through the currents of the river, so I stopped near Fort Saint Joseph to liberate one of their horses. Sadly, the horse was having none of it in my present condition which alerted the men inside of the garrison. I was able to steal away in the night rather easily even with a couple of hounds on my trail.

I spent two more days walking the riverbank to the northwest toward the big lake. I was able to sneak passed a few trappers and fishermen who sensed my presence but shrugged it off. It was a chore to not taunt them with a spectral haunting. The more I travelled, and the more time dragged on I felt ever hungrier but not from the lack of food. This constant desire that would not go ignored was driving me to the brink of madness.

Chapter Thirty-One

"Lieutenant," Wenonah said, tugging at the man's jacket sleeve as he held the reins of the wagon.

"Yes, my dear," he replied with his customarily whiskey laced breath.

"May we rest, please? My bottom is getting a little sore. This rough road is hard on these old bones," she said and flashed him her best mischievous little girl smile.

"Hold," he called out and held his hand up.

The small party came to a halt and went about the task of setting camp. Wenonah and her two companions meandered away from the group and prepared themselves a meager meal of salted fish, hard tack, and tea. She hated tea. Elijah would never make her drink tea. She felt a tinge of pity for the man, but it soon dissipated into nothingness. There was nothing to worry about, he was just fine and would meet up with them soon enough. And boy, that was going to be something to see.

It had been several days since the incident of my murder and the young soldier was sinking lower by the day. It was the first time he had seen a man killed and to witness it in such a brutal fashion was tearing him up. The man had been one of their own, how could they have killed him over simple disagreements? Marigold wished himself back to his family's farm in the Saint Lawrence Valley where the biggest danger was frostbite and wolves. He feared he was living amongst those very wolves and they were far scarier than the furred beasts.

Wenonah cast him a sympathetic eye. While she relished in the darkness of humanity, she also found herself quite intrigued by the way some would not turn, would not stray from the path of goodness no matter the circumstances. Sure, the young man had succumbed to the pressures of the others, but in the very moment of truth he refused to let go of his conscience and could not commit murder. And yet, he suffered the same guilt as if he had shot the man himself. The burden of the righteous. She wanted to hold him, comfort him and caress him, right before she snapped his weak, pathetic neck.

She had only dared once to partake of an innocent soul and it nearly destroyed her. The pain was more agonizing than could be described. It was as if a war were being waged within her very depths. She had been warned, but she had also been very curious as children sometimes have a tendency of being. She shuddered at the memory, finished her tea and wandered over to where the lieutenant was talking with the big, scary man with a mangy red beard. They both ceased their conversation as she neared them.

"You could have buried him, it would have been the proper thing to do," she said.

"He didn't deserve no proper burial," Faust replied.

"Now, corporal, she is right, no man deserved to be left arse up to the wind," Gagnon said with a smile and nudged Corporal Faust with an elbow before taking a long pull from his whiskey bottle.

"That stuff will kill you, you know," Wenonah said.

"This?" the lieutenant said, holding up the whiskey bottle.

"No, your darkness," she said, drinking in his aura and doing everything within her power not to strike him dead that very moment.

Lieutenant Gagnon shifted himself to face her. He was unnerved by her brazen attitude and knowledge beyond her years. If it hadn't been for her two lumbering fools, he would have left her to rot next to Morgan's corpse.

"My two lumbering fools do not protect me, I protect them. And as for rotting, dear Elijah is not rotting as you should hope."

"Little girl, I have had just about enough of your shenanigans. Come daylight you and your two fools will part ways with us," he said and waved a dismissive hand.

"Ah dear Phillipe, that would not bode well for you."

Gagnon searched through his half-drunk mind and could not find one recollection where he had told the little girl his first name. There was something about her that filled him with a sense of foreboding.

"And why pray tell not?"

"You are a stranger in these lands, you barely know how to say hello. People around these parts are not so receptive."

"May I remind you that you are not one of them either."

"Ah, but dear Phillipe, I am of all peoples from all lands."

"Shut up! You are but an insolent child and nothing more," he said, waving another dismissive hand.

"We shall see, dear Phillipe, we shall see," she said and turned away to hide her smirk. She made her way back to her two attendants, one of whom began brushing her long, brown locks which had just a hint of gray.

Chapter Thirty-Two

Shadowman, Shadowman,
Where have you gone?
Shadowman, Shadowman,
Turn away from the dawn.

Wenonah's sing song taunts brought me out of my slumber and back into the reality of my world. I truly wished the child-crone would quit speaking in riddles and just come out and say what was on her mind. Hell, if she possessed the power to taunt me within my own mind, she could surely draw me a damned map.

After a few moments of rubbing my eyes, once I could find them, and some time trying to get over my craving for a cup of coffee I thought about her taunt. Away from the dawn? Of course, that meant away from the east and directed me to head west. But due west? Northwest? Southwest?

I had stopped for the night at a crossroads hoping for an unsuspecting traveler to cross my path so I could borrow some supplies from them, but it was to no avail. I stood at the intersection, got my bearings from the stars and the pinkish hue on the horizon, it was then I saw a cairn of stones with what appeared to be tea spat on them set off away from the path. She was a wily one that is for sure. I followed the first marker for about an hour and as the sun crested the horizon it was directly at my back. Could she not have just said follow the stones? Maybe she did not have a rhyme for rocks or stones or boulders.

I hoped that not only was she leading me in the right direction but that she was also doing whatever she could to slow them down. I'm not sure if it was my hunger or my absolute desire to kill both Lieutenant Gagnon and Corporal Faust that was driving me onward, but I was able to ignore all physical pain and exhaustion. My mind was filled with images of how I would dispatch each of them. Each one of them took turns going first in my fantasies finally settling on eliminating the bigger threat first.

My thoughts often drifted to my growing hatred of this unforgiving, god forsaken land. I longed to be back in civilization once more. Sipping fine wines and bedding beautiful women, as if those things had ever actually occurred. The more my mind drifted the more I feared I was becoming delusional. I laughed out loud when I recalled my mother screaming at me, claiming I had demons running around inside of me. "Dear mother, if you only knew," I said to her memory on the wind.

It was the third, maybe fourth day of following the trail west when I caught scent of them. Not a scent smelled through my nostrils but an essence wafting through the breeze. As I was still an apprentice with my newly acquired talents, I had no idea how to interpret those signals. Was I only a mere few hours away from them or days?

I followed the markers Wenonah was leaving for me which made my travel much faster not having to scout the trail. By the signs on the markers I was getting closer to them, no more than a day out. I would have to remember to ask her exactly how she slowed them down so much. By that evening I had drawn close enough to smell their campfire. I climbed a small ridge that overlooked their campsite to get my bearings and formulate a plan of attack.

Faust and Gagnon were sharing a bottle by the fire, the young soldier was off by himself. From the looks of it he was on watch but not doing his best due diligence. Wenonah was preparing her evening tea while her companions tended to their bedrolls. Judging by the sun's position it was about an hour from sunset, so I settled in for a short nap before deciding on my course of action. I was hoping the young man would be taking first watch. *Hatred, Fear and Lies.*

When I awoke several hours later things were just as I had hoped. Both Gagnon and Faust were passed out in a drunken slumber and the young lad struggled to stay awake as he stared off into the night. I crept through the scrub brush more out of habit than necessity until I was a mere twenty feet from the young man. I stashed my pack of stolen clothes by Wenonah who threw a quick wink in my direction which made me question just how visible I was to her.

I knew I had to act quickly as I would only have mere seconds to accomplish my task with optimal results. I unsheathed my tomahawk and carried it in my right hand across the darkened camp to where the young man was keeping guard. Just as his head tilted back in a half-asleep posture, I swung the handle of my weapon up across his neck and applied as much pressure as I dared. He did not even have time to struggle before he succumbed to the lack of blood flow to his brain.

Quickly I dragged the young man over to where Faust was passed out with his hand outstretched. Using the tomahawk, I lopped off the big man's hand in one quick swing and shoved the weapon into the young man's hand as he started to regain consciousness. The encampment exploded in a flurry of activity.

Faust screamed in pain and leapt to his feet which startled the now awake young man who held a tomahawk in his hand with the Hessian's blood dripping from the blade and the man's severed hand in the other. Confusion reigned supreme. I stepped into the shadows to watch in all unfold. I felt a tinge of pity for the young soldier as Faust's good arm with a mallet for a hand bashed into his face. Blood spurted from the young man's nose as Faust dropped on top of him and gripped his throat until his knuckles were white.

"What did you do that for?" he screamed and shoved his bleeding stump into the smaller man's face.

"Corporal, stand down," Lieutenant Gagnon ordered.

Faust ignored the man's orders and was at the precipice of killing the young soldier. Reluctantly I assumed the role of his knight in shining armor, especially since I had caused him this torment. I withdrew from the shadows and positioned myself, so the moon shone straight through me. I snatched the tomahawk from the kid's hand and lopped off the big man's other hand at the wrist.

The corporal screamed and instinctively grabbed for his newly wounded arm with his already handless arm. He gazed up at me with confusion and fear. In that moment I think he saw me or was at the very least aware of my presence. I kicked him over onto his back and put my face so close to his that he could smell my fetid breath.

"You should have killed me when you had the chance," I taunted.

I had relished in his hatred and his anger but now, his fear was absolutely intoxicating. I let his luxurious essence swirl around me as I felt his strength waning. He had lost a lot of blood and would soon be seeing the harbinger of death. He was mumbling something be it was too soft to understand.

"Are you reciting the Lord's Prayer? You of all people?" I asked.

His eyes opened and I felt his demeanor start to change. Before he could get even one more iota at peace, I lopped his head off with one quick blow. His essence was instantly coursing through my veins. I felt his rage. I felt his torment. I felt his fear. I consumed his darkness.

I was in a euphoric state for several moments and when I began to regain my balance Lieutenant Gagnon was pointing his pistol at my chest.

"Shall we not go through that again, it is such an inconvenience," I said with a smug grin.

He stood there for several minutes with his finger on the trigger and a look of bewilderment twisted on his face. More than once I prepared myself to feel a musket ball pierce my heart once again. The young lad had darted away from camp and was cowering in the darkness.

"Well done dear Elijah," Wenonah said, looking up at me with a smile.

"How?" was the only word that managed to escape Gagnon's lips.

I just shrugged in response.

"Magic!" Wenonah said with a shrug, raising her hands palms up above her shoulders.

"But you were dead?"

"Most certainly. And now I am not."

"I must have missed. Must have just wounded you."

"No, you were on target. Hurt like the dickens really, so please, do not do that again or I shall become terribly angry with you. Angrier than I already am I suppose," I said, dropping his musket ball to the earth in front of him.

"What sort of trick is this?" he asked, the barrel of his gun wavering back and forth.

"If you shoot me again, I will have to reap the same vengeance upon you as Corporal Faust over there," I said, pointing to the headless soldier still oozing blood from his neck stump. As I pointed, I realized I was rapidly resuming my normal state, and I also realized I was buck naked when Wenonah giggled.

I gave the girl-crone a disgusted look and she tossed me my pants after several moments of snickering. I went about my business in a nonchalant manner as if I did not have a pistol pointed at my chest and no clothes on.

After getting my pants back on I said, "Please stop pointing that thing at me before you accidentally shoot me, and we have to go through this trouble all over again."

"What kind of a trick is this? I killed you," he asked once more, stiffening his posture.

"It is no trick, you indeed did put a musket ball into my heart, and you most certainly killed me. Therein lies the trick, I cannot die. Now, you are starting to get my dander up and when my dander gets up, I get quite reckless. Wenonah here says we need you, but I tend to disagree."

"Dear Elijah, have some tea," she said, handing me a cup of putrid, watered down oolong.

I felt the lieutenant's cloud swirling all around me in a beautiful sea of blackness. It was filled with anger, hatred, but most of all fear. Delicious fear. I fought with every fiber of my being to keep from ending the man's miserable life right that very moment. I slipped my tomahawk back into its binding and gave him a warm smile. But my eyes painted a much grimmer tale which he must have understood as he lowered his weapon.

"Marigold clean up Corporal Faust would you please?" he said with a dismissive hand.

Wenonah nodded and her two companions joined to assist the young man who was having quite the difficult time dragging the behemoth's body away from the camp.

"Sir, shall I bury him?"

"No, no need for that. Just take anything identifiable off his clothes and bag up the head, we will dispose of that further down the trail. Make sure his backside is to the dirt in case any Brits happen upon the body."

"Sir?"

"Nothing, just a poor attempt at some levity in a dark moment."

The lieutenant plopped down on a rock and pulled his bottle out of his bag. I dusted myself off, straightened my clothes and joined him for a drink. Wenonah shot me a wicked grin and wandered off to do whatever it was she did when she was not tormenting me.

Chapter Thirty-Three

Conversation was held to a minimum over the course of the next few days on the trail. I could sense that Gagnon was still stewing and chose to distance myself to let the kettle simmer back down. Nothing would be achieved by killing him too early. And I still did not have a clue what it was we were trying to achieve other than creating chaos which was perfectly fine with me given the way I was feeling after absorbing dear Mr. Faust. I could not even begin to imagine what the exhilaration would be if magnified a hundred-fold.

I was admiring the countryside of lush green meadows that surrounded us. I was fond of the seclusion the forest offered, yet nothing could beat the sensation of the sun beating down on a man as a cool breeze blew across his nape. Butterflies were flitting on the new blossoms and katydids serenaded us from the underbrush. From the outside we appeared as harmless as field mice. I was wandering through my many reveries when the young lad made his way over to me.

Sheepishly he said, "Good morning, sir."

"It's Elijah. Just call me Elijah. No need for formalities," I said, giving up the charade of my pseudonym.

"Sorry, it's a habit. My name is Robert, Robert Marigold."

"You're not a Frenchie, are you?"

"No sir, I mean Elijah."

"Nor a Brit."

"I was born here in the colonies."

"Well good for you. What's on your mind?"

"Excuse me?"

"You didn't mosey your way over here just to gossip so what is on your mind?"

"Are you going to kill us?"

"Why on earth would you ask such a question?" I heard the words as they came out of my mouth and completely understood where the lad was coming from. "You, probably not. Him, most definitely," I said, pointing my thumb in Gagnon's direction.

The young man walked along side of me staring into nothingness while contemplating my words. I could sense the goodness emanating from deep within him and it sickened me. Not morally or emotionally, no, he physically sickened me, and I wanted nothing more than to wish him away.

"Listen son, I like you, I really do. You seem like a fine young man and quite frankly, I have no use for you. I strongly suggest that the very first chance you get you slip away from this little caucus of ours and get as far away from us as you can. Things are going to get ugly from here on out."

"Desert? I can't desert, they will hang me."

"I never said desert. Get away from us, find your way to another fort. Make up some story or another about being captured and you escaped or something."

"But the lieutenant will have me branded as a deserter."

"He will never get that chance. When you find another unit or fort just tell them he was killed, and you were captured. Tell them you got lost during your escape."

"I'm not a very good liar Elijah."

"You had better learn to be one. If you stay with us you will most assuredly die, maybe not by my hand, but you will die just the same. If you think I am evil and scary, the lieutenant there is far worse than I could ever be."

"That I do know. In fact, he scares me to death."

"As he should. Now, like I said, you light out of camp tonight. I will get him good and drunk and by the time he realizes you are gone in the morning you will be too far away to go after."

He nodded and started slowing up to head for the rear. "Elijah, you be careful and do not trust him in the least," he said.

The innocent look of true concern glaring back at me through his eyes set me at ease. Maybe there was hope for me yet. He was genuinely a good person and I wished him no harm. I would make certain he escaped the evil intentions of our little gathering of lost souls.

The day was long and hot and by the time we entertained thoughts of making camp we were all in dire need of a rest. Funny, Wenonah could make me immortal, yet she did nothing to keep my feet from hurting. I sat down and took off my boots. My feet were a criss-cross of cracked, torn flesh that were tender to the touch. These boots were definitely not made for walking.

"How long must I tolerate him?" I asked Wenonah when we had a moment alone.

"Dear Elijah, do you not yet feel the power that courses through your veins? Do you not desire even more power?"

"To an extent, but I also wish to be practical."

"Why?"

"Because it is the smart thing to do."

"Smart for a mortal maybe, but you, you must learn to abandon such precautions. I thought the big man would have finally awakened the beast within you. Maybe I consumed too much of him and for that I apologize."

"Or maybe my soul is not as dark as you thought. Maybe I'm not such a lost cause after all."

She let loose one of her little girl giggles and said, "Oh, no dear Elijah, your soul is about as dark as they come. Even the corporal with his propensity for eating brains was not as dark as you."

"Come now, he must have been ten shades darker than I. He devoured dying men's brains as they begged for mercy for Christ's sake."

"Ah, but what you see him doing out of evil intentions is not the proper assumption to make."

"Not the proper assumption? Why else on earth would the man have done such a dastardly thing?"

"Fear dear Elijah, fear. The man knew that someday his luck would run out and when it did, he was going to answer for his sins."

"So, he committed the dastardliest sins possible? That doesn't make much sense."

"Men who know they are doomed for all eternity think they can make deals."

"Deals with whom?"

"I don't know that dear Elijah. Maybe God, maybe the devil himself. As you witnessed, in his final moments on this earth the Hessian reached out to a god he had ignored for most of his life. You on the other hand, you are an anomaly. Even with a musket ball cleaving your chest you made no deals and showed not one single shred of remorse. Therefore, I have chosen you above all others. Why are you second guessing that which is inside of you, that which is a primal part of you?"

Never in my life as far back as I could remember had I ever questioned my actions or my motives. I lived every single day riding on the back of my impulses never giving God nor the devil much of a thought. I had careened through my days believing that the only higher power that existed was the man who was powerful enough to rule the roost. Kill or be killed. My life has been governed by survival of the fittest followed by an eternal dirt nap and nothing more.

Maybe that was it, in convincing me there was an evil higher power she forced me to believe that pure good must also exist because one could not possibly be without the other. The light cannot exist without darkness to illuminate. And maybe, just maybe I was a part of that master plan. I had to be the darkness so the light could then exist. I found it particularly peculiar how immortality had me suddenly questioning my own mortality and reason for existence.

Had I really lived such a wicked life that a demon from hell would seek me out? I let myself drift through time to a place in my memories that seemed almost too hard to find. I never remembered my childhood being anything other than a normal childhood. Playing. Working. Killing. I remembered the killing and if I were to be honest with myself, how much I enjoyed the killing.

Almost from the time I could walk I would accompany my father to the woods to hunt game around our little cabin. Rabbits first, then various breeds of fowl and eventually deer and elk. I loved the exhilarating sensation of triumph from a successful hunt. But most of all, I enjoyed watching the animals kick and flail about as their lives bled out into the dirt. I learned how to merely wound the animals by gut shooting them to prolong their deaths. Their shrill screams of pain and anguish were songs to my ear. I shuddered as I recalled the look in my father's eyes the day, he came to the realization there was something off about me.

At some point, when I was about thirteen years old or so my father recognized this bloodlust in me and stopped taking me on his hunts. He had taken all my weapons away from me, even my knives. To humiliate me further he left me at home with the womenfolk to cook and clean and do chores around the house. Even worse, he made me study the Bible and report to my mother what I had learned. That was when the seed of hatred was planted deep within me.

We lived by a small band of natives and although we had little or no contact with them, I watched them as they went about their lives. Explicitly I would steal away out into the woods to watch them hunt. I was fascinated with their weaponry which may not have been as deadly as a musket but so much quicker in that they were able to plant half a dozen arrows into an animal before a musket could be reloaded once. And their wooden shafts did much less damage to the meat than a musket ball. To my chagrin the weapon and the hunters were so much more efficient that the animals died quickly, with little or no pain.

It had taken me at least a dozen tries to replicate their bows. I used different boughs, some too stiff, some too flexible. The strings they used proved to be the most difficult. None of the vines I used seemed to hold up to the extreme pressure of the bow and would snap or simply shoot the arrow toward my toes.

One day my patience panned out and I spied a father teaching his son how to make a bow, something my father had not bothered to teach me. After learning the proper materials, I went to work on my juniper bow whittling and working the wood as time permitted. I would stash my materials in a hollow oak stump deep in the woods and would steal away each day working a little bit at a time. I was able to trap a few rabbits to make the string. I was fascinated by the inner workings of the animals and how far their intestines could be stretched. I scraped, dried, and braided the rabbit guts into a perfect bow string. By my fourteenth birthday I was ready to give myself a valuable birthday present; freedom.

I was yanked from my reveries by an icy wind blowing over me, yet the sun was blazing overhead. She was right. Wenonah was right, I was evil through and through and had been since I was just a young lad. I recalled the warmth and stickiness of the blood as it clung to my skin and how I savored the metallic smell and the salty taste.

Defeated I wandered over to where she was making coffee, sat down and said, “So what do we do now.”

“One must die so another can live.”

“What in the hell does that mean?”

“That person you once were, even though a dark soul, still carries a small ember of goodness. You must cast away remorse, cast away regrets and douse that ember once and for all so that the all-powerful you can exist.”

“So, I have to choose to condemn myself to hell for all eternity?”

“Dear Elijah, were you not already in hell before I rescued you?”

I thought about what she had just said while scanning through my ever-fading memories. Although I had pushed it away from my mind, I still remembered the scars of guilt I wore every day. I remembered suffering through the pain of remorse knowing I could never undo what I had done. An image of my little sister writhing on the ground with three arrows in her tormented me suddenly and tears began to stream down from the corners of my eyes.

"Embrace your new life and all those memories will fade over time until you have none left. All the pain and hurt will vanish," Wenonah said.

"You mean a new life filled with murder and mayhem."

"Have you not killed before?"

I just nodded my head. I was finding it exceedingly difficult to cope with the fact that I was such an evil human being that a demon from the depths of hell would desire to recruit me into her envoy. Perhaps this was my true destiny after all. Maybe I was just like Wenonah and had not realized it yet. Why should I be remorseful for simply fulfilling my own destiny? It was time to embrace the darkness and shed all facets of light including remorse.

That evening I made sure to refill the lieutenant's glass more often than usual. He was feeling no pain about an hour after the sun had dipped below the horizon. I made my way out to where Robert was standing watch. Poor lad was standing watch with no one to relieve him. I guess Gagnon had let that little fact slip his mind.

"Evening," I said, startling the young man.

"Good evening sir, I mean Elijah."

"Are you ready?"

"Ready for what?"

"Ready to get the hell away from here and back to your life. I assume you have a wife, children?"

"No, nothing like that."

"Not even a girl you fancy?"

"There is one back in town, she's quite pretty and we seem to get along just fine. But I'm too shy and nervous."

"After your ordeal here, I hope you have learned that life is something special, something to be cherished and is ever fleeting. Go back to town and sweep that woman off her feet."

"But if I leave," he started.

"Your leaving is much less of a problem than if you stay. If you stay, you will die of that I can assure you. Now hold still and hold your tongue," I said and quickly slashed my tomahawk across his face laying open a large gash. I gave him a cloth which he applied to the wound while shooting me a look of wonderment. "You were attacked by a band of cutthroats, the corporal and lieutenant were killed and you were left for dead. That is what you tell them when you get back to the fort. That and nothing else, do you understand?"

He nodded his head while fighting back his tears. I put my blade into the fire until it was red hot and brought it to the wound on his face to seal it up. I fought back my own tears of pity as he struggled in pain. Not one for goodbyes I stuffed his pack into his arms and shoved him out into the night alone. I truly hoped he made it back to civilization in one piece and lived out a long and prosperous life far away from the clutches of the French army. Far away from the clutches of me.

Chapter Thirty-Four

Late that next morning found us standing on the shores of an enormous body of water looking west. Seagulls cried an eerie tune as they argued with one another over morsels of food while several deer had come out of the woods and were drinking at the water's edge. With my rejuvenation I was simply enjoying everything about the day.

I studied a small golden locket with a broken filigree chain I had found lying on the ground in the camp that morning. It might have belonged to the Hessian, but I doubted it as the picture of the woman inside was a young beautiful lass not likely to be caught dead with a man such as him. No, this must have belonged to young Marigold and this was who he was running to. It made my heart feel good knowing that I may have saved the young man's life this day.

Lieutenant Gagnon had not said a single word about young Marigold running off in the night. Maybe he had expected him to flee a long time ago. Maybe he wished he had gone with him. Either way it was a conversation we were not having this day.

"Poussin would have frolicked in this place," Gagnon said, splitting the silence which startled me.

"Poussin?"

"A French painter extraordinaire."

"Huh, never heard of her," I said, still in the mood to throw stones.

"He. And of course, you haven't, you are a cretin below anything of such remark."

"Cretin? And you are a drunken fool, what makes us that much different?"

"I have not always been a drunken fool, but you have always been a cretin," he smiled and handed me the bottle which I declined.

"What is your plan?"

"It's not my plan, it's hers," he said pointing at Wenonah.

"So now you are taking war council and diplomatic advice from a little child?" I asked.

"Come now, we both know she is so much more than a little child. Appearances can be deceiving you know."

I nodded, caught Wenonah's attention, and beckoned her over to where we were sitting. She frolicked like a young lass sniffing the blossoms and chasing butterflies as she made her way through the field of wildflowers. I sensed it was all just an elaborate act, but then a part of me had to wonder if it wasn't. Was this little girl-crone just that, a multitude of things rolled up into one?

"Yes, dear Elijah? Phillipe?" she said with an elegant curtsey followed by her handing me a bouquet of pink lady slippers.

"We have made it to the lake, where do we go from here? How do we meet with the tribal elders?"

"We head north, many days north to where the big waters meet."

"Big waters meet? What does that mean?"

"This is not the only big lake, there is another to the east. Both of them meet and share water far to the north."

"I've never heard of such a place," I said, suddenly fascinated by the thought.

"You will see."

"And then what? We just wait? Do we look for them?" Gagnon asked, clearly irritated that he was having to get his direction from someone else let alone a child.

She ignored him and said, "We take canoes to Minis Gitigaan."

"What is this Minis Gitigaan?"

"It is an island in the big lake."

"I have never heard of such a place," the lieutenant barked.

"Of course you haven't, it is a secret and sacred place."

"You know how I feel about water, how far do we have to canoe?"

"About a day, maybe less depending on the wind."

"A day to canoe to an island? Just how big is this lake?" I asked.

"Bigger than you can imagine," she said, spreading her arms wide for emphasis.

"Let me get this straight, we are going to be trapped on an island with several different hostile tribes, most of whom don't care too much for Frenchmen? That does not seem to be the most prudent of plans to me," Lieutenant Gagnon said.

"It is the only plan there is. This is the only place these leaders will meet."

"What is so special about this island?"

"It is where many ancestors are buried from many, many tribes. It is said that their spirits live in the trees."

"Great, we are going to a haunted island to be slaughtered," Lieutenant Gagnon said.

"We will not be slaughtered. As I said, the island is sacred to many tribes so there will be no violence. By anyone," Wenonah expressed in a motherly tone while staring Gagnon down.

"I hear there is a French fort on the lake north of here, we will stop there and pick up some additional men for the journey to the island."

"There is no need for that," she said.

"Au contraire my dear, there is a great need for that. I am not going over into hostile territory without any troops whatsoever."

Wenonah shook her head, "If you bring troops and weapons, they will kill you before you ever make it to the island. If you must, gather a couple cooks and maybe someone to help carry supplies for the feast, but no men in uniform."

"Why do I feel like we are lambs being led to the slaughter?"

"Dear Phillipe, do you recall it was you who proposed this little arrangement, not I. This is a very volatile situation and you must do things my way if you wish to succeed."

He huffed and stormed away knowing full well that she was correct. Out on the water they would be sitting ducks in a canoe, now if he could commandeer a warship from the fort that would be an entirely different story. Those thoughts passed with each gulp of whiskey that poured into his gullet. I watched from a distance that afforded me a respite from his constant chatter.

The following morning brought with it storms blowing in from across the lake. At times it seemed as though the winds were picking up every single drop of water from the lake and dumping it directly upon us. Howling winds bit through my jacket, through my skin and clear down to my bones until I ached to my very core.

The day in front of us was bleak and gray with no signs of life other than us retched travelers. Most sane critters had dug deep into shelter somewhere to wait out this storm. Not us, we moved into the miniscule shelter provided by the tree line and trudged on wordlessly, driven by a desire I had yet to grasp the meaning of.

Shadowman, Shadowman,
Why do you fret so?
Shadowman, Shadowman,
For us to reap, first we must sow.

Wenonah's words taunted my brain. I was looking at the back of her little head, but I could still see her sarcastic sneer. Like a parasite she wormed around in my brain, hiding within the shadows of my every thought, squirming and burrowing through my soullessness. There was something for a man to endure. I had no soul and yet I had many and there were bound to be many more. Would I be able to reconcile with a horde of souls residing within me or would it drive me completely mad?

A few hours later the storm subsided, and we exited the forest to follow the lakeshore which was much more easily traversed. The storm had left the air hazy and visibility was down to just a few mere feet in front of us. Gulls sang their eerie melodies as they drifted unseen above us. It sounded as though they were laughing, mocking us as we slogged onward. The once roaring waves of the great lake were now nothing more than kittens lapping the shore. It was the proverbial calm before the next storm I presumed.

As the fog dissipated with the rising of the morning's sun it revealed huge piles of sand up and down the coast of the great lake. As more of the day was revealed these were not mere piles of sand, but mountains, mountains that seemed to be endless. The golden grains pushed their way westward until they met the water's edge and left us with no other option than to climb upwards. It appeared to be a battle between the water and the earth of who could eat who first.

My legs were burning by the time we crested the dune. Whatever sense of triumph and relief I felt was washed away as one dune led to the next. An expanse of sand lay before us as far as the eye could see. Looking back over the water I spied a couple of large islands off to the west, fog still clinging to their shores.

"Have we arrived at our destination?" I turned and asked Wenonah through gasps of breath while wiping sweat from my brow.

Undaunted by the climb and as fresh as a spring daisy she smiled and replied, "Oh no, dear Elijah, we are not yet close enough to see. Another few days, maybe even a week I would imagine."

"What are those islands called," Gagnon asked.

She shrugged. "Don't know if they have names or not. If they do, I have never learned of them. But I do know they are filled with walking spirits."

"Walking spirits?" Gagnon asked.

"Ghosts," I said.

"The fantastic tales you natives weave," Phillipe dismissed the discussion with a simple snort as he turned away.

"Us natives? I take it you have never heard of Cazotte or Corneille, both of whom penned tales of ghosts," Wenonah shot back.

"Child, you baffle me so. How on earth would you know of such men?"

"Oh, dear Phillipe, I know of all men."

As her words fell on my ears a chill wind ran up my spine leaving layers of gooseflesh in its wake. Where Phillipe Gagnon simply dismissed Wenonah as a prankster, I knew she spoke the truth. But how much of the truth remained a mystery that would transcend time.

As if Phillipe was not even there, she turned to me, "My dear Elijah, do you see that small inlet between the two islands?"

I angled myself to get a view straight down her crooked finger. "Yes, I see it, a bit difficult with this fog though."

"Strain your eyes and look at the surface of the water between the two islands for it is on days such as these the spirits love to wander."

I glanced at her with a suspicious eye not sure if I was being drawn into a web of a child's mind or into the demon's lair. She smiled a girlish smile which set me a little at ease, that was until I saw what she was talking about. From my periphery I spied movement across the water between the two islands. My logical self-explained it away as simply the wind or water currents but my imagination saw ghosts dancing across the water's surface with elegant ease. Once more I was clearly rattled and once more, she was visibly amused by this fact.

Chapter Thirty-Five

We broke camp early that next morning and set off northward across the dunes. In any other setting this would be considered a desert, but with a massive body of water nestled up to the expanse of sand it was merely one seemingly endless beach. Sand and water as far as the eye could see and yet, very few signs of civilization which suited me fine.

As we travelled Wenonah regaled me with tales of a sleeping mother bear waiting for her cubs to cross the lake, underwater jungle cats, a cervidae who blessed women with fertility and a flesh-eating creature who punished evil men. The latter she vehemently defended as being more truth than legend when Gagnon scoffed aloud at her tale. I desperately wanted to ask her if there was a legend about me in my current manifestation but truly feared her response, so I maintained my silence.

We weathered a storm or two which cost us some travel time as did circumventing a small town here and there which tested my patience on a grand scale. I did not like little sips of my travel company let alone being stuck with them for hours on end with nothing to talk about but trivial nonsense. The longer this dragged on the more I needed to feed which was made apparent to me by Wenonah's constant nagging of my psyche.

I shifted my thoughts to the breathtaking scenery stretching endlessly in front of me. Granted, I had sailed the oceans, so I was no stranger to open water, but this was different. This freshwater sea licked at the sandy beach little a kitten trying a bowl of milk for the first time. And the sands were almost pristine, no dead fish or clumps of seaweed rotting away in the hot summer sun drawing swarms of flies. No smell of decay wafting on the winds, only freshness.

Suddenly I was drawn to my knees by the vilest odor I have ever experienced. It was as though the entire beach had been transformed into a long strand of decaying human flesh. I retched violently as Gagnon looked on with confusion painted on his face while Wenonah sported a sneer that told me she was the culprit of my current dilemma. Once again, this tiny little creature had found a way to terrify me to my marrow. How could she possibly invade my very sense of smell? And it was quite obvious she thoroughly enjoyed tormenting me by the voracity of her sniggering.

For the next couple of days, I kept my distance from her. Our small entourage grew by way of rogues and drifters we had picked up along the way. We had grown our posse to more than half a dozen men and one small child-crone. Having grown weary of the extended travel, we spent the days mostly in silence. The air was starting to take on a slight chill, meaning we had travelled quite a bit north and must be nearing our destination. When night fell, I could see a sliver of light glowing on the horizon.

"What is that?" I pointed out through the darkness.

"We must avoid that place. We will be heading inland until we hit the lake again," Wenonah commented.

"Why not just continue to follow the lake?" Gagnon asked.

"Did I not say we must avoid that place?"

"Why, is this another of your places of evil?"

"You could say that Frenchy. But it is not my place of evil, it is yours."

"So, that means we are almost to land's end then," he said. "And that would be the glow of Fort Michilimackinac."

"Yes Frenchy, that is your evil place."

"We need to forge forward and gather supplies," he argued.

"No, we shall not. We shall not go near that place. There will be a council there and if they see us our plans and our excursion into this accursed wilderness will be for naught."

"We need supplies and the fort can't be more than a mile or two away."

"And we shall have them. I have already made arrangements and supplies will be waiting with our boats on the shores of the big lake to the west," Wenonah said. Phillipe moved his lips ever so slightly. "I said no and that is all I am going to say."

Gagnon was a smart man and noticed her companions had assumed an aggressive posture, as did I. He was not sure what they were capable of, but he was well aware of what I would do to him and he wisely dropped the issue. As he turned away from us, I noticed a glint in his eye that let me know the issue may be over in a verbal sense, but he had in no way erased it from his mind. I would have to keep my eye on him.

An hour or so later I was tucked beneath a blanket next to the fire. I could see the flames dancing through my skin. I knew I had begun to fade earlier in the day, but as night fell it had accelerated to the point of being noticeable. At first, I had not understood Wenonah's insistence at bringing every rogue we had encountered along the way into our fold against Gagnon's stiff resistance and my hesitation. Now I understood. Now I could sense these men's inner being and they were filled with darkness.

I knew Phillipe was up to something as he had been pacing like a restless cat for the better part of two hours. I picked a fight with one of the ruffians and gave him a good thrashing during which I noticed Gagnon slipping off into the darkness. I had given him the diversion as bait and like the rat I knew him to be, he took it. I laid down in the darkness and awaited the inevitable retribution from the ne'er-do-well whose pride I had stolen so easily in the daylight. This night, I would steal his soul as well.

I was still burying the body in the scrub when I caught sight of Gagnon's shadow creeping back into camp. I began to regret my not following him as I was certain his visit to the fort was bound to do us more harm than good. I hoped he had just slipped out for a little after hour's recreation with a vixen or two. He ruffled his bedroll and began making coffee as if he had just awakened for the day.

I walked down to the beach to watch the moon setting on the water as the sun came up at my back. Gulls cried in the distance as they dove into the depths for wriggling bait fish. I was stretching and scratching when I first spied a reflection from the water's edge about a half a mile down the beach. I tucked up into the shadows of the dunes looming over the beach and ambled toward the shimmering in the distance. I hunkered down and watched until my ankles were too sore to crouch anymore. Nothing. I didn't spy any movement whatsoever. I deemed it safe and walked upright the rest of the way.

There were boats, canoes to be more exact, but large canoes. Five of them in all, two were brimming with supplies. The boats were beached at the bow and were filled stem to stern with barrels and sacks which held a variety of trinkets and food. But how did they get here? I surely would have heard men rowing this many boats through the still waters of the night. It was then that I noticed there were no footprints in the sand other than my own. How in the hell did men beach large, heavily laden boats without making nary a sound or disturbing the beach and then just disappear? I was pondering the situation while absent mindedly staring off into the horizon when Wenonah's crackling voice startled me from behind.

"What are you contemplating dear Elijah? Are you thinking about that cold, dark night off the coast of Montserrat?" she asked, sending chills reeling throughout my body.

I ignored her question and stuck to the matters at hand. "How did these boats get here? Where did they come from? And who brought them here and where did they disappear to?"

"Ah dear Elijah, so many questions, so few answers."

"I am not in the mood for your games this morning, Wenonah."

"This is far from being a game, Shadowman," she spat, her voice laced with contempt. "You keep asking questions like you are in control. You have never been in control. You will start to do as you are told and quit asking so many questions."

It took me a moment to gather what she had just spewed from her tiny little mouth. I had to resist the urge to gut the little urchin with every fiber of my being.

"Still a doubting Thomas I see. What will it take to convince you that you have no choice but to follow me? Would gutting me convince you? You may not want to bear witness to what spills forth from out of my belly," she said with a sneer.

How did she read my every thought? How could she have possible known I had contemplated gutting her, it had been a brief whisper of a thought, nothing more? Once again fear invaded my soul. I would lay claim that this allegiance would be the death of me, had it not done so already. I briefly contemplated what it might take to dissolve this partnership. The Lord Jesus flashed but for a moment in my embattled mind.

Shadowman, Shadowman,
Embrace the darkness anew.
Shadowman, Shadowman,
For His darkness has consumed you.

I just glared back at the little miscreant who simply giggled for a moment, but then her face took on a sternness I had not seen in all our time together.

"Never again will you think those thoughts, or I will educate you on the scope of my power. I will do unto you that which you cannot even imagine to be possible. The time for doubt has long passed. Accept your fate as it stands, or you will be forced to accept a fate far worse."

I turned away from her without a word. I really had nothing to say. Fear had gripped me so tightly that I feared if I were to open my mouth I would start to vomit and not be able to stop.

"Phillipe stole away in the night," she broke the unnerving silence.

I just nodded in agreement. "He slipped back into camp just before sunrise."

"Where do you think he ran off to in the middle of the night?"

"I think we both know exactly where he went."

"Why would he go to the fort, other than to go drinking and whoring?"

"Safe money would wager it was to betray someone, or everyone involved in this little soiree."

"I agree. You must be wary of him, even more than you already are," she said, her face lined with concern.

I nodded. "So, what is the plan?"

"I saw torchlights in the night coming from the west. The elders have gathered on a small island next to Minis Gitigaan to await our arrival. When the fog lifts, we will take the supplies over to the small island and meet with the elders. There we will prepare a feast in the name of good faith before we canoe over to Minis Gitigaan for council."

"I know we cannot trust Frenchy, but are we able to trust the savages?" I asked.

"Savages?"

"The natives."

"Why do you call them savages? Do you consider yourself a savage? I am certain you have committed far more heinous acts of savagery than any of the elders."

"Probably so, but they are heathens and do not believe in God, not in Jesus Christ."

"They believe in God, just not your God as you portray him. As for Jesus, the ones who have heard of him certainly believe in him, but as a man and not so much the son of God. As for you, are you not a heathen as well?"

"Absolutely not, I have been baptized."

She laughed, "Oh dear Elijah, simply having someone dunk your head in the water and say a few words from a book does not make you any less of a heathen than someone who has not. Do you live by the doctrine and laws set forth in that very same book?"

"I try," I replied, my voice taking on a much softer tone as apprehension took hold of my thoughts.

"You try? Thou shalt not murder? Did that not count the day you cleaved that Hessians skull? Or thou shalt not steal when you stole the man's very soul? You my dear Elijah are more of a heathen and more savage than any of the natives I have ever encountered in any land. At least when they are savage it is with a higher purpose other than to fulfill their own bloated egos. Do I dare mention blasphemy or adultery?"

"You've made your point," I said and turned my back on her.

My nose led me to the camp where fresh coffee had just started to boil. I sipped at the bitter brew while gnawing on a piece of salted venison and tried to ignore the jumble of thoughts spiraling through my brain. The saltiness of the meat eased the bitterness of the coffee and I was able to drift away for a moment. Phillipe joined me in silence, but I could tell he was studying me, probably trying to decipher whether or not I was aware of his late-night departure from the camp. Not wanting him to be able to read me I kept to myself and avoided any eye contact. I wanted to see if he would try and push the issue which he did not. Wenonah was right, he was up to something and I was certain it would prove detrimental to our cause.

When breakfast was finished, we secured the campsite by staking down the tents and stowing all of our gear as our plan was to return the following day. Gagnon remained unusually quiet and began taking on the persona of Wenonah's man servants. I used his aloofness to my advantage and stole away to my tent where I checked my pistols for a clean load and slipped them under my vest. Within an hour we were loaded into the canoes and on our way to the island of the dead.

Chapter Thirty-Six

The very moment I set foot on the sands of the small island I felt an overwhelming sense of dread. I was immediately shrouded in the darkness of hatred and fear sending a shiver rippling through my body. Wenonah smiled at me through her crooked, blackened teeth which made the sensation that much worse. Over time I had realized she could alter her appearance and would do so in the most subtle of ways just to unnerve me. With every step I took across this unborn land I felt death underfoot.

"Where have you brought me?" I asked her once I had helped her out of the canoe.

"I told you that already, this is the land of the dead."

"But I feel such an ominous presence, surely not all who died here were dark souls."

"All of the dead have their places."

"And just what does that mean?"

"As in life, in death, the purest of souls are sheltered from those inflicted with the blackness."

"So, you chose to make our camp in the company of evil spirits?"

"Why of course, dear Elijah. Have you forgotten who you are? Who you once were? And who you will be for an eternity?"

I thought about her words in silence. A knot formed in the pit of my stomach. What had I done? Surely my mortal sins could have been forgiven, but this, this unholy alliance I had so naively entered into, could it be forgiven? Could this pact be broken?

Shadowman, Shadowman,
You do amuse me so.
Shadowman, Shadowman,
The answer to your riddle is a resounding no!

I turned my gaze to the hag-child and nausea overwhelmed me. I barely made it to a cluster of Pitcher's Thistle before emptying my stomach onto the delicate purple petals. I could somehow feel her hot, fetid breath on the back of my neck even though she was more than a stone's throw away from me. Once again, my thoughts turned to regret and escape.

"Dear Elijah, it is best to focus on the task at hand and not dwell on your woes. What is done is done and cannot be undone. Embrace what has become of you."

I nodded and went about unloading supplies from the canoes. Even though I had provoked one of the ruffians and dispatched him the previous night I was now starting to fade once again. It was not enough for anyone other than myself to notice, but it would set me on edge if it were to progress in the middle of this summit. I had yet to learn the intricacies of my malady. Was my transgression into the shadows a set parameter of time or were there many influencing factors? I had not had the time to conduct experiments and Wenonah's lack of guidance had left me a mere babe in the woods. But she was right about one thing, it was time for me to embrace this darkness that had become of me. If for no other reason than it seemed I had no other choice. If I were going to spend the rest of eternity living in the shadows, I had better accept it and use it to my advantage.

"Shall we head to the other side of the island to meet with the others?" I asked.

"No, dear Elijah that will not be possible."

"Why not?"

"That is where the others reside."

"I thought you said this island was uninhabited?"

"It is inhabited by spirits."

"Like Minis Gitigaan?"

"Similar but different," she said.

"How? Are not both islands burial grounds?"

"Not in the literal sense. The bones are on Minis Gitigaan, but the souls remain here, where the living made their final journey."

"So, we are surrounded by the dead?"

"Yes, and it is the dead to the north that we must avoid."

"Oh great, another secret I know nothing about."

"You are such an impatient creature. When will you realize that you are now immortal? You have lifetimes to learn, you need not know all there is to know in one day."

"But this is important information, knowledge I should be privileged to."

"For now, simply understand that it would not bode well for you to be in the company of the pure."

"Pure, meaning good souls?"

"Innocent souls to be more precise."

"I feel a hunger burning within me, am I to feed on these dark souls swarming around me?"

"No dear Elijah, those souls already belong to me."

I saw torchlight flickering over the horizon to the north and assumed it was where one of the camps had been set up. Wenonah's men busied themselves with setting up camp, gathering wood and lighting a campfire. They set up blankets with small benches around the fire. Finally, they brought out cooking equipment and set up a makeshift kitchen. Once their clamoring was finished sounds of men laboring drifted in from the western shore.

"What is going on over there?" I asked Wenonah.

"Oh, that is a surprise. And I must admit, it is my favorite event of the evening."

"Another surprise."

"Patience is a virtue you truly struggle with dear Elijah."

Tired of her enigmatic babbling I wandered off to be alone for a moment. I felt her eyes following me as I walked away from her. I sensed they were not the eyes of a child, nor of an old hag but those of a creature eyeing its prey. I forced myself to clear my mind of all cohesive thought. I sang songs, I admired the blue waters, and I skipped stones and sipped of the freshness that lingered in the air. Anything to avoid having a thought about that wretched beast I had so ignorantly become tethered to.

Shadowman, Shadowman,
The ties that bind are stronger than leather.
Shadowman, Shadowman,
You are bound to me forever.

I ignored her taunts and meandered over to where her confidants were working a large pot onto a bed of hot coals. I attempted to help several times and was rebuffed so I took a seat on one of the benches and took the opportunity to hone my blades. I studied the men, for lack of a better term, as they toiled. Neither broke a sweat nor did they tire, they simply went about their tasks without falter. They would stop to eat a nibble of jerky or a sip a water skin so they must be alive. But I did the same and I was as dead as dead could be, or so I perceived myself to be dead. I was so confused by this perplexing series of events my life had become that I was not convinced this were all nothing but I nightmare I refused to wake from. Maybe I had been hit in the head and none of this was real.

There was a certain tension in the air which instilled such discomfort in me that I wanted off the island. There was a myriad of emotions running through me, not just through my mind and thoughts but literally through every fiber of my being. My nerves were as taut as the strings on a fiddle and were being plucked at a tremendous pace. Overwhelmed I left the encampment for some much-needed solitude.

I walked the shoreline of the island until I came to a very narrow peninsula. I walked for what seemed like miles surrounded by the big lake with the only land in sight being the island we were on and what I could only assume was Minis Gitigaan. The peninsula reached out its long tendril toward a peninsula on the larger island doing the same. It reminded me of a painting I had once seen that depicted God reaching a finger out to Adam. I chuckled to myself at the imagery my mind had created which was so far from my reality.

After an hour or so of mindless walking I found a secluded patch of tall bluestem grass to disappear into. Away from the bustle of the day I began to feel much more subdued and once again in control of my faculties. I watched the clouds roll by while listening to the waves washing over the singing sands and the haunting melody of terns on the wing. The sweet scent of lilac floated on the breeze piquing my curiosity as I had yet to see a bush filled with the delicate purple flowers.

I must have dozed off for it was nearing dark when my thoughts came back to me. Torch light painted an ominous glow over the small island and even with my cat nap I still felt uneasy. It was as if the island itself were alive and in conflict with itself. I felt both the darkness and the light swirling around me as though I were walking through a field of a thousand tiny tornados. I did not relish staying in this place for even one moment longer.

When I arrived back in camp, I saw that Wenonah's men were working with Phillipe to load the canoes. They had emptied the cauldron into smaller pots and were loading the prepared meal as well.

"What are they doing?" I asked Wenonah who had taken an overseer's posture.

"They are ferrying the supplies over for the feast."

I was confused so I asked, "Why would we have not just stopped there in the first place and prepared everything there?"

"In terms you may understand, it would be considered blasphemous to interrupt the slumber of the ancestors by cooking and building on their island without being invited first."

"Won't the feast and the talks interrupt them? And how the hell are the dead going to invite guests for dinner?"

"No interruption, they will be invited guests as well. Tribal elders from each tribe must perform rituals to request the use of their island. That is the purpose of the blue torches you see on Mini Gitigaan, they are to signal to us that we have been allowed to conduct business."

“That seems more than a tad bit absurd doesn’t it? Do you believe we have to be invited first?”

“It does not matter what you or I believe, it matters what they believe,” she said, pointing to the tribal members gathering for the trip to Minis Gitigaan. “They will not proceed without authorization from their elders. No invitation, no meeting.”

I shrugged her off and went to help to load the supplies into the canoes before climbing aboard one of them to take up a paddle. I purposefully chose a canoe that was well ahead of the canoe in which Wenonah sat smirking at me. The helmsman kept us tight to the pointing finger, leeward of the wind until we hit open water. Butterflies invaded my gullet as we hit the open water. I slowed my stroke and peered down into the green-blue waters and was relieved to see that it was not all that deep. Memories of Martinique, Montserrat and the Caribbean still haunted my waking moments, awakening a deep-rooted fear of the water. As we neared Minis Gitigaan I saw how many had already arrived and were awaiting our arrival. Many more than I had expected. These were families, there was unquestionably something Wenonah was keeping from me.

I saw the banners of the Three Fires, the Potawatomie, Odawa, and Ojibwe on the beach in front of us as soon as we cleared the fog. I lowered my head and scanned the coast but did not see any indication there were any other tribes represented. Maybe the others had changed their minds, or maybe they were not there yet. I heard the laughter of children playing as a whisper on the wind, their voices obscured by the sound of the lake. Children, I questioned?

Shadowman, Shadowman,
Be sure to mind your tongue.
Shadowman, Shadowman,
You mustn’t corrupt the young.

As soon as we beached the canoes on Minis Gitigaan Wenonah's men set crocks and large stones in a bed of hot coals that had already been prepared at the center of the encampment. The island was stunning, so I took a short walk to familiarize myself with my surroundings. As I neared the southern shore, I caught sight of land to the south of the island. I wasn't sure if that was the mainland, but I doubted it. It was much closer than the path we took so I was certain it was another island. Once again, I was in awe of this immense body of water and its parallels to the Caribbean.

I was busy and was not keeping an eye on Wenonah or Phillipe, so I didn't see them disappear into the woodland. I still saw only the woodland Indians of the north gathered and no others. This was not going to be much of a peace council, or war council for that matter.

I caught sight of Phillipe who was of course busying himself by passing out bottles of rum which I had no doubt was well watered down. The tribal elders strictly controlled how much their attendants imbibed, only allowing each man one swallow before giving the bottles back to the Frenchman. They themselves did not partake of the grog, instead sat stoically against the night. I could see wisdom on their faces and in their eyes as the firelight glistened. This put me at a little more at ease, these were honorable and prudent men, much unlike myself.

Other groups began to join our little congregation and I immediately sensed apprehension from the leaders of the Three Fires. It was apparent they did not like these newcomers but thankfully had put their emotions in check. It was quite evident there was some bad blood between them, especially the Meskwaki and the Potawatomie elders. Even though all weapons had been confiscated and locked away for safe keeping I had no doubts these men could kill with their bare hands if necessary.

"Welcome all, I can see that some of you have already been acquainted," Phillipe said, eliciting a raised hand from Wenonah which curbed his tongue.

She moved to the center of the clearing that had been arranged for council and addressed the elders, "Shall we begin with a prisoner exchange?"

The men nodded and their attendants disappeared for a moment and returned toting two men each bound at the wrists. From the looks given back and forth from the Meskwaki elder to one of the captives there was a connection. The men were bloodied, bruised and what little clothing they wore was tattered and torn. I had heard about captives being forced to run a gauntlet through the capturing village where women, children and old men would beat them with various objects. It appeared the Meskwaki village treated their captives much more brutally than the Anishinaabe.

"I must apologize, we have no prisoners of yours, so we offer you our best slaves instead," the Meskwaki elder said.

From the looks on the elder's faces I sensed there was a bit of chicanery, perhaps half-truths from the Meskwaki and Sauk leaders. One of the slaves was obviously an Anglo, though I was not sure of his origins. I assumed French because he was the only captive with a gag in his mouth leading me to believe he did not know when to shut up. The other slave was a native but appeared to have mixed heritage as he was quite light skinned. The attendants met in the center, traded captives, and then returned to their respective groups. The captives were then led to a scaffolding which had been erected when our party first landed.

"What now?" I leaned over and asked Wenonah under my breath.

"My favorite part. These men will be tested, if they pass the test and are deemed worthy by the elders they may be adopted into their new tribes."

"And if not?"

"If not, we may get to feed for free," she said with a sinister grin.

Gagnon passed in front of the tribal elders and I immediately swooned. There was an angry wind swirling about me that threatened to choke me. I glanced over at Wenonah who was sitting there with a smile on her face and only the whites of her eyes showing. After several minutes, the sensation subsided.

"What in the hell was that?" I asked.

"Our dear Phillipe is so arrogant he has failed to learn history. All the men in this conclave hate each other with a passion. Fathers have killed fathers, brothers have killed brothers, and sons have killed sons among other, more dastardly depravities. But the one thing they all have in common is that they hate the French even more as the French have killed many on both sides. The Fox will never agree to this union."

"So, you knew this was doomed from the start?"

"A girl can dream, can't she?" she said with a smile and a dismissive wave of her hand making it clear I was to partake of the festivities unfolding in front of us.

The captives were stripped naked and forced to climb up to the scaffolding which was only eight feet off the ground and made from sturdy saplings with gaps between each of the beams. Three of the captives seemed to know what fate awaited them and stood arrow straight once their bindings were cut. They took off their moccasins, set them nearly aside and waited patiently. Within minutes they were handed bowls of food to eat. The Anglo who had been struggling with his captors from the onset was given nothing.

"I fear he won't last very long," Wenonah said in a mocking tone, jabbing a crooked thumb in the man's direction.

Four children were brought out from each tribe and given blunted saplings just long enough to reach up through the openings in the scaffolding. The children were blindfolded and told that the first one of them to get a captive to cry out would be rewarded. At this point the gag was removed from the Anglo and immediately I understood why he had been gagged in the first place.

"What are you doing? You cannot do this to me. I am a lieutenant in the French army, and I demand you free me at once," he cried out which caused Gagnon a great deal of pleasure.

The tallest of the children took his cue and followed the man's voice. Instead of poking through the slats like the other children he began jumping up and swinging with all his strength in a downward motion. Within three or four swings he connected with the Frenchman's little toe with a loud crack. I was certain the digit had been broken, a belief that was immediately confirmed by the man's howling. He grabbed his foot and dropped to a fetal position quickly grasping what a mistake he had made when all the children formed en masse and began shoving their sticks into his eyes, ears, and groin. His tender spots were left vulnerable and were fair game as far as the young warriors were concerned. The three other captives tried hard not to smile as they knew what that would mean for them but were also relieved, they had been spared the rod so to speak.

The children continued to poke, the Frenchy continued to cry out and the elders broke out into raucous laughter. Two women emerged and began passing out what looked like little cakes to the children while two men roughly brought Frenchy back to his feet. He began to protest and one of the more muscular of the men whacked him across the lips with one of the sticks, effectively shutting him up. He struggled a little, more of simply just a twitch which earned him a sharp blow to bare buttocks.

Wenonah giggled and said, "That Frenchman has no idea what he is in for. You may want to say a little prayer for him."

The young children sat down to enjoy their well-deserved snack and three older children from each tribe were brought out and given carefully measured saplings that were no longer blunted but sharpened to a fine point and hardened in the fire. From my estimation they were long enough to jab the bottoms of the feet and penetrate the flesh no more than an inch or so. Each of them chose their victims, the Frenchman of course getting the brunt of the attackers.

The first of the captives took the first direct hit. As the stick dangled from his bleeding foot, he uttered no sound and made no movement. The same with the second and third captives. Now the older boys were toying with the Frenchman, they were making sure they didn't actually break the skin.

One of them finally sunk one of the points into his foot causing him to scream out, "You little heathens, may you all rot in hell."

The oldest of the boys held the others back and stared down the Frenchman. I could not imagine what the man was feeling but the boy's icy stare gave me the goosebumps. And then he smiled long and wide before crouching as low as he could get to the ground before releasing into a jump. Instead of holding onto the stick he used it like a spear which buried six inches through the man's foot. He yelped in pain and fell into the fetal position once more. The boy gave a loud, triumphant cry and quickly directed the other boys to follow suit. They crouched and launched their spears into the Frenchman who writhed in agony. The boys returned to their respective camps and were congratulated bý their elders.

The attendants once more scaled the scaffolding with plates of food for the captives, even one for the Frenchman who flung his plate away in anger. I had the inclination that he had just wasted his last meal and felt a tinge of pity for the man.

"What do you think Misko? Will you adopt that one?" the Meskwaki elder, Huritt, said with a snide sneer.

Misko Nodin chose to ignore the dig and instead stood and retrieved the Frenchman's plate, refilled it and took it to him. The Frenchman seemed to understand the importance of the gesture and reluctantly accepted the plate of food which he picked at with trembling hands. I believe at that moment he realized that his situation had gone from his merely being treated inhumanely to a matter of life and death.

"Who are those two?" I asked.

"Misko is the taller one who gave the food back to the Frenchman. He is the delegate from the northern bands. The other is Huritt of the Meskwaki."

"I have heard the word Misko, but what is Huritt?"

"It translates to handsome."

I shot her a sideways glance. The man was anything but handsome. He had narrow set, angry eyes with no eyebrows to speak of. His mouth was crooked and upturned on the left side. Scars slashed across his face, some self-inflicted, others not so much.

She clicked her tongue at me. "It's like calling a fat man Slim."

A group of young men began to assemble and were admiring each other's fashioned spears. These were much sturdier than those given to the children and were designed for hunting, designed to kill. Some were merely hardened shafts with a wooden point, others had flint tips similar to arrowheads and there was one that I would wish upon my worst enemy. It was designed to penetrate and then deploy barbs into the flesh to keep the spear from backing out and to maximize internal damage. I had seen similar spears used for spearing fish in the West Indies.

The warriors counted out twenty paces and faced the captives on the scaffolding in what I could only describe as a rudimentary firing squad. Two women appeared and began blindfolding the young men. They then walked to the scaffolding and offered blindfolds to the captives. The Frenchman started to accept until he noticed that the others had declined. He was beginning to understand that this was a test of their bravery and commitment.

The mood had turned from somewhat festive to quite somber. Drums began to sound in a cadence that had me falling into the rhythm with them. Slow and methodically they echoed in the night accompanied only by the crackling of the bonfire. Without warning the first spear was in flight and connected with its target hitting the man just above the elbow in his bicep muscle. The man did not so much as flinch he simply stared forward at the hurler and said something in a language I did not understand. The man who had thrown the spear nodded and took a step back off the line and adjusted his stance one step to the left. I then understood that his victim had simply told him where the spear had found its mark so he could have better aim with his next throw.

The next man to throw faced his target, a lighter skinned man who stood next to the wobbling Frenchman. He stood stalwart in the face of his fate, much more defiant than the others, almost daring the man to hit him with a kill shot. As with the other, he did not even twitch when the spear was thrown. It went wide if its mark just grazing the man's thigh. As with the other he uttered one word, but then surprisingly he said something else which seemed to anger the young man who had thrown the spear and he flung another, this time skewering the man's lower abdomen.

Immediately the elders erupted into chaos and Huritt stormed over to berate the man who was of his camp. I did not know what was said, but it was clear the elder was not pleased he had thrown a second spear out of anger. He then turned his ire to the scaffold but only stared down the light skinned man. I thought I caught a smirk crease his lips just a little. I didn't know the relationship, but it was apparent the Meskwaki elder had been greatly dishonored.

Dark energy swarmed around us like angry bees. A thousand silent voices screamed at me from all directions. I glanced over at Wenonah who seemed to be lost in a cloud of bliss. And although it was quite agitating and nerve wracking it was also soothing my aching hunger. It was converting anguish and pain into pleasure. Huritt flicked a dismissive hand in the air, turned his back on the men and took his seat.

With that gesture the wounded captive yanked the spear from his side and jumped from the scaffolding in one quick motion. Once he hit the ground, he took two long strides and launched the spear. Before the man who had originally thrown it could react it was buried deep in his eye socket. He dropped to the ground without a sound, a look of surprise forever etched on his young face. The captive returned to his perch on the scaffolding and the ritual continued.

Seeing all of this unfold before his eyes the Frenchman urinated out of fear which drew a raucous round of applause and accolades from the small gathering. The man on the line hefted his weapon several times to get a feel before letting it fly. It hit the other captive dead center in the tender flesh just below his Adam's apple. The force of the blow knocked him backward and he started to drop. The two captives on either side of him held him up as he stood unyielding until death finally won the battle. His body was carefully lowered down in front of the scaffolding where the women immediately seized upon him with hatchets and knives, cutting his flesh into strips and chunks.

Gagnon neared the scaffolding and the Frenchman seemed to recognize him. He asked under his breath, "Why in God's name are they doing that to him? They already killed him for Christ's sake."

"Hold your tongue man or you will be served right along with him."

"Served?"

It finally dawned on the bewildered man what was transpiring as the lieutenant walked away with a smirk to disappear into the shadows. The Frenchman dropped to his knees in prayer and watched in horror as his fellow captive was dismembered and cooked over an open flame. The light skinned captive looked down on him with disgust, fish hooked his nostrils with two fingers and yanked him painfully back to his feet. When the Frenchman tried to protest the man gave him a short punch to the rib cage taking the wind right out of his sails.

I glanced over at Wenonah and saw that she seemed a bit uncomfortable and asked, "What's bothering you all of the sudden?"

"His was not a dark soul, at least not dark enough. Let us hope that does not happen again," she said in a tone that suggested she was trying to spit something bad tasting from her mouth.

The ritual moved into another phase as plates of freshly roasted meat were passed around. I was smart enough to know that it would have been considered a huge insult to not only those in attendance, but to the spirit of the dearly departed should I not partake of his offering. I sniffed my plate and it smelled of sweet maple, I shrugged and placed one of the smaller chunks in my mouth. With each bite I was reminded of the look on the man's face as he stood dying on the scaffolding and gagged just a little. I washed it down with some rum which allowed his face to fade from my vision a little. Wenonah was eating but not very heartily.

With some rather physical prompting by the light skinned captive the Frenchman managed to swallow three bites before regurgitating his fellow captive all over the scaffolding. This brought more raucous laughter and while I did not fully speak the language I was able to decipher that the theme of the joke was that the dead man did like the Frenchman and was trying to get away from him.

Suddenly Lieutenant Gagnon interrupted the festivities. "Gentlemen, and ladies," he said as he glanced over at Wenonah. "Can we please get to deliberating on the matters at hand?"

"It is not time for talk. There is much yet to do," Misko Nodin, the Ojibwe elder said.

"Oh, come now, what more is there to do? Kill another of these captives? Hell, let me start it off," he said and moved to draw his saber. He was quickly set upon by two warriors who relieved him of his weapons.

I noticed both sides of the camp were none too pleased with Phillipe's outburst. Without realizing it he was doing more to bind these two factions than any talks could do. All the elders hated this white man. Sadly, for him he was uniting them against the wrong front.

"Let me apologize for the lieutenant's drunken outburst. He cannot handle his rum," I said while exaggerating a drunken buffoon raising laughter from the elders. "But it is important that we get to the matters at hand. Is it possible to discuss this during this lull in the ceremony? Give your brave warrior a chance to escape the Frenchman's gullet," I gave a wink and they laughed again.

The most stoic of the elders spoke, "Are you in charge?"

Caught off guard I said, "I wouldn't take that liberty, but I do know what the desired outcome of this council would be for all parties involved."

"Then speak, you have already proven yourself a far superior negotiator than the Frenchman over there."

"I think I could have done that without opening my mouth," I said in jest.

The elders all laughed, and Gagnon slinked off into the shadows. I knew I shouldn't have made a pun at his expense, but I also knew it would loosen the elders up a little and give me some credibility. Besides, this was a joint operation, not a one man show. Wenonah's eyes sparkled and she gave me a discreet nod.

"Honored guests," I started. "We all sense the growing animosities between the Frenchmen to the west and the red coats to the east because we are trapped between the two of them. This has not proven profitable for any of you and has kept many of us, you especially, at odds with each other to the point of meaningless wars and senseless death."

I glanced around at the elders who had stopped everything they were doing and were now giving me their full attention. I was not sure what to say next and the long silence was making me nervous.

"I agree, this practice of our two peoples killing one another over a war that is not even ours is pointless and no good can come of it. But what is it you propose?"

"That is simple, you choose."

"Between the arrogant, smelly Britons or the even more arrogant, more smelly Frenchmen?" one of the younger men asked.

I shrugged and replied, "I know, it is not much of a choice, but it is a necessary one. You, Huritt is it? You side with the red coats and yet that only strengthens your eastern enemies."

An elder nodded and grunted, "The Iroquois Nation."

"So why do that? I know you are a wise man and you know that if the red coats victoriously drive the Frenchmen from the western lands then the Iroquois Nation will share in the greater spoils and even that will be meager. You will be given nothing more than scraps not worthy of a cur."

I let my voice take on a stern, urgent tone to drive my point home. Hell, I had no clue what the British would do if they beat the French, but my objective was to turn these men against the British, although, I was starting to doubt my allegiance with the Frenchman. With a fleeting glance Wenonah reminded me of the purpose for this gathering. It was not to make alliances or to promote peace, in the end it was to create utter chaos. I was not here to make them allies of the French, rather, even bigger enemies of the Iroquois and eventually the British so that all sides, every faction of humanity in this young, growing land would be consumed with hatred for one another. My mission was to perpetuate a blood bath.

Chapter Thirty-Seven

I was pouring myself another rum when I noticed something odd in the faces of the elders sitting across from me. Then a familiar feeling washed over me, and I glanced over at Wenonah who was sitting there with her eyes rolled back as if she were in the throes of passion. It was as if the world had stopped turning and we were all frozen in place. The warriors behind the elders were the first casualties of the betrayal as a volley of arrows whispered from out of the darkness. A recognizable scent grabbed my attention, Gagnon.

I started to get to my feet but was pinned down by several sets of hands.

"Be careful of that one, he is shifty and dangerous," Phillipe commented as three warriors set upon me with leather thongs and ropes. "And bag that vicious little creature," he said.

Something happened to Wenonah as her attendants set upon her attackers and were beaten down. Warriors attacked the two with lances, pinning them to the ground before chopping at them with their tomahawks until there was little left of them that was recognizable as having once been human. But had they even been human? She screamed out and started biting and clawing at the warriors who struggled to get her diminutive frame into a burlap sack.

"Phillipe, you let me out this instant. You do not want to see me angry."

"Be quiet you old hag or I will throw you into the river like an unwanted litter of kittens."

I felt something stirring inside of me, something I had not felt in a long time. Something I had not really felt since my first encounter with the hag child; fear. Sure, I had been afraid, and had moments where I thought about fear, but never the brand of fear that grips you, that sends butterflies careening through your gullet. I started to speak but one of the men instantly rapped me on the back of the head with the blunt end of his tomahawk effectively silencing me.

"What is the meaning of this Frenchman?" Huritt let the words hiss off his tongue.

"I'm glad you asked. We want your cooperation. We want you to join us in defeating the British."

"You have a strange way of asking, first you dishonor us and then you ask for our allegiance?" Misko Nodin injected.

Phillipe laughed until he brought up phlegm, "Ask? Oh, I wasn't asking. I was giving you an option."

"And what option would that be?"

"Join us and live, that is your only option."

"My warriors will have your heads on their lances."

"My good man, no they won't they are being dispatched as we speak. And yes, your tribe does have enough warriors to eventually make good on your threat but by then, it will be your head on my pike. I believe these men will need a little more convincing," Gagnon said, motioning to two Mohawk warriors closest to him.

Wanting to rub the newly formed lump on my skull that ached like a stubbed toe I flexed my muscles and tried to move but was held fast. I watched as the two warriors disappeared into the shadows. Gagnon was wearing that smug, dastardly grin of his while the elders were stoic, but I could also sense they were weighing their options. I could still hear Wenonah cursing an unseen entity from somewhere out of my line of sight. Things sure went bad in a hurry. Did she know this? Was this all part of the master plan? Even if it were, I was in no way prepared for what happened next.

"Gentlemen, I've always felt that a good chef should always present the cut of meat served at dinner for his guest's review. I am truly sorry I did not do this prior to service, but they were still a little less than cooperative at that point,"

Gagnon said, his evil washing over me like a warm bath. My body felt luxurious, but my mind screamed in agony.

Before us were two young men in their late teens, planked and carved like pigs from the waist down. I could see that whoever carved them up took great care not to cut any major arteries as the young men were still alive, their eyes widened with horror. I recognized them from earlier in the night, as the sons of the elders.

Misko Nodin began to rise out of his seat but was held fast and a spike ended tomahawk was driven through his hand into the wooden table when he resisted. Huritt stirred but was quickly subdued with a blade against his neck. Phillipe was in complete control and his ego demanded their full attention.

"Gentlemen, as I have already made perfectly clear, this is a non-optional agreement. You will pledge not some, but all of your warriors to the cause."

"We will do no such thing. Torture us, kill us, you will not get the results you desire. You sought to gain allies and instead have made blood enemies," Misko said, reaching his free arm over and placing his hand on Huritt's shoulder. The Meskwaki elder returned the gesture in solidarity. Both men expressed a courage I know I myself do not possess, yet they could not contain their tears as evidenced in the glistening rivulets filling in the creases on their faces.

"Gentleman, I must warn you, it will only get uglier from here on out unless I have your full cooperation."

I do believe it was at that very moment that both the elders and I came to the tragic realization that sounds of the children playing had abated. The women were no longer scurrying about doing this or that and the night had settled in around us as if we were the last human beings left on earth.

Phillipe gave a chuckle and said, "Ah, I see you brilliant men have sensed that something is amiss, rotten in the state of Denmark so to speak. And I can assure you from your perspectives something is greatly amiss."

"What have you done, Phillipe?" I asked through clenched teeth which earned me another, even harder, rap to the back of my tender skull.

"Hold your tongue Shadowman, this is no longer any of your concern," he no longer made any attempt to mask the contempt in his voice.

"We did not come here to harm anyone, especially not women and children."

"Shut him up please," he said. A leather thong was tied through my mouth and a sack placed on my head. "Good, peace and quiet, I could not gather my thoughts with all of his chattering.

Swirls of dark energy performed a ballet across my every nerve ending propelling my mind into a jumble of confused thought. I felt like a beast dying of thirst caged at the edge of a sweet flowing river unable to slake an insatiable desire. A desire that would not relinquish its grip on my very soul. The overload of sensation caused me to thrash and squirm which earned me yet another blow to my tender skull. This in turn fed my growing anger which only served to add one more ingredient to the stew.

"You will capitulate and see the world through my vision, or you will suffer dearly."

"We will not send our young men to die for your senseless war."

"Au Contraire, it is far from senseless, it will make me and my colleagues here extraordinarily rich men. You will return to your respective homes and prepare your warriors for war. Then you will send them to Michilimackinac where we can gather forces and strategize a battle plan to take out the British in the area first and then move eastward."

"We will do nothing of the sort. Kill us if you wish, but we will never fight for you."

"I was afraid you were going to say that," Phillipe said. "Take that sack off of Mr. Morgan's head, I want him to see what is in store for him."

Being a man of little conscience myself I was surprised at my own reaction of dismay to the scene unfolding in front of me. Phillipe had brought one of the women out in front of the elders. She was not old enough to have been one of their wives but not so young as to be one of their small children. It was then I saw she was bearing a child, and quite far along by the looks of her distended belly. The sheer terror on her innocent face caused my heart to ache. He brought out a long plank and laid it on the ground in front of the elder's table.

An anger burned inside me unlike anything I had ever felt. But a fear as well. Gagnon was well aware of my adeptness at avoiding the angel of death and his being a shrewd tactician I was certain he had concocted a solution for this dilemma. One that would certainly involve an inordinate amount of discomfort on my part.

"Gentlemen, this is only the beginning of what I hope, for your sake, turns into a truly short negotiation. From what I have been told she is neither your wife nor your daughter but is a captive recently betrothed to your boy over there," he said and pointed to one of the mutilated boys who had all but stopped squirming. "I pray your feelings for your future daughter in law do not run too deeply. Spike her."

With that two Mohawk warriors roughly took her by the arms and dragged her over to where a six-foot-long wooden plank was lying on the ground. The woman was biting and kicking and screaming all of which earned her a bloody mouth and a hard blow to the shin from a wooden club. One man held her down by the shoulders while the other man nailed her feet to the plank with long nails through her feet high up near the ankle.

"This here gentlemen is your timer. An hourglass so to speak. When I stand her up your time to decide begins. You will have until the nails rip through her feet to make a decision."

Gagnon then bent down and lifted the plank from the end where her feet were nailed, and her head pointed toward the ground. She was already moaning in pain but let out a piercing scream once all her weight was being supported by her damaged feet. After several moments of thrashing about she realized it was much less painful to just lie still. To keep from crying out she bit into her forearm until it started to bleed.

"Oh, she is a brave one isn't she?"

"She does not deserve this. She has done nothing to harm you," Misko said, standing up from the table earning himself a blow to the head that drew blood and knocked him off his feet.

The woman's instinct for survival began to take control of her pain, letting her think more rationally. Whenever Phillipe wasn't paying attention to her, she gripped the sides of the plank and used her arm strength to leverage herself up which lessened the weight on her impaled feet. Gagnon had been enraptured by his own diatribe and failed to notice her for quite some time. I found myself silently rooting her on. One of the warriors caught his attention and pointed out her ploy.

"Come now, we can't be having any of that," he said.

I felt his anger surge across the distance between us and the darkness within him was cold and bleak. He took a wooden club from one of the men and smashed her elbows until I was certain he had obliterated the joints. She yelped in pain at the initial blow but somehow managed to choke back her pain. The Frenchman was beginning to make the Hessian seem like a decent bloke. He slammed the club on the table on front of the elders causing them to startle.

"Gentlemen," he changed to a softer tone. "Just how ugly does this thing have to get? If need be, I will bring out each of your children one by one until I finally run out of them and must start on your grandchildren. They seemed to be extremely near and dear to you, cute little bugs I might add."

I saw something transpire between the two elders that Phillipe had missed. Just the briefest glance passed between the two. The Ojibwe elder gave a slow blink. With that Huritt used all his might, broke free from the warrior holding him and dove across the table to where the woman was hanging upside down in agony. He pulled a small knife from his waistband and slit her throat before Phillipe could react with a blow across the man's jawbone with the club. I watched her fade into peace. And then

I felt something very odd, extremely uncomfortable and I swore that I could hear Wenonah screaming.

Shadowman, Shadowman,
Why hast thou forsaken me?
Shadowman, Shadowman,
I demand you set me free!

"Maybe I did not make myself clear," he said, clubbing the elder in the stomach several times. "Bring me the smallest female child, we will start with her."

Misko Nodin wrestled himself free from the men holding him down, ripped the tomahawk impaling his hand, stood up and said, "That will not be necessary. We will do as you ask."

The men released their grip on him, and he went to tend to the dead woman and Huritt who was still writhing in pain. Misko laid the plank back down and gently closed the woman's cold, staring eyes.

"And as a gesture of good faith I will allow you to take your eldest sons with you but the other shall remain in my good care until our task is complete."

"No, that is not agreeable. Our word is our bond," Huritt said, pulling himself up onto his elbows.

"Unfortunately, that is not an optional part of this agreement. See, I know you do not trust me which causes me not to trust you, so I need leverage. Your families are that leverage. I expect to see you at Michilimackinac in two weeks' time, so I suggest you get cracking," Phillipe said.

"Gagnon, you will not dare to harm those children," I called out as he walked away.

"Or else?" he said, spinning back on his heels to look at me. "He bores me. Bag him and knock him out if he gives you trouble, just do not kill him, it would be pointless."

I heard the cries of a newborn infant echoing into the night as I was dragged away in darkness.

Chapter Thirty-Eight

"I'm so cold," I heard a little boy's voice echo within the walls of my foggy mind.

Was it my voice? Had I travelled back in time? Or worse, had I become a gnome-child the likes of Wenonah? My head ached and the pain threatened to destroy any coherent thought I may possibly conjure the ability to latch on to. I slowly opened my eyes and found I was in a darkened room. I tried to move but could not. I jerked at my arms but could not free them and was immediately wracked with excruciating pain for the attempt.

"Watseka, there it is again. I told you there was a ghost in here with us."

"Relax, Sugnog, it is just the wind I told you," Watseka said.

"The wind cannot rattle chains."

"No, but the wind can shake a door or even a wall which in turn would rattle the chains."

The fog encapsulating my brain was slowly dissipating and the horror of my reality came sharply into focus. Not only had I been chained to a beam, but my wrists had been bound with leather straps that shrunk as they dried. And as if that were not enough, spikes had been driven through my hands into the beam as high as my arms would stretch. I tried to maneuver to get more comfortable and quickly realized my feet had been spiked in the flat-footed position as well. Although I could not see my body, I knew the predicament just the same. How long had I been here?

"See, look," the young boy blurted out and pointed to where I was sitting in the darkness. "I can see its breath."

"That is just the frosty morning air creeping in through a broken board."

"Nuh uh, that's a ghost, and he is watching us."

"First, ghosts do not have to breathe and second, how do you know it is a he? Maybe it is an evil witch who eats children who like to argue."

My eyes should have adjusted to the darkness, but I was still blinded. I tried to move my head side to side but it too held fast to the beam. I tried to speak, but the only sound I was able to manage was a low, guttural growl of sorts.

"Did you hear that?"

"Relax Zhigaag, it is only the wind."

"Watseka, I'm scared. And I told you not to call me that, I do not stink."

"There is nothing to be afraid of, Sugnog. See, stop this nonsense, you are scaring your little sister. We are already in enough trouble without you making it worse."

I wagged my tongue around in my mouth to find I had a leather thong with a ball of something hard like bone in the center preventing me from doing much other that breathing or grunting. That damned Gagnon had thought of everything either to keep me from escaping or to torture me endlessly. This was a predicament so depraved even I could not have imagined. One of the children coughed, raspy and deep.

"Gigyago is getting sick."

"I know," Watseka, the eldest said.

"I'm hungry."

"I know you are Zhigaag, I am too. Here, you can have my apple," she said, using the boy's less than desired nickname. He hated it, but she loved it and using it comforted her so she could keep her fears hidden from him.

"But you gave us your apple yesterday," the smallest of the three said, her voice weak and distant.

"And the day before that," Sugnog interjected.

"I'm fine. I can hold out until my grandfather comes for us."

"What if he doesn't? What if he cannot? You saw those men, they wanted to kill us right there, maybe they killed everyone, and no one is left to come and get us."

"Stop it! You are scaring the little ones."

I listened to their bickering for quite some time before I nodded off. When I came to it was even darker and the room had grown quiet except for the sounds of children sleeping. As I lost myself in thought, lulled by the rhythms of the night I could make out something dark in the room. Darker than the shadows. Darker than even the night itself. And then one of the children coughed in that low, deep, wet cough I had heard earlier, and the darkness seemed to glow. How in the hell does that even happen? How can darkness glow? But it did just that.

They coughed once more, and their darkness glowed in unison. Each time this phenomenon occurred I felt a sense of both melancholia and jubilation at the same exact instance. Was this their sickness I was seeing? Experiencing? Was this the same sickness that Wenonah had shown me was living inside of me?

"She is getting worse."

"I know."

"What are we going to do, Watseka?"

"There is not much we can do."

"And we are running out of food."

"I know that as well."

"What are we going to do about that? Are we going to starve to death?"

"Listen, I am not father, I am not grandfather. I do not have the wisdom of the elders. I do not see a way out of this so all we can do is pray."

"Pray for the spirits to help us?"

"No, pray they are merciful and take us quickly in our sleep, so we do not suffer."

Listening to these children was placing a burden on my heart the likes of which I had never felt before. They did not deserve the evils being thrust upon them of which I was partially to blame. Their blood would forever be on my hands.

What in the world was Phillipe up to? I can see him abandoning me to an eternity of torture, but these children were nothing but innocent pawns in his sadistic game. Would he actually sacrifice these poor children who had done nothing to harm anyone?

I was lost in the rhythms of slumber when the darkness rudely awakened me. But this was different. The glowing darkness has changed. It was not something I could see, more of a tangible feeling about the air itself. I felt a profound sadness invading my soul and I tried to back away from its assault. But still it came, forcing itself upon me like nightfall, giving me no choice but to endure the onslaught.

My beating heart felt as if it were clenched in someone's fist, beating ever harder, trying to break free from the bond. Trying to break free of my chest itself. Being a man who had rarely felt remorse it was proving impossible to process this level of sadness and regret. I was made fully aware that a little child was suffering, dying because of me. Because of my actions, my inactions and what part I played in this mechanism. The most difficult aspect to process and accept was that I was helpless to do anything about it. And then the poor child coughed no more.

Elijah, Dear Elijah,
Fight against the light.
Elijah, Dear Elijah,
Resist with all your might.

Chapter Thirty-Nine

"Andres Phillipe Gagnon, you release me at once!" Wenonah spat.

Phillipe sat at the other end of the canoe and grinned at the hag-child as she struggled against her bonds. Smiling on the outside but filled with dread on the inside. How had she known he had been called Andres after his grandfather? He was certain he had never offered that information to her.

"Because I know everything about you," she said, mimicking his twisted grin.

"Bag and gag her again. If you cannot behave you will be dealt with as such," he said. Phillipe gathered his nerve and scooted right up next to her. "I do not know what kind of demon you are, but I do know that you will not win this battle. I have stripped you of your defenses and when we get back to our camp on the little island, I will put an end to you all together. You will no longer be able to spin your webs of magic."

It had been nearly a week since the betrayal on Minis Gitigaan and Philippe had progressed beyond annoyed with the situation. Even with his senses dulled by alcohol he knew Wenonah was a force not to be reckoned with. Although she was his captive for the moment, he knew he could not maintain the upper hand for long, so he bided his time awaiting the arrival of reinforcements from the mainland. Reinforcements of the religious nature.

A set of canoes pulled up beside Gagnon's filled with several men dressed in ornate regalia. Two of them were quite elderly with one being on almost the complete opposite end of the age spectrum. Phillipe imagined he was an apprentice of some sort. *Great, they had brought children to an adult party.*

"Ah, I see our guests of honor have arrived. I hope you enjoy their company," he leaned in and hissed into her ear.

In a soft, childlike voice she whispered, "Do you really think your priests or witchdoctors or whatever you want to call them are going to be able to help you? You were mine long before you even laid eyes on me and nothing is going to change that. Just remember one thing Phillipe, you are a dark soul and your fate has been sealed by your own actions. As for your little excursion, there are as many allies as there are adversaries."

Gagnon moved back away from the vile creature and took a long pull from his flask. How did she know everything about him, about everything he was planning even before he had planned it? Was she the antichrist instilled with the same attribute of second sight as Jesus Christ himself? Was he her Judas? A wave of nausea washed over him, and he leaned over the canoe to empty his lunch into the dark waters. The elders watched this unfold from their canoe and were gravely concerned.

Under her hood of burlap Wenonah's face was creased with concern. She may not have known where Elijah was being kept but she could sense he was surrounded by innocent souls. Souls of those sick and dying. Souls who could sever her ties to him and undo all of her handiwork. She must get to him before it was too late. But even with all of her power she still had rules she had no choice but to follow, one of which was that she could do no physical harm. Mental anguish, yes. Manipulate others to harm in her stead, yes. Make one harm themselves, of course. But she was not able to raise a hand to the living herself.

"Is she a wendigo," the Meskwaki elder asked.

"No, Huritt, I do not think she is from any of our legends or tales. I think we are in more trouble than I first imagined. Nothing good will come of this and I can assure you, that Frenchman will show no mercy."

"Is she the white man's devil, the one they call Satan?"

"She takes the name Wenonah from us, but she is not one of us."

"Wenonah? First daughter? Maybe she is the daughter of the white man's Satan?"

Misko Nodin just shrugged. "Whatever she is, I believe the Frenchman has angered a beast he foolishly thinks he can control. I am not fearful for myself but for the children. When she kills us all there will be no one to rescue them and they will starve."

"What about the other white man? The one they took away with the children."

"I feel he is in an even worse predicament than we are."

Phillipe gathered himself into a blanket and shivered against the darkness. His plan was coming to fruition and yet he was not elated as he should be. There was something terribly wrong. He severely underestimated this little hag-child and had not recognized the true danger she posed. His arrogance had blinded him and forged him forward without ever considering the consequences.

"Phillipe, it is not too late to undo what you have done. I am a forgiving person. Unbind me and we shall talk about what to do next."

"Silence child, thing, or whatever the hell you are," he barked. Phillipe swore he could feel her anger swelling up inside of him. She was a devious little trickster.

He was not one to believe much in the God of the Bible or of Eden or Heaven, so he most assuredly had not given much thought to the darker denizens of the underworld. Mainly because he did not believe in an underworld, or Hell as the preachers would have you believe it was called. Until now. Whatever kind of creature Wenonah was she was assuredly not of this earth. He had not had any doubts until she put them in his head to manifest and grow until they were out of control.

Phillipe could not see her sinister grin beneath the shroud, but he knew it was there, taunting him. He peered over the bow of the canoe into the darkness looking for the orange glow of torchlight. Looking for anything to divert his attention away from Wenonah and her devious tricks. Was this the smartest plan he had ever concocted? No, but it would prove to be the most lucrative if he could pull it off, so it was worth the risk. Besides, what could that little tyke do to him? She merely had a way of messing with a man's mind, nothing more.

"Oh, dear Phillipe, I am capable of so much more than you give me credit for. As of right now I am merely perturbed by your insolence but as the minutes drag on my anger grows. You do not want to see me angry," she cackled, mimicking girls pretending to be witches.

There was a small giggle when she giggled, and Wenonah realized she had an unwitting ally on the canoe. There was a child, for whatever reason she did not know, but that did not matter. A child was not as easy to manipulate but she had a few tried and true schemes. She breathed in deeply and partook of his essence. A boy child not yet close to being a man. He would not be very strong, but he would be useful enough. Yes, he would serve aptly.

Gagnon was relieved to see an orange glow over the water about a half a mile away and waved the other canoes over to him. It took them more than a week to gather supplies and for the shaman to be summoned. Phillipe himself did not believe in most of their superstitions but the natives were right about one thing, he did not dare chance just running her through with his sword. There was something magical about her that he was not willing to toy with. Had he not witnessed Morgan's resurrection firsthand he would have dismissed the lot of it.

An eerie feeling washed over him as he stepped onto the shores of the island for the second time in his life. He had a sudden premonition that he did not belong in this place and yet he somehow knew this was where he would spend eternity. He took a long pull from his flask and shunned the foreboding portent from his brain. Two men dragged Wenonah from the canoe kicking and screaming all the way down the beach to where the camp was still set up. Embers still smoldered in the white ash.

"Why is that Frenchman so fearful of this little child? Unruly but surely not a demon," one of the Mohawk men commented.

Putting a gentle hand on the man's shoulder and speaking in a fatherly tone one of the shamans said, "She is deceiving you. She is making you see what she wants you to see and think what she wants you to think. She is the most dangerous of all demons for she can turn a man against himself. Do not spend any more time with her than absolutely necessary."

With that the two men bound Wenonah's hands and feet to two large totems that had been erected in the center of a common circle. There were four pyres burning around the circumference, one to the east, west, north, and south. The air was filled with the smoke of medicinal herbs being burned in vessels made of bone. The shamans, four of them, took great care with these herbs. Each of the shamans assumed their role as the protector of the east, west, north, and south respectively and burned a different blend of plants for each direction starting with the east.

"Smells lovely, what is for dinner?" Wenonah taunted.

The young boy giggled, unheard by all except her well-tuned ears. He was sitting in the smoke of sweet grass, so he was to the north and she to the south.

Dear little warrior,
I am as fearful as a fawn.
Dear little warrior,
You must save me before the dawn.

Migizi heard her words but the pretty little girl had not uttered a single sound. He gazed at her with a curious glance and she seemed to look right back at him even though her head was covered. He moved slightly to his side and her head followed. A breeze blew across the water causing a chill to run up his spine. He peered out into the darkness and saw that the lake was black and still. There was no breeze. He shuddered.

The shamans stood in the wafting smoke of cedar, sweet grass, sage, and other medicinal herbs while chanting softly in unison. One of them slipped the cowling from around her face and flashed a tender, concerned look in her direction. She responded with a defiant sneer. Wenonah looked down upon them in amusement while parroting their words. They maneuvered the smoke to swirl around her using a large feather. Eagle, she imagined, however, vulture would have been more apropos.

She quickly became bored with their meaningless ceremony which soon went from a minor annoyance to downright aggravating. The shaman had begun poking at her bared stomach with totems made from bone and bird talons. She hoped they were not chicken feet, she hated chickens with a passion. Each of them dipped their hand in a bowl of powder and rubbed them against her belly. It tickled which lifted her spirits and put her in a playful mood.

One of the shamans let out a yelp and jumped back away from her causing the others to do the same. Cautiously he outstretched his arm and placed his hand on the child's stomach once more. Almost as quickly as he had extended his arm, he withdrew it in near panic. He glanced at the others who were confused as to why he was being startled. Each of them in unison touched her as well and felt nothing.

The shaman gave a nervous laugh and placed a shaking hand on Wenonah's belly once more. Something moved inside of her and again he jerked his hand away, only this time, his hand would not move. It was held fast in place by some unseen force. Her stomach stopped moving suddenly and the shaman breathed a sigh of relief which was momentary at best. His hand began to grow warmer and warmer until it became searing hot and it trembled as he tried to jerk away from her. Tendrils of smoke began rise from between his fingers and the smell of cooked flesh permeated the air. The others stood in frightened amazement, not really believing what they were witnessing.

Wenonah's power was waning, and she could not continue to torment the man, so she relinquished her control on the man's mind. He was bewildered when he brought his hand to his face as there was not a single mark, it was not even reddened from the heat.

"You saw that, right?" he asked the others holding his hand palm out to them.

The other shaman simply nodded in agreement. Wenonah feigned pain and discomfort when in fact she felt not much more than irritation.

"It is true, a demon lives in this child," a shaman said to Phillipe.

"I was already quite aware of that fact. How do we rid ourselves of it?" Gagnon replied.

"We must prepare a cleansing ritual."

"Great, perfect, we are surrounded by water," Gagnon said, spreading his arms like wings.

"Not with water, with fire."

"And it must be done properly if we are to save the girl."

"Who said anything about saving the girl, I just want whatever the hell this creature is gone and out of my life forever."

The small group of men stood around her discussing what steps they must take but she never heard a single word. She did not even see them; she was staring right through them and into the face of her new friend. She smiled and winked at him and after several moments he returned the gesture. She assumed her most innocent expression and blew him a kiss. He blushed and blew her a kiss back.

"You must help me," she mouthed, and he nodded.

Chapter Forty

I awakened to more coughing in the night. Another child was sick and sounded as though they did not have long in this world. I had been concentrating on the voices, but it was difficult as they did not communicate very often. I counted at least five children not counting the dead child or the one who was now sick. I wracked my brain trying to get a sense of time and how long I had been chained to this wall. I could not be certain how long I had been out, but the dead child had already begun putting off a very displeasing odor.

"That Meskwaki boy sounds like he is sick now."

"I know," Watseka said.

"Do you think that grandfather has forgotten us?"

"Absolutely not, he would never forget about us. Something is preventing him from coming to get us."

"Is he dead?"

"Did his spirit tell you goodbye?"

"No."

"Then he is not dead," the girl spoke with authority, but her tone was also tender. From what I gathered she was the eldest of the children but was just a child herself. A very brave child.

There was a long pause during which I contemplated saying something, but I did not want to frighten the children any more than they already were. The position I was in was beyond painful. My hands and feet ached from where the spikes had been driven through the bone and flesh but also the rest of my body was in agony from not being able to move. I rotated my shoulders to try and ease the stiffness in my neck and then I rolled my head from side to side. I heard a gasp in the darkness.

"Did you see that?" the boy asked.

"Yes," the girl whispered back.

"I told you there was someone in here with us."

"Okay smarty, where are they then? Only the bag moved, not a person," she said, not wanting to scare the child with what she really suspected, rats.

"A bag can't move unless there is something in it, like a ghost."

She wanted to say, "Or a big fat, hairy, hungry rat." But instead said, "Sugnog, you are letting your mind play tricks on you."

"Maybe because I am so hungry. How much food do we have?"

"There are eight apples, two small corn cakes and a few pieces of salted meat."

"That is all we have left?"

"I am afraid so."

"That won't last two or three days, even if the Meskwaki boy dies. How much water?"

"The same, about two or three days."

"That's not enough. They left us here to die. What are we going to do, Watseka?"

"First, we don't panic. Second, we stretch it out by rationing to the little ones, you and I must be strong."

"We will do the others no good if we get sick too. We have to be strong for them and that we cannot do if we give them all of our food and water."

"It is how it must be. Grandfather has taught you about faith."

"But these three aren't even our blood. Our blood has already died," he argued.

"Grandfather has also taught you that we are of one blood no matter the tribe, even the white tribes and the dark tribes from far away."

"Grandfather did not teach me to die without a fight."

I listened to their bickering for as long as I could stand. I knew the situation was hopeless but dwelling upon it was doing them no service. At least if they passed, they could pass with honor and dignity. Also, I saw this as an opportunity to try and free myself from this prison.

"You must eat the sick one. Do not eat the one already dead," I said and although I could not see I knew the boy was pointing at the sack over my head. My throat was dry and scratchy causing my voice to sound hollow and hoarse. It was eerie enough to myself, so I knew it had a worse effect on the children. I was certain I sounded what they imagined a ghost would sound like.

"I told you there was a ghost in here with us."

"That is not a ghost that is an evil demon. We will do no such thing," Watseka said to me.

"They will die anyway. And then another will die, and another until it is only the two of you left," I said.

"Then we will eat them after they die," the boy said in defiance.

"No, once they die their bodies will become poison. You must consume the flesh before they expire."

"You mean kill them?" the girl said.

"No, I would rather die of sickness or starvation than die as a frozen Wiindigoo heart," the boy screamed.

"A what? I don't know that word," I asked.

"It is a legend meant to scare unruly children with, nothing more," Watseka said.

"No, it is real. If you eat human flesh you will become a flesh-eating monster," Sugnog countered.

"I am sure that as with any religion or culture exceptions are made when it comes to survival. Besides, I've known of several men who were shipwrecked on a deserted island with no food and were forced to eat their sick comrades in order to survive and they did not turn into monsters," I said, choosing not to mention to the boy that these men were already monsters to begin with and that one of them was me. And had I not, in essence, become a Wendigo.

I felt an overwhelming sense of dread wash over me. That the day I opened the door to Wenonah, all those years ago. Was my meeting her beneath a council rock simply a coincidence or was it retribution for the unthinkable acts I had committed to survive? But did I really do them to survive or purely out of greed?

"Now tell me about this place. Do you know where we are?"

"We are underground I think," Watseka said.

"Do not talk to him, he is an evil ghost trying to make us do something very bad," Sugnog said in defiance.

"No, I am trying to save your lives. Underground, like a cave?"

"No, like a cellar but with wooden walls like a small house."

"Are you children chained like me?" I jerked at my chained as best as I could. I could hear them both gasp and scoot away.

They whispered back and forth to each other but could not make out any of the words. Maybe my choice to reveal myself to them was not the most prudent of choices. But I knew I had to convince them to kill the sickly child for two reasons. One, I was not lying to them, it was their only hope of survival and two, the surge I felt when the first child died made me very aware, I needed more. I hungered for more. But this was a different hunger, far unlike the hunger Wenonah had so graciously gifted me with. There was a force greater than myself compelling me to consume this child's soul.

Chapter Forty-One

"Dear Phillipe," Wenonah called out in the darkness having managed to work the gag out of her mouth. "What of those poor children? It has been nearly a week since we departed and left them behind and by my count you did not leave any men behind to ensure they were provided with food and water."

She repeated her statement numerous times, raising the level of her voice with each repetition. She knew the answers already and her soliloquy was not for the benefit of the treacherous Frenchman rather for the elders whose precious loved ones were slowly being starved to death. She knew that Elijah was becoming desperate and would be forced to devour one of the children's souls and that could quite possibly sever her control over him. And that she could not allow.

"Do the elders know that you have abandoned their children? Left them to starve to death, alone and afraid."

Lieutenant Gagnon burst from his tent and stormed over to where Wenonah was trussed up in the middle of the encampment. She started to taunt him, but he clamped his hand tightly around her mouth. Even though he could not see her mouth he knew by the glint in her eye that she was smiling. He raised his fist high and aimed for her temple.

"Do not hurt that child," Misko Nodin said.

"Let her speak, I am interested in what she has to say," Huritt added.

"She is just talking gibberish trying to stir up trouble."

"She said something about my grandchildren. You promised no harm would come to them if we cooperated with you. Where are they?"

Phillipe leaned in and hissed in Wenonah's ear, "You keep your damned mouth shut about those children. You reassure them that you were only trying to cause trouble, or I will gut you like a pig."

He felt strange sensation against the palm of his hand and realized she was licking his hand. He clamped down tighter and shoved upward on her jaw hoping to force her to bite her own tongue. She nodded her head in agreement and mumbled something he could not make out, so he slowly unclamped his hand from around her mouth.

By this time, a small crowd had gathered from the commotion and watched in horror when Gagnon removed his hand. Wenonah's mouth was no longer on her face. There was nothing but a smooth piece of flesh under her nose where her mouth had once been. Two of the warriors cried out something unintelligible and dashed off into the darkness. The elders suddenly understood the Frenchman's trepidation about this child. She was no child.

"Dear, dear Phillipe, you still do not comprehend the predicament you are in do you?" Wenonah said.

Gagnon heard her voice, but she had no mouth. He tried to shake the rum from his brain. Was it her voice he had heard or was it just in his head? He turned to face the others; confusion was scrawled on every face.

"Did you hear her voice?" he asked, his voice trembling with fear.

She giggled her little child giggle, "Silly Phillipe, down here."

Slowly he turned his gaze to where her voice had emanated which was the palm of his hand. She stuck her tongue out and licked a circle around her lips before laughing long and hard. Phillipe trembled and stared at his hand, frozen with awe. He must have gotten into some peyote or something. Maybe the rum was bad. One of the Mohawk warriors swung his club smashing Gagnon's hand.

"Ow. Son of a bitch! What in the hell did you do that for you crazy bastard," Phillipe cried and lashed out.

"Hey, that hurt," Wenonah cried out, a trickle of blood running down both her mouth that was now imbedded in the Frenchman's hand and the stretched taut skin on her face where it had been only moments ago.

The elders began chanting what Gagnon could only imagine was a prayer of sorts. The mouth, Wenonah's mouth, began mocking them at first and then began screaming and gnashing her teeth at them as if their prayer was upsetting her. It was all that Phillipe could do to keep his hand from flailing around. And then she laughed.

"I'm just playing. Sing and chant all you want, it doesn't mean anything to me. I do not know why I frighten you so, I am just a little girl after all," when she finished everything was as it had been before Phillipe had clamped his hand over her mouth.

"Why did you bring that beast here with us?" the leader of the Mohawk warriors asked.

"I didn't know what else to do with her. You see that she is not what she appears to be, and she is quite dangerous. I couldn't just leave her behind."

"If you were thinking she would serve as an advantage to us you were mistaken, she is a liability and will kill us all if given the chance."

"What kind of creature do you think she is?" Phillipe asked.

"I do not have a clue, she is a beast of your gods, not ours."

None of the adults were paying attention so the young boy fetched some water and carried it over to Wenonah who had been mouthing the word "thirsty" at him while pleading for kindness with her eyes. He moved a small bench over to where she was, so he was tall enough to get the skin to her mouth. She sipped at the cool water droplets.

"What is your name?" she asked.

He fearfully backed away from her without a word.

"I will call you Ogichidaa."

He cocked his head slightly to the left, thought about it for a minute and then smiled an awkward smile of a boy who had lost several baby teeth and was now growing his adult set.

"You do not need to fear me my child, I am not much older than you are."

The boy eyed her up and down not sure what to think. She looked like a normal little girl, even talked like one, until she spoke through that Frenchman's hand. He wasn't very old, but he was old enough to know when to stay away from trouble. He turned to walk away.

"Do you have any brothers or sisters?" she asked.

He nodded.

"I'll bet you have a big brother."

He shook his head.

"Ah you have a little sister, I can see it in your eyes. It is why you are such a brave warrior, you have to protect her."

He nodded his head.

"Do you have a puppy?"

He paused and then shook his head.

"Ah, he's not a puppy he's a dog."

The boy nodded. He understood her, but he refused to speak to her. It was only mildly annoying and made for a fun game to while away the time.

"Is your father here?"

He nodded his head and pointed at a Mohawk tribesman speaking with the Frenchman.

"Can you kill him? I need you to kill him."

The boy stepped back in horror and shot her an angry, yet inquisitive glance.

She laughed, "Oh no boy, you misunderstood me. Not your father, the Frenchman."

He thought about it for a moment, nodded his head with a smile and darted off into the darkness.

Chapter Forty-Two

I could feel a presence with me in the darkness. It wasn't the children or even anything I could put my finger on. It was her. Wenonah was trying to peek into my soul but for some reason she was stymied. I hated to admit it, but I really did need one of her childish sing song chants of guidance.

The sickest of the children was getting sicker and my window of opportunity was closing. I knew I could never convince them to kill a healthy child, so this sick kid was my only hope to worm my way out of this mess. I needed a soul, any soul, to feed my dark demon. Maybe then I could gather enough strength to free myself from my bonds.

"Maybe he is right, that little boy is really sick," Watseka said

"Don't even say what you are thinking. Why are you listening to an evil spirit?"

"He's going to die anyway. We are out of food and almost out of water. This may be our only way to survive."

"We will be cursed for all eternity if we do this."

"That is just a silly superstition. Besides, I do not think it applies when it is a person's only chance for survival."

"How?"

"How what?"

"How are you going to kill him? We don't have any weapons and neither of us can reach him."

The room fell into an eerie silence with the only sound being that of the sick child wheezing with each labored breath. Being sightless was maddening as was the growing hunger raging in the pit of my soul. I needed to feed. Once again, I found myself contemplating what death meant for me. Would I simply wither slowly away until I just ceased to exist? Would the agony and torment grow exponentially as the days fell away into oblivion driving me over the brink of madness?

I was lost within my own thoughts, trying to devise a plan to get these children to murder one of their own and did not hear the child's last breath, but I felt it. I felt a warmth growing inside me both physically and mentally. Was I consuming this child's light? Could I feed on good souls as well as the dark? I felt something stir inside me as if I had a raccoon trapped inside of my shirt.

Shadowman, Shadowman,
At all costs resist!
Shadowman, Shadowman,
Or we will both cease to exist!

Was this a delusion brought on by dehydration and my insatiable hunger burning through my very core? Was the little she-demon speaking the truth, or was this just another one of her tricks? I could not resist, my hunger was too great and the sensation much too satisfying.

But then another feeling washed over me, a sense of dread. Not dread in the sense of fear for my own safety but a terrifying sense for the child who had just passed. Had I just robbed them of their chance to go to their great spirit? Had I just sentenced them to purgatory, or worse? I was feeling guilt, remorse, both emotions I was not familiar with at all. It was agonizing yet liberating at the same time. I felt the tether between Wenonah and myself begin to weaken. I no longer felt the unending desire to survive, it had been replaced with a burning need to be free, free of her.

Chapter Forty-Three

Wenonah sensed something was amiss. She felt the bond between her and Elijah growing ever weaker. It had not dawned on her until that very moment that she was in a predicament she may very well never survive. Gagnon and the Mohawks had been chitter-chattering all night long about what to do with her. Gagnon wanted to lop her head off with his sword, but the much more superstitious, and wiser, tribal elders were reluctant. They felt that killing her would do more harm than good, if killing her were even possible.

"Then what do you suggest we do with her, before this entire plan is ruined?"

"We could bury her up to her neck and let the birds finish the job," one of them said.

"No good, she could forever taint the ground, or worse."

She watched her little warrior as he paid close attention to what the adults were saying. Each of them seemed to fear her in a different way. Afraid to kill her, afraid to let her live, afraid to let her go and terrified to keep her. They all had a myriad of ideas and opinions yet not one of them offered a true solution to the problem. And then the child spoke.

"Mishi Gammi," he said. When the adults ignored him, he said it again, only louder until he caught Gagnon's attention.

"What was that you said little man?" Phillipe asked.

"Mishi Gammi."

"Michi-gami," one of the elders corrected the boy's pronunciation.

"What does that mean?" Gagnon asked.

"It is what many call the big lake. It means Great Water."

The boy smiled, pointed at Wenonah, and then pointed at the lake. She felt a sudden chill slowly settle over her. She had been gravely mistaken in thinking this child would be an ally.

"Do you mean we should set her adrift in the water?" Gagnon asked.

The boy shook his head and then stabbed a finger into the palm of his hand. When the Frenchman still did not understand he took a stick from the fire, cleared a spot in the sand with his small hand and began to draw an image with his stick.

"The boy is a genius. He thinks we should put her in a canoe and set her adrift."

"But will this be a solution to our problem? Might she find her way back to shore?"

Again, the boy shook his head. He gathered some pebbles from the beach and put them in his sand canoe. Then he took his stick and began stabbing it into the sand repeatedly.

"I think he means we should put her in a canoe, fill it with rocks and then shoot it with arrows until it sinks. That just might be a solution to our problem."

"We will lash her to the canoe so that she cannot get loose," Gagnon added.

"This creature does not seem to fear death."

"Then we shall send her bravely to her grave. I am not about to let some little ragamuffin spoil our plans."

"When one does not fear death it usually means that they believe they cannot die in battle."

"I don't really care if she dies or not just so long as she is out of our hair. We stand to make a fortune from this little venture of ours and I'll be damned if I will let a runny nosed child ruin this. I think the bottom of the lake is a very good place for her to spend eternity regretting the day she ever met me," Gagnon sneered at her through the flickering flames of the campfire.

"What about the Anishinaabe elders? What will we do with them?"

"I'd love to see them at the bottom of the lake as well, but sadly we still need them," Gagnon said, tousling the young boy's dark hair as he walked by.

Wenonah watched as the men busied themselves cutting strips of rawhide and gathering stones in a pile, they would load into a canoe later. She caught the eye of her betrayer and each time he unnerved her. Someone who betrayed another did not usually possess the fortitude to look them in the eyes after their betrayal. But the little warrior made it a point to catch her eye every time he walked by with another armload of rocks. Defiant, smug, exuding his pride with confidence. She was beginning to dislike him even more than she hated the Frenchman.

The men chopped a large spruce, cut it again into five-foot-long sections which they then split and fashioned into framework that resembled a cross. The men continued to toil and bicker about whether they should be approaching their problem in this manner as the night slowly gave way to the morning. The sun began to breach the horizon and bathed the island in an eerie red glow. A storm was brewing, and it appeared it was going to be a monster.

As they began lashing the structure to the canoe Wenonah screamed out above the din of the rising storm, "My God, my God, why has thou forsaken me?" each of the men jumped and stared back at her in unadulterated fear. She cackled in the face of the mounting winds.

Warrior, dear Warrior,
It is time to make them see,
Warrior, dear Warrior,
They must not bury me at sea.

Wenonah was almost convinced that this was the worst predicament she had ever encountered. While she would not drown, and the waters would protect her flesh and bone vessel for a time she wasn't prepared to spend eternity with fish plucking at her eyeballs. There was a strong current which would push her toward the shallows, eventually. And while being fathoms beneath the surface of the lake was not much more appealing than having her head lopped off or being consumed in a lake of fire it was the lesser of those evils.

The lake had begun spitting up whitecaps and the winds howled across the open beach. The men laid the lashed Wenonah down into the canoe and prayed the white caps would not cause them to take on water and sink long before they made it to their destination.

"We need to do this now, before that squall makes it to us," one of the men pointed to the horizon where a large swath of the water was nothing but a black cloud rolling towards them.

Gagnon had to wonder if this was not just another one of Wenonah's craft tricks. Was this really happening or was she toying with their minds?

"Where is the deepest point, beyond all of these reefs?" Phillipe asked, pulling his collar up against the wind.

"To the south about an hour, hour and a half against this wind. We will have to navigate through several shallows and then portage one larger reef before making the open water."

"Can we get there before this storm hits?"

"Yes, the question is, will we be able to make it back to land ourselves."

They had lashed three canoes to hers and were towing her though the choppy water as Wenonah taunted and cackled at them the entire trip. Once they came to a reef several men happily jumped out of the canoe and guided them through the shallow water, anything to put a little distance between themselves and that demon-child.

Wenonah could not see him, but she knew that her little Ogichidaa was watching her. She never felt his eyes waver from her. But more disconcerting was the fact that she not once sensed even the slightest shred of fear. In fact, she felt that he was amused by her.

Phillipe was becoming quite annoyed with this little adventure. His knees were screaming in pain from kneeling on the bottom of the canoe which was the only way to keep from getting his crotch soaking wet. The bow of his canoe slapped a wave at an awkward angle and sprayed his face with icy waters.

"How much further?" he asked.

"Once we clear that big island, I have heard it called Amik, we will be into open waters beyond the reefs."

"How deep?" Phillipe asked.

"No one knows, no one alive anyway. Only the dead have ever found the bottom. It is deep enough that you will not see her, and she will not see you," he replied.

"I wouldn't count on that even if she were at the bottom of the deepest of oceans, I'm afraid."

Gagnon lost himself in the rhythm of the canoe paddles splashing against the whitecaps as they dipped into the black water. He reflected on his many bad choices which had led him to be out in the middle of an expanse of water at night with a storm fast approaching in the company of a demonic child. Granted, it was not one of his best decisions but if it rid him of whatever that creature was it was well worth it. A gust of wind danced across the lake and straight down his collar, chilling him to the bone. He faced away from the gusts and peered into the black waters.

Phillipe gasped aloud at what he saw in the tumultuous waters. He averted his face to shake the image from his mind. He had not thought about her in years, probably a decade, so why now? Why was his dear Perrine haunting him now in such a desolate, god-forsaken place? She had never wanted to come to the New World, she was content being the wife of a simple vintner, but he had bigger aspirations, much bigger.

He slowly turned his face back to the murky depths, her deep chestnut eyes smiled back at him under her auburn trusses. He had forgotten how beautiful and radiant she was. How she could wish away the darkest of storms with her laughter. He closed his eyes and breathed in her essence, the slightest hint of lavender tickled his memories. Phillipe's heart was wandering back to when it still beat pure. He loved his Perrine so.

He opened his eyes and gasped once more, catching the attention of one of the oarsmen who shot him a puzzled glance. He returned a weak smile and played it off as if he had fallen asleep. Phillipe watched the man for several moments and got the impression he was averting his eyes from the water at all costs.

Once more he braved the ebon canvas as his heart thumped against his breastplate. The image was still there, although this was something he did not want to see. It was the last day he had set foot in France, it was the last day he had laid eyes on his precious love and it was the last day his darling Perrine graced this earth. He tried to shake her bloody image from his mind, but it was as fresh as the day he had murdered her.

"To hell with you," he screamed across the water at Wenonah. He could not see her, but he knew damned well she was sporting a triumphant smirk. He was also certain of her culpability in his torment.

With tears streaking down his face Phillipe turned to brave the foaming waters once more. There was nothing but an empty blackness. There was no smiling face, there was no haunting aroma, there was only a deep, dark void looming forever in front of him. The longer he stared into the nothingness the larger the void within him grew.

He laughed aloud but to himself, startling the oarsman. His mind was simply toying with him as a result of being fatigued. These were simply memories, not visions. As he was turning away, he caught a flicker of movement, a miniscule spot of light undulating with the waves. Slowly their campsite from the island came into view across the surface of the black water and he was suddenly enraged. The elders were no longer tied to stakes, they were gone.

"Sink her now!" he cried out.

"But we are in waters that are only two or three fathoms."

"We need to get back to the island, the prisoners have escaped."

"How do you know this?"

"I just know it, trust me. The sooner we get this creature out of our lives the better."

They set Wenonah's canoe adrift with a hard shove. As soon as she was free of them a strong wind started blowing to the south, pushing her further and further away from the other canoes before the archers could ready their bows. They fired off a volley of arrow and all but a few arrows missed their mark. They fired off another volley and most of those arrows fell harmlessly into the water. They dropped their bows and began paddling toward the wayward vessel. The howling winds were so loud they drown out Phillipe's orders as he barked.

"Dear Phillipe, is this all part of your master plan?" Wenonah cackled over the screeching winds.

The canoes stopped, the men picked up their bows and fired several more volleys, none of which were effective in bringing down the canoe which continued to drift away out of range as they readied. On the third attempt the oarsmen dug in hard and deep to pick up speed before ditching their paddles for their bows. The moment the men dropped their paddles the little warrior leapt to his feet, grabbed a spear from the bottom of his canoe and dove from the bow into the black waters.

"What in the hell is he doing?" Phillipe screamed.

His father shrugged and donned a fretted expression. Within minutes the boy had disappeared into the darkness. They could hear his arms chopping at the turbulent water, so they knew he was still swimming toward Wenonah. The men picked up their paddles and started after him.

As their canoe neared the other, they saw the boy climb from the black waters into the canoe. He hoisted the spear above his head with the point directly over Wenonah's heart. Gagnon shuddered from the look on the boy's face, he was a ruthless killer. He drove the spear home into the bottom of the canoe again and again. Cold water spilled up over his ankles.

"O:nen ki wahi," Phillipe heard the boy call out over the storm.

"What did he say?"

"He just said goodbye to a friend," the boy's father replied.

The boy stared down at the little girl as the water flowed up around her. Her hair drifted around her head, forming a halo of auburn. He had no fear of her whatsoever. She had called him Ogichidaa, had she not? So, a warrior he must be. As the water flowed up over Wenonah's face, she continued to stare up at him through the dark waves. She smiled and let a tiny bubble escape from her lips.

His brow furrowed in confusion. Why was she not breathing? Why was she not drowning? Why was she not afraid as she was surely about to die? She mocked him even as she descended into her grave. How dare she? He raised the spear one more time, only this time his intention was to pierce her little heart. She would not rob him of this coup.

The boy drove the lance home with all his strength. Wenonah let loose a shriek that caused him to clamp his hands over his ears. Her eyes were no longer that of an innocent little girl but that of an enraged demon. The lip of the canoe finally gave up its struggle and allowed the water to flood the tiny vessel. It broke from the surface of the water with a plop and began to descend into the murky depths. The boy treaded water while locking eyes with the dying beast. He was no longer a little warrior; he was a conqueror.

The boy's father plucked him from the water once their canoe reached him. He trembled as the others patted him on the back, tousled his hair and wrapped blankets around him. He took a moment to compose himself before glancing up at the Frenchman.

Gagnon's blood froze in his veins and his stomach roiled with fear. The boy was looking at him through her eyes, through evil, demon eyes. Then the boy smiled at him, adjusted the blankets, and turned to face waters where Wenonah had disappeared into the darkness.

All at once the clouds opened up a deluge upon them and the winds began to shriek. The sound was almost human, and the volume was deafening. The canoes were filling with water fast than they could bail.

"What is happening?" the father asked his son in a tone that seemed to reverse their roles.

"She is angry."

"There is nothing we can do about that. We have to paddle faster," Gagnon cried out over the shrieking winds.

"Oh, but there is something we can do," the boy said, turning to face Gagnon.

"What? What can we possibly do about a storm?"

"This is not a storm, this is her anger. She wants something."

"She always wants something. Ask her what she wants."

"I do not need to ask her, I already know."

"Then what in the hell does she want?"

"She wants you," he said and drove the spear up into Phillipe's ribcage using the leverage to shove the man overboard into the angry, black water.

Chapter Forty-Four

The remaining children had been quiet for quite some time. I could hear them breathing and moving about in their sleep, but as for conversation, there was little to none. I tried to engage several times, but they did not have the energy or wherewithal to respond. By my count they had not eaten in several days and had gone without water for even longer than that. Sadly, their auras were growing darker with each passing moment with the smallest being the darkest of them.

My consciousness wanted nothing more than for me to be able to just give up and fade into oblivion. My subconscious wanted nothing more than survival and it was winning the battle as I struggled to find a way to set myself free from my bonds. I tugged at the leather thongs until I felt my own blood running down my arms. I strained to look out of curiosity, but there was nothing there that I could see. I wrenched at my bindings until I fell asleep from exhaustion.

I awakened to warm little puffs of air on my face. I slowly opened my eyes to find that the cowl had been removed and I could see. At first my heart tightened in my chest and nerves went on alert when I saw my savior was a small child. Had Wenonah come to rescue me from one hell only to thrust me back into hers? I looked into the child's eyes and she skittered away like a tiny mouse.

"I won't hurt you," I said as softly as I could. Not only did I want to set the child's fear at ease I also did not want to wake the others. I did not want any interference.

"But you wanted them to kill me. And eat me."

"I thought you were going to die."

"But I didn't," she scowled back at me with beautiful, but angry hazel eyes.

"You sounded very, very sick and I was trying to help your brother and sister."

"They are not my brother and sister, they were the enemy."

It was then that I noticed two things, the room had grown eerily silent and the little child's face was covered in blood. "Did you hurt yourself? Come closer so I can see if you are alright," I said, not really wanting to know her response.

She looked down at the floor and said in a barely audible voice, "I couldn't do it."

"You couldn't do what?"

"I couldn't kill them," she said, looking up from the floor and catching my gaze.

The look in her eyes sent a shiver through me. Was I mistaken? Was the myth of the Wendigo actually truth? The child had a hunger in her eyes, a hunger that reminded me of Wenonah. My stomach lurched.

"That is fine sweetie, not many people have the fortitude to kill another human being, even for survival's sake. And these were your friends."

Again, her face took on a look of confusion. "They are not my friends, and I could not kill them because I felt bad, I could not kill them because I am not strong enough and this piece of metal is too dull," she said, and threw a rust colored hunk of metal off into the shadows.

"Can you untie my bindings?" I asked.

"No, I tried when you were sleeping. They are too tight."

The more I drifted back to consciousness the sharper everything came into view. My skin felt taut and sticky. I was smeared with dried blood, but it could not have been my own. It was then I realized this must be the children's blood.

"Am I covered in blood?"

She nodded her head.

"Their blood?" I asked with a bob of my head.

Again, she nodded at the two children lying still on the blood-soaked floor, red lines running across their throats from ear to ear.

"Why did you rub their blood on me?"

"I want to be able to see you," she replied.

I became aware of a dull throbbing in the tender part of my inner thigh. I wrenched my head the best I could, but I could not see down into my own lap. I felt a familiar sensation spreading down my leg.

"Am I bleeding?" I asked.

She simply bobbed her head slowly up and down and wiped her arm across her lips.

"Why am I bleeding?"

She shrugged without looking up at me.

"What did you do?"

"I was hungry, and she told me to. But you tasted awful and I spit you out."

"You bit me? Who told you to bite me?"

"A little girl."

"A little girl? Where is this little girl?"

"Gone?"

"Where did she go? How did she get out of here?"

"She was never here so she didn't have to get out."

"If she was never here how was she able to talk to you?"

"She sang me silly little songs," she replied and dropped exhausted into my lap.

I never had a chance to react to what the blood-soaked child curled up on my lap had revealed. The door burst open and the children's patriarchs absorbed the scene laid out before them. I almost did not recognize the elders as a myriad of emotions had tormented their features into grotesque masks. Even before seeing them I had felt them, and their darkness nauseated me. I should have been reveling in their blackness, but I was repulsed.

I opened my mouth to speak, to plead my case but they were upon me before a sound crossed my lips. The first blow was to my temple and dazed me to the point I never felt the others. With tired, weary eyes I gazed upon the little girl who was now smiling down at me. She leaned her head back and seemed to breathe in my essence of life as it left my body. The men were still pummeling my battered body as I succumbed to the darkness and for the first time in my life I felt at peace.

Chapter Forty-Five

Consciousness came screaming back to me like the first taste of oxygen for a drowning man. It took several minutes before I was able to ascertain my surroundings. I was still on the floor of the cabin's cellar but no longer trussed up like a Christmas goose. The room was deserted and cold due to the fact that half of the structure had deteriorated and collapsed. There was not even the slightest hint of smoke drifting on the wind leading me to assume my immediate surroundings were deserted as well. I shook my head in disgust, once more I had managed to become marooned on a deserted island.

I raised my hand to wipe my face, but it missed the mark as it did again on a subsequent attempt. Feeling something was off I ran my hand down my arm to my elbow where my arm took a sharp turn outward away from my body. I wiggled my fingers and gladly they still moved.

The beating the elders gave me was coming back to me in pieces, they must have broken my arm and it healed wrong. How long had I been out? I would have taken weeks to heal like this. I looked down and realized a visual assessment would do me no good at all, I was completely translucent, even the blood the child had smeared over me had dried and fallen off. I settled on the logical reasoning that they had beaten me to death.

It took several days for me to regain enough strength to be able to leave the cabin and walk the island. But where was I to walk to? From shore to shore, top to bottom and then what? One of my legs had been badly damaged as well which made walking awkward and uncomfortable as my foot jutted away from my body in a forty-five-degree angle. I found it somewhat of a blessing that I could not see how battered my body really was.

I wandered the desolate white sands for hours embracing the cold wind in my face which I found quite odd in the fact that I no longer had a face. The extreme hunger of my hollow soul tormented me to no end. I tried to occupy my mind by cleaning up the building, which was more of a shack and much more run down than was my first impression of it. I used the lumber from the collapsed portions to plug holes as best as I could.

Along the beach I erected wind breaks to shelter me from the winter winds that I knew would be coming soon. Even though I had my bearings from studying the sun during the day and the stars at night I still had no idea which direction would be the optimal route to take to evacuate myself from this island or even how I might accomplish such a feat. I cursed myself for not paying more attention to my surroundings on the voyage over.

A sadness gripped me as I toiled about the derelict edifice. Even though I had disposed of every last remnant of the children from my mind their spirits seemed to linger in every square inch of the place. I would have dismissed it as my memories feeding my guilt, but it was much more than that. It was not something as intangible as a thought or idea, it was physically real. I could feel the warmth of their touch on my skin.

I found myself sitting on the southern shore peering across the great water at a decent sized land mass. I was not sure if it was the mainland or just another island, either way, having learned from life's mistakes I knew it was too far to swim especially with only one good arm and one good leg. I waded out into the frigid waters just to feel something other than this burning hunger invading my every thought. I was taken aback by the imagery of the ripples created by my movement with no visible sign anything was even there.

I spent the rest of the day gathering driftwood for a fire on the beach even though I had a fire going in the cabin's fireplace. I was feeling oddly melancholy and sound of the waves was soothing as was the crackling of my campfire. As darkness set in, I spotted several pairs of glowing orbs easing out of the forest. I chuckled, even though the critters could not see me, they still knew I was there. I tossed a big pile of dune grass on the fire to get it burning a little hotter, but I threw too much on and it started to billow huge plumes of white smoke right into my face.

I was amazed to find that while most of the smoke from the fire passed around me, re-creating my shape and form, some seemed to pass straight through me. It allowed me a little bit of comfort being able to see my invisible body, so I endured the acrid tendrils tickling my nostrils. A few gulls cried out over the din of the lake, the howl of wolves drifted over the island's dense forest and so began the night's concerto.

Around the beginning of the third movement I caught just a hint of sounds drifting from the other side of the sheltered cove. I meandered over the beach of white sands and shells to gaze out over the expanse of dark water. There were many sets of the strangest ripples I had ever seen dancing across the surface of the water. Each set seemed to lead away from the island out into the deep water, and yet, the winds were at my face.

I was lost in a reverie so deep I cannot even recall what I was thinking about when I felt a presence in the dark with me. I held fast and listened. This affliction of mine was a constant source of learning and a gunny sack filled with questions. Even though I was invisible to the eye would creatures who hunted by scent, like wolves, be aware of my presence? Would they be able to attack me without seeing me? And if completely eaten and digested would I then still be able to return to walk the earth?

From my haunches I spied a crippled old woman carrying something in her arms. Her breathing was labored but her movements deliberate and steady across the loose sands. She was walking straight toward me as if she knew I were there. The hunter and its prey indeed. Was this yet another incarnation of the little devil-child who had condemned me to this hell on earth?

"Can you spare an old woman a spot of tea?" she called out into the darkness in an accent that smacked of the Meskwaki.

Tea? She could not possibly be that evil little ragamuffin for she abhorred the black leaves. But she was also a sly, crafty little demon who had fooled me on more than one occasion. And this old woman was no seer, she simply knew someone had to be here because of the fire. I admonished myself with a chuckle and moved down the beach away from the fire.

"Will you not get cold down there, away from the fire? Or do you not get cold?"

She moved closer to the fire which allowed me to get a better look at her so I could assess the situation. She was old, too old to determine her true age and was hunched over from too many years of hard work on this earth. She cradled a small bundle in the crook of her left arm and rhythmically tapped at the ground with a gnarled cane in her right hand. Her hair was yellowed and flayed out away from her head in all directions. She seemed harmless enough, but I had travelled down that road already one too many times.

She moved a little to the left as if to give me a better view of her. It was then that I noticed her eyes were the color of calf's milk. I moved and her eyes moved with me. She laughed a wet cackle.

"Did I get it right?" she asked.

"Get what right?"

"I like to guess which way people move and then make them think I can actually see them. It is one of the last pleasures I have in this life."

I laughed. "So, you only pretend that you can you see me?" I asked, holding my translucent hand in front of my own face.

"In a manner of speaking."

"And just what do you mean by that?"

"I know where you are, I know about how tall you are and about how many stones you weigh but I do not know the color of your eyes as you know mine."

"Curious. Please explain."

"I see you with my mind, not my eyes. I know how old you are by your voice, I know how tall you are by where your voice comes from and I know how much you weigh by the sound you make walking in the sands. Don't look so stunned Elijah," she said.

"Stunned? How would you know if I looked stunned or not? And how do you know my name?"

"Most do. I was told a magnificent tale from some little children many, many years ago. Is it true that I could not see you even if I had just one good eye?"

I nodded out of habit. I began to get an eerie feeling burning down deep in my gut, somehow this craggy old woman reminded me of a venomous little urchin I had no inkling to ever see again in my life no matter how many years that turned out to be. At least this old hag was not plaguing my mind with sing-song nursery rhymes. I sensed that something was amiss, there was something about that bundle she carried that worried her.

"What is that you carry?" I asked.

"The very reason I am here."

"No offense, but I am tired and weary of vague answers so if you do not wish to share please leave me to my own."

"Very well," she said and turned away, walking, and tapping down the beach. She turned back to say, "You know, I met her once too. She is the reason I do not see what I wish to see, only what she wishes me to see."

I remembered the sack of eyes Wenonah carried and a shiver rippled through me. I moved away from her and the fire.

"Do not be alarmed, she no longer sees through me, I stole them back," she said, holding out her hand with two petrified nuggets in her palm. "That sure made her angry," she laughed until she doubled over to catch her breath.

"Did she send you?" I asked, backing even further away from the woman who still unnerved me by following my movements with her eyes.

"No, she did not send me. From what I have been told she lies at the bottom of the lake."

"So, then she is dead?"

Once more she cackled through wet lungs, "No, I am afraid that creature cannot die, at least not in the mortal sense. She can only be destroyed through you. You must extinguish your own flame in order to extinguish hers."

"I do not understand. If you know as much about me as you claim, then you know I cannot destroy myself. And how is it that you come to know so much about me?"

"When the children spoke of you, I knew what you were because I am a lot like you."

"So, are you immortal as well? As far as I knew she only took the eyes of children, and you, well you are not a child."

"No Elijah, you can rest assured that I will be dead soon enough. But I have been compelled to share what little knowledge I have with you."

"Compelled by whom?"

"That I cannot say."

"You can't or you won't?" I asked, starting to get perturbed by the back and forth conversation.

"I cannot say because I do not know. I do not know the particulars of how I arrived at this point in life, but I can say that ever since I parted ways with that demon child I have been guided by a hand unknown to me."

"Guided, how? And please join me, you must be cold," I said, moving back to the warmth of the fire.

As soon as the old woman neared within ten feet of me, I felt an ominous presence, a malevolent darkness that permeated the distance between us. I jumped up and backed away into the night.

"Do not fear, it is not as it seems."

"What is that bundle you carry? I sense it is evil, like her," I said.

"It is but an infant child. She is afflicted with a malady, several in fact."

"What are you doing with her?"

"She is in my charge. This is what I do."

"Just what is it you are doing?"

"I am bringing this banished child to this sacred place in hopes of saving her soul."

"What is wrong with her?"

"I do not know, I am not a doctor."

"Then how do you know she is not well?"

"I know you feel the darkness within her just as I do. That is her sickness."

I moved back to the fire where the old woman had taken a seat on a log. With each step the intensity of the darkness grew, roiling within me like a mass of angry vipers. She uncovered the child who glared up at me with flaming red eyes. Her skin was like that of a porcelain doll, unnaturally white as from her features I could tell even from her young age that she was a native child.

"She is not what she appears. She is quite harmless, to others."

"I do not understand. How did you come by this child?"

"She cannot harm you, but she harms herself. She has a disease growing within her that is causing her to suffer. I am a wanderer, a gatherer of sorts. I travel throughout the lands collecting lost souls such as hers."

"How is her soul lost?"

"Many of the tribes are very superstitious and when a child is born to the world such as this child they are abandoned, left for the wolves to claim. They are abandoned before they are welcomed into this world by religious leaders be they white men or the natives. I will put it in more familiar terms to you, they have never been baptized so their souls are condemned to walk the earth. I bring them here to a special place on the island just for them."

"What does that have to do with my saving her soul?"

"You must kill her. You must take her soul unto your own."

I peered into her milky white eyes looking for malice but found only benevolence. Tears streamed down her face and she sucked at little sips of air to keep from sobbing. I felt a tinge inside of me I had rarely ever felt in my life. I was suddenly laden with a heaviness that had no reason.

"I will not kill that child. I cannot."

"But you must, it is your destiny. This little one's soul will never find peace in heaven otherwise."

"That is all hogwash, nonsense to control the masses. When we die we simply die and nothing more."

"Ah yes, you are using God's greatest, and also his most destructive, gift to mankind."

"What is that?"

"Freewill. But truthfully, after what has happened to you do you still believe in nothing at all? Why would she have gone to all of the trouble to trick you into giving her your soul? Why would it matter to her to steal anyone's soul?"

"Because that is how she feeds."

"But then she would be able to feed on anyone would she not?"

"She said they had to be dark souls," I said, sensing I had walked into a trap.

"Ah, in therein lies your answer. If she only wanted dark souls, then there must be souls that are pure as well. The age-old battle for balance, good versus evil."

I found myself trapped in a war in which I am directly in the middle between two opposing forces. And it is precisely where I wish not to be. How could I have ever believed I could just walk away, just hide from everything. Deep down I knew this would never be over, at least not until I found a way to make it end. Maybe this old woman was the way, the only way.

Chapter Forty-Six

We travelled so deep into the forest of the island that I could no longer hear or see the lake. Our excursion began even before first light, before the sun had winked at the horizon. The further we traversed the tangle of trees the colder the air became which should have been the complete opposite. It had been the better part of an hour before I noticed something very peculiar about the child.

"She does not cry. If she is sickly as you say, she should be crying."

"She cannot cry. But she is trying to, believe me."

"Why can't the child cry?"

"Because her tongue has been cut out and her vocal cords have been removed."

"Who would do such a thing to a little baby?"

"I do not know for certain, but I imagine it was the tribal shaman."

"Why on earth would they commit such a dastardly act?"

"As I said, they can be very superstitious, and I am quite certain her cries were not that of a normal baby. It is believed that children afflicted such as this communicate with demons, providing them with information on the tribe."

The trek once again fell silent save our footfalls on the forest floor. The air was fragranced by the many cedars making their homes in the swampy loam and a gentle wind whispered through the boughs lending a serene, peaceful atmosphere. And then I remembered the purpose for our journey. The irony of my life was not lost on me. Wenonah found me because of my darkness, but in doing so she put me in a situation in which I had found at least a sliver of light and now this woman wanted me to revert back to committing evil. I was most certain this was another of the child-hag's deceptions and was alert for betrayal. Suddenly I felt lightheaded and stopped walking.

"You can feel it can't you?" she asked, looking directly at me as if I were visible.

"I just felt a little weak for a moment. I have not slept or eaten properly in God only knows how long."

I didn't want to tell her that I had no idea what condition I was in as I had not been able to assess the damage reaped upon me by fists, clubs and whatever else was used to batter my body. It had been weeks, maybe months since I had seen myself with my own two eyes. I knew the obvious injuries that did not need to be seen to know they were there, mangled fingers, arm and an ankle that didn't know if it were coming or going.

"What you are feeling is her weakness."

"Her? You mean Wenonah?"

"Is that what that thing is calling itself now? I knew her as Mahneerah."

"How did you come to know of her?"

"We met innocently enough. She came wandering through our little encampment one day seeking shelter. She and I were about the same age, so we played games together."

I saw a tear glisten the milky white orbs that filled her eye sockets and felt my own heart express a tinge of pity.

"She had been there a few days when she started asking about a warrior, we called Moswa. He was one of our bravest and strongest fighters, but my father banished him for killing another out of anger. It was a simple game, a test of strength and even though Moswa was the stronger man he lost because the other warrior outsmarted him. Moswa killed the victor while he was sleeping."

"He was a dark soul, not unlike myself," I said for my own benefit.

"When my father told her this, she seemed agitated but then smiled and offered my father some tea. His teeth had been bothering him, so he refused which angered her greatly. She then summoned two warriors who had been outside the camp unknown to us. They tried to first provoke my brother into a fight which my father did not let happen. They then tried to provoke my father and again, he would not engage with them. This infuriated her and she demanded to know where Moswa was. When my father said he did not know she flew into a fit of rage and her two companions beat both my father and brother very badly and threatened to do the same to my mother and me if they did not tell."

"Interesting. I had not seen that side of her. I knew she was manipulative and crafty, but not brutish. Was this how she stole your eyesight? Did she have her men beat you?"

"Unfortunately, no, that would have been the end of the nightmare. No, she coerced me into giving them up willingly under the false pretense of sparing my family. And she did not lie there, she did spare them, but they were no longer themselves but mindless beings that followed her like orphaned puppies. And since then I have travelled this earth seeing only when she wants me to see. I have to be honest, she did let me see you, but I do not think she intended to."

There was a small glow ahead of us, so I asked, "What is that glowing up there? Torches?"

"You will see soon enough," she said with a smile.

A few hundred yards more and the narrow path opened into a small clearing. There were dozens upon dozens, no, hundreds of fireflies dancing through the air. I watched in awe as one would light up and then several would light up seemingly in response to the other.

"Are they communicating with each other?"

"I never really thought about it," she answered and after a few moments she said, "I believe they might be. How perceptive of you. It's good to have a fresh set of eyes once in a while."

"I thought you were sightless, but you can see them?"

"No, but I can hear them, and I can feel them."

"Now I sense you are just being a jokester with me. Fireflies do not make any noise, at least not any a human would be able to hear."

"Look closer, Elijah, those are not fireflies."

Out of habit I dropped to my haunches to offer a stealthier profile as if being invisible was not of adequate stealth. I maneuvered myself closer to the flitting, flickering lights until a snapping twig betrayed my surreptitiousness and alerted whatever creatures these may be. All at once they stopped moving and hovered in midair until one of them closest to me lit up brighter than all the rest and they darted off in all directions like rats when a lamp is lit.

"Fascinating," I said.

"Fascinating indeed."

"What kind of creatures are they?"

"The most pitiful creatures of all. They are lost souls."

"Woman, you are daft. You are battier than Wenonah."

"And yet you believe in her do you not?"

I thought over her words and when said aloud they made me sound like I had gotten into a bad batch of rotgut. But she was right. My circumstances, while bizarre, were what they were and there was no denying that. Up until now all this peculiarity had been forced upon me through chicanery but now if I were to believe her, I controlled my own destiny.

"You called them lost souls, why are they lost?"

"For a variety of reasons, but to put it short, they were denied any path to their spirituality and died before they could make that choice on their own. They were not allowed to grow into the dark souls Mahneerah had sown."

"So, they are all infants, like this one?"

"For the most part, yes."

"Assuming I agree to go through with this, what happens to them? What happens to me?"

"I do not have a clue."

"So then this could go very badly?"

"I imagine it could. But really, look at the three of us, how much more badly could it go?" she let loose another long, phlegm inducing laugh.

"I suppose you are correct on that point."

I stared up into the night sky through a crown of pines. The storm had cleared, and the stars were out in mass to the point it was difficult to discern a specific constellation. The little flickers of light were nestled within the boughs, fearful yet curious. I had come to yet another crossroads in my life and I too was fearful, the last choice I made did not work out too well for me. My life up until now had been a series of romps with the seven deadly sins and I was no stranger to murder, but murdering an innocent child was something far more egregious than any of my acts thus far.

"I can sense your apprehension, but do not fear, you are not murdering this child for she is already dead."

"That is, if I am to take your word for it."

"Oh, come now, Elijah, you know better than that. I know you can sense the blackness growing within her."

I gave a slow but deliberate nod, "But what of my soul? Will I not be condemning myself to hell if I have not already done so?"

"No, quite the opposite is true. By putting this child out of her misery and rescuing her soul you will be on the road to rescuing yours as well."

I took the swaddled child from her and was shocked to feel she was thrashing about, her mouth agape in a silent scream. Her eyes were clamped shut, her legs were kicking non-stop and her tiny chest heaved with each breath. I set the pitiful creature gently on the sandy ground and clamped my good hand around her neck. Immediately she stopped thrashing, looked up at me with her fiery red eyes and smiled.

Tears flowed down my cheeks the moment she wrapped her delicate fingers around my pinky. And even though she was suffocating by my hand she smiled up at me with a tenderness I had never seen in my lifetime. She made only one small gasp and then she was gone. I let loose and rolled over onto my back as I felt her spirit invading my body. At first the pain was intense, so intense I felt it would surely kill me. A swirling blackness enveloped me, and I was certain the old woman had hoodwinked me.

And then a sensation washed over me that I cannot explain. Tears burst forth from me in heaving sobs, but they were not tears of sorrow, they were tears of joy. I felt as though two gentle hands were caressing me to my very core as I felt the little one leave me and all was at peace.

Lying on my back staring at the stars, tears streaking down into pools around my neck I tried to fathom what had just transpired. The old woman was smiling down at me with the full moon framing her in a halo. I smiled back in pure contentment.

It was then that the first of the fireflies dropped from high in the boughs and raced toward me. It hit me with a thump and immediately I was overcome with a sense of sorrow followed by intense joy. And then another, and yet another until the trees were completely void of the star-like beings and my heart was overfilled with tranquility.

Chapter Forty-Seven

The warmth of the sun beating down on my face brought me out of a deep slumber. I rolled to my side and realized I was no longer transparent, I was no longer the Shadowman. My exultation was short lived once I could see the damage that had been done to my body.

"How long was I out?"

"Today marks the second day."

"And you just sat here the whole time?"

"Where else was I to go?"

After burying the infant's corpse, we wandered the bleak graveyard for a few minutes and I found it wasn't so dreary or sad anymore. The heat of the sun felt good as we slowly made our way back to my beach encampment. The old woman offered me her shawl with a grin, somehow knowing I was stark naked.

"What was it that happened back there? I feel so different."

"You became the vessel they needed to get home."

"I felt something else, something other than them."

"I do not know, I didn't feel what you felt. Their guardian angels perhaps. Maybe something even more wondrous and powerful."

I disappeared into the forest. I needed to be alone to digest everything that had happened up until that point in my life. I found it much harder to snare rabbits while in my current visible state and with only one good arm, but I did manage to rustle a couple nice sized ones. I carried them back to the camp to cook for lunch.

"I'm tired of calling you old woman, do you have a name?"

"I do not recall hearing you ever call me that."

"I said it mostly to myself."

"Marie," she said with a thick French accent that came out like *Mah-Ree*.

"You are a Frenchy? I thought you were a native."

"A little of both. My mother was from France, Paris in fact. Her husband died of dysentery when they were here less than a year. They had befriended a local tribe who then took her in out of pity. Eventually she caught the eye of my father and soon thereafter I began my bizarre and eventful life."

"It is nice to meet you, Marie."

I was lost without my tomahawks and struggled to clean the rabbits, one armed with a dull knife while she looked on with a vacant stare.

"You are going to have to fix that thing sooner than later," Marie said.

"What thing? This knife? It was all I could find, and I don't have a sharpening stone."

"Not the knife, that near useless arm of yours."

"How can I fix it, it has healed in a very bad position and I cannot do anything to straighten it out. I may not die from my wounds, but I do not regenerate broken or missing limbs from the looks of things."

"But you do heal."

"Yes, I heal."

"Then the solution is obvious."

"Maybe to you."

"You must break your arm again, and maybe again until it heals in such a manner that it is useful to you, or at least not so cumbersome. Otherwise you will be stuck on this island for an eternity and that just will not suffice, you have work to do."

"I do believe that I would prefer to be in the company of a physician if that is the route I am to take."

"Look around, do you see a physician, because I surely do not," she said, moving from her head side to side scanning the horizon, she even put her hand above her eyebrow for effect.

Her laughter was as pure as the glistening snow and I had to join her.

"You could seek one out on the mainland."

"And just how are we getting back to the mainland?" I asked her.

"I am not, I never had any intentions of going back. I am old, incredibly old, it is time for me to see what is in store for me in the next world."

"You must have come here by boat?"

"That I did."

"Then I could use it to get myself back to the mainland, could I not? It sounds like you do not plan to use it any longer."

Again, she laughed at my expense. "Oh, what I would not give to have my eyesight back just long enough to witness that."

"Witness what? And just what in the world do you find so amusing?"

"A one armed many paddling a canoe in circles whilst cursing at the wind," she said, laughing so hard she had to clutch at her sides and take little sips of air.

I saw her point and kept my mouth shut, but she had given me an idea. Being a seafaring man once upon a time I knew a thing or two about sailing. I recalled there were things I could use back at the cabin I was held captive in. If only I could find my way back there.

I jumped up from my log and gave Marie a soft slap to the shoulder, "Keep an eye on dinner for me, I'll be back soon," I said, running off down the trail as fast as my contorted ankle would carry me, her laughter following close behind.

I had to stop several times to get my memory back in order and my bearings straight. I was in such a mood when I started wandering the island that I never gave much thought into surveying the place. I spent more than an hour looking for the trail that led to the small cabin. I felt defeated the moment I stepped into the place. The few blankets I had spotted were gone. They probably used them for burial shrouds or to keep the living children warm on the way back to the mainland.

All was not lost, I found a few timbers that were small enough to use for a mast and yardarm. Scraps of rawhide that bound me and the children were still tied to posts but badly deteriorated. A wind blew hard across the southern wall and the timbers groaned. From out of nowhere I was suddenly overwhelmed with a sense of dread and something else I could not quite bring into focus. There was nothing else of use in the shack so I trotted back down the path as best I could.

I followed the tantalizing aroma of freshly roasted rabbit back to our camp. Borborygmus erupted without warning as I set my armload of materials down. This of course elicited a belly laugh from Marie who offered me a plate of wild rice and a leg which I eagerly took. I was into my third mouthful when I realized she was staring at me, well, sort of staring in my direction anyway.

"Am I sounding like a pig? I apologize, I am not used to dining in the graces of such astute company," I said with a greasy smile and elegant bow.

"No, no, Elijah, you are not making a pig of yourself, you are just complimenting the chef."

"I sense there is something you wish to say."

"There is, but I am not sure how."

"Just open your mouth and let the words tumble out, that's how I usually do it. Etiquette and restraint be damned. How do you think I earned most of my scars?"

"What are these things that you have gathered I heard you scatter about the camp," she said, effectively changing the subject.

"I have an idea on how to get off this island."

"And just how, pray tell will you do that?"

"I will fashion a sailboat out of your canoe, and we can both sail to the mainland. Of course, there are probably many people over there wanting my head on a pike so I have to be careful and travel at night or wait until I can disappear into the shadows once again."

She looked upon me with a look of sorrow even though her eyes were void of any color. A sadness passed over her and I felt it inside of me. I studied her haggard face for long minutes before it dawned on me.

"You see it now, do you not?" she said.

"I believe I do, and yet, it is unbelievable."

"But it is so."

"You are that little girl, from the cabin."

"One in the same."

"But how can that be? That was but a few days ago."

"No, Elijah, that was decades ago."

"Have you been here the whole time? What happened to the rest of you?"

"No, my grandfather took us back with him after they," her voice trailed off.

I was left speechless. What she said could not possibly be true. When I took the musket ball in the chest from the Frenchy it was just a matter of days and I was good as new, or at least I thought it was only days. Maybe Wenonah was the key ingredient, without her near me or her sing songs in my head I was left to the mercy of nature. Or the unnatural as it were.

"So why now?"

"Why did I tell you now?"

"No, why did you come back to the island after all these years?"

"To die. And it always nagged me about you. I felt bad they left you the way they did. They thought you evil, and I thought you magical."

"You came here to find me?"

"I came to bury your bones. I stopped believing in your magic more than fifty years ago."

Her revelation was damning to me, had I really been dead for decades? Maybe I had been wandering for decades with no recollection. Was it possible that my body recovered but my mind did not?

"So why on earth would you come all the way out here to die alone?"

"No matter where I would be, I would die alone. I have no family except for those I ferry back and forth to the island."

"You brought all these lost souls out here?"

"Some, most, but not all. Mine is a tradition carried on for many generations."

"How soon after you left the island did this Mahneerah come calling on your village?"

"Not more than a year."

She got up from the log we were sitting on and began wandering an open field near the water's edge. She began picking at various plants and saplings until she had a small sack filled to the brim. She put them in a small clay pot which she then placed near the coals of our fire.

"Just what are you up to?"

"I am making us a special tea."

"I see you have birch and nettles, what is that other stuff."

"Ancient secrets."

"Really?"

"No, I have no idea what these are, I decided to experiment a little so do not drink too much tea until you know what it will do to you."

"That's comforting."

I watched her toiling about as if she were a young woman with two good eyes. It was amazing to see just how helpless she was not. I was absent-mindedly rubbing a spot on my leg that seemed to be missing a chunk of flesh. It was healed and not sore to the touch but oddly, I could not remember where the wound had come from and did not recall it even being there. I was looking it over very closely when I realized what it was, and a pang of guilt shot through me. It was a bite mark.

"Was this my fault?" I asked, my head never moving.

"Was what your fault?"

"You, your eyesight, your family. Did she track you down because of me? Was she looking for me?"

"That is so far in the past it is a long-forgotten memory. Besides, it was I who chose to eat you was it not?"

"But because of my actions. So, are you just like me?"

"I was for a time. I was not completely honest with you earlier out of shame. See, I was once like these lost souls you saved today. My own people cast me out once they realized what I had become."

"But you said you came here to die?"

"And I did. When I gave her my eyes part of the bargain was to cleanse my soul of you. She mocked me later, saying that it did not really matter, that without the proper ritual and her special spices I had managed nothing by consuming you. I guess we will find out soon enough."

"But you do not fade into the shadows over time as I do?"

"No, I do not."

There was a long pause between us before I gathered the nerve to just come out and ask her, "Are you immortal as I appear to be?"

"I do not really know the answer to that question, I have never had the courage to put that to the test, though I have tried," she replied, showing me jagged, ugly scars across her wrists. "I never had the strength to go through with it."

"Sometimes it takes more courage to stand and face your adversities that it does to escape them."

"Well said. But I do not believe I am like you. See, I am old and withered while you appear the very same as you did when I was but a girl."

We sat for another hour or so watching the sun dip lower in the sky without a word between us. We nibbled on rabbit and wild strawberries and pondered the world in front of us. We had both travelled on different paths around the same black sun intersecting until we collided on a deserted beach in the middle of a freshwater ocean. Lost and aimless the only thing we had left in this world was each other.

"I will not let you die alone on this island," I said.

"Ah, but I will not be alone, I will have you to keep me company."

"You're talking nonsensical again old woman," I blurted before I could stop myself.

She got up from the log she had been perched upon and began rummaging around in her meager belongings. My heart felt heavy, laden with guilt and a tear formed in the corner of my eye. I was so tired of being alone and friendless.

"Marie, I am sorry, I didn't mean to call you an old woman."

She turned around with a smile, "But I am an old woman and getting older with each passing of the sun." She came back to her perch and handed a battered leather pouch to me.

"What is this?" I asked, dropping two oddly shaped pebbles into my hand, nearly putting them back into the bag once I realized what they were.

"If they worked for her, maybe they will work for you."

"What do you mean by that?"

"We can play a game akin to what I heard colonial children call hide and seek. You keep these and I will go off somewhere unseen and you use my eyes to see of you can track me."

"I think you may be a bit off the hooks, but I will entertain your wild notions as I have nothing better to do at the moment," I said with a sarcastic smirk.

"No peeking," she said and disappeared down a deer trail that led into the forest at the interior of the island.

I puttered around for five or ten minutes before I decided to play along with her little game though I was not really in the mood. I opened the small leather pouch and dumped two small, odd shaped pebbles into the palm of my hand. I rolled them around in my hand and quickly bored of the exercise. I was ready to dump them back into the bag when I felt the first one move and I almost dropped it into the sand. The petrified orbs began to shift and take shape as they filled into round, tear-glistened eyeballs.

It took me several minutes to regain my composure before I could investigate the palm of my hand once again. I held my hand out high in the air and then came to the realization that I had no idea how this trick was supposed to work. I felt movement against my palm and lowered my hand to where I could see what was occurring. The petrified pellets had morphed into two round globes, puffy and shimmering with mucus.

I investigated the orbs criss crossed with hair thin lines of red exploding off in every direction. I pressed down on one with my fingertip and found it was firm yet spongy. This was indeed an eyeball though for the life of me I could not imagine how this was at all possible. I turned both hazel tinted irises outward and concentrated, trying to discern where Marie had wandered off to.

Nothing. There was no connection between her now opulent eyes and my brain. All I saw was the whites of her eyes and the backside of them at that. The hair on my neck stood straight out and my arms were pure gooseflesh as the two orbs slowly rotated until they were facing me. Almost immediately they glistened over, and a pool formed in my cupped palm and I realized she was crying. I held them up to my eyes and gazed into her distant stare.

A strangeness washed over me, and I wavered on my feet. My vision was blurred as if I had been clunked on the head a time or two and nausea gripped my gullet. Instinctively I closed my fist around the spheres and averted my gaze. I felt them wiggling around in my hand like a puppy's eager tongue licking at my palm. Fluid forced its way between my fingers and dripped down my arm until it left darkened stains on the white sands. I forced my hand open and peered into her world.

Once again, I felt woozy and had to catch myself against a small tree. I did not enjoy this sensation in the least. I managed to gather my wits about me and stared into the disembodied orbs until I was able to discern my own reflection. They seemed to dance around from side to side a bit and I realized they were watching gulls soaring and diving behind me. I felt a punch to the gullet when I came to question just how long had it been since she had been able to see this wondrous world.

Slowly, as if emerging from a fog, a reflection of her sightless face stepped into my vision. Although the bitter winds of winter were blowing across the sands she was spinning around and prancing through the scrub like a little girl on a spring day after being cooped away for a long winter. She sported a smile, a genuine smile as she plucked autumn's dying blooms from the sandy soil. I was sporting a genuine smile of my own, a rarity of late.

I wandered a few yards into the forest to cut the glare of the sun. Sitting in the shade of a mighty oak I studied her romping figurine, more for clues as to where she was rather than her. After all, this was a game and I intended to win. I could barely make out a land mass behind her so she must be on the southern shore of the island. Black clouds rolled behind her setting the stage for this macabre dance.

I gazed into her eyes and said aloud, “You might want to head for the shelter, a storm is coming.”

She smiled, cocked her head at me and mouthed, *you have my eyes, not my ears!*

All the sudden the image I had been watching turned black. I closed my hand and shook the orbs around a few times and then opened my hand. They were spinning left to right, right to left until they finally settled down enough for me to look into them once more. I laughed aloud when I spied her belly up in the sand, both hands clamped to the side of her head.

I was still laughing at her youthful exuberance when I spotted the bow of a ship emerging from the clouds and moving toward the island. My first instinct was to run for the beach, run toward my only means off this accursed island. By the time I made it to where Marie was still dancing in the sand my outlook had changed and I no longer thought rushing headlong into this was the best approach.

“Marie,” I said, grabbing her arm and tugging her with me until we reached the safety of the forest. “What do you know about those people on the land across from us?”

“What is the matter, Elijah? I sense tension in your voice.”

“There is a ship coming from the south heading straight for us.”

“What kind of ship?”

“One unlike anything I have ever seen. While it does have sails, they are furled and yet it still moves. And there is smoke billowing out of it as if it were on fire yet there are no flames that I can see.”

"Ah, there is so much I did not get to tell you, Elijah. The world has changed, some for the better and some not so good. Though I have never seen one, I imagine what you are describing is a steam ship."

"A steam ship?"

"It has a furnace onboard which then heats a big kettle of water producing steam which is then used to spin a big wheel on the side of the ship that propels it through the water."

"Fantastical! What say you about the men who may be sailing this vessel?"

"I say we must be wary. No men come to this island that do not still use canoes and especially none from the big island."

"Why not?"

"Because they are either wicked, or Irish, and most are both. Now never you mind, that is all hearsay to me as I do not make a particularly good eyewitness."

"Irish, you mean from Ireland? I thought this land was nothing but Frenchies and the Brits, and of course your people."

"Men from Ireland started coming here to fish our great waters about twenty years ago or so, when I was a young girl," she said with a smile.

"Are these going to be friend or foe?"

She shrugged, "I do not know, maybe friend, maybe foe, maybe both. Tell me, why is your desire to be free of this island so strong? Do we not have enough food, water and shelter for the two of us?"

"There burns a hunger inside of me that cannot be sated with anything found on this island, at least not anymore. Besides, I have a thing about being trapped on an island, I am not particularly fond of being marooned."

"Even if it means you get to live a life of peace with no war or violence?"

"I am afraid, my dear Marie, that violence and war always manages to find me."

Chapter Forty-Eight

Marie and I hid within the shadows of the forest as the vessel drew closer. Without a dock on the island the ship was forced to drop anchor and moor out beyond the shallows. My heart was pounding in my chest and it took every bit of resolve I had to not run toward the beach with my arms flailing begging to be rescued. I had already suffered one musket ball to the chest I did not relish another.

We watched as they dropped a lifeboat into the water and then began tossing heavy bundles down into the boat. Three men climbed down a rope ladder into the small craft and began rowing for the shore. The sun had already dipped below the horizon and night was fast approaching. The men beached the rowboat, heaved it over onto its side and dumped their cargo onto the beach.

"Smugglers?" I asked.

Marie shrugged and said, "Or pirates."

"Pirates? On these waters?"

"Oh yes, some meaner that Ol' Blackbeard himself," she whispered.

Two of the men began dragging their cargo up the beach toward where we were cowering in the shadows of massive cedars while one man stayed behind with the boat. I assumed he was their leader of sorts the way he barked orders at them. He was a towering, commanding figure indeed. The men returned to the beach and grabbed two more of the white canvas covered bundles and dragged them up with the others. Marie and I used their grunting and groaning to cover our egress deeper into the woods.

With the men's backs to me as they returned to the beach, I used the opportunity to creep closer to the shore. *Exodus* was the name painted on the hull of the thirty-footer. With the sun now completely set I was able to edge close enough to get a good look at what the men had dragged up from the lifeboat and found the revelation disconcerting at best. One of the bundles had a pair of shoeless feet protruding from the white canvas. These were not smugglers, they were murderers plain and simple.

I choked on the blackness emanating from the group of miscreants. Their vileness was intent on invading my soulless husk and that was something I simply could not allow. I was never going back to the creature Wenonah had intended me to be. And especially not after absorbing the purity of those innocent lost souls.

"Grab your rifles and make sure the job is done," the lanky, gruff looking sailor barked.

The two men grabbed a pair of muskets from the floor of the lifeboat and walked back up the beach to where the bundles were piled one on top of the other. I heard the click of the hammer followed by a roar of thunder from each musket. The bundles jumped from the sand with the force of the balls at close range. My chest ached in remembrance.

The men were reloading their muskets when I first saw her shadow emerge from the forest. Before I could react, Marie had left the shelter and safety of the forest.

"I demand you cease this at once," Marie cried out through the din of the howling winds that had begun to blow across the island.

I was frozen in time. Did I dare risk leaving the safety of the shadows? Would they simply see her as a harmless old blind woman? I sighed in relief, the men did not hear her, nor did they even look up from reloading their weapons. She had drawn to within twenty yards from them as they raised to fire another volley.

"Did you not hear me? I said you cease this at once. This is a holy place, a place of reverence, not one of violence," Marie cried out.

She startled one of the men who raised his musket and fired. I saw the flame shooting from his barrel and the cloud of smoke billowing up around him and my heart ached. It ached even more when I watched Marie's body slump into the sand.

"You imbecile!" the captain shouted and stepped forth. "She is but a blind old woman you fool," he pulled a pistol from his waistband and aimed it at her head as she writhed helplessly on the ground.

Without a single thought of apprehension, I threw all good judgment to the wind and dashed from the woods. "If you harm her any further, I will kill you," I screamed as I ran.

The man who had yet to fire quickly swung his musket in my direction and let loose a ball that only grazed my thigh but had enough force to put me on the ground. The two men began reloading as I struggled to get to my feet. Retreat was my only option at this point.

"There may be more of them, don't waste your time with him and get to the boat," the captain said, firing his pistol into Marie's skull before loping off down the beach to help get the boat in the water but not before I got a very good look at the lanky bastard with a fiery beard down to his chest.

"We will meet again," I vowed as the *Exodus* steamed away. Again, in this bitter lifetime I had found myself alone on a deserted island surrounded by death.

Chapter Forty-Nine

I watched the lights of the vessel disappear into the darkness through tear glistened eyes. I could still hear the wheel slapping the water so they were still close enough that I should have been able to see their lights which meant they had doused their lanterns. With great effort I managed to get myself back to my feet with only one good arm and two damaged legs. Blood poured from my thigh down onto my foot making the sand clump around me which made it even harder to walk. I hobbled over to where Marie's lifeless body stained the earth.

I brought her head delicately into my lap and she moaned. Tears streamed down my face and I realized that maybe for the first time in my life I was crying for someone other than my own self. And while this was not of my doing, I couldn't help but feel culpable just the same.

"Do not cry for me, Elijah. I came here to die, and so die I shall," she said, a weak smile creasing her face.

I pulled her hair away from the wound in her head and realized the bastard had only managed a glancing blow. Her scalp was torn and there was a crease in her skull, but her brains were still intact.

"Fortunately, I have a very hard head, or so I have been told," she pat the back of my hand. "Unfortunately, my stomach is not so hard."

I had forgotten all about the first man's shot. I peeled her blood-soaked hand away from her wound and let loose a small gasp. Her wound was one I had seen many times over and I was aware it was a mortal wound.

My adrenaline surge was wearing off and I became acutely aware of the winds bellowing across the island. If I had any hope of saving Marie's life, I would need to shelter her from the coming storm, or she would surely perish before the next sunrise. I knew she was too damaged to be able to get her back to the ramshackle cabin so I dragged one of the bodies up to where she lay, freed it from its canvas cocoon and used the canvas as a blanket. I dragged the other bodies over and stacked them like cord wood to shelter her from the wind.

I limped off into the forest and returned with several sturdy limbs to stake the canvas into a makeshift tent. Autumn's vibrant brush was all but gone from the island. Flakes of snow started to float down from the heavens and the temperature had dropped a good ten degrees. I combed the beach for driftwood, just enough to get a fire started but I had no means other than the coals in our fire across the island, if there were indeed any embers left.

I dug through the pockets of the man I had exposed looking for anything that might be of use. I found nothing so I shredded his shirt into strips and put them in my pockets. If I wound them tightly around a stick, I might be able to restart a fire with whatever embers remained back at camp. I checked Marie's wound and saw that the cold was helping to slow the bleeding.

"Marie, I am so sorry, but I have to leave you. I must try and make it back to camp before all the coals of our fire die out. We need a fire and I cannot move you."

"Don't you mind me, get yourself to shelter."

"I will not leave you to die alone on this accursed island. You hang on until I get back, everything will be fine, you'll see."

"I can only see what you let me see."

"Are you delirious? Why do you speak in riddles and jokes?"

"Humor an old woman, let me see this world one last time before I am called away into the next."

"As you wish," I said, dumping the two petrified raisins from their leather pouch I pulled from my pocket. "But I'll be damned if this will be the last time. You will not die here this night," I said and struggled to my feet.

"I fear the decision is not yours to make, Elijah."

I ignored her and went about unwrapping another of the corpses. I undressed him and put on his clothes for the trek across the island but found they were much too small for me and could only get one arm in his shirt. He had a small knife in his pocket, so I used it to cut small squares of the canvas to use to carry the embers back with me. I toiled, all the while trying to ignore the two glistening orbs sitting on Marie's chest, intent on watching my every move. I was interrupted by her raucous laughter.

"Are you mad, woman? Why do you laugh?"

"I was just thinking that you were a sight for sore eyes."

I could not help but chuckle. "You are truly mad old woman."

"Why are you so resolute in this quest for fire that will take you all the way across the island in a snowstorm?"

"Because one, if not both of us will die without heat and I have no means to make a fire."

"But you do, Elijah," she giggled.

I was certain death was creeping in on her inch by inch and was driving her completely insane. I could respond with nothing more than an exasperated expression.

"Lucifer," she said, barely audible above the shrieking winds.

"I shall start to pray for you dear woman. Why are you spouting on about the devil?"

"I am not speaking of the devil. I said, a Lucifer, not the Lucifer. The dead man had a Lucifer in his pocket which you have laid upon the ground."

I followed where her eyes were looking at a menagerie of belongings I had dumped from the dead man's pockets. There was not much of anything for her to have gotten so excited about. A few coins, a broken comb and some sticks wrapped in paper. I flipped the coins over in my hand, most of which I was unfamiliar with. There were a couple of half cent coins, a half dime coin, and a quarter dollar with an eagle on the one side, and a lady's likeness on the other. It was when I saw the date that I was hit with the realization of just how much time had passed.

"There is nothing of Satan in this man's belongings."

"I did not say Satan, I said Lucifer."

"Are they not one in the same?" I argued.

"If we were speaking of beings or Bible stories, yes, but not in this conversation. Those sticks are called Lucifers. Though I have never seen one work, I have only smelled them after they were on fire."

"And just what is their purpose?"

"To light lanterns or in this case, to light a fire. Now hurry, this old woman is freezing."

I dropped everything but the odd sticks back onto the ground and began preparing the wood for a fire. Using the small pocketknife, I scraped the dry driftwood into ribbons of kindling and made a bundle of them with pieces of the dead man's shirt. I then tied a small bundle of twigs followed by a larger bundle of sticks and arranged everything into a small pit I had dug into the sand to protect the fire from the wind. I held the "Lucifer" in my hand and looked it up and down with no clue as to how it was supposed to operate. I was certain she was having her last laugh on earth at my expense.

"I have never seen one of those work but from what I have heard they are very dangerous," she warned.

I studied the device for several minutes before coming to the conclusion that this would be a two-man operation as I was only half a man with one good arm.

"I think one merely has to remove the paper from the wooden portion. Maybe the air has something to do with it. But I cannot do it with one hand."

She held out her hand and I placed the rough paper between her fingers. I made sure I had a good grip on the wooden stick and pulled it quickly towards me and down to the kindling pile. Suddenly the small shelter was illuminated in a great ball of white smoke and instant flames. Startled, I dropped the stick which immediately ignited the kindling.

Within fifteen minutes we had a roaring fire that would keep at least one of us alive for the night. I chuckled at my own irony, the only one the fire was going to keep alive this night was the one who could not die a permanent death. But I did not wish to be found a frozen corpse come spring either. Before long the lean-to was roasting so I got rid of the dead sailor's clothes. They were much too tight on me anyway.

"How are you feeling?" I asked.

"I'm better now, the fire has taken the chill off. Though I doubt I will be dancing an Irish jig any time soon."

"I promise you, I will get the sons of bitches who did this to you," I said.

"You will do nothing of the sort. What is done is done and vengeance will not undo it. Besides, I was dying anyway, they only sped things along."

"That is neither here nor there, I will kill them for what they have done. Vengeance is deserved."

"For me or for yourself?"

There was a long silence between us interrupted only by the crackling of the fire, the shrieking gales snapping at our canvas shelter and the slapping of the waves against the coastline.

"Elijah, you cannot seek vengeance by killing them. Seek justice instead."

"Killing them would serve justice."

"No, it would do an injustice. It would deliver you back into the maw of the beast."

"They deserve to die a slow, painful death for what they have done."

"And you deserve to live a life without her chains binding you," she said, reaching out to take my hand in hers. "Promise me, you will never kill out of anger again. That you will never more consume the darkness."

"I am not sure I can make that promise and even less sure that I could honor it."

"But honor it you must."

I thought about her words and she was right. If I learned one thing on this island it was that I was not bound to be an evil being, I could be pure of heart if I so desired, I only needed to traverse the correct path. I bundled up and trotted down the coast a little further collecting as much firewood as a one-armed man could carry. It sure would be a hell of a lot easier had I possessed any tools or at the very least, my tomahawks.

My fingers were numb by the time I returned, and I knew I would have to go back out in an hour or so. Marie had dozed off and was so quiet I had to check to make sure she was still breathing several times. It was going to be a very long night, hell, a very long winter.

Chapter Fifty

I awoke to more than two inches of fresh snow and nothing but a few coals in the fire. The wind had subsided so collecting firewood proved to be much easier. I gathered enough wood for about an hour and checked on Marie before venturing away from camp to set up some snares. The critters would be out and about storing up food before the next storm hit the island which was precisely what I intended to do as well.

Save for the snow it was a beautiful day. Although, this accursed lake had shown me its propensity to change moods in an instant, so I did not allow myself to get comfortable in the notion that the worst had passed. I set about gathering wood from even further down the beach while constantly scanning the horizon for any signs of more unwanted guests.

While warming my bones beside the fire I contemplated my life's choices. Why I had ever left the turquoise waters of the Caribbean escaped me, until I replayed the memory of the blood sucking bugs, the ever-present blazing sun and numerous people who wanted my head on a pike. But why here? Why did I choose this God forsaken place that was nothing if not brutal and unforgiving? Once the feeling returned to my fingers I ventured out for more wood and to check the snares.

I hobbled my way back to camp with an armload of dry wood and a scrawny varmint whose skull I caved with a rock. I cleaned the rabbit and carefully saved the innards so I might use them to draw in some fish I could spear. I cut the rabbit into long thin strips with the pocketknife and hung them over a makeshift rack above some coals I had moved away from the flames of the fire. I would need to do a lot better as a hunter and gatherer if we were to survive the winter.

"Are you able to eat? Would you like some rabbit for breakfast?" I asked Marie. I asked her again, a little more loudly the second time.

I reached my hand under the canvas I had covered her with and gripped her hand. It was as cold as the snow surrounding us. I dropped down onto my haunches with a sigh. She looked so peaceful. For a moment I questioned my sadness, was I sad for her passing or simply because once again, I was utterly alone in a miserable world? I realized my heart was truly aching for her. At first, I started to cry, but then I was forced to smile. Not many get to make peace with the world and leave it on their terms, but Marie did exactly that.

"I'm kind of fond of rabbit myself. And I am famished," I heard a voice call out.

I swung around in an arc, brandishing the small pocketknife as it was the only weapon I possessed. There were no footprints in the snow other than mine in any direction. Especially none close enough that I would be able to hear who made them. It was silent once again and I began to think myself mad.

"Who is out there? Show yourself," I said.

"I would, but I cannot," the voice responded.

The second instance of the voice brought me to the realization it was much closer to me than I had first thought. I rummaged around my wood pile and found a hefty stick and began poking at the three canvas bundles piled up around me. When my efforts went for naught, I jammed the stick into them even harder.

"Ow. Was that really necessary?" a voice called from the bottom bundle.

"Is someone alive in there?" I asked, poking the bottom canvas again.

"Would I be talking to you if I weren't?" he responded.

I gave a weak laugh, "If you only knew half of what I have seen in one lifetime you would not ask that question."

"Could we discuss this after you have freed me from this damned death sack? I am getting tired of pissing on myself and I fear that I am close to doing something much worse."

I rolled the two canvases containing the dead men stacked on top of him off onto the sand and began cutting away at the ropes binding the third bundle. The pocketknife was quite dull, and the ropes were well made making the task of sawing them loose a difficult one at best.

"Not to bellyache too much, but you do know the difference between the sharp edge of a knife and the dull?"

"Keep grumbling and I will show you I know which end is the pointed end. Your bellyaching is not making this any easier or any quicker."

I took a break from gnawing at the ropes to get a nibble of rabbit and drink a few swallows of water. I had half a mind to go gather some more firewood and check my snares but then imagined myself in his position and resolved that expedience was the honorable thing.

"And just because I am arse up to the wind don't mean you can go getting any fancy ideas in your head."

"I am starting to understand just what it was that landed you in such a precarious position. Too bad they didn't gag you before shooting you."

I was so engrossed in freeing the man from his bindings that I did not notice the black clouds forming over the western horizon. It was the temperature dropping that got my attention. Soon after the winds came howling. With my barrier down the wind threatened to blow out the campfire and was directing the heat away from me.

"Is it me or is it getting colder out there?" he asked, it was then that I noticed his bare feet wiggling out the end of the cocoon.

"It is not you, a storm is brewing. I need to get you out of there so we can take shelter," I said, spinning him around so that his exposed feet were inside the warmth of the canvas but propped up on Marie's chest. I did not see as if she would mind given the circumstances.

Between gathering more wood and cutting him loose I was exhausted, but the task was complete. Once free the man helped me secure the new scrap of canvas up to create a better wind break. He dashed off to relieve himself while I fixed him a meager plate of rabbit and cold beans. When he returned, we both sat, wordlessly, eyeing each up and down while we ate.

He was a brutish man with wild hair and tired eyes. He looked to be pushing forty, but in this harsh environment that could mean he was only in his twenties. He had the hands of a man not afraid to work or break a knuckle when need be. There was something oddly familiar about him though, but I could not place where we may have met.

"Dear merciful Lord, you look like you have been to hell and back, mister," he said with a sympathetic grin.

"I do not suppose you have had the opportunity to check yourself in a reflective glass as of late," I quipped in return.

"I reckon I have not. Mister, just what in the hell happened to you? If you don't mind me asking."

"You can call me Elijah."

"It is a pleasure to meet you Elijah. Name's Robert Marigold in a long line of Robert Marigolds. But you can call me Goldy."

I studied his face and tried to imagine him without the beard, the dirt or the blood as the more I looked upon him the more familiar to me he became

"Pleasure to meet you, Goldy," I smiled, but it quickly disappeared. "When?" I asked, nodding a head toward Marie's corpse.

"I think I heard her death rattle about an hour after you left camp the first time. Were you two close?"

"In a manner of speaking, yes."

"I am truly sorry she left this world in such a violent manner."

"She went out on her terms and I suppose she was at peace in the end. How badly are you injured?"

"They cracked my skull pretty good, but it is made of stone so I will survive. I guess I owe you two my life as even hard as rock it wouldn't have stopped a musket ball."

I nodded. "You owe her not me, regretfully she will never be able to collect on that debt."

I handed Goldy a few strips of the rabbit and offered some more beans which he politely refused. We melted snow for water and took shelter under the tarps as the latest storm blasted the island. It was already dark by the time the storm let up and we went out scavenging for more firewood. At least I now had a mule to cart the wood.

"Looks like we are going to be spending the winter together on this island paradise," Goldy said.

"Kind of looks like winter has set in for good," I agreed.

"I am afraid we can't stay here near the water, we will freeze to death. We need to build a shelter in the protection of the forest."

"I agree, but we will not need to build a shelter, there is a rundown old shack about a mile from here."

"Lead the way," Goldy said with all the eagerness of a child wanting to explore.

"We should leave at first light. But we have to take her with us, and I don't think I can manage."

"You don't really intend to keep a dead woman in a cabin with us all winter?"

"No, we will wrap her in a canvas and store her outside until I can take her to her sacred burial ground in the interior of the island."

"It is a fair and noble cause and I am more than willing to carry her when the time presents itself. She must have been a good woman."

"I truly believe she was."

The winds died down over night and we awoke to three more inches of fresh snow. We spent the next morning building a travois to cart Marie's body with us to the cabin where we could move her to the cemetery come springtime when the ground thawed. We stripped the dead men and piled all their possessions on the canvas with Marie's body. Before setting out we dug a couple of shallow graves in the sand where the fire pit had been because the earth was thawed.

"Would you like to say a few words or mark their graves?" I asked.

"Wouldn't know what to say. Hell, I only knew one of their first names."

"I got the impression they were acquaintances."

"I was merely acquainted with the older brother, Seamus Doyle. And he and I were merely business partners, not friends," he said and lifted his pole of the travois. I grabbed the other and we started off for the cabin.

"Nothing too illegal I hope."

"Depends on whose laws, yours or the King's."

I stopped in my tracks and turned to face him. "So, the Brits beat the Frenchies and now the King of England lords over this land too?"

"What in blazes are you talking about? No, the King of England does not rule here, this is the United States of America, the president rules here."

"But you clearly mentioned the King's laws."

"I meant that peckerwood what calls himself the king over there on the big island."

"Was he the man I saw on the beach, the one with the long red beard?"

"One in the same. He hated those Doyle's something fierce and wanted to see for himself they would never be a bother to him or his kind ever again."

"Why did he hate you just as much? I mean, you did seem to be sharing in their fate."

"He must have thought I was a Doyle too, or at least blood related somehow.'

I looked down at Marie, caressed her frozen hair and said, "I guess we survive the winter and come spring I will pay this King a visit."

Chapter Fifty-One

It was nearly two hours later by the time we made it to the cabin and my ears were numb, not from the bitter cold rather from the man's constant chatter. It was not that I didn't appreciate his company, but I already had a thousand conversations going on inside my own head. We put Marie's body against the north facing wall, covered her with another of the canvas tarps and then piled stones on top to keep the critters from munching on her through the winter.

When I stepped through the doorway the air inside stole my breath. While not very strong I could still feel the dark energy in this room. It was ingrained in the wood itself. A dark stain steeped in my very essence spread out across the middle of the floor. It seemed to glow in recognition as I crossed the threshold.

Another storm was looming on the horizon so Goldy and I went to work patching up the small fireplace and got a fire going. Quickly the room filled with noxious smoke which sent Marigold scrambling for the roof. A few moments later a large bundle of fur, feathers and bones burst through the chimney and down into the fire. It appeared something got stuck and then something enjoyed an easy meal and got stuck themselves.

After airing the place out, we began boarding up windows and patching holes in the roof of the only part of the building still standing. I was never known as a man proficient with his hands, but one-handed carpentry was not a skill I possessed. It was after the third time I dropped a board on his foot that Robert suggested we take a break.

"What happened to you in here?" Goldy asked, startling me by breaking the silence.

"I am not sure I understand just what it is you are asking?"

"Listen, let us get one thing clear, I am by no means the smartest man in these parts, but I am far from being the most ignorant as well. There is something very odd about you and about your situation."

"I will not deny that I am quite the odd conundrum that is for certain, but I still do not see what you are implying."

"What I am implying is this, if it were one thing, I could shrug it off, but there is a litany of oddities surrounding you."

"For instance?" I asked.

"For instance, how did you end up on this island buck naked with an old Indian woman?"

"I was not naked."

"You were covering yourself with a baby's blanket and wearing a shirt three sizes too small for you, I consider that naked."

"I had a boating accident."

He shook his head and shot me a discerning glance. "It appears we are going to be stranded on this island for near six months, I would much rather spend that time with someone I can trust than alone. But I will spend it alone if I cannot trust you. I do not care what it is you have done; I just need to know. Lord knows I am not proud of every one of my actions in this lifetime so I will not judge you, I just need to know what is going on."

"If I told you, you would not believe a word which would tarnish us even further and create an even bigger mistrust."

"I have had many jobs in this lifetime, one of them being a sawbones for the Army so I know a little about the human anatomy. And one thing I know for certain, the scars you wear would have killed any man deader than dead and yet, here you stand. Also, I look around this room and I see it was used to house captives and you bear the scars of that very same captivity. Your wrists were bound here," he said, pointing to the post where I was tied decades ago. "And your feet were nailed to the floor here."

"Okay, so I was a prisoner in this very room, I admit it."

"But it is not that simple. Your wounds are too far healed and this shack far too decrepit for this to have happened recently."

"You are correct, it was a few years ago," I said, trying to appease the man and get him away from his interrogation.

"It was more than a few years ago judging by the scars on your feet and the age of these bindings. There are dried blood stains everywhere and not just from you. What in the hell happened in this place?"

"Have a seat. I wish I had coffee, or better yet, rum to discuss this over."

"And that is another thing, your language just is not right, and you seem out of place. I cannot even begin to comment on the certain pigment of your skin, there is an opaqueness I have never seen in all my days. I am not one to believe in legends or superstitions, but I might make an exception in your case. I have half a mind to think you're one of those flesh-eating beasts I've heard the natives speak about."

"I assure you that I am not a wendigo and have no desire whatsoever to partake of your flesh."

"That is a good thing for you, I am certain I would taste horrendous."

"No, I am not a flesh-eating beast of Indian lore, mine is a fanciful tale you will most assuredly deem preposterous and less believable than that."

"As long as it is the truth, I will give you your say without interruption."

I regaled the man with the tale of my life as a pirate, as a bounty hunter and eventually the events that brought me to this point in my life. From his eyes I could tell that he was listening to my every word, but also that he doubted many of them. I think the moment where his opinion of my story turned from fiction to fact was when I shared with him the scar left in my chest when Gagnon's musket ball pierced my heart.

"I must admit, I am having a very difficult time swallowing all of your tale, hell any of that outlandish story."

"As do I. But you did ask for the truth."

He studied me up and down, paying very close attention to the myriad of scars adorning my body before he said, "So if I were to kill you right now you would come back to life?"

"Eventually. But I really do not feel like slumbering for the next few decades so please do not test your theory."

"Do you plan on dining on my soul?" he asked while absent-mindedly stoking the fire with his back to me.

"I hadn't given it any thought to be honest with you."

"What do you see? Is mine a dark soul?"

"I do not see into souls; I simply sense their essence. With you, I do not sense anything, yours is neither wholly bad nor wholly good I suppose."

"Fair enough."

With that, he ended the conversation about who the Shadowman was and where he originated. I took that to mean that he did not care just as long as I did not attempt to eat him or abscond with his soul.

"So, do you think this Wenonah who did this to you is dead?"

"Honestly, I do not believe she can truly die, at least not by conventional means. Possibly with a divine intervention of sorts."

"You mean God?"

"I mean something I have never believed in until all of this began. I am not certain if it is God, the Great Spirit, Buddha, or all of them combined but I believe it will take something far more powerful than a man to do away with her. Even a shadow of a man."

It was three days before the snow let up which gave us the opportunity to walk of the shoreline which revealed the lake had iced over at least ten feet offshore. Before leaving I checked Marie's body and found it was safely tucked under a foot of snow and there had been no signs of animals disturbing her slumber. We were out of food and needed to forage for something other than dust mites.

I was comforted to see that the trail leading to the cemetery was void of any footprints in the fresh snow indicating that we were still alone on the island. I wasn't too keen on desecrating a burial ground, but we were in dire need of equipment and food. The spirit houses had all been covered with fresh snow and I was relieved to see there were no tracks of any kind leading away from any of the mounds. Not that I expected to run into any ghosts, but it would not surprise me either.

I gently moved away the snow from the roof, blowing it off as I got down to the house itself. It was three feet long and eighteen inches wide. Cedar shakes covered in green moss and dead pine needles formed the roof. There was a small hole in the front of the edifice to place belongings of the loved one intended for use on the other side.

"You didn't tell me you were a grave robber too," Marigold commented as I rifled through a spirit house.

"We are not robbing, we are simply borrowing. We will return whatever we take before spring and no one will be the wiser."

"No one but the spirit residing here," he laughed. "It is kind of a strange custom don't you think?"

"What is?"

"To just leave valuable things out in the open like this."

"No stranger than leaving flowers on one's grave or the wealthy being buried with their money and jewelry dressed in fancy clothes. Or for that fact, kings buried with their crowns, even a crown of thorns. This is far more practical if you believe there is another place our souls go when we die."

"Aren't they worried the things would be stolen, like they are being right now?"

I shot him a sideways glance and uncovered another spirit house piled with fresh snow careful not to disturb the structure itself. There was nothing but trinkets and mementos, so I did not bother with the contents.

"Finally, the house of a provider," I said, sliding a bow and quiver of arrows from the hole in the front of the house. I was glad to see he was a true sportsman and there was some gear for fishing as well.

"How will the poor soul eat on the other side?"

"Quit your bellyaching and grab me a few of those pine boughs to mark this grave with. I want to make sure we return his possessions as soon as we are able. Make sure they are tall enough to see over another foot of snow, I have a feeling we will be getting a lot more snow as the winter marches on."

"At least we won't die of thirst," he replied and headed into the woods with the small pocketknife to cut some branches.

A rude cacophony echoed from the forest and Goldy came spilling out, arms loaded with pine boughs.

"I said a couple boughs, not the whole forest. We are merely marking a grave not building a house," I laughed at the sight of him sprawled in the snow.

Suddenly my laughter was rudely interrupted by the call of the largest raven I had ever laid eyes on perched on a limb above the fallen man. The creature was the deepest ebony and as large as a vulture. Goldy scooted away as fast as he could and scrambled to his feet.

"God, I hate those things," he said, brushing the snow off from himself.

"It's just a bird."

"No, it's a raven."

"Which is just a bird," I scoffed. "If he scares you, just shoo him away."

"Nevermore," he cawed at the bird.

The raven let loose a loud caw in response.

"Nevermore," Goldy reiterated.

"What is that all about?"

"Have you never read 'The Raven'?"

"The what?"

"The poem by Edgar Allan Poe."

"Can't say that I have ever had much occasion to peruse any poetry and definitely not any as of late."

"It's creepy, that's all I have to say," he said as he bent over to scoop up some fresh snow that he compacted between his hands.

Marigold threw the snowball as hard as he could at the raven who simply lifted aloft and drifted on the wing, coming to rest on the peak of one of the spirit houses still covered in snow. Three more snowballs all ended with the same results, the raven took to the skies and landed back on the very same spirit house.

"Maybe the spirit of an old warrior is trying to tell us something," I said while making my way over to the spirit house the raven had been perched upon.

Goldy kept a wary eye on the bird as I dug through the spirit house and pulled its contents out into the light of day. I was startled enough that Marigold noticed, and my reaction spooked him.

"I hate cemeteries and you are not making it any better. Why did you react like that?" he asked.

"I'm not sure how to say this that will not set you even more on edge."

"We are traipsing about a cemetery, putting our hands inside of miniature tombs all the while a raven mocks us over head. Can it get any worse?"

"Yes, I believe it can. These are my belongings," I said, hefting my two tomahawks. They were quite rusty, and the leather wrappings were falling away, but they were definitely mine. A golden locket with a broken filigree chain was wrapped around one of the shafts.

"Let us leave this place now. I am not one to believe in magic, but something is just not right here."

I nodded and began to gather up my long-abandoned belongings. The raven swooped down and landed on the peak of the spirit house just a mere inch from my face. Its eyes were gone from their sockets.

Chapter Fifty-Two

"Kill him. Shoot that damned bird," I said.

Goldy raised the bow and fired an arrow at the raven. The first arrow missed but the raven was so large that he was slow to take off and Marigold's second arrow found its mark. The ebon bird laid bleeding in the snow, a victim of its own hubris.

"You seemed pretty adamant about killing it. Is there something more to the story?"

"Look at the eyes."

"The damned thing doesn't have any. How the hell could it see us if it were blind?"

"It is that foul demon trying to track me," I said, lopping the creatures head off with my tomahawk.

"Was that really necessary?"

"If for nothing but my own piece of mind, yes, it was completely necessary."

I buried the head of the beast face down in the sand as soon as we were free from the cemetery grounds. I did not want that abominable creature to be in the same hallowed ground tarnishing the good, honorable people interred there. On the way back to the cabin Marigold managed to get a deer with our newly acquired bow so dinner was going to be a fancy feast compared to what I had been used to as of late.

"So, tell me more about this king," I said between mouthfuls of perfectly roasted back strap.

"Not much to tell, except that he is a strange fellow that is for sure."

"Not much to tell? He had every intention of killing you so he must have had a reason."

"Not a good one. He and his followers don't like Irish folks too much and they mistook me for an Irishman."

"Followers? That sounds more like a preacher man than a king?"

"He is both. He leads some kind of newfound religion, I don't know enough about it to share the particulars, but I can say that other, more traditional church leaders have not taken too kindly to it. From what I have heard the man tells tall tales of finding golden books and other sorts of odd claims. Many well-established church leaders were so angered that they even killed a fellow named Jones in Chicago for spreading the word. It was told that the man killed was the founder of the new religion. That was when Kingston Lewis split from that sect and moved to the island with his followers and soon after declared himself the King of Beaver Island. Actually, it was one of his followers who first called him king, but Lewis never corrected her, and the designation stuck."

"How did you manage to get tangled up with him in such a manner that he wanted you dead?"

"I was guilty of nothing but associating with the wrong crowd. I was in need of a grubstake to get me started on my new life and Doyle, an Irishman was quick to lend me some cash. At a high interest rate of course. But he was patient in my being able to pay him back, though he did knock me on the noggin more than once for being late with a payment."

"Is that why this king fellow killed the Doyle's?"

"It was more complicated than that. Seems this new-fangled religion preaches that men can have more than one wife."

"Absurd! More than one wife? What man in his right mind would want or could handle more than one woman? How did this involve Doyle?"

Goldy laughed and nodded his head. "It started when Doyle's youngest sibling joined Kingston Lewis' church and Lewis took a fancy to her. He had plans to make her his fourth wife which Doyle vehemently protested. Lewis retaliated by coaxing Doyle's betrothed to join his church and then ultimately made her his fourth wife, then Doyle's sister his fifth."

"How was this man able to get away with these deeds? What about the law?"

"They are the law. I have heard tales of him being dragged off to trial in Detroit for treason, but he was acquitted. Lewis is not only vindictive, but smart as a whip which is a dangerous combination. Soon after returning to the island he beckoned more of his followers from Wisconsin to join him on the island. Once he had the numbers on his side he ran for political office and won thus securing his foothold on this island."

"Sounds like a fairy tale."

"In some ways I suppose it is. It can be difficult to separate the fact from the fiction. But I myself have borne witness to his domineering hand. He is a strict disciplinarian and is no stranger to having men flogged. Two of whom I saw given lashes because their wives refused to wear attire prescribed by Lewis."

"Sounds like a place we should avoid and if it weren't for vengeance I would do just that."

"Did I not hear you make a promise to the old woman that you would not do such a thing?"

"You did."

"Was she wrong in asking you to make that vow?"

"Not in the least."

"Then I shall see that you honor it. Any vengeance to be had against Lewis will be my own, after all, it is me he wanted dead, not you."

I nodded, not because I agreed, but because I was tired of this conversation and wished to sleep. The man was right about one thing, if this Kingston Lewis were anything like he attested him to be then his soul would be black as night and most assuredly would be able to seduce me into devouring it. I was going to have to keep my wits about me and my anger at bay lest I fall prey to Wenonah's darkness once again.

I struggled to bring in another armload of wood for the fire and managed to drop a decent sized chunk on my ankle. As I stood there cursing my bad luck, I felt Robert's eyes on me and had endured more of his sniggering than I cared for.

"I'm glad you find watching me struggle so amusing," I said.

"That statement assumes I can see you to watch you."

I glanced down at my hand and saw that I had regressed further into my shadow state. Marigold seemed to be taking my transition a lot better than I thought he would have.

"I've been thinking, we really have to do something about that arm of yours. If you are truly immortal as you claim, it is going to prove to be one hell of a nuisance for all eternity."

"What do you suggest, Sawbones, hacking it off? I told you I am not like a lizard, it will not grow back."

"Hear me out. I am a doctor of sorts and have dealt with all sorts of cuts, scrapes and broken bones."

"No, absolutely not."

"You have not heard what I am about to suggest."

"I know what it is you are about to suggest. And, as I have told you, I am immortal yes, but immune to pain I am not."

"I think we will only have to break it a few times to get it straight again."

"A few times?" I bellowed. "And just how do you plan to accomplish this? Beat my arm with a log until it is smashed?"

"In a manner of speaking, yes. Let me take a look at that monstrosity," he smiled and beckoned me over.

Goldy ran his hands carefully over my arm, paying close attention to my elbow. Several times he nearly earned a rap on his forehead by bending my arm further than it wanted to be bent.

"What do you have in mind?" I asked, knowing that what he said was true, my arm did need straightening even if it never worked properly again.

"You know that tree out front with the two trunks we use to snap smaller logs with? After looking at your arm I don't think the bone is the problem, it is your elbow joint that is out of place. It was broken loose from the socket and then healed out of place over time. I think a time or two can fix it."

"A time or two of what?"

"If you put your arm between the two trunks of the tree, I can probably snap it back into place, but it may take a few times depending on how much the cartilage has healed around the bone. I'm afraid it not only dislocated the ball from the socket but then was twisted sideways out of the hinge as well."

"You are being serious about this aren't you?"

"Very serious."

"With no rum, no whiskey, nothing to ease the pain?"

Goldy shrugged, "On the bright side, it won't kill you and I doubt I could make it any worse."

"I'm beginning to think that just lopping it off might be the better option."

"If you'd like, I am pretty good at that."

We spent the rest of the day cutting strips of canvas from the last sheet that was not being used to protect Marie's body. Goldy remembered something he had heard from the Indians on the island about fermented birch sap, so we raided the cemetery until we found three small bottles. I hoped the spirits wouldn't mind being sober on the other side but was soon disappointed to learn the concoction held no intoxicating properties, but Marigold assured me it served a purpose.

All in all, it took three attempts before my arm finally decided to cooperate, each one more painful than the last. The "treatment" as Goldy had called it lasted all of November and most of December during which I slept nearly all of it. He managed to keep venison on the table and was a hell of a good cook, ensuring I rousted up for meals.

It was nearing Christmas if my calculations were correct and with my arm feeling much better, I went about decorating our shelter with whatever I could find. I fashioned a crude chess set from deer bones and carved a board into the floor with my little pocketknife. I spent Christmas Eve sipping on a tea made from birch and winterberries while getting lessons from Goldy on how not to play chess.

Marigold spent hours every day regaling me with tales of how the upstart rebels managed to beat back the British. Of how there was no more king trying to impose his will on these lands, save for one of course. He told me about how the land was divided up into more than thirty different territories called states and more of them being added every year. I found it hard to believe the course of events as he related them, but he assured me it was all true and I had no cause to disbelieve him.

"How long before the ice breaks up enough to get to the big island?" I asked.

"Assuming this is really Christmas I'd venture to say we still have at least three more months before we can get off this little piece of heaven."

I nodded. "That leaves another especially important question, just how in the hell are we going to leave? We have no boat after that bastard king destroyed our only canoe and it is too far to swim."

"These waters come alive with ships in the spring. We can simply borrow one of them."

"Ships going where?"

"Hauling lumber, furs, whiskey, you name it back and forth between the cities on either shore. From the tales you have told me you are no stranger to piracy so it should be no problem hijacking a vessel."

"Two men, overrun and commandeer an entire ship?"

"These are not the ships of your day, they are smaller and have a much smaller crew. Besides, we do not need to steal the entire ship, merely a lifeboat. I did learn a thing or two from the king who is nothing more than a freshwater pirate with many crafty tricks in his bag. We will simply lure them to us."

"And just how do we manage to do that?" I asked.

"We will mimic the pier at Lewistown on the big island by arranging lit torches out in the water. The ship will think they are heading into port and instead they will run aground. They will abandon the ship to cut timbers to free themselves and that is when you abscond with one of their lifeboats."

"Me? Why me?"

"Because they will not be able to see you. They will blame one another for not mooring it properly and think it just went adrift. If done properly you will be out of sight before they notice it missing because they will be too busy gathering materials to free their ship from the reef."

"No wonder you beat me so handily at chess, you're a pretty good strategist."

I felt something stir in my pocket and reached in to clutch the small leather pouch holding two human raisins. They were perfectly still and lifeless, so I put them back and dismissed the sensation as my overactive imagination. Ever since our encounter with that raven I dreadfully awaited Wenonah's sing song rhymes and childish giggles. I feared it was only a matter of time.

Chapter Fifty-Three

January was a long, lonely month and February was not much better. But we were nearing the Ides of March and spring was no longer an unrealistic fantasy. Once the snow was passable again Marigold and I scoured the forest for pine sap, fungus caps and limbs long enough to shove into the sands beneath the lake. We melted the pine sap and mixed it with charcoal which we then layered on the sticks with canvas strips and the clothes we had salvaged from the dead men. They would make fine torches indeed.

We put Marie to rest in the cemetery and returned the borrowed belongings to the spirit houses once we had enough meat to last until our egress from our island prison. I took the small leather pouch from my pocket and placed it in the grave with her. The need for vengeance burned hot in my heart, but so did my hunger and her passing words of wisdom. I made a vow to her and I was bound to honor it.

It was in early April when the lights of a ship appeared on the northwest horizon. We hurried and set out the torches in a pattern to resemble the pier at Lewistown harbor and Goldy disappeared through the forest to the eastern side of the island. I blended in with the shadows and waded as far out into the frigid water as I dared.

Goldy's plan worked to perfection, the ship headed straight between the rows of torchlight and before they knew what had happened, they had run aground on the rocky reef. The sailors all abandoned their vessel and headed for shore to defend the ship allowing me the opportunity to slip onboard, sight unseen. I crept past the lone sentry who kept dozing off, climbed into the lifeboat, and dropped it into the water below. I had to laugh at the look on the man's face as he peered over the stern to see an empty boat drifting away.

"It is far too early in the season to be soaking wet and naked," I said as Goldy was climbing into the boat.

He tossed me my dry clothes and said, "I think it would be best if we steer to the western side of the island away from the port of Lewistown. There is a conclave of natives near the western shore, we will be safe there."

"You mean, you will be safe there, I am sure they would not welcome a phantom into their village."

"Then I suggest you try to stay out of sight and keep the talking to a minimum."

I could not see his grin in the darkness, but I knew it was there just the same. We rowed the boat around the western point of the island, disembarked and then shoved the boat back out into open water. It would be found somewhere far south of the encampment and would not inadvertently make the natives suspects.

I hung back in the forest while Goldy made his introductions. It was obvious by the way they received him that he knew a couple of them, and they were friends. He made certain to leave a blanket out by the fire before he retired into one of the small huts with a woman who appeared to be quite familiar with his company. My mind was racing around in too many circles to be able to sleep so I scavenged around the fire for something to nibble on and took a spot on a log. I was shivering against the cold breeze blowing of the still icy lake but did not want to risk covering up with the blanket lest someone see a blanket warming itself by the fire and stone it to death.

I watched the beach at Minis Gitigaan as it glowed with fire light. By now I was certain the sailors were aware their beaching was no accident and would be searching for the culprits. I hoped they would just shrug it off as they had not been robbed nor looted save for a missing lifeboat. The captain would surely blame the sailor on watch for the loss of the boat and the sailor surely would not put the blame on a ghostly intruder. I was startled by a noise behind me and saw that a young boy had come out of a hut and took a seat on the log next to me. I could tell that he had been crying.

"Are you a spirit or a demon?" he asked.

I took a moment to gather my thoughts before answering, "I am neither. How did you know I was here?"

"Your breath," he said, pointing to a plume jetting from where my mouth should be. "I didn't think you could be a spirit because they do not need to breathe. But I think demons might have to," he observed, wrinkling his face as he pondered my origins.

"I am not a demon, at least not anymore."

"Then what are you?"

"I am a man I suppose. Like you, but much older. My name is Elijah, what is yours?"

He looked at where he assumed I was for several moments before responding. "Elisha."

"Why are you out here alone, Elisha?"

"I could not sleep."

I went and grabbed the blanket which was cozy warm from the fire and draped it over the two of us. This young boy jerked away, and I thought I had startled him.

"I apologize, I sometimes forget that people cannot see me."

"I saw you, I might be young, but I do know that blankets cannot float through the air."

I reached over and lifted the back of the boy's shirt, there were thick red welts going in every direction. The angry marks oozed with his bodily fluids and glistened in the moonlight. I found myself suddenly enraged.

"What in the hell happened to you?"

"Nothing. I was punished. I deserved it."

"No one deserves a flogging like that, and especially not a child. Who did this to you?"

"Some of the king's men. He told them to do it."

"Why on earth would he do that? What could you have possibly done that warranted this?" I said, so incensed that spittle was flying from my mouth.

"I used some of our tithe money to buy some apples for the horses and a little doll for my baby sister."

"Tithe money?"

"Money my mom pays to the kingdom. I was delivering it for her when I saw the doll in the king's store. I did not think they would notice a few missing coins but when I got to the church office the man there counted it. When it was short, he immediately summoned the king."

"Why does your mom have to pay the kingdom?"

"Everyone has to pay the kingdom, it is our duty. King Lewis says so every time we go to church."

"What does your father have to say about this?" I asked.

"My father is dead."

"I'm so sorry, what happened?"

"He was a fisherman, people say he drowned. But I know better."

"Why do you say that?"

"Because he was the best swimmer on the island. He would swim to Minis Gitigaan and back every morning before breakfast. Some of the king's people were angry that my father caught so many fish when they would catch but a few."

I must have been talking loud enough to wake the boy's mother who came out to the fire with Goldy in tow. I could see by the grin spreading across his face that the situation of her not being able to see me amused him to no end. Perhaps to unfoul my present mood I played along. I put a gentle hand on her shoulder and whispered in her ear which I expected to startle her, but she did not startle in the least.

"Nice to meet you, Shadowman," she said with a smile. "I am Jewel. It is not my birth name, but Robert cannot pronounce my real name properly and it sounds like something really bad when he says it."

"How . . . "

"I could see your breath when you were talking to my son who I know is not crazy enough to be sitting out under the moonlight talking to himself. At least not yet. And he gave me a little warning," she said with a nod of her long, dark, raven hair at Goldy.

"You do not seem to be very alarmed, given the current circumstances," I said.

"What is there to be alarmed about? You just spent an entire winter cooped up with this heathen and there's not one single bite mark on him," she replied.

We spent the next hour talking about nothing that I could recall. Even before dawn lit its lamp on the small fishing village of about fifty people, most of the natives had disappeared in small boats out on the lake where they lit pine tar torches affixed to the front of their canoes. The firelight attracted fish to the canoes where men would then spear them. Some of them even employed nets with stones attached to drag whitefish up from the depths. I was the last one left awake and listened to the calming sounds of *sploosh* each time a net was tossed. I felt an unfamiliar peace settling in over me and I slept.

Goldy and I spent the next week recuperating from our long winter on Minis Gitigaan during which Jewel explained the history of the island and the arrival of the *king* several years earlier.

"He was not a bad man when the first few of them arrived. But the more of his people came the more influential he became. Eventually the more brazen he became as well," Jewel said as she served us a breakfast of fried eggs and flatbread.

Between mouthfuls and without warning I asked, "So why was the boy flogged? Seems a severe punishment for a slight crime," I asked.

"For the same reason, my husband was killed, the king wants me for his wife. He first tried to buy me from my husband with land and when he refused, he went missing out on the lake. I have no proof, but I know what happened. Some months later the king came to me with his proposition and I refused. I told him I was still mourning the loss of my husband."

"He beat your boy because you will not lay with him?"

"He also bought our land from a corrupt tribal elder and then charged me a rent he knew I could not afford. When I fell behind, he proposed a ludicrous arrangement. This was about the time I had the pleasure of making acquaintance with Mister Robert Marigold here and he paid my back rents and purchased this land. I declined the king's offer once more and moved here with Robert."

"I never pegged you for a softy, but I am getting a sense of why he dislikes you enough to kill you." I smiled at Goldy.

"It was a little more involved than my Jewel tells. I was one of Kington's first followers many years ago in the state of Wisconsin. Once we got here things started to change and I left the congregation which displeased my one-time friend. He took it as a personal affront, and I suppose it was. He did a few things to retaliate which rubbed my nerves raw and when I met Jewel, I saw a chance to get a little retribution. Besides, look at her, she is beautiful, kind and makes great eggs. So, I killed two birds with one stone."

"So that was the end of it? From what you have told me, this Lewis fellow does not seem to take kindly to the word no, or to being bested."

"No, as you can see from what he did to Elisha it is far from over. You and I are going to settle it once and for all, that is, if you are still in agreement," Robert said.

"I agree more than ever now. This man needs to pay for what he did to Marie, the boy, his father and only God knows what other crimes he is responsible for."

Our discussion was interrupted by a little one's wailing coming from their small hut. Jewel got up from the fire and returned a few moments later with a small child. She appeared to be about four years old, but sickly and frail. I recoiled immediately when they had drawn close enough to me for me to taste the little one's darkness. There was such a blackness enveloping the child that it choked me.

"Is something wrong?" Jewel asked.

"I was just startled, that's all," I replied as I slid away from them.

Truth be told, the child was completely consumed with a vile darkness that was choking off my airways and constricting my chest. And although Jewel could not see me, I knew she had sensed my recoil. The child was flailing and screaming so violently that her mother could barely hang on to her. And then she looked up at me and stopped. She reached a delicate hand over and touched my face with such a tenderness it welled up tears in my eyes. I had no understanding of how she knew I was there. Could she see me? Or did she just sense my presence. And then she smiled.

A calm, genuinely happy look washed over Jewel's face and she waved a dismissive hand. Goldy took his cue, gathered up the boy and disappeared down toward the lakeshore. The child reached her little arms out to me and I collected her up into my arms. The sensation rushing through me was nothing short of repulsion, and yet, I was bathed in an essence from this child that was masked by the shroud of darkness. For the life of me, I could not understand this gift, this curse that had been bestowed upon me. Once a man with no emotion, now even the slightest of breezes set me into tears.

"So, it is true about you?" Jewel asked.

"I am afraid I do not understand what it is you are asking."

"Goldy told me about the old woman who was shot by King Lewis."

"Marie," I said.

"Yes. I knew her, well, I had met her once or twice before."

"How?"

"She would pass through here on her way to Minis Gitigaan every so often with a small child. I always found something sort of magical about her. There was more than met the eye, I am certain."

"Yes, there definitely was more to her than one could see."

"She told me tales about a man who could turn into a shadow. About a man who was once as dark as the night but was dark no longer. She said he was a savior of lost souls."

"She was also very skilled at telling tall tales."

"She said you were on Minis Gitigaan but that you were sleeping. I found it very odd because she told of meeting you when she was but a girl and yet she was an old woman. That would mean you should be dead, not sleeping."

I had wrapped myself in a blanket somewhat for modesty's sake but also to keep the child warm and so Jewel wasn't gazing upon nothingness. The child stared up into my eyes and caressed my face with her tender touch. Little tear drops formed in the corners of her eyes and my heart felt as though it were in the grasp of a giant beast. I tried to give the child back to her mother, but she thrashed about and started screaming the same word over and over again. She did not calm down until I resigned to keep her on my lap.

"What was it that she was saying?" I asked.

With tears in her eyes Jewel answered, "She said please, please release me. She has not spoken a word since she was born, I did not think she knew how."

Chapter Fifty-Four

I spent two days wandering the forest around the encampment with escape at the forefront of my mind. Every time I put the child down she would scream and wail as if in excruciating pain. Even out here, away from everyone I could still hear her cries echoing in my brain. And I could still see the pained look in her mother's eyes who loved the child dearly but also wanted to end her suffering which tore at my heart with talons of remorse.

I was staring out at the open blue water when I heard someone coming up behind me. It took every ounce of restraint to keep from darting off into the woods like a madman.

"How long are you planning on staying out here by yourself?" Goldy asked.

"How did you know I was here?"

"I've learned how to read the tell-tale signs. You still leave footprints, disturbed leaves, and the like. Takes a little more effort, but I can find you when I want to."

"That's comforting to know. Did you come all this way for anything in particular or just to say good morning?"

"I see someone got a good night's sleep last night," Goldy said.

"Sorry, but there is nothing to be cheerful about," I said.

"Elijah, you are wrong about that. You have been given a gift, you just need to realize just how precious of a gift it is," Jewel said as she came up behind me. I felt her warm breath against my skin, and it made me shudder.

"I have looked at my life in every imaginable way and the one thing I see for certain, this is not a gift."

"Ah, but it is. And you must embrace it. Do you believe in God?" she asked.

"Which God? I have heard of so many."

"There is only one God, he is called many things by many people, but he is one in the same."

"If this God is so great then why does he allow so much killing in his name?"

"Because he gave us the freewill to stop it if we so choose. At some point goodness must triumph over evil and when it does, evil will be cleansed from this earth."

"And you honestly believe this? It has always been my experience that only the strong survive."

"It is said the meek shall inherit the Earth. It takes more strength and perseverance to walk the narrow path of light than it does to run the wide road of darkness."

"To the victors go the spoils."

"And the meek will be the victors when the war is over."

"What is this war that you speak of?"

"Between good and evil, heaven and hell of course."

"Are you telling me that you subscribe to the white man's bible?"

"The parts, which are many, that mirror my own traditions and beliefs, yes. It is just a book after all, but a book of thoughts and ideas that do no harm. And it is not the white man's Bible, only the white man's translation. The Bible was written for all mankind."

"There is no war between the devil and God, there is no heaven or hell, we are just stuck on this god forsaken chunk of dirt. Some of us much longer than others."

"Elijah, do you truly believe that after all you have witnessed?"

"Absolutely. I have begun to think none of this is real and I am completely insane."

"Am I to believe that I am just imagining that while you are solid to the touch, I cannot see you with my eyes?"

"Maybe you're insane too. Or you are a product of my own insanity."

"Then is the whole of the world insane?"

"I believe the whole of my world is incredulous at the very least."

I tried to ignore her words and retreat back into myself. I wanted nothing more than to cease to exist and it was the only thing that I was certain would not happen. This sun was nearing its apex for the day and its warmth felt good on my transparent skin.

"What is wrong with my daughter?" Jewel asked, startling me back from my withdrawal.

"Why do you ask me that?"

"I ask you because I know you possess a gift. A sight that can read a person's soul."

I cursed the long, cold winter spent on the island with Goldy with nothing to do but talk. I revealed far too much to the man but once I started to relate my tall tale, I felt a weight being lifted and could not stop which I was now regretting.

"She is black inside, almost completely black."

"Her soul?" she asked, choking back her tears.

"No, I don't think so. But I do not know. Usually when I see that kind of blackness it is permeated with an evil I can taste. I do not taste that with her. But I can sense there is a light behind the blackness."

"What does that even mean?"

"I do not know. I do not know if the blackness is a sickness growing within her or if her soul has been corrupted somehow. I just do not know."

"Is that why she cries all the time? Is she in pain? Does she have a sickness that is eating her alive?"

Tears were streaming down my face. "Jewel, I wish I knew. I would tell you if I knew. I just know what I see and what I feel."

"I should have listened to Marie years ago."

"Marie? What does she have to do with your daughter?"

"Marie would stop here on her travels to Minis Gitigaan. She would always have a sickly child with her. She was such a lonely creature, she would go to the island and wait for the child to die before returning. She said there was no one but her to give the child a proper burial and that she did not want them to die alone."

"But what does that have to do with your daughter?"

"I think she saw the same thing you saw. She kept asking if she could take her to the island, but I refused. She never pressed me, only asked. I see now that I was wrong to refuse."

"A mother giving up a child is a near impossible task."

"But I was refusing for myself, not for my baby's sake. I see the way she is with you. She knows what you can do for her doesn't she?"

"I think she understands, yes."

"Then you must do it."

"Do what?"

"Take her to the island and free her from her sickness."

"I cannot heal her."

"I know that. But you can release her and that is what she wants."

"Release her? I have no power to release her from her illness. I am not a doctor nor a shaman."

"If it were that simple, I would agree with you, bundle her up and take her to Chicago or New York where we might find a doctor that could help her."

"Why isn't it that simple?"

"Because she is not ill with any sickness known to man. She has an evil growing inside of her."

"Are you insane? The child is merely sick."

"Are you merely sick?"

"What kind of a question is that?" I said, becoming quite agitated with the woman's incessant questioning.

"After everything that has happened to you why would you not believe that she could be filled with an evil spirit? You have been given a gift to seek out this evil and destroy it."

"No, I have been cursed with an affliction. I will entertain you long enough to ask, how did such a thing happen that your daughter became cursed?"

"She did not become cursed, she was born with it already inside of her. I knew from the very first day I held her."

"How did such a thing transpire?" I asked, not wanting to hear her answer because as much as I wanted to dismiss her rant as the ravings of a lunatic, I did not want to know the truth.

Jewel got noticeably quiet and walked away from me. I watched her walk down the beach, her feet in the cold water. Guilt tugged at me. I had no cause or right to be so harsh with her just because I was frustrated with my own situation. She picked up a few stones from the waterline and skipped them across the almost glassy surface. The *splish, splish, splish,* of the stones was soothing to my mind, it seemed to bring order to the chaos. And my life was nothing if not chaos.

"You have to do this. Not for Jewel and not for me, but for the child," Goldy said, emerging from the trees to hand me a fresh cup of hot coffee. I had to chuckle as he was handing it to no one, I was ten feet away. Eventually he found my hand.

"Do you understand what you are asking me to do?" I said, the laughter quickly disappearing from my voice.

"Yes, we do, but it has to be done," Jewel said as she slid up and put her arm around Goldy's waist. "She becomes less and less of her and more of the vileness every day. Even more so since you came here. I think it senses who you are."

"It?"

"The thing residing inside of my child is not my daughter."

"For the sake of argument, are you insinuating that your daughter has been possessed by a demon of sorts?"

"I am not insinuating anything, I am stating facts."

"How did she come to be possessed by this demon?"

"Because I allowed it to happen."

"How could this possible be your fault?"

Tears flowed down her cheeks. "Because I allowed myself to be filled with a demon's seed."

"Do you realize how outlandish all of this sounds?" I asked.

Goldy gripped my bicep in his meaty hand, gave it a shake and said, "Might I remind you that you are near invisible and cannot die? How outlandish is that? Would it seem a lot less outlandish if I were to tell you the culprit in all of this is familiar to the both of you?"

His words sent my mind racing. I knew exactly what he was implying, yet I had never given any thought to the fact that I may not be alone in the misery spread by that little demon hag. After all, she was more than willing to hurt as many innocent souls as it took to achieve her goals. They were just means to an end.

"Are you implying that Wenonah had something to do with your child's illness? That is absurd."

"Is that what you called her?"

"That is what she called herself," I replied.

"Do you know what that name means in my language?" Jewel asked.

"Please, enlighten me."

"It means first-born daughter."

"She was the first child born of her parents that is no great revelation."

"It is if you take it in more literal sense. What if she were the first-born female ever born of this earth?"

"You already know my feelings on religion, and I will say I do not believe in the good book or the stories told within its pages. But even the Bible says the first-born woman was a daughter of Adam and Eve."

"Born of Eve, yes. The Bible does in fact say that Eve is the mother of all living. But it never says that Adam was the father of all living."

"What are you getting at?" I asked, casting her a raised eyebrow, a suspicious glance that she could not even see.

"What if the serpent was the father of the first-born female child?"

"Please do not ever repeat that anywhere the king or his men might overhear as he will surely have you flogged for blasphemy," Goldy said, genuinely nervous.

"I am only pointing out what the scriptures actually say, and moreover, do not say. It has always struck me odd that in the Bible Cain, the first-born son, is able to take a wife before the birth of any woman is mentioned."

"I do not know the Bible well enough to argue its nuances. Is there a specific point you are trying to make?"

"Maybe without any realization Adam and Eve created the chaos that is the world today with a seemingly innocent act. There was not the slightest bit of knowledge of evil until they partook of the forbidden fruit. And once that act was committed evil was imparted upon the world forever more."

"Are you trying to say there would be no murder, no wars and no Wenona without that first bite of the apple?" I asked.

"Just that there may be two sides to that story, the side of Yahweh that we all know and a side we have never heard; Satan's side. Perhaps it was not an apple, not even a piece of fruit at all, but something far more sinister. Perchance the fruit mentioned in the Bible was merely a metaphor for evil."

"Is it your contention that evil did not exist until they ate of the fruit?"

"No, evil existed, but their knowledge of it was nonexistent therefore it could not harm them until they were made aware its presence."

"My time with Kingston Lewis afforded me access to his library which was filled with religious texts and each one of them, including his newly found religion, tell the story of our creation and ultimate fall from grace," Goldy said.

"That is a simple matter of the Bible parable being told first and other religions just mimicked it."

"If that were true, then at least one of those religions would have altered the story to suit their needs but none have," Jewel said.

"In the beginning there was both God and Satan, one good, the other evil?" I asked.

"That is my theory, yes. God created mankind and Satan corrupted it."

"If God is the creator of all beings, did he create evil as well? And if so, why?"

"You are asking me questions only God can answer. Are you one to believe in coincidence, fate, and kismet, whatever you wish to call it?"

"Not much, no."

"Then how would you categorize my having met Marie after I birthed a sickly child, a pregnancy which happened after I met your Wenonah and that all four of us now have one another in common?"

"Is this one big chess match and we, mankind, are the pawns?" I asked.

"Some of us are pawns, others are knights and bishops. And then there are those who are kings, like yourself. Pieces that can win or lose the game," Jewel said.

I thought about what she was saying, and it posed the question to my own mind, was my encountering the descendent of Robert Marigold just a coincidence or was it all part of some master story being written as I lived it?

"You said you met the same Wenonah who did this to me?"

"I can only imagine her being one in the same. She was just as you described her to me, although, instead of two seemingly dead Indian braves with her she had a ghostly pale Frenchman, in uniform, and a little blind Mohawk boy."

My heart froze. "Where did you see her?"

"Here on the island, she came over with the king several years ago. Before he was the king of course."

"And she had a Frenchman with her? A solider?"

"Yes."

"When was this?"

"Maybe five years now."

Fear spread through me like a wildfire on the prairie. But why? Why should I even fear that incessant creature? She could not kill me, she could not even harm me herself by her own admissions. And then my mind wandered to all the things I knew her capable of, yet it was the unknown that frightened me even more. I knew it was time that I must abandon my stubbornness and look at things in a more celestial light. Jewel was right, there was more at work here than sheer coincidence or circumstance. If I were part of some scheme, then maybe these people were all just pieces in the puzzle.

"Do you think the king is as I am? Has she found another to do her bidding?"

"No, I do not believe so. There was a time when I spent as much time with him as I have with you and he never took on the appearance, or lack of, that you do," Goldy said.

"But how long ago was that? She may have bewitched him in the time since you last saw him."

"No, I do not think she can. I recall you telling me that according to her only one of you could exist at one time. Maybe this is why you are so important to her, maybe she cannot create another until she destroys you."

"That is comforting," I replied.

Wordlessly we made our way back around the point to the camp. The sweet smell of cedar hung in the crisp morning air as we crunched on shells beneath our feet. I found myself wanting to be back on that island alone for all eternity, it was so much more appealing than the road that lie ahead of me. When we got within a few hundred feet of the camp the child's cries met my ears. She was wailing at the top of her lungs. He brother eagerly awaited our arrival, needing a respite from his sister no doubt. It would surely drive me insane within minutes.

"Here, I made you something," he said, handing me what appeared to be a bundle of leaves and vines.

"What is it?" I asked after turning it over in my hands several times.

"It is a mask, so we can see you. Put it on and I will tie it for you."

I slipped the leaves up onto my face after checking to make sure he was not tricking me with poison ivy or the like. I knelt so he could reach the vines and tie them behind my head. A few adjustments later and I could see and breathe just fine. I was now a creature from the forest.

I peered in on the little one and instead of being frightened by my mask her spirits picked up and she let loose a giggle. But then she frowned and reached to tug my mask off. As soon as it fell away from my face she smiled, reached her tiny fingers up and delicately caressed my cheek. This child could somehow see me.

"You see, you are the only person who can calm her because she knows what you can do for her," Jewel said from behind me.

"You mean do to her."

"No, I mean for her. You will be freeing her from her agony."

"How can you so calmly ask me to do this to your child?"

"I am not calm; I am a nest of angry vipers inside. Believe me, I have struggled with this for far too long I might add," Jewel said, wiping a tear from her eye. "You need to do this before I change my mind. It is said that love is as strong as death, I believe it to be even stronger."

I picked the child up and was immediately assaulted by the blackness growing within her. It was angry with me, fighting with me. The malevolence within her knew I could destroy it. She kicked and writhed in pain and yet, she still smiled up at me. She knew I could destroy it as well.

Chapter Fifty-Five

Jewel spent a solid three hours saying her goodbyes to her precious child during which my heart seized in my chest and I vomited multiple times. I came ever close to calling off our arrangement several times but each time the thought even flitted into my mind the child would burst into raucous fits of sobbing. Goldy put Jewel to bed and then brought the child to me and set her in the canoe. He shoved us off into the night, his cheeks glistened with tears in the flickering torchlight.

My arm was still not in the greatest of shape and took two more paddle strokes with the bad arm to compensate. The child lay in my feet staring up at me with the most peaceful, contented look drawn upon her face. But every so often I would see a flash, like the fire and brimstone I had seen in Wenonah's eyes blazing at me from the child's innocent orbs. If the goodness in her was aware of my motives so, then was the evil as well.

There was not a single cloud in the sky, so I gazed up at the stars until I found the Big Dipper. From there I followed the stars until I located Leo, my birthright sign. I felt more like a whimpering cat than I did a majestic lion at the moment. Where was the nobility in murdering an innocent child?

"But are you truly an innocent child? Is it as simple as that?" I asked the big brown orbs staring back up at me.

She cocked her head to the side at my words as if she understood them. And maybe she did. She was a toddler after all and not an infant. That thought invaded me like an army. Did this child know exactly what I was going to do to her? Was she aware that I was about to be her killer and not her savior? She smiled and yet something in her eyes glowed an even angrier red.

I dug deep and hard into the water to gain some momentum and then set the paddle down to rest for a moment. I unwrapped a small cloth that had pieces of sweet fried bread. I broke off a piece for me and smaller one for the child. She tried to sit upright but every time she did her body was wracked with pain. I wondered what infirmity ailed this poor thing and did it have a name. Or was it merely the evil trapped within her that caused her such discomfort that she could not even sit upright. She sucked crumbs of cornbread from my fingertips and smiled. What if I could rid her of this evil?

"I truly wish I could rid you of the monster lurking inside of you. I wish no harm had to come to you, but this is the only path I know to take."

She reached her little arms up to me, so I lifted her into my arms and hugged her. I could feel her tiny heart beating against my chest. What nature of evil could possibly exist that would force a man to slay a child?

Was this another of Wenonah's tricks? Was she using this child to lure me back into the depths of her depravity? Were there more children with this malady? I had so many more questions than I had answers so I cleared my mind as best as I could and focused on getting us to Minis Gitigaan safely.

I felt a certain reverence surround us once we reached the outskirts of the burial grounds. It seemed to be brighter here, the air crisper and my heart oddly felt more at peace.

The very instant we stepped into the hallowed grounds of the cemetery I was blasted with a surge of dark energy emanating from the child. She began to struggle with me, trying to claw her way out of my arms. Exasperated, I set the child down and stormed away from her. At that moment I had every intention of just leaving the child there on the ground and letting nature take its course. But then Marie's infectious laughter drown out the echoes of the child's screams and I knew I must see this through.

I turned to look at the child and she was smiling at me, reaching her arms for me out of love, yet her eyes screamed anger and hatred. The conflict thundering through that poor child's body was putting her through hell. Without another thought I took three long strides and jerked her up from the ground.

A warmth surrounded me as if there were a dozen hands on my shoulders, there to give me strength. The child's eyes flashed a beacon of understanding as they pleaded for me to finish what I had set into motion. Again, her tiny fingers wiped the tears from my eyes as I clamped down tighter and tighter on her throat.

Suddenly the clear, star filled sky let loose a warm, gentle rain and I felt the ebbing of the darkness within her begin to recede. A small chuff of air passed her lips and her fingers slid slowly down my cheek. My chest heaved from my sobbing as I laid her down in a bed I had prepared. I relaxed my grip on her throat and kissed her tiny, still warm lips.

A shriek unlike anything I have ever heard before escaped her lips with a voracity that caused me to cover my ears. A surge of blackness forced me to my knees, and I swooned over onto my side. With this she halted her retreat and went on the attack. She scampered across the decaying leaves and onto my chest where she gnashed her teeth at me in anger. Her eyes spit hatred at me as she dug her little fingernails into my tender flesh.

There was a brief respite from her attack, and it was her adoring eyes that caught mine. In the language I had first heard her speak she said, "Please. Release me. Send me home."

Without giving myself any time to think about it, I sat up, spun her around and applied pressure to the top of her head until I felt her little neck snap. She went limp in my arms and I in turn went limp to the ground. A roar began to swell in my ears until it reached a deafening crescendo as her life force surged through me. I was dazed and incoherent as both the vile blackness and her sweetness entered me and tried to take hold. I could smell and taste the anger as it swarmed my every cell. It was tempting, powerful and satiating. I wanted to consume it as it was consuming me.

"Do not fall victim to her again," I heard Marie's voice on the wind.

I looked and saw her coming toward me, floating gracefully across the pine needle carpet. Her smile was as infectious as the day I met her. I fought back against the wickedness trying to infiltrate my persona and allowed the child's virtuous spirit to take hold in my barren soul. Immediately I felt myself swelling to the point I thought I would burst. Tears flowed from my eyes as I vomited the vile blackness onto the soil. I am not sure if what I saw was real, but I swear I saw the abomination scurry off into the forest as if trying to escape the hallowed ground beneath us. And then I succumbed to sleep.

When I awakened the sun was beating down upon my face and I found myself naked on Minis Gitigaan. I would not have felt self-conscious except for two facts, I was completely visible, and Marie was standing over me gazing down at me with the pretty hazel eyes I had left in her spirit house.

Quickly covering myself with the woven leaf mask I said, "I did not think you were like me."

"I am not like you," she responded.

"But you did not die so you too are immortal."

"No Elijah, I am as dead as dead can be."

"But I can see you just as plain as day."

"Yes, you can, but this is not me. Not my physical form anyway. I roam this island as a caretaker of the spirits thanks to you."

"But then why can I see you if you are but a ghost?" I asked.

"I am not a ghost; I am much more than that. But you can see me merely because you want to. Your mind's eye has painted you a picture and that is what you see."

I felt a leaden weight on my heart. I had somehow condemned this poor woman to spend eternity walking alone on this island.

"I am not alone, Elijah. I have many, many souls to keep me company. In fact, I have one more precious soul who you have delivered to me. Do not be saddened, you have brought me more joy than my life ever did."

"I must be dreaming or having a nightmare."

Her laugh echoed across the cemetery. "I would slap you if I could. You are not dreaming silly man. If you are modest you can find some clothes to wear in one of the houses."

"There are some in the cabin, we can go there."

"No, we cannot. I cannot leave this hallowed ground."

"Then let me run back to the canoe. For once I was prepared for this and brought a change of clothes."

She nodded and I took off down the trail. I returned clothed and feeling much less vulnerable to her gaze.

"How do you feel Elijah?"

"I am a little hungry, but that will pass."

"I was referring to your soul."

"I feel different. This was different than with the child you brought to the island."

"They will each be different in their own little ways. But each will make you stronger."

"Each? You speak as if this were an ongoing thing. It is not," I said.

"Oh, but it is. You have found the reason for your curse as you call it. It is not a curse, but a cure, a blessing."

"Murdering children is a blessing? I do not think I can agree with you on that point."

"It is a gift, Elijah. And you did not murder that child, you freed her. She was murdered a long time ago by the demon who has been spreading its seed across the land. I have learned so much in such a short amount of time. I truly do pity you, though I have been assured I should not."

"What are you talking about?"

"When I shed my earthly chains, the knowledge, the answers I was gifted with were beyond my comprehension. All the questions I asked throughout my life have been answered with so many other answers to things I never even so much as pondered. I am saddened that you will never feel that satisfaction and joy."

"I have never had a lot of questions, until now that is."

"You have to continue your vocation."

"What is this vocation you speak of?"

"There are many souls you must save."

"I should just wander around killing children until I find one riddled with evil and bring them back here?"

"No, you will know where they are, and they will find you. As for bringing them back here, that is not necessary. The deed may be accomplished anywhere. However, if you wish to save the child's soul as well, I suggest hallowed ground such as this place."

"This is insane."

"Elijah, you still fight it. I am here to tell you that you must embrace this side of your affliction. Before they are certain of your true intentions, they will not bestow their gifts upon you."

"Who are they?"

"I do not know. Angels maybe? Gods? When they speak to me, I do not even hear their voices. Thoughts just form in my head and the knowledge is suddenly there."

"If you are not as I am, and you are not a ghost, this must all be a dream."

All at once Marie disappeared and a swirling mass of leaves, dead pine needles and sand formed into a column. She had turned herself into a ghostly cyclone. Then as suddenly as the tornado appeared it blew apart into millions of particles. I glanced about over each shoulder and then behind me, she was gone.

I staggered to my feet, gathered up the child's corpse and ambled over to the pre-dug grave I had prepared earlier in the evening. With each step I felt a tickle at the back of my neck, and then warm puffs of air causing my hair to stand on end. And then I smelled her unmistakable scent. I buried the child and marked her grave the best I could with pieces of bark and her blanket so Jewel would be able to find it if she wished. More puffs of air followed by a pinch.

"You can quit playing."

"But it is such fun."

I tried to ignore her taunts, tickles, and pokes as I heated water for coffee over a small fire. I had to smile, she acted more like a younger sibling than she did a dead, old woman.

"I will let you get away with that one," she said.

"You can read my mind too I see."

"Not really. I sense your thoughts and the emotion, not really the literal words. I can also sense the confusion that is tearing at your brain. I have another trick I have learned since you left me here all alone," she said.

I was about to protest the fact that I did not leave her there alone when I was catapulted from one plane of existence into another. I wandered down a path which led to the water. Beside me was a tall, lanky man with a flaming red beard, the king. To the left of me was a diminutive woman flanked by a French army officer. I quickly understood that I was not me. I was not seeing this scene unfold through my eyes but through another's.

Even in this ethereal dream I sensed the darkness surrounding Kingston Lewis. I could sense it spreading to my beholder as well. He was influencing my host, though I could not hear what they were saying. The vision continued as they boarded a vessel and headed out into the open water finally arriving at their destination, the island.

My heart turned to ice when Wenonah turned her head and gazed directly into my eyes, not the eyes of my host, but my eyes. She was somehow watching me within this vision of her.

"What was that all about?" I asked, tearing myself away from Marie's trickery.

"I am trying to show you how this all came to pass and why you must continue your quest to rid this world of her seeds and to destroy the King of Beaver Island."

For the next hour I drifted in and out of Marie's clutches. I watched as Wenonah manipulated this man into meeting Jewel and taking her for his wife. For some reason the seed was not planted with the son, but with the first-born daughter. I watched as Kingston Lewis became ever darker over the passage of time and under the guise of religion manipulated his followers into committing the most heinous of acts.

I watched in horror as he had men flogged because their wives would not dress the way he mandated. Women flogged because they refused his advances and rebuffed his marriage proposals. And children flogged for many reasons, none of which were appropriate. All of this in the name of God.

The scars on my back flamed in remembrance of my own encounter and dreadfulness of the cat-o-nine. No man, woman and especially not a child deserved to be put to the leathers, it was cruel and inhuman.

We were interrupted by the popping of distant gunfire. At first, I thought it was a hunting party but then a cacophonous boom echoed across the channel between the two islands.

"Was that a cannon?"

"Yes. The king will sometimes use his cannon to disperse crowds and settle the rabble. It is a small thing, but quite effective."

"Why would there be rabble rousers if they are his followers?"

"Not all are content as sheep. There were a lot of island locals who were displaced as the king and his followers took control of more and more land. He will go after the woman soon."

"Which woman? Jewel?"

"Yes. He has coveted her for many years."

"That I will not allow."

I stood and gathered my things. I felt Marie's presence until I stepped outside of the hallowed ground of the cemetery. I took a step back inside and felt her warmth caressing my face.

"Remember, you cannot kill him yourself or you will become her tool of evil once more which is precisely what she wants."

Chapter Fifty-Six

I decided it best to wait until nightfall to make my way back to Beaver Island. I was not sure if the king knew about me or if he was aware, how much did he know so I felt the cover of darkness was my safest option. As I slowly paddled toward the northwest edge of the island, I felt this newly collected energy surging through me. It was so much more exhilarating than when I had consumed the dark souls in the first days of my curse. A certain warmth fell in all around me like a cocoon and I caught myself smiling for no apparent reason on more than one occasion.

The pangs of guilt were less intense and subsided within a few hours. While I still felt remorse for killing the child there was a certain solace that came with it as well. Her very essence circulated throughout my body and made it clear that I did not inflict that poor child with the illness that haunted her, but I did release her from it.

I also felt a piece of Marie within me as well even though it was not I who had ended her life. For the first time in my life I genuinely believed there was something beyond death that far surpassed the stories we had been told since childhood. But this newfound perspective also left me feeling hollow. Marie was right to pity me as I would never be able to bask in the glory of the promised afterlife.

I left the canoe about a half mile south of the encampment and made my way back through the thick tangle of forest. Despite my prudence I stumbled into the camp like a rampaging bull. There was no fire, no torches, nothing to indicate life. I moved through the shadows from tent to tent and found no one. Not only were Jewel, Goldy and the Elisha gone, but everyone in the small village were also gone.

I grabbed my tomahawks, threw on a pair of moccasins that were much too small for me and started back into the forest. Within a mile I came to the shores of a large body of water. At first, I thought I had accidentally made it to the east coast of the island but then was able to make out the flicker of torchlight across the water. I followed the vacant shoreline south for half a mile until I was able to smell the saltpeter from the canon's firing and left the open for the safety of the trees. I stayed within the shadows of the trees until a thick, boggy marsh stretched out in front of me with black water as far as my eye could see.

Ahead of me the edge of the forest was bathed in an orange glow and the murmur of voices began to catch my ear. I slowed my progress moving from tree to tree until I was close enough to see that there was a large bonfire in front of what appeared to be a very large church. King Red-Beard stood on the long porch of the building with two men flanking either side of him. All four were armed with long rifles.

The king began to address the crowd as men began throwing furniture onto the blazing fire. "Do not think you can just waltz back onto the island after betraying your congregation and go about life as nothing ever happened."

"We just went to visit family in Mackinac," I heard a woman's voice call over the roar of the fire.

"Does your woman speak for you too, Peter?"

"We were just visiting her ill mother."

"You mean her ill mother who also happens to be the mother of Chauncey O'Rourke who conspires against us?"

"There was no conspiring against you, not on our part. Please, we will leave the island, just let us take our belongings."

"These things here?" the king pointed to a pile of furniture, dishes, toys, and personal belongings piled up around the fire. "These things belong to me and I will do with them as I see fit. Do you not remember pledging all your worldly possessions to the church in exchange for your land? Land you gave up willingly when you left the island against my wishes."

"Please, show us some mercy," the man begged.

"I am going to show you more mercy than was recommended. I will not kill you this day. But you will be sent back to the mainland with a message," his voice boomed with authority.

He flicked his wrist and two men from the crowd took the man by the arms and dragged him up to the long porch. They flexed and tightened their grip on the man. The king flicked his wrist and added a head bob. A brutish man slipped a double-edged dagger from a scabbard on his chest and effortlessly sliced one of the man's ears off. He put the severed appendage in an ornate wooden box and set the box on the ground in front of the writhing man.

"You have one hour to vacate my lands, or I will have the same done to your entire family. I have been gracious enough to provide you with a rowboat and some rations for the trip. Give the O'Rourke's my best."

The man lingered but for thirty seconds or less which earned him a rap in the knee with a blackjack. Several of the men strong-armed him and his family down a dirt path and out of my view. I assumed that was the direction of the port. I studied the faces in the crowd and saw that there were more than just a few disapproving faces. I might have some allies I did not count on.

"Bring on the next order of business," the king bellowed.

There was a lot of movement behind them on the porch. Even from my distant vantage point I could hear boots scuffing against the hardwood floor and a ruckus from inside the structure. The door burst open and Goldy went spilling out onto the porch. One of the men unleased two brutal kicks to his ribcage before Kingston Lewis raised a hand to stop him from delivering a third. Jewel fought, kicked, and screamed as she was dragged out of the church by her hair.

"Careful, do not damage my bride on her wedding night," Lewis sneered.

"I will not marry you, you're a pig and a heathen," Jewel spat.

Her tirade earned Goldy another kick to the ribs which seemed to calm her down a bit. Tucked behind the men I could see Elisha with tears flowing down his reddened cheeks, it was obvious he had been roughly handled.

"As you all know, this woman's husband Joseph was a dear friend to me," the king started.

"You liar. You betrayed him and then killed him."

He waved a dismissive hand and one of the men holding her took off his belt and used it as a gag.

"As I was saying before I was so rudely interrupted. This woman's husband was a dear friend and he confided in me that should anything happen to him it was his wish that I assume the responsibility of getting her through the gates of Heaven. I made an oath to bear this responsibility and I take that oath very seriously. So, tonight, with your blessing, I will wed his widow and ensure she will fall under my family graces and be allowed into the here ever after."

"Why not marry her to one of the single lads?" I heard a voice cry from the back of the crowd.

"Mr. Wilcott, do you cower your head in shame or fear? If you have the courage to say something, have the courage to own up to your words. You know full well that I was commanded by the Lord to spread and grow his flock. However, if you wish to join the wedding party, there is always room for one more," he said, the loathing thick in his voice.

The man who had been brave enough to jeer from the shadows was not as audacious once the attention was thrust upon him. The crowd parted and the man disappeared into the night.

"Now, on to other business. Mr. Marigold, you have been accused of adultery, with my future wife of all people. What do you have to say for yourself?"

Goldy laughed long and hard before spitting a wad of phlegm into the ground at the man's feet. "Do you even see the irony in your own words?"

Again, the king motioned to the others with a dismissive wave. They dragged Goldy off the porch, down the dirt to a place in front of the fire. They dropped him to the dirt and moved out of my view for a few moments. When they returned, they were dragging a set of stocks which had crude wheels fastened to the bottom. They picked Robert up from the dirt, each man taking an arm until they had him shoved up against the wooden structure.

Once they had him locked into the device, they wheeled it into position near the steps of the church. I maneuvered myself in the shadows to get a better view and my movement must have caught Goldy's attention as he looked directly at me. He gave me a smile, apprehensive, but a smile none the less. I put a hand on my weapons and started out of the shadows, but he stopped me with a quick shake of his head.

I let my anger subside and soon knew he was right. The better part of valor was indeed discretion. I moved back into the shadows and prayed for the strength to see this through.

Kingston Lewis moved down off the porch and walked around the stocks until he was facing Robert Marigold. Being a very tall man, he had to stoop in order to be face to face with his adversary.

"Mister Marigold, do I have your blessing in this union?"

"It is not my blessing to give. Jewel and only Jewel can make that decision and I will stand by whatever decision she makes."

"But she listens to you. She will do as you say."

"You are mistaken there. The good Lord has provided her with the same freewill that he has bestowed upon all of us and she will exercise her own freewill in this matter. Like I said, it is her decision to make, not mine."

"Well then let us help her make that decision, shall we?" the king bellowed with his arms raised to the heavens in a show for the crowd.

Lewis walked back up to the porch, his heavy boots clunking against the loose wood planks. He reached a hand to Jewel and she recoiled as if he were brandishing a hot iron. He nodded and the men firmed up their grip on her and then grabbed something from a case sitting on the ground. My heart sunk the moment I recognized the dastardly tool. I breathed a small sigh of relief when I saw that it was a smaller version of a cat-o-nine referred to as a pussy. There were only three strands of knotted rope cord, slightly less painful and less deadly than a full cat-o-nine.

King Lewis had his men peel up the back of Goldy's shirt and hold it out of the way. I saw his arms muscles flex as he swung the abomination in a high arc, landing the lash across the man's shoulder blades. He winced, but nothing more. In anger he swung again, and again, four, five, six. On the tenth a female in the crowd cried out, "enough." Not once did Goldy make a sound.

"What have you to say now Mister Marigold?"

"Why are you asking me, I already told you, it is the lady's decision to make?"

He turned to face Jewel, "It is your decision. Shall we end this, or would you prefer to continue?"

Goldy yelled out, "Tell him to kiss your ass. You hit harder than he does."

This infuriated the king which was exacerbated even more by a wave of laughter from the crowd. He went back to the case and pulled out another whip, this time it was not only a cat, but a cat designed to tear flesh. There were several knots on each tail and tied to random knots were shiny objects. From where I stood, I could not see exactly what they were, but they were either metal or glass and were designed to not only inflict damage to a man's skin but cut deep into the meat.

The man's face was as red as his beard as he stomped back over to the stocks. A rain had started to fall and some of the lookers on retreated for the safety of cover. One of the men stepped in to help with Goldy but Lewis shoved him backward hard enough the man landed with a splash. The king, incensed and wanting more than just to hurt Goldy, ripped his pants off and dropped them to the mud. He did not even bother to take aim but swung the whip in a backhanded motion as he distanced himself. I readied my weapons and once again Robert stopped me with a glance.

I have never felt as helpless in all my life as I did at that moment. A man whom I had only known a short time had become a true friend and I was allowing him to be flogged. A second crack from the whip landed flush on the man's buttocks and a fine mist of blood covered the front of the king's shirt. This seemed to excite him, and he swung once more, only harder. Rivulets of blood cascaded down Goldy's legs and swirled with the muddy water at his feet. I readied myself to charge the man should his arm swing upward one more time.

"You stop that this very instant," a brazen woman said, lifting her powder blue, oval hoop skirt to move forward through the rain-soaked mud. Her face was lined with age, even more so in her angered state.

"You stay out of this Mrs. Brookens, this is none of your concern."

"It is my concern. My husband would not tolerate this behavior and you are well aware of that."

The king craned his neck around several times before saying, "I do not see Sheriff Brookens anywhere in the crowd so he must not be too upset with us."

"You know full well that he is ill and cannot be down here or he would put a stop to this just as sure as the sun will rise tomorrow."

"This is none of your concern," he said more forcefully.

"It very well is my concern. Not everyone in this community is part of *your* community. You may strut about here like you are royalty, but you are only self-proclaimed."

During this minor uproar I watched as a very large vessel slowly pulled up to the dock some hundred yards away more or less. The sailors all wore uniforms, so I assumed they were military of sorts. A few of them disbursed into the crowd and several more stayed behind to guard the vessel.

One of the women with Mrs. Brookens broke ranks and made her way up to where Goldy hung limp in the stocks. She gently pulled his pants back up and secured them. One of the king's men stormed toward her and gave her a shove. From the expression on his face it was much harder than he had intended, and she went careening backward into the mud.

"You take your hands of her," Mrs. Brookens ordered, drawing, and pointing a small revolver at the man.

A shot rang out and the Brookens woman fell to a slump next to the fallen woman. My back was turned to the porch, so I did not see who fired but from the king's reaction I knew it was not him. The crowd surged forward in anger and two of the sailors ran forward with rifles at the ready. Kingston Lewis revealed the depths of his depravity by snatching Elisha and pulling him toward him as a shield.

"This is not your concern; it is a local matter. Go back to your ship," he directed at the sailors while putting a revolver to the boy's head.

One of the sailors and a man from the crowd I assumed was a doctor went to the aid of Mrs. Brookens who was hurt badly but still alive. The other two sailors raised their guns and were ready to fire. Kingston Lewis had such a tight grip on the boy that all the thrashing about in the world was not going to set him free. Someone had freed Goldy from the stocks and he was now charging at the man cowering behind the child. Lewis fired a warning shot into the ground and quickly brought the revolver back up to rest against the lad's temple. Goldy stopped in his tracks and one of the men on the porch put a rifle butt into his breadbasket.

"Go get the captain," the sailor tending to the wounded woman ordered and one of the men ran off toward the ship.

I had endured more than I cared already and be damned, I was going to put a stop to this. I dashed from the shadows and ran toward the lanky coward. Jewel saw this and planted a foot into the rear of his knee causing him to buckle hard. The hand with the revolver flew up for just a moment but it was all I needed. I let my hawk fly which caught his wrist and pinned it to one of the porch columns with the spike end. I was readying the second tomahawk to lop off his head when something caught my eye from the shadows.

A sharp toothed Wenonah stood at the very fringes of the crowd with a sinister grin spread across her face. She was flanked on either side by Phillipe Gagnon and a young boy whom I did not recognize. I felt a surge of dark energy chewing its way toward me as Kingston Lewis discovered who had attacked him. I felt yet another surge of energy, but this came from deep within me, incapacitating me long enough to stop my swing. As I was frozen in time and unable to react the king reached for the boy and gripped him by a handful of hair. He was dragging the boy's face toward the blade end of my tomahawk.

It was as if time had slowed. I saw myself on the very edge of a precipice and being pulled in every direction. No matter the consequence I could not let the boy perish. I broke free of the bond and raised my weapon for another throw.

"Elijah, do not do this!" Goldy screamed out over the growing din of the melee.

Once more I found Wenonah's gaze. She was reveling in the chaos swirling about her. The death and mayhem were more than exhilarating, it was euphoric. I shot her a look of contempt and charged forward with my blade arcing through the air. I readied myself for an onslaught of vile blackness, but it never came.

Kington Lewis hung limp from the tomahawk embedded in his hand, my second weapon was buried harmlessly in the column above his head. I saw a jagged crimson line drawn across his throat and Jewel standing behind him with a bloody knife in her hand. The king's blood mixed with Goldy's as the rains pelted the earth seemingly to cleanse the earth.

One of the men raised a rifle at Jewel but before he could fire the weapon Goldy had swung the cat-o-nine and caught him square in the face. A maelstrom of pent up anger and frustration exploded all around us. Bullets had started to buzz about like angry bees as both sides regained their composure and squared off on one another.

"Come on, we have to get out of here," I said, grabbing the boy up from the porch.

The four of us ran toward the ship and blended into the crowd of others who had the same idea. Once most of the townsfolk were safely on board the ship began firing their cannons into the mob of the King's followers effectively disbursing the crowd. As the boat edged backward out of the harbor the smoke began to clear. A feeling of dread washed over me as the only thing left on the street was Wenonah with Gagnon standing next to her and the boy motionless at her feet. She stood stalwart in the rain staring back at me with a smile on her face but pure hatred in her eyes. Phillipe raised his rifle and fired once.

Port Oneida
Mid 1800's

Chapter Fifty-Seven

That all seemed so long ago, a lifetime in fact. The changes I have gone through both physically and mentally have been exhausting. My only desire was to leave all those memories behind and find some peace. Not only did my memories follow, they gave chase. I was stealing away from the island under the cover of a moonless night with my pilfered supplies when a sense of Déjà vu overwhelmed me. I looked back at the torchlight on the island and stepped back in time.

Never in a thousand lifetimes will I manage to forget the primal scream that erupted from deep inside Robert Marigold when Gagnon's bullet found Jewel's heart. It was all I could do to keep him from diving into the waters of Lake Michigan to go after her as she sank into the murky depths. With Gagnon's shot others began firing as well and we were forced to take cover. The king's followers began firing at the boat and the sailors fired back at the crowd. Through the sulfuric cloud of haze, I caught a wicked, wicked grin. She had somehow managed to grab Elisha in the chaotic maelstrom. She turned and the three of them simply faded away in the night.

I watched Goldy spin out of control after that and it was all my doing. In fact, I was so concerned with my own situation, my calling as it were, that I never even gave his grief much thought at all. I was too wrapped up in saving all the poor lost souls I could find. And Robert, he just followed me like a puppy eager to please his master.

Goldy and I had moved around the small towns near the lake at first, but it was fruitless. I felt compelled to move into more populated areas, so we made our way to the cities, Grand

Rapids first, then on to Detroit and eventually Toledo. I was so out of control by the time we got to Toledo that I had thrown caution to the wind which eventually drew the notice of the authorities. In retrospect, I wonder if I were truly saving lost souls or merely killing innocent children.

I made it back to the mainland shore and spent the next several hours ferrying my ill-gotten gains back to my camp. I was careful not to take too much of any one particular item and left the one-of-a-kind items alone. Even so, I carefully erased my tracks on the beach, dismantled the raft and carried it up the dunes where I burned it. While rearranging my small storeroom and storing my new cache of staples I ran across an old burlap sack and smiled. I fell prey to irony.

Inside that sack was enough gold to let me live like a king, a Beaver Island king anyway. And yet, there was no way I would be able to spend it without succumbing to the beast within me. I imagined the poor shopkeepers face as he watched a purse of gold float into his store and merchandise float out. Poor bastard would be ridiculed if he ever dared tell the tale.

The first couple of years, while still on the coast before moving east for Detroit I would make trips back and forth to Minis Gitigaan just as Marie had done before me. I was curious to see what had become of Beaver Island, so I stopped at the local tavern on my way back to enjoy a drink. I kept to myself and listened to the gossip. I was glad to hear that right after Goldy and I departed the townsfolk aided by mainlanders took the island back and drove the king's followers back across the waters to Green Bay and beyond.

It was on one of these nights I learned of an intriguing tale. Some of the townsmen were arguing about lost treasure. One of the men claimed he saw the king and a few of his followers sinking something into the bottom of Lake Geneserath. Although he never saw what it was, he swore he heard them talking about gold.

One night after partaking of too much rum I made my way out into the lake in a borrowed boat. I borrowed several lengths of rope as well. I tied knots at five-foot intervals and found the lake to be much deeper than I had anticipated. From the description overheard in the bar the point where the men had sunk the treasure was in about forty feet of water. Had I been sober I am most certain I would not have tied the anchor around my ankle and tossed it overboard.

Choosing the dead of night for this endeavor was not the most brilliant idea I had ever concocted. Not to mention I had no working knowledge of how my body would react to breathing water like a fish. The depths were murky at best and seeing my own hand in front of my face was a chore let alone finding anything on the bottom. I think I died a dozen times over that night each one worse than its predecessor. When the sun crested the horizon, I found myself regurgitating lake water by the buckets full. But I also found myself in possession of six burlap sacks weighing nearly one hundred pounds each filled with gold coin, jewelry, and other sparkling artifacts.

The coins had proven difficult to spend as they were minted by the king himself and held no real monetary value other than the gold. Robert located a man in Toledo that smelted it all down into small ingots, for a hefty price of course. So here I sat in the wilds of Michigan with tens of thousands of dollars in gold ingots and yet I was reduced to thievery. What an existence this has turned out to be.

The night was a restless one as I was repeatedly awakened by nightmares of drowning. Every time I bolted awake the dream was right there just out of my grasp, so I did not know the details. At first, I assumed I had brought bad memories to the surface but there was something off about them. I needed Goldy's camaraderie now more than ever. It was during a particularly troubling nightmare that I was finally able to discern why these dreams troubled me so. They were not my own.

That despicable creature had somehow condemned my only friend on the world to a fate worse than death. Talons clutched at my heart as the realization formed itself into reality in my mind. And then it began again.

Shadowman, Shadowman,
Just as he,
Shadowman, Shadowman,
You will never be free.

I gazed up at the Big Dipper and ascertained it was roughly two in the morning. My breath chugged forth into the cold night air like the steamship *Exodus* as it passed my lips. I started water to boil for coffee as I knew sleep would elude me for the remainder of the evening. As I watched steam rise from the kettle, I thought about her sing song words. Had I really heard them or was my imagination toying with me? I did not feel her omnipresent tug on my psyche, but I sensed she was close. Closer than I wanted her to be.

As for Goldy, I was convinced my visions of the poor bastard condemned to an unthinkable fate were more reality than fantasy. The pure evil that was Wenonah continued to find ways to haunt me to the very core of my existence. Sleep took me before the sun made even a hint of color on the landscape.

Chapter Fifty-Eight

I awakened to a thin veil of snow covering me in icy white dust. Another thing I had learned over time, my body temperature was not that of the living which allowed the snow to stay on my skin and not melt away. I brushed myself off and fed the dwindling coals of my fire a few pieces of kindling to bring it back to life. Within a few minutes I had enough flame to reheat my coffee from earlier.

As the ice-cold kettle groaned against the heat of the fire I stood and stretched my aching body. Life was hard enough on a man's body when he only had a few decades to live. But in my case, eternity was taking an insurmountable toll. It was during my third yawn I noticed that I had been visited in the night by my tiny voyeur.

But there was something different, they were no longer trying to hide. There was some sort of pattern in the snow made by tiny handprints. I walked in a circle around the crystalline artwork trying to decipher its meaning when it dawned on me, it was an arrow of sorts, pointing me in the direction of the tree line. I gathered my clothes, got dressed and poured a cup of coffee before warily heading out of camp.

Even though I was not visible I was aware my feet still left footprints in the snow, so I tried to keep my steps within the directional arrows without obscuring them. With each step my apprehension grew. It felt as though I were walking straight into a trap and yet, I had no other choice but to follow.

Once I was less than fifty feet from the tree line I hunkered down on my haunches and carefully scanned the forest for tell-tale signs of an ambush. I judged where shadows would be cast in relation to the sun's position and paid close attention to the bases of the trees. I started with the front row and worked my way back as far as I could see. If there was an ambush set it was deep into the thick of the forest.

The first pinecone landed harmlessly at my feet, the second caught me square in the forehead as I was looking at the first. Being the person I am, I was enraged in an instant. Who dared to play games with me on such a blustery morning? I took the last drink of my now cold coffee and allowed myself a moment to calm down. I laughed. It was nothing more than the wind in the trees. That is when I saw it.

I small shadow I had thought was a rock began to stand and take shape. Initially I took a defensive stance but when the rock stood no taller than a child I relaxed. My circumspection returned the moment I realized the cloaked shape was the exact same size as my parasitic adversary. I dropped down to my haunches and observed the figure. Mockingly it did the same.

There was something familiar about the person's movements, so I edge closer but stayed on guard. I chuckled to myself, what did I plan to do if it were her? The figure stood and a beckoned me with a tiny arm to I stood upright and made my way toward the woods. Narrowing the gap, I stopped in my tracks when I recognized who this mysterious creature was, and my heart sank.

I quickly scanned my memory. How long had it been since that fateful night on Beaver Island? Ten, twenty, thirty years? When a man is immortal time becomes a blur. No matter the amount of time, Elisha would no longer be a child no matter what. I livened my pace and dropped to my knees as soon as I realized my assessment was correct, it was Elisha standing in the forest before me.

My lips parted but he immediately put his finger to them to silence me. Through teary eyes I scanned him up and down. Once again, I opened my mouth to speak and once again, he silenced me. As my eyes adjusted to the darkness of the woodland, I saw that he was wearing a blindfold. My blood turned to ice once I determined the reason why, his beautiful eyes were now as shriveled as raisins. The blindfold was to keep her from seeing that he had found me.

We spent the better part of an hour conversing via stick figures drawn in the sandy soil. I learned of Wenonah's fray with Gagnon which, as I had already discerned, did not bode well for the Frenchman and of her obsession to locate me. The more questions I asked the more frustrated he became. I sensed he wanted nothing more than to rip his blindfold off and talk to me until he could talk no more, answering every single one of my questions and then some. But we both knew he could not do that.

Elisha erased the drawn images from the sand leaving him with a large, clean slate with which to work. At first, I was at a loss as I watched him scratching here and scratching there while creating no real decipherable image. Within several minutes I realized he was drawing me a map of the area and wanted me to follow the same coastal path I had first taken with Wenonah. When he came to the place where the big waters met, he kept dragging his stick across the wide water and drew in another large land mass. Once across the water he dragged his stick to the east and stabbed it into the ground as an indicator of where I should go.

After studying the crude map for several minutes and deducing it was well over two hundred miles, he wanted me to travel I shrugged. He must have sensed this as he grabbed me by the hand and led me through the dense woods until we came to a ridge overlooking a clearing. In the small valley below lie a homestead I had yet to discover. I was still at a loss until he pointed a small finger toward a barn, a barn with horses. With hand gestures he indicated that he would let one of the horses out after the sun set so I could sneak down and take it. My mind started assessing all my options and opportunities and he suddenly stopped me. He made it quite clear that it was dangerous for me down there. She was down there.

Not one for sentimentalities I started back toward my camp with a weak smile and a nod of my head even though he could not see me. He stopped me, reached he arms out and wrapped them around me in a bear hug. He was as cold as the snow piling up on his shoulders. I tousled his hair and headed back for my camp with tears streaming down my face until they hardened into tiny ice crystals.

Chapter Fifty-Nine

I had travelled better than twenty miles on foot before the nag would let me mount her. I guess at some point she resigned herself to her fate and capitulated. Her cantankerous nature had me reminiscing about an old, lost friend.

I arrived where the big waters met on the fourth day, which I learned was called the Straits of Mackinac from eavesdropping on some locals. I steered well clear of the fort even though the French flag had been replaced with the stars and stripes which now represented this land. I still found it hard to believe that a handful of scrabble defeated the British army and sent the king whimpering back into his kennel. Freedom was a great motivator. The irony was not lost on me, being immortal offered me more freedoms than I could have ever imagined and yet, I was a slave to it as well.

I hung around the docks until I overheard a worker loading a steamer say they were crossing the straits for the town of Saint Ignace on the other side. I could not resist the fun of walking my nag onto the boat seemingly of her own volition and completely alone. As soon as the ship's crew were distracted by her presence I stowed away to a comfortable spot below decks for some much-needed rest.

I led Marie, sentimentality won out when I finally decided to name the nag, off the vessel just as nonchalantly as we had arrived leaving the sailors scratching their heads and me holding back a chuckle. Saint Ignace turned out to be a bustling fishing and logging town with more than its fair share of dark souls that I could taste with each step I took. I quickly made my way inland away from the riff raff on the docks. The last thing I needed was to consume any of that dark energy. Sadly, there were many afflicted children in this town as well whose souls were crying out to me.

I broke Marie into a full gallop down the shoreline toward the east hoping to distance myself from the depravity and sorrow pervading the town. Once away from civilization I was able to enjoy the ride and I was astonished at how much these waters looked like the islands of the Caribbean. There were dozens of elongated strips of land jutting southward from the mainland. Each of them was lush with deep green forests with little to no habitation in sight.

I walked Marie from island to island having to swim but a few times and then only a few strokes as the water was quite shallow in most places. I was taking a drink of the cool lake water while surveying the landscape when I spotted the first cairn Elisha had drawn on his crude map. It was hidden in a clump of sea oats but if one knew what they were looking for it was easy enough to spot.

I traversed the lake until I made it to that cairn and once again surveyed the horizon. Further out I saw yet another pile of stones that led me toward one of the larger islands. At the water's edge I realized it was too deep, so I let Marie alone to wander the small land mass and began my swim across the channel. I hoped she would be there when I returned.

The lake had not begun to freeze yet, but it sure felt like it was only a degree or two away from being covered in ice. Thankfully, the swim was a short one and I was smart enough to carry a blanket as I backstroked my way across the channel. I walked the beach for more than a mile but could not find any more cairns. I was beginning to grow angry with myself for misreading the waymarks and prepared to swim back across when I noticed something dangling from a large maple.

I had seen these before in villages I had wandered through. It was something of legend to protect children as they slept. It was made of willow fashioned into a hoop and not very large, about two inches in diameter. Tied across the open circle were many strands fashioned into what resembled a spider's web.

I moved deeper into the forest and scanned the trees until I found another one, and then yet another. Why were these talismans meant to protect children in such a desolate, uninhabited place? I did not relish the correlation it suggested with my own situation. I was turning the latest one over in my hands admiring the handiwork when a voice came from nowhere in the form of a single word.

"Asabikeshiinh," whispered through the pines.

I glanced around but could not see anyone. I listened but heard nothing but the rustling of pine needles in the soft wind. I had just about given up and blamed my overactive imagination when a pinecone bounced off my head. And then another. I took several steps back and looked up into the tree but caught a glimpse of nothing.

Every time I moved, I was pelted with yet another pinecone. Who or whatever was in that tree could see me, or at the very least sensed my presence.

"I have had enough of your shenanigans, show yourself or I shall retrieve my axe and fell this tree."

I heard rustling and caught movement in the branches. I was squinting to see as high as I could when a cone found its mark at the back of my head. Somehow this imp had managed to get all the way through the trees and around behind me. I spun around and hurled one of the pinecones up into the tree which accomplished two things, it fell back down and hit me right between the eyes and my actions elicited laughter from within the boughs alerting me to the voyeur's hiding place.

"Why do you come to my island, Elijah? Or should I call you Shadowman?"

The hair on the back of my neck stood up and I was on high alert. Had I walked into a trap set by an impish demon?

"Do not worry, Elijah, I am a friend. I knew you would be coming sooner or later."

I watched in amazement as a human being appeared in the trees where there was none before. He was not translucent as I, but he was well disguised. He was a spry, wiry creature who climbed down out of the trees not unlike monkeys I had seen in the Caribbean. He dropped down in front of me as silently as a jungle cat.

He was much smaller than I, nearly two heads shorter. He had wispy, white hair that fluttered around him with the breeze. His skin was tougher and more grained than the leather on the bottom of a boot. He stared up at me with coal black eyes as if he could see me.

"Are you able to see me?" I asked, scanning my own arm up and down. I could barely even see me, and I knew I was there.

"In a manner of speaking. I cannot see the color of your eyes nor the shape of your face, but I can see your essence before me," he replied, his voice more of a young man's than that of an old withered soul.

"Who are you?"

"Who I am is of no consequence, it is who you are that truly matters."

Great, another old Indian who speaks in nothing but riddles. "Please, I am too tired for riddles and games."

"Very well, I understand your frustration. It has been a long, eventful life has it not?"

"Indeed. Who exactly are you and why am I here?"

"You are here because we share a common enemy, one that must be reigned in."

"Are you referring to the little imp I have come to know as Wenonah?"

"One in the same. We have met, you and I," he said, a sly expression greasing his face.

"I think I would remember that."

"It was a long time ago, at the very beginning of my life and here we are nearing the end of it. And you look exactly the same."

"You have me at a loss. And again, with the riddles."

"It is of no fault of yours. I was but a few minutes old and you never truly laid eyes on me."

I thought back through all my fading memories. "You were the child born that night?"

"One in the same."

"You must be," I paused to think of the word I wanted.

"Ancient," he said with a wrinkled, toothless smile.

"But how, how has all of this transpired?" I asked, but not really of the old man, just in general as I plopped down to the ground, exasperated. "How did you come to be here and what has led me here to you?"

"Come, it is a long story, and I am tired," he said, leading me down a small trail further into the interior of the island.

The old man gathered things along the way, birch bark, some winterberry, and a few other ingredients. I found myself reminiscing about shared tea with Marie on Minis Gitigaan and an odd feeling washed over me.

"Don't look so surprised," he said. "I knew your Marie too. And no, I cannot see your face, but I can sense your mood."

I laughed. "Yes, it is obvious you knew Marie because you are just as odd as she."

I started a fire using the hot coals in his bed of ash while he gathered kindling and dry firewood. He put water in a small pan and put that on the coals off to the side of the fire itself. He said what I can only imagine was a prayer over the ingredients cupped in both hands before carefully immersing them in the water.

"What do you believe this Wenonah to be?" he asked.

"A demon from hell," I said, but then sighed. "But even then, truthfully, most of the time I do not believe that. Sometimes I believe this is all just one long nightmare I cannot wake up from."

"But yet, you really do not fear her."

"No, not her, but I do fear what she can make me become."

"Why do you not fear her?"

"Because she cannot physically harm me, or so she has told me many times."

"It is true, she cannot lay a single hand on you. But she can trick and manipulate you and others."

I nodded. "Is there a point to this?"

"Yes, if you believe in the darkness, then you must also believe in the light. You must embrace what you are, what you have become."

"And what is that?"

"You have spent many years on this earth, many more than I and travelled great distances have you not?"

"More than some, not as much as others."

"Ah, which of us speaks in riddles?"

"Fair point. Yes, I have seen more than my fair share of days upon this earth."

He rubbed at a tuft of scraggly white hair covering his chin. "And you have seen the extent of the sickness this demon has sown across all of mankind."

"Unfortunately, yes, I have."

"You were actually part of that sickness for a time, it is what makes you so special."

"I don't feel special, mostly I feel tired."

"That is only because you are drifting aimlessly through this unique life of yours without a higher purpose."

"Higher purpose?"

"Just as Wenonah travels through this world corrupting the hearts and minds of people, mostly children, for the sole purpose of using them as tools to further spread her evil, her father's evil. You too need to accept your role as a tool to put an end to her venality."

"Her father's evil? Do you mean to tell me . . . "

"Yes, she is the daughter of the angel Lucifer and continues to grow his army day by day. It is an army you must conquer, and you have been managing a little of that along the way."

"For the sake of an exceedingly long argument let us assume that I believe you, then why me? Of all the people on earth why did the devil choose me?"

"Because you were already his to choose."

I pondered the old man's words while poking at the fire with a stick. Red hot embers floated upward into the gathering darkness until they lost their lives and disappeared into nothingness just as I longed to do. I wanted the ability to float upwards and away from this place on the wind. Not just this place, but this everything. I found I was tired, so very tired.

"What do you mean, already his to choose?"

The old man poked at the fire with his own stick, causing embers to rise into the night sky. He took a peculiar amount of glee in the action, as if he were a mere child seeing this for the first time.

"Your fate was sealed even before you were born. You had a brother you never knew; he came along a few years before you. He was a sickly little boy and didn't last through two winters."

"Not a story I was ever told, but what does that have to do with me?"

"After losing the child and trying for several years to have another your mother was told, wrongfully so, that she was barren. Your father began drinking heavily and threatened to leave her if she could not bear him a son. Your mother was desperate, and evil has a way of finding desperate souls," his words trailed off into the night as he thought of what to say next. "Your mother made a desperate plea, a bargain of sorts."

"Your tale is getting more far-fetched by the minute old man. Do you expect me to believe that my mother made a deal with the devil and I was born from that pact? Is Satan my father as well?" I asked with a belly laugh.

"No, your mother did not make a deal with the devil nor is Satan your father. Your father is your father. The deal your mother made was with Wenonah. But as you would suspect, the peculiar creature beguiled your mother into trading a soul for a life."

"Are you saying that my mother sold her soul to give me life?"

"Yes, that is what your mother thought she was doing. But what she didn't know was that the soul she was bargaining with was yours."

Chapter Sixty

My mood was sullen as I gazed out over the expanse of water adorned with a curtain of deep purple. Night was stubborn to relinquish its grip but eventually daybreak won the battle and a tiny sliver of sun broke free of the horizon washing the deep hues with bright orange and yellow. Could the paths of my life have be so predetermined as to not afford me any chance for a different outcome?

The old man's snores were singing in unison with the gentle lapping of the waves as they osculated the island. The colors reminded me of the seas I once roamed. The air here was crisp and clean, as fresh as the day was new. Such as my life was, brand new with the start of each day. Just because my fate had been sealed did not mean I had to accept it for what it was.

I must have been daydreaming for quite some time because the sun was now well above the horizon and the aroma of birch bark tea floated through the air. There was also a sweetness that I recognized as sap from a maple tree. My stomach growled in protest, so I broke from my morning's reveries and walk over to the fire where whitefish was cooking on cedar bark.

"Smells good old man," I said and took a seat by the fire.

"You can call me andookomeshiinh, not because that is my name, but because I like the way it sounds. Marie would call me that when I would scamper up into the treetops to steal nuts from the squirrels. She never told me what it meant but I liked the sound of it."

"How about I just call you something a bit easier to pronounce, like Old Man," I said with a chuckle.

"Suit yourself. Fish is about done," he said, basting the meat with more of the maple sap.

When the whitefish was done, we wordlessly picked at the sweetened flesh and washed it down with a tea that hinted of pine. My belly was full and no longer rumbling. I feared I would purr like a sated kitten and embarrass myself.

"So, Old Man, since you seem to know more about me than I know about myself, what is next for me?"

"I am afraid that is a question I do not have the answer for. Ask me something of where you have been, and I will reveal as much as I know. But as for what your future holds, that is entirely up to you and is a mystery to me."

"If it were up to me, I would not have been sent here to find you. You must know something," I said.

"I know a lot of things, and yet, there is so much more that I do not have knowledge of. This I do know; you must do something. You must choose one path or the other. The light or the absence of it."

I knew what the old man was saying in his roundabout way. Sadly, either choice I made would have to involve Wenonah. It was clear that I did not have the option to just walk away and ignore the losing hand fate had dealt me. I felt a surge of energy within me and I knew the answer.

"How do I kill her?" I asked while tossing a few more pieces of deadfall onto the fire.

He shrugged and said, "I do not know the answer to that question, but I would wager you cannot kill her. I would imagine she is already dead in a sense, at least not alive as a human is alive."

"If I cannot kill her then what am I supposed to do?"

"You have to weaken her to the point she must relinquish her power over you in order to survive."

"And then what?"

He looked upon me with a sadness and I understood. "And then you die."

I stirred the fire for a few minutes, picked at another piece of whitefish and thought about my situation. Ironically, I had spent years, decades, wanting nothing more than to die but now that I stood on the precipice of death, I wanted no part of it. But I also knew I had no other choice.

"How do I weaken her?"

"You have to keep her from feeding. You must keep both of you from feeding. She will eventually have to draw from your soul in order to survive which will weaken you even further. Eventually you will fall from her control and die leaving her nothing to feed on. There is the possibility that if you are successful in weakening her enough, she will be too weak to break her bonds. She may not die, but you may be able to prevent her from spreading her malignancy."

I thought about that for a moment and said, "Possibility? Won't she just move on and find another to feed on?"

"Not if you prevent her from being able to."

"And just how will I do that if I am dead?"

"Water is her enemy. While she can survive a drowning and even swim short distances, once you have her weakened, she will not have the energy to escape."

"Escape what?" I asked, afraid of what his answer would be as it would be also condemning me to a fate worse than death.

"An island. You must trap her on an island far from shore and far from civilization."

"In this ever-expanding world, where would I accomplish this miracle of marooning an angry demon away from all humanity?"

"I know of such a place far to the north."

"There is a lake big enough to keep her from swimming to shore while also avoiding civilization?"

"Look out across these great waters, there is yet another lake to the north known as Anishinaabewi-gichigami and is much larger and much deeper than this wonder. It is truly a sight to behold, or so I have been told."

"Just how long will I have to endure being trapped on an island with that creature?"

"Until you can endure no more and then a lifetime longer."

"In my lifetime I have seen civilization grow beyond any imagination so how will I manage to keep her from feeding?"

"That is a conundrum you must solve yourself. The remote island is surrounded by many rocky reefs, the land is too harsh to farm and there is not enough timber to make it worth building a settlement, so it has remained uninhabited for centuries. I assume it can remain that way for at least one century longer," he said with a sarcastic grin.

We walked down the beach in silence, I contemplated my next move while he just picked through the stones until he found one he liked and dropped it in a sack tied to his waist. Far off on the horizon the makings of a storm was brewing. The clouds were rolling up together into a thick, blackened mass that appeared to march straight for us.

"Just how remote is this island you speak of?"

"A day or two out in a canoe, maybe three if you had a demon thrashing about in the bottom," he laughed.

"Speaking of which, just how do you expect me to get her to the island, she will not go willingly."

"Ah but she will with the proper coaxing. But you are not going to like what I have in mind."

The old man did not say another word and I began to suspect he was formulating his plan as we spoke and was not ready to unveil it. I watched him from the shallows as he swam several hundred yards out from the island like a spry teenager before diving into the depths of the frigid waters. I began to get nervous at the length of time he had spent beneath the surface. In fact, I had held my breath and had to breathe a third time before he broke the surface and sucked in a lungful of air. He swam back to the island on his back with something perched on his chest.

"Get the coals good and hot then put a big pot of water on to boil," he said while trying to catch his breath.

I saw that the old man had retrieved a trap brimming with crawfish and my mouth began to water. I had only tasted the succulent morsels once or twice in my extended lifetime and I was more than ready for a third. Once the water had begun to boil, he dumped a couple of handfuls of the writhing, snapping creatures into the roiling water. He held a few of the snapping beasts up to his hair and clipped them on as adornments.

"I can't help but feel as though you are feeding me my last meal. What exactly is this plan of yours?" I asked between bites of juicy crawfish.

"You will need to lure her to you with the only thing she will respond to."

The sad look in the old man's eyes revealed to me what he was thinking. "She will follow my dark soul, won't she?" I offered and he simply nodded.

The rest of the meal was a somber affair in which I spent most of my time reflecting on all that was my life. I had embraced the darkness at an early age and then even more so after meeting Wenonah. Honestly, before meeting Marie, I had never even so much as brushed up against the light. Not that it was an enigma to me, it simply did not exist as far as I was concerned.

But now, now that I had the innocence of a thousand blessed souls coursing through my very being, I no longer wanted to embrace the darkness, I feared it. I had always lived my life like there was nothing more than the dirt below my feet and the clouds above my head. But now I knew differently, and I was not willing to give up my one and only chance at redemption.

A killdeer ran ahead of me on its spindly legs and then dropped to the rocks and feigned a broken wing. It did this several times, always staying a good twenty yards ahead of me. I knew it must have a nest somewhere and picked up my pace to put distance between myself and the bird's charge. It lifted quickly into flight abandoning the broken wing performance and shrilled off in a half circle landing somewhere out of sight behind me.

I was sitting all alone tossing small pebbles into the lake when the old man came up from behind me and put his hand on my shoulder. Immediately I felt a rush of energy pass through us and my thoughts were filled with Marie and the promise I made to her to never embrace the darkness again. I also recalled the melancholy she exhibited when we spoke of other planes of existence and how I was doomed to never leave this place.

"She wants me to tell you that she was wrong," the old man said, tears streaming down both cheeks.

"When did you speak to her?"

"While you were walking down the beach. I did not speak to her like you and I speak, she talks to me in my head."

I nodded. "Why does her talking to you make you cry? Do you miss her?"

"Yes, of course I miss her. Every single day I miss her. But that is not why tears flow down my face."

"Then what makes you cry?"

"You do."

"How do I make you cry?"

"When I touched you, I felt the sadness, the sorrow that lingers inside of you. I only felt it but for a brief moment, but you feel it constantly don't you?"

"Yes, it is always present. Even more so knowing what I must do. What I must give up. For most of my life I simply passed time on this planet, I did not live, nor did I care about the sanctity of life. For me, waking up was nothing more than sheer luck. I did not believe in heaven or hell, God or the devil. All that changed when I had the misfortune of meeting Wenonah. But it changed again a hundred-fold that day on Minis Gitigaan with Marie, when she opened my eyes to the light. I did not know what joy was until that moment," I explained.

"Even more powerful when the joy you feel is for someone else. When you released those poor lost souls, you did something for them no one else could do."

"I felt their sorrow first, but then an overwhelming sense of elation that brought me to tears. It was the first time in my life I had ever felt true happiness. I don't want to ever want to embrace the darkness ever again," I said, tears forming in the corners of my eyes.

"But you must. And remember, this is not something you are doing for personal gain or even self-preservation. You will be sacrificing yourself for those poor, innocent souls a thousand-fold."

I nodded and went back to picking at my dinner. My throat was so constricted I could not swallow so I just nibbled at the pink flesh. I must have fallen asleep by the fire because I awakened well after dawn and found myself all alone on the island. Marie was tied loosely to a tree and snorted when I finally got to my feet. She could not see me, but she knew I was there just the same. I had half a mind to ask her how she managed to get over to the island but I knew what her answer would be, so I kept the questions to myself.

I spent two hours scouring the forest looking for the old man but there was neither hide, nor hair of him even high up in the treetops. I gathered my things and secured them to Marie. As a last chore I carried a few pans of water and poured them over the bed of coals and then buried the ashes beneath a blanket of sand. I was gathering up the last of my clothes when I found a piece of birch bark stuffed into one of my pockets. The old man had drawn me a map to the island as well as a pictograph of his plan. Did a plan really matter? No matter the plan I followed the result would be the same, I would be dead.

Chapter Sixty-One

The long ride back to my camp was more cathartic than I could have imagined. I talked Marie's ear off for most of the trip, running the various plans and scenarios past her most of which she did not even bother to comment on. A few received subdued snorts and a shake of her head. A week after dining on succulent crayfish with an odd little man I found myself on the outskirts of the forest leading to my underground dwelling scrounging for winter berries and chewing on frozen venison jerky.

The weather had turned from a mild, refreshing chill to brutal winds not fit for man, beast, or even immortal beings. After all these years I still did not know how Wenonah was able to track me, so I opted to stay away from my camp and brave the night without a fire. While the cold was no threat to my survival it still wracked my body with pain. With a little coaxing I was able to get Marie to lie down with me to help keep the both of us warm. She ceded after a bitter argument making herself clear she had no use for a shadow of a man.

I watched the farmhouse for almost a week before I was content in the knowledge that Wenonah was no longer there. I was ready to give up my surveillance and return to camp when I overheard voices coming from an outlying barn, so I carefully made my way over to investigate.

"I don't like that strange little child is all I am saying."

"You best be quiet about that; you know how Tobias feels about her. And I am not so sure I would call her a little child."

"I know how Tobias feels, but that don't mean I have to like her."

"George, you never mind that. Tobias is the boss and he owns this place. If he were to get angry and toss us out, we would have no money and no place to live just like that. In the dead of winter at that. Just keep your distance from her."

"I try, but she knows I don't like her, so she hangs around. The only way I get rid of her is to start reading my bible. I read it aloud even when I don't want to just to annoy her. Where did her and that creepy little blind kid go anyway?"

"I heard Tobias say they were heading over to Manitou Island to check on the progress of the lumber mill."

"We need to get away from this place. Ever since that woman and child showed up Tobias has been acting differently."

"Differently how?"

"He is up all hours of the night, he yells at the womenfolk more than ever and I am afraid he is into something illegal out there on that island?"

"I know and I don't like it any better than you, but winter has set in. We've got no choice but to ride the season out."

I quietly abandoned my eavesdropping and headed back for my camp. There I gathered a few supplies, bundled up in my best winter clothing with layer upon layer and started out for the shore. Night was falling and I had to make my move sooner than later. I found myself hoping that this Tobias was a dark soul, it would save me a lot of trouble if he were.

Under the cover of darkness, I commandeered a small rowboat near the farmhouse that had been pulled up onto the beach and turned upside down for the winter. I turned it over and tossed my pack inside. The big lake had a large sheet of ice extending from the shore and that was covered with several inches of snow which made tugging the rowboat across the ice shelf much easier.

It took me more than an hour to reach open water where I gently rowed the boat around to the western side of the island away from the glowing lamp lights of civilization. The ice shelf extended a good half mile out from the island forcing me to tug the rowboat the rest of the way to the island. I would have left it on the ice, but I really had no plan and figured it might be needed later if things went sour.

After a bit of scouting, I learned there were only three men on the island within a mile of the beach in an encampment. It appeared they were constructing a mill, one of the men seemed to oversee the timbering operation, the other a boat captain which left the third and largest of them to be Tobias. The man was six and a half feet tall and as sturdy as an oak, not a man I wanted to tangle with.

I watched their camp for nearly half an hour before catching sight of Wenonah. She was squirreled away in the shadows tinkering about on something I could not see. Then I caught sight of the boy lingering in the shadows by the fire and it occurred to me, she was using Elisha to spy on the men. What harm was there in letting a little blind boy warm himself by their fire? I made certain to stay out of his cone of vision. Even though I was obscured I did not trust the she devil's inability to sense where I was.

My heart had been racing and my mind raced even faster on my journey across the ice. The fear of the unknown had my every nerve tense and aware. As I sat in the shadows, I allowed myself to shrink back and relax. I continually had to remind myself there was no rush to any of this. Wenonah's constant insistence on my patience was not lost in the moment. I breathed in the woodsy smoke from the fire while letting my mind drift. It was then I sensed a dark aura settled over the campfire, it was the presence of a hatred, deep and dark.

Wenonah had moved close to the boy and whispered something in his ear. He nodded and she handed him a piece of paper. Elisha felt his way around the three men until he came to Tobias. He then handed the crumpled piece of paper to the large, bearded man who immediately began to rage.

I could not hear what they were saying but the smaller of the three, the ship's captain, appeared to be pleading his case. Seeing that Wenonah had become enthralled with this display of machismo I made my way around the small landing until I was almost directly behind her. I looked across the fire and saw that the boy had covered his eyes with a dark cloth. He knew I was there. He pointed at the wood pile.

My eyes followed the boy's finger and I saw the big man turn his head toward the wood pile as well. A pike pole was stabbed into one of the top logs and Tobias was reaching for it. Seeing this, the captain began to back toward the dock while digging into the deep pocket of his peacoat. Tobias' dark energy swirled around me as if to tantalize me into consuming it. I could not let that happen.

The boy somehow sensed I was up to something and turned his blind gaze upon the two quarreling men. As their argument grew more and more heated so did Wenonah's rapture. She had already drawn a considerable amount of the dark energy to her and was now shrouded in a dark cloud of ugliness. With no time to waste I quickly covered her with the sack the old man had given me, knocked her over and bound both her feet and the sack with heavy rope. I then threw the monkey's paw end of the rope over a nearby branch of a cedar and hoisted her into the air. I quickly turned my attention back to the fray.

The captain of the boat had freed a revolver from his pocket and was pointing it at Tobias who was lunging at him with the pike. I was already on a dead run to intervene when Wenonah screamed out.

Shadowman, Shadowman,
You will NEVER be free.
Shadowman, Shadowman,
Your soul belongs to me!

This was no longer a sing song little girl's rhyme in my head, but a banshee's shriek heard by all. I managed to make it to the captain just as he removed the revolver from his pocket and fired. It was a wayward shot that hit me high on my left shoulder and threw me to the ground. Both men were stunned by the fact Tobias had not been shot and yet there was a pool of blood forming on the ground in front of them. While the captain checked the cylinder for a misfire Tobias regained his composure and started at him with the barbed pole once more.

I swept the man's legs and took him to the ground before he could take a swing at the retreating man. I quickly knocked him out with a well-placed blow behind his ear. Before he could take off on a dead run out of fear, I did the same to the boat captain.

"What do we do now Shadowman?" Elisha asked, gazing up at me with his hands covering his eyes.

I looked down upon his quizzical expression and my heart was gripped by a sadness I had never known. Not once had I thought of this child and what might become of him if I were to succeed in destroying Wenonah. I had only concerned myself with the mission at hand. It was now obvious that my plans would have to somehow include him.

"We will gather our little bundle of joy and head for the big lake they call Gitchi-Gami," I said with a head bob toward the burlap sack dangling from a tree looking as though it were filled with a hundred wet, angry cats. "Do you know how to drive a boat?" I asked with a smile that he somehow saw and returned.

Chapter Sixty-Two

After several days we finally reached the shores of the big lake, I commandeered us a vessel that would make the journey to the remote island. I spent weeks waiting for the right boat, one stocked well with dry goods, pelts, construction tools and materials and a whole lot of coffee. I was able to wander around the streets of the small port town and eavesdrop on conversations, one of which gave me the day the vessel was to depart. I snuck on board, dispatched the skeleton crew and tied them up. Once safely away from civilization I put them into a lifeboat, untied them and set them free no doubt wondering for the rest of their lives what had happened.

Within a week's time we arrived at the island where the boy and I went to work unloading as many provisions as I felt we would need to get us through the next winter. I then steamed the boat alone out past the shoals. After making certain that the rest of the supplies were sealed and watertight, I fired the small signal canon into the hull of the ship and let her sink to the bottom of lake Gitchi-Gami to serve as an underwater storeroom.

The next few months were a bustle of chaos preparing for an eternity in exile. For a sightless creature Elisha had become adept at swinging an axe and felling trees. We constructed a small shack with a very deep, well-hidden cellar in which to imprison Wenonah. I did not have the heart to spike her feet and hands as had been done to me, so I tied her securely with ropes and chains salvaged from the boat. In time I planned to use other materials I reclaimed to build a cage to house her in.

My transparency allowed me the freedom to wander about my island home and reside in the shack without the complication of arousing suspicions should the occasional thrill-seeking wanderer make it out this far into the middle of the big lake. The cellar was large enough and comfortable enough for the lad and me to take refuge if the need arose or the weather became ugly.

As a matter of routine Wenonah tormented me daily with visions of Goldy buried in the silt on the bottom of a murky, black river. Many times, it was all I could do to keep from going out to search for him. I do not know how the she-devil fabricated the visions I was seeing because if my friend were alive still, he would have to be in the same state of body as I and would not be visible to me. It was merely more of her chicanery.

Deep within my heart I was certain he was truly there suffering unspeakable horror. The demon never let me forget that he endured an existence filled with suffering and anguish all because of me. I had been the cause of the poor man's anguish.

Throughout that first year I was terribly busy developing a persona for the island I hoped would discourage visitors. Early on the few visitors to land on the shores were curious native youngsters off on a grand adventure. I sent them scurrying away by haunting them around their camps. I will admit, I was having much more fun than I should have been.

Next came fisherman who strayed too far from the mainland and needed to take on wood for fuel and water to continue their voyage. Oddly, these white men were easily discouraged by a few hauntings as well. Over time the reputation of the island spread, and the visitors became much sparser.

There were a few who had come to these shores wearing the blackened veil of evil. It was during those times I was the most diligent. Wenonah writhed, gnashed, and screamed as their decadence tantalized her senses. I was careful to waylay them with the minimum amount of violence possible and set them adrift on the open waters.

The months had turned to years and then into decades in which I watched Wenonah slowly grow weaker and in turn so did I while the once vibrant and young Elisha aged into a feeble old man. Eventually, Elisha passed leaving only her and myself to talk to. We complained during the heat of summer and begged for its return when the ice formed on the lake, though it was usually a one-sided conversation. One thing did amaze me about the cursed place, even in my state of being the black flies could find my flesh to dine upon.

With nothing to do but wait I stood on the shore day after day looking out into forever not even certain what it was I was waiting for. Although it was my deepest desire, I highly doubted Wenonah would just pass gently into the night like Elisha had done. Her torment of my mind has diminished little by little over time until I felt a tinge of pity for the beast. She was, after all, just an animal of sorts with her own set of instincts she was destined to follow.

It was nearly ten years after Elisha had been laid to rest that I began to realize just what an arduous undertaking my mission was. Could I outlast her, or would she eventually out last me in the end? I found myself praying to a god I had never even given much thought to, let alone believe in until I met the demon child. The irony was not lost on me, it took the devil to bring me to God's doorstep.

With each passing year my loneliness became easier to tolerate though there were times when I teetered on the brink of insanity. Unless I had already toppled over the edge and this was all a series of a madman's nightmares. I toiled around the island planting small gardens from seeds that were on the boat. I planted them in a hodge podge manner as to not arouse suspicion from the occasional visitor, most of whom were government officials and university students. As luck would have it the island was eventually designated a nature preserve making it off limits to hunting, trapping, and even fishing.

As the years passed Wenonah continued to weaken, but so did I. I lost track of the years more from a lack of interest than paying attention. I did not care to determine just how many decades made up an eternity. This truly came as a blessing at a time when civilization continued to march forward at a breakneck pace.

Even being far removed from civilization I found myself reveling in the advancements of mankind. Every year the boats got larger and larger until they could block out the sun. But most of all what astonished me the most were the flying machines that crossed the sky. Small and rarely seen at first, they sputtered through the air as if they would drop out of the sky without warning. Many years later came the larger, gleaming silver machines that streaked across the sky so high into the clouds I could barely see them.

I found myself on many occasions deliberating a jaunt to the mainland just to see what had become of the world. But with every thought of escape, Wenonah reminded me of the dire need for my exile. Walking down the empty beach I started up into the night sky and wondered, now than man had learned to fly, would they ever be able to visit the moon. I laughed so hard and loud that when I stopped the island was enveloped in an eerie silence. A man on the moon, I had truly gone mad.

The End of Eternity

Chapter Sixty-Three

The cold November winds howled through the derelict vineyard I had given up on decades ago. The grapes were sour, and I found no enjoyment from wine anymore. Winter was coming early as I had suspected and the gathering season much too short to refill the pantry. The garden had given up a meager yield this year, which was even more meager than the last. This endeavor had lasted far longer than I could have ever imagined and while I would not starve to death, an empty belly was still quite an uncomfortable thing to endure.

I did not spend much time topside as of late, so I made my way back down to the cellar and plopped down on a makeshift chair fashioned from an old stump. My lifelong companion, my only confrère in life for as long as I could remember, lay curled up like an aging dog in the corner. She was void of any semblance of humanity she may have once had. Steam from a freshly brewed coffee whispered in the morning air and I felt compelled to light a cigar to complete the ensemble just to taunt the little fiend.

The weather caused my mind to drift through a snow-covered path of distant memories. Although we were adversaries, we had also traversed through time connected as one. Through the years we had many exploits together, some successful, some not, but all were bonding experiences that bound us together like a leather tome. Stories interwoven within the fabric of time.

I penned my thoughts onto one of the few remaining pieces of parchment. Around the room were scattered sheaves of my most inner thoughts. Somewhere in all of this was a story, a story that would one day be told. And when it was told it would be regarded as an astonishing work of pure fiction no matter how steeped in fact the story was.

I felt writer's block trying to creep in and realized that the silence was deafening and was stealing my thoughts away, so I set my metronome into motion and succumbed to the mindless ticking away of my life. The coffee was bitter but welcomed on this dreary day. There was no sun even though sunrise had been three hours prior. Bleak, gray clouds hung in the sky from every point on the horizon like a wicked comforter blanketing the earth. It seemed even the heavens knew.

I was restless as was usually the case and the cellar smelled too much like a cemetery plot, so I moved us upstairs for the day. The dingy light was not much better, but it did match my mood. I felt a stirring at my feet and glanced down, there was still some life left in the old girl after all. She gazed up at me with longing eyes, eyes that begged to be free.

Fleeting memories of us roaming the lands together in a new fallen snow creased a crooked smile across my lips. Even though I had brought Wenonah up from the depths of the cellar to ease my loneliness, I kept her tightly bound. She gave me someone else to talk to other than myself though lately she could only manage to grunt and growl in response.

My coffee empty I struggled to my feet to brew another. I didn't really need another, and my stores were running dangerously low, but it gave me a small sense of pleasure knowing the aroma tantalized the foul beast. My bones hissed and cracked, telling me my body had grown much too old and that this was a younger man's world, not one for the likes of me. Wenonah's labored breathing echoed from the other room accompanied by the metronome's ticking and the scream of venting steam blended into a symphony of the macabre.

I gazed out the cabin window at the light fluffy snow that the heavens had suddenly given up. Large snowflakes rested gently upon the layer of old snow, covering up the last remnants of green in the yard. I shivered against the cold and went into the other room for another sweater as lighting a large fire in the fireplace was not prudent during the daylight hours. The cabin was well hidden, buried mostly beneath the ground and the rest of the way beneath the snow but smoke from a fire large enough to heat the cabin would be a dangerous beacon even in this vast nothingness. I hugged the warmth of the cashmere and draped another blanket over my unwilling confidant who must surely be freezing from the lack of sustenance coursing through her.

"Are you hungry?" I asked, setting the remaining bowl of rabbit stew on the floor in front of her without giving her a chance to refuse. She lapped at it grudgingly with a long, raspy tendril that was once her silvery, sarcastic tongue.

I could sense a myriad of emotions in her eyes. Behind the tears of rage, I could see pure fear manifesting itself. I was certain she was getting sips of her own mortality with each labored breath and death was giving her a taste of her own medicine. A medicine I too would one day partake, sooner than later I hoped.

"Snow is coming down a lot harder now. Looks like maybe a couple of feet before this squall moves on. But, after all, winter has set in up here in the great white north so what else should we expect."

I was not sure if the sound she made was a reply to my comment, or merely an involuntary response to pain. I lit a small candle, more for ambiance than necessity, and pulled up a seat on the floor next to her. I looked her over and saw that she had deteriorated even further since the last time I had looked her over. There was not a shred of her original appearance left, the little girl was lost.

The creature before me was merely a bag of bones covered in a thick, brown leather of sorts. No real hair to speak of, just pock marked skin that was also laden with abnormalities across every inch of surface. Her eyes no longer sparkled with the mischievous nature of a child but burned black with venomous hatred.

"Sometimes I miss that sarcastic little girl," I said.

Slowly, methodically she stretched out her thin bony hand and lashed out at me with a long, claw tipped tentacles that had once been the delicate fingers she used to pluck wildflowers from the field. She was so weak and slow that there was no danger of her making contact, but I reflexively jerked away from her none the less.

Shadowman, Shadowman,
Do not think you have won.
Shadowman, Shadowman,
Your nightmare has just begun!

The sing-song childish nature of her rhymes had all but disappeared. Over time the voice chanting in my head grew aged and filled with wet gravel. I was drawn to her coal black eyes filled with hatred and loathing. I had to wonder, had she ever been that playful, laughing little girl or had her exuberant persona been a façade all along.

"Oh, no, my little pretty. It is your nightmare that has only just begun," I said and turned away from her to go take a much-needed nap.

~ ~ ~

The morning brought with it a gorgeous sunrise glinting hints of angry red in with the golds. It was not unlike the sunrise before the storm which condemned me to a deserted island all those years ago. And here I sit, watching another sunrise filled with ominous portents of the day to come. The weather in this God forsaken land has always perplexed me. Bitter cold and snowing in the morning followed by thunderstorms in the afternoon. It is what one must endure when they take up residence with the devil I suppose.

I stood on the southwestern shore of the island mesmerized by the methodical blinking of a lighthouse about a mile offshore of the island proper. The beacon rotated slowly around until a flash of light would explode when it was positioned straight across from me. Even though the sun was up, it was overcast and gray, so the beacon continued to warn ships of the dangerous reef surrounding her.

My reverie was interrupted by a strange sound coming from the clouds. At first, I thought it was thunder, but then I saw a flash of silver in the sky. It was one of the flying contraptions I had seen on occasion. It seemed to be having trouble staying aloft. The wings wobbled from side to side and the front of mechanical beast kept bobbing up and down.

The closer it got to me the more I realized it was trying to land on the water. There were what appeared to be two canoes lashed to either side underneath the craft. It was still too high to land on the water and I was not sure if the craft would clear the cliffs. As they crossed over the island the nose lifted slightly and it soared over my head less than fifty feet above the cliffs.

Just as it cleared the cliffs and was over the bay a blinding flash streaked across the sky and struck the front of the soaring contrivance. It screamed in anguished and streaked on a downward trajectory toward the water. The two canoes hit first and then broke away from the craft sending it skipping across the water like a round stone until it crashed into the lighthouse island.

~ ~ ~

"I think my leg is broken," a skinny young man said while cautiously trying to stand.

Aimee bent down to check out the injuries to her cohort's leg while wiping blood from her own forehead. "It's not broken, Jimmy, you'll live," she said, coughing as the acrid smoke from the plane's wreckage invaded her lungs.

"Did you see Murphy?" Jimmy asked, working his skinny arm free of the wreckage.

"Screw Murph, did you see what happened to Travis?"

"I didn't get a chance to see much of anything once we hit the water. I don't think Murphy was able to get his seat belt unbuckled."

"Good. It would serve the prick right to sink to the bottom of this lake."

"Damn, Aimee, that's pretty cold hearted."

"Shut up, Jimmy. Get up off your ass and help me look for the Travis, he's the only one with the account numbers."

"Sure thing, sis, you're the boss."

Jimmy hobbled along behind Aimee as she frantically searched the wreckage for the other passengers. She bolted on a dead run across the tiny island and dashed straight into the water. She up righted an airplane seat with a passenger still buckled in, it was Travis. Jimmy helped her get him unbuckled and dragged him up onto the snow-covered sand.

"He doesn't look too good," Jimmy said, running his hand over his greasy, jet-black hair.

Aimee bent down and put her ear to the man's mouth. "He's still breathing. Find me something to cover him up with," she said, stopping long enough to put a hair band around her thick, black hair.

Travis was bleeding profusely from a cut to his upper arm. A piece of wreckage protruded from under his arm pit. Aimee knew enough about first aid to know she couldn't remove the metal shard, or the man might bleed to death.

She slapped him across the face several times. "Travis. Travis."

"Come on, Aimee, that's not going to do any good."

"Neither is him dying with those account numbers in his head. We didn't pull this job to end up with nothing."

Aimee worked on keeping Travis warm while Jimmy scoured the wreckage for their partner. A large man stood in the shadows of the lighthouse keeping his pistol in the ribcage of the lighthouse keeper. He gave the old man a hard nudge.

"You folks need to get him inside before hypothermia sets in," the lighthouse keeper called out as he appeared on the porch of the lighthouse. "I've got a fire going and we can call for the coast guard to get you some help."

The older man held the door open as Jimmy and Aimee dragged their injured partner into the cozy keeper's quarters.

He was much taller than either of them, but blind and frail. Jimmy found himself wondering how useful a blind lighthouse keep could be.

"Shouldn't we go back out and look for Murph?" Jimmy asked at the doorway.

"I said screw Murph. We need to wake up Travis and get those account numbers before he dies, and they die with him. Don't go near that radio old man," she commanded, drawing a pistol out from under her jacket and jabbing him in the chest with it.

"Easy young lady, there's no need for that gun. I was just going to call the Coast Guard and get you some help," he said with his hands in the air.

"I don't need the Coast Guard. I need this man to talk. Living out here by yourself, you must know something about first aid."

"A little. Enough to bandage a cut or splint a sprain but that is the extent of my limited knowledge."

"What is wrong with him?" she asked, jabbing the barrel of the pistol at Travis who lay at her feet.

"What's wrong is that he was just in a plane crash. Jesus, sis, put the damned gun away, can't you see the old man is blind and damned near deaf," Jimmy said. "We need to find Murphy."

"I said fuck Murphy. I hope he's lying dead at the bottom of the lake. This is all his fault. Go north, he said. Canada instead of Mexico, he said. Now look at the bullshit mess we're in."

Saloon doors on the kitchen burst open and before Aimee could react Murphy planted a left fist squarely on her jaw which put her on the floor so hard it snapped her hair band. It would have been a comical sight under any other circumstances. Murphy was a big man, but much smaller than Charles which was apparent by the borrowed clothes he was wearing. The legs of his pants had been hacked off with a knife and an electrical extension cord did double duty as his belt.

"Better than being eaten by hammerheads in the Sea of Cortez isn't it?" the big man said.

"Murph, that wasn't necessary," Jimmy said and stepped forward in defense of his sister.

"I've got a right hand too if you want that," he said, curling his hand into an anvil sized fist.

Jimmy stopped in his tracks and bowed his head to the floor in capitulation.

"You bastard, you broke my last hair band," Aimee said, wiping the blood from her mouth with her sleeve.

"You hope I was dead?" Murphy said, bending down to pick up the pistol Aimee dropped when he hit her.

"You know I didn't mean it, Murph. You know I love you and couldn't live without you," Aimee said, unable to tame all of the sarcasm from her voice.

"Oh, you meant it alright. I know you meant it," he said, pocketing the pistol. "Charles, how long until the coast guard arrives?" Murphy asked while pulling assorted debris from his thick, red beard.

"Chatter on the radio says they are about thirty minutes out," the lighthouse keeper said.

"You two know each other?" Aimee asked.

"No, not really. We just recently made each other's acquaintance, but I happen to be a little more cordial than you are, so I was able to communicate with the man. Charles, do you have a boat? One besides the one you normally use that the coast guard wouldn't notice was missing?"

"Yes. It's around back."

"What is over there on that large island?"

"It is deserted, so nothing save for a small, decrepit shack and some small out buildings that were used when they created the nature preserve."

"Good, and what about this boat of yours?

"It has a few supplies, but not much. It's light so you can drag it up into the woods once you get to the big island. There is a map of the island in the pack with the supplies. The old shack is deep in the forest, it might be safe to lay low there for a few hours, but no longer than a day before the coast guard starts looking for survivors."

"Jimmy, help me get Travis to the boat. Aimee, you will drive so I can keep an eye on you. Charles, you keep the coast guard busy, and keep their eyes to the north if possible, if you wouldn't mind of course."

Charles nodded and followed the others outside. He grabbed the remaining seats and drug them to the north end of the tiny island. He lit the seats on fire and tossed in an old tire swing for good measure. He gave a soft wave to Murphy as the small Zodiac screamed away from the lighthouse island.

~ ~ ~

I ran back through the forest as fast as my ancient legs would carry me. By the time I made it down to the cove with my spyglass the metal beast had sunk beneath the water's surface and the fires were almost all burned out. I scanned back and forth across the front of the lighthouse but did not see anyone or anything other than a few pieces of wreckage.

And then I caught sight of two people, a man and a woman, combing through the wreckage. I watched as they dragged something out of the lake. My heart threatened to burst from my chest. I prayed they would stay on the tiny island and seek help from there. The tiny island had a dock, and a man I had seen wandering around the grounds. I assumed he was there to take care of the lighthouse. The group had all they needed right there and did not need to invade my sanctuary.

I had been watching them for quite some time before I was given my first taste. A darkness was on that island now and it was seeking me out. I put away my spyglass and ran back for the cabin as fast as I could. I had to get Wenonah back down into the cellar.

~ ~ ~

Aimee drove the Zodiac into the cove as fast as it would go with her long, dark hair flowing behind her. She hit the beach at full speed and ran the boat high up onto the sand. Like clockwork the team jumped out and dragged the boat into the forest where they concealed it with a built-in camouflage tarp and debris from the forest floor.

Jimmy and Murphy carried the injured Travis who they had strapped to a stretcher they found at the lighthouse while Aimee took the lead. The trail through the woods was nothing more than a deer trail making the travel frustratingly slow. They had to stop several times to attend to the man's wounds and to apply new bandages.

"I don't hear any boats?" Jimmy said, checking his watch.

"That's good, maybe the authorities were further away than Charles anticipated. The more lead time we have the better."

"We need to get those account numbers from Travis before he dies," Aimee said.

"We are not going to get anything out of him until we stabilize him which means we need a place where I can patch him up so get moving," Murphy commanded.

Shadowman, Shadowman,
I sense your growing fear.
Shadowman, Shadowman,
The end of your charade draws near.

I shoved her mocking words out of my head as I watched the group bushwhacking their way through the dense forest. The man was right, there were no sounds of any boats out on the water so I might still have a chance of chasing them off or waiting them out. I knew I was only kidding myself, these were not the types to be scared off by rudimentary fabricated ghosts. My only hope was that the authorities would show up and intervene before I had to.

I shadowed the entourage as closely as I dared as they made their way through the forest to my hideaway. I could feel Wenonah struggling about inside my brain, trying to worm her way back in as a sea of ebon energy swirled around me. From what I could decipher these were all dark souls, except for the injured man being carried. Panic set in, I could not allow them to find the creature in the cellar and more importantly, I could not kill them.

It took less than ten minutes for them to arrive at the shack. I waited for them to go inside first before sliding in after them. It was one of those times where my transparency was a blessing rather than a curse. Although, I did feel self-conscious about hanging my assets out there in front of a beautiful woman. It had been so long since I had seen myself in the light of day that I could only imagine my manhood closely resembled the color and texture of the beast in the cellar.

"Aimee, get Travis's coat off him. And Jimmy, get a fire going I'm sure Travis is in danger of going into shock from hypothermia," Murphy said.

Murphy went about assessing the man's wounds and treating him the best he could with the equipment available. Murphy had been spent several years as a combat medic while serving in the military as a member of the Special Forces so battle dressing wounds was second nature to him. Travis had taken a significant blow to the head in the crash and there was a deep laceration in his forehead. Both arms were broken but only the wound in his armpit was potentially life threatening. Murphy was committed to ensuring the man would survive this day long enough to take a bullet to the brain.

"Shhh," Jimmy said. "Do you hear that? Sounds like a boat, and a big one at that."

"Get up on the roof and see what you can see while I work on Travis."

I followed the skinny young man out of the shack and up on to the roof. At one point he stopped and looked around in all directions. I had to resist the urge to tickle an ear or two just for my own amusement. There was a red boat with a large white stripe skipping through the waves headed toward the lighthouse. Black smoke billowed up from the north end of the lighthouse island, no doubt drawing their attention.

I waited until the man dropped down from the rooftop before doing the same myself. I retrieved the spyglass I had hidden in the scrub and climbed back onto the roof as quietly as possible. I might be invisible, but I still sounded like a bull wearing steel boots when I walked.

Shadowman, Shadowman,
We have guests.
Shadowman, Shadowman,
They are quite the tasty pests.

I shook Wenonah's torments from my brain and concentrated on the boat heading toward the lighthouse island. Perhaps I could somehow divert them over here and they would chase off these interlopers for me. I raised the spyglass to my eye and saw that my worst nightmares were coming to fruition. By no means did I want that boat coming to my island, but in my heart of hearts I knew that was exactly why it was even here in the first place. It was then I realized her little sing-song rhymes were evolving, reverting to when I had first heard them in my head. She was regaining her strength. Something was wrong, very, very wrong.

"What did you see?" Murphy's voice carried up to the rooftop.

"Definitely the Coast Guard. Canadians it looks like. Headed for the lighthouse island," Jimmy responded.

"Hopefully, Charles can satisfy their curiosity. Now get us a fire going," Murphy said.

"Something isn't right about this place, sis. There is someone else here," he said while building a pile of kindling gathered from the yard.

"What in the hell are you talking about Jimmy? Look at this place. It has been deserted for years, probably even decades," Aimee said.

"Murphy, the fireplace bricks are still warm. Someone had a fire in here just a few hours ago."

"Relax Jimmy, I'm sure it was just Charles. Maybe he has a propensity to wander about when he gets bored."

Jimmy poked around in the fire pit while the other two tended to Travis. "And there is no dust on the table?"

"So, Charles wiped things down for us."

"Yeah, but he didn't know we were coming."

"Jimmy, please, give it a rest. I am trying to concentrate on what I am doing here."

From under his breath Jimmy said, "And what is that God awful smell?"

~ ~ ~

I sat in the darkest corner of the shack listening to them bicker back and forth. I sensed a stirring beneath us that was not of this world. Dark energy was swirling about the room in malevolent tornados and I knew I had better formulate a plan before all was lost. I could feel Wenonah getting stronger with each bitter word spoken.

Something clawed at my throat from the inside threating to choke the very life from me. As quietly as I could I rushed for freedom and fresh air. I stopped dead in my tracks, Wenonah was coming up the forest path with two men in uniform and a blind old man stooped over with age. She turned and said something to her entourage. The two uniformed men nodded and stepped back into the shelter of the trees.

I maneuvered through the thick brush until I was close enough to see her face. She looked like Wenonah in stature, but her face was not the same. She did not have the same cherubic glow of a child that I had come to know. No, she resembled a loving matron with flowing silver hair. But her eyes, her eyes were as wicked as the smile that suddenly creased her lips. The blind man turned his head to the thicket, looked at me and smiled at me as well.

I was confused but for a moment until I recalled Jewel's story about the visitor to her village and it had not been

Wenonah as I had believed. This was Mahneerah. She turned and looked at me through the trees and wagged a boney finger back and forth while her forked tongue slithered over her needle-sharp teeth. I was surrounded by an icy cold wind that gripped my soulless core to the very pit of existence. She and the old man turned back around and continued up the path to the cabin.

Shadowman, Shadowman,
Meet the second daughter.
Shadowman, Shadowman,
Little lambs led to the slaughter.

Wenonah's intrusion into my brain was much stronger. I could sense her plotting and strategizing. Was this Mahneerah able to inflict harm or was she bound by the same rules as Wenonah? I found myself feeling like such a coward creeping though the shadows, but I had no plan. I had not anticipated this turn of events and I was completely at a loss as to what to do. One thing I did know was that I had to stop this apparent rescue at all costs.

"Charles, what are you doing here? And how did you get here?" Murphy asked of the blind man standing at the threshold of the shack.

"And who is your little friend?" Jimmy asked, nodding to the diminutive woman standing behind him.

"I am Mahneerah, and I have come to help you."

"Help us? How on earth are you going to help us?" Aimee asked.

"Charles informed me of your predicament."

"And just what predicament might that be?" Murphy asked.

"Your dying friend there, and of course the secrets he keeps."

"Who in the hell are you lady?"

"Who I am is of no importance. What is of importance is what I can do for you, or do to you, it is your choice," she sneered.

I did not like the way this situation was progressing. I knew she had deep, dark intentions and I knew that more than likely those intentions included me. Her being here was no coincidence, of that I was certain.

Murphy cocked his pistol and stuck it in her face. "I do not have time for your games old woman. State your business or get the fuck out of here."

"You have no choice but to make time," she said.

Mahneerah gave a subtle nod to Charles who disappeared for a moment only to return with the two uniformed men. They took up position on either side of the crone. Once I saw them up close, I knew how dire my situation was. They both had the same distant stare of the Indian braves Wenonah had in tow when she and I first met. I feared the end was near, just not the end I had imagined or prayed for.

"She brought the damned coast guard with her," Aimee said.

Murphy quickly averted the pistol away from Mahneerah and aimed it at the larger of the two men. "Get your damned hands up," he ordered.

Neither man complied, of which I was well aware would be the outcome of Murphy's demands.

"This is your last warning."

"Easy Murph, we can't be shooting the coast guard. That will bring a shit storm down on us," Jimmy said.

"So will being arrested and going to prison you idiot."

"Murphy, baby, for once I agree with Jimmy. We can't be starting a war with the military," Aimee said.

"Need I remind you which of us it was who killed that cop?"

"He would have killed Travis. I had no choice."

One of the uniformed men took a step forward.

"I am not telling you again, put your damned hands up," Murphy said, pulling the hammer back on the pistol. The fact that neither man so much as flinched had him unnerved.

Again, neither man complied.

"Have it your way," he said as he fired a round into the larger man's chest.

The pistol was a forty-five caliber which packed a mean punch and would put most men on their backs. The shot caused the man to recoil, but he did not drop. And strangest of all, he did not bleed.

"What the fuck!"

"You missed," Jimmy said.

"How did you fucking miss him?"

"I did not miss Aimee. Didn't you see him stagger? Look at the hole in his chest," Murphy said, pointing at the large hole in the man's uniform shirt and a grotesque stain on the wall behind him.

The room filled with the laughter of a cackling old crone and I felt the creature below me stir. I had positioned myself in the furthest corner and did all I knew to do, simply watch the events unfold. A myriad of energies swirled about the room, some much darker than others. I could sense their growing anger, but most of all, I tasted their fear. And with that taste a part of me longed to embrace the darkness once more.

"Sit down, we are all going to have some tea," Mahneerah said with a wave of her hand.

With that Charles unpacked a small bag which held a teapot and a small leather pouch. He set out five small teacups on matching saucers and then put a pot of water into the fire to boil. Mahneerah reached into the pouch and put a pinch of fine powder and dried, black leaves into each cup.

"And for you, a little something special because you are so cute," she said, putting a pinch of something from inside her jacket into Jimmy's cup.

I could think of nothing to do in this situation, but I knew I had to do something, so I resorted to a tried and true parlor trick used to chase off visitors in the past. I swiped my arm across the table sending cups and saucers flying about the room. A chill ran up my spine when Mahneerah caught my eyes and a smirk creased her lips. The three fugitives bolted up from their chairs in a screech while Mahneerah sat unfazed.

"What in the hell was that?" Jimmy said. "Is this place haunted? Was that a ghost? I told you there were ghosts." The man's hands were trembling, and I half expected him to soil his trousers.

"That was no ghost I assure you," Mahneerah said.

"What kind of games are you playing?" Murphy said.

"I am not the one playing games," she said, again shooting an evil smirk in my direction. "It was merely a harmless wind. Please sit back down so we can enjoy some tea."

Trembling, they took their seats as Charles went about the task of resetting the table. Mahneerah put a tin of butter cookies on the table as well as a small coffee cake on a platter. Confusion spread across their faces as they watched this ritual. Again, their cups were filled with tea leaves from her pouch and the kettle filled with boiling water was pulled from the fire. Charles began filling the cups but missed the tiny vessels, spilling scalding water across the table with each attempt.

Mahneerah laughed. "I would forget my own head if it was not attached to this gorgeous body," she said and took two small black marbles from a pouch tied to her belt.

"What the hell?" Murphy gasped as the two shriveled raisins slowly regained their shape into two glistening eyeballs.

They made an awkward series of motions and I knew they were blinking even though there were no eyelids. The eyes followed Charles' movements around the room as he filled each cup up to the brim with boiling water.

"This is some creepy shit. I want to leave, now. Right now," Aimee said, getting up from the table.

"You may not leave until we have all had our tea," Mahneerah's voice took on a stern, maternal quality.

"Lady, I don't know who in the fuck you think you are, but this ends right here, right now," Murphy said, raised his pistol and fired.

The gun exploded in his hand, blowing two of his fingers clean off and breaking the others. He screamed out in pain, anger, and frustration. He glared over at the old woman and the look in her eyes terrified him. Aimee stood in shock for several moments trying to digest what had just happened before turning for the door.

Mahneerah flicked her wrist and the uniformed coast guard strode over and before she could react, he put a firm hand on her shoulder. Aimee struggled at first but a glance from Murphy cradling his mangled hand and she capitulated. Jimmy just stared on, mouth agape with disbelief.

Why did she need them all to drink this tea? I knew enough about this ritual to know that she had already chosen Jimmy, a move that had me baffled as I sensed his aura was not blackened like the others. I considered that I might be misreading him as he was sitting between Murphy and Aimee and they were both a swirling mass of exquisite darkness.

Shadowman, Shadowman,
A gleaming silver knife.
Shadowman, Shadowman,
Time to take your own life.

I could feel the situation, the entire situation slipping away from me. Was it Wenonah's voice chiming in my head, Mahneerah's, or was my very own mind toying with me? I grabbed the knife from the table and let it hover in mid-air for several moments, watching the confusion and dread spread across their faces which resulted in their spewing delicious fear all around me. I put the blade against my radial artery and sliced down with all my might. Seemingly from nowhere red, hot blood spewed across the room and into the faces staring aghast at the events unfolding before them.

There were two things I did not count on in my haphazard plan. I became coated in my own blood as well which made me quite visible to the gallery and I had fortuitously committed suicide. The last thing I saw as I slipped from consciousness was Mahneerah's sneer.

~ ~ ~

I had no recollection of time but when I resurrected from the dead the scene before me was pretty much the same as when I left this world. Although, the energies in the room had become darker and more violent. I shook the cobwebs from my brain and eavesdropped on their conversation while playing dead.

"Welcome back to the living Elijah," Mahneerah said without ever glancing in my direction.

"Okay, we waited for him to come back just as you said he would, now when are you going to explain all of this?" Murphy said.

"Explain all of this? Does it really need an explanation?" she said.

"You bet your ass it does. I had better start getting some answers pronto," Murphy demanded, knowing full well he was way out of his league without any leverage.

"Sister be a dear and join us please," Mahneerah said.

Charles climbed down the cellar ladder only to return several minutes later carrying Wenonah cradled in his arms. Her long, spindly arms hung loosely down toward the floor. The uninvited guests gasped at the sight of her horrific appearance. I gasped at how much less of a beast she was. She was quickly on her way to reverting to the impish little demon I knew and loathed.

Charles pulled up an extra chair to the table and set Wenonah down. She looked across the room with an almost sad expression painted on her leathery face. The beast's nose twitched back and forth as drool dripped from the sides of her drooping maw.

"Soon enough, dear sister. Soon enough."

Aimee and Murphy scooted away from Wenonah and rose to their feet in a panic.

"What the fuck is that thing?" Aimee said.

Obviously offended, Wenonah did something I did not think she was capable of. In a lightning move she reached over and sunk her teeth deep into the woman's side. Blood spewed forth and Aimee screamed.

Murphy cried out, grabbed the gun from Aimee's waistband with his undamaged hand and swung the gun around. Without hesitation he fired three rounds point blank into Wenonah. An ear shattering scream resounded off the walls followed by raucous, maniacal laughter. Wenonah spit the bullets out and tossed them onto the table. The gun made a resonating thud as it fell from the dumbfounded man's hand and hit the wooden floor.

In what I can only describe as a tone of boredom, Mahneerah uttered a single word. "Jimmy."

I saw he had the same distant, blank stare as the men in uniform possessed. It was the same expression worn by Wenonah's braves as well. His teacup was lying on its side and empty. Without hesitation he reached down and retrieved the pistol from the floor, put it to the man's head and cocked the hammer back. Murphy was given just enough time to realize what was happening. Enough time for anger to set in and enough time for fear to swallow him whole before the bullet entered his brain.

Aimee screamed, "Jimmy, what in the fuck are you doing?"

She too had just enough time for the fear to set in before her brother turned and the next bullet he fired entered her brain. I was immediately bombarded by the flux of dark energy spewing about the room. I felt myself absorbing it and quickly returning to my corporeal self.

I knew I only had one chance to right all that was going wrong. I sensed the man who lay dying was filled with light energy. I grabbed one of my tomahawks from the wall and charged across the room with reckless abandon. Marie's voice invaded my thoughts, and I stopped dead in my tracks.

Elijah, sweet, sweet Elijah,
The light you see does not gleam.
Elijah, sweet, sweet Elijah,
It is nothing but another scheme.

Was this another of Wenonah's tricks? Mahneerah's? I launched myself into Charles who had been blocking the way while Jimmy looked on in confusion. The man on the floor was gasping and choking for air and each breath sounded like his last. With no more hesitation I raised my tomahawk high above him and drove it home into his heart.

For a moment there was nothing. He simply died from his heart being pierced. And then I felt a growing surge of blackness swirling around me. I glanced at Mahneerah who was smiling a smile a satisfaction. It was then I noticed the teacup beside the dead man and realized I had made a fatal error in judgement.

Shadowman, Shadowman
There can be but just one.
Shadowman, Shadowman,
Your gift has been undone.

I felt another swirl of dark energy in the room, more horrifying than the last. It gnawed and chewed its way up my legs, tightened like a belt around my waist and clawed up my shoulders.

"Jimmy," I heard Mahneerah say.

I broke my gaze from the dead man to Jimmy who had now trained his weapon on me. I saw the muzzle flash and smelled the acrid smoke as my skull splintered into tiny shards. A million needles were jabbing at my brain. And then all went dark.

~ ~ ~

Our small entourage left the shack with Wenonah in the lead, me by her left side and Jimmy on her right. Travis, the dead man, trailed a few steps behind us asking questions a mile a minute. I wanted to scream at him to just shut up for a moment, but my voice had been stifled. As with the receding tide I felt little pieces of what were once me slip away into oblivion. My worst nightmare had come to fruition.

Events from my life flashed before me like pages being torn from a book. The loose sheets of parchment burst into flames and were gone forever. With each passing page I felt more of me disappear. I heard Wenonah's childish giggle when the pages also revealed it was her pulling at my puppet strings all along. Elisha, the monkey man in the trees, even Marie, they were all her guiding me here to this very moment, to this very fate. The hellishness of it all was the realization that my entire existence had been all for naught. I was but a useless speck of dust to be blown about in the wind without a second thought.

But none of those pages contained my one true friend in life so there had to have been some meaning. For one very brief moment I was allowed a single glimpse at poor Robert Marigold spending his miserable subsistence on the bottom of the Maumee River and then that memory was ripped away with the rest of them.

I felt my energy surging from my soul into the wicked beast's. Her eyes were rolled back in her head in pure rapture. She let me have one final glimpse of my twisted reality. She revealed that I was merely a vessel to collect that what she must feed upon. And once that vessel of pure chaos was filled, it was time for it to be emptied.

Shadowman, Shadowman,
Your world will never be free.
Shadowman, Shadowman,
Every soul belongs to me!

The voice echoing throughout my body was not that of a spry little girl, nor that of an arthritic old crone. No, this malevolent voice was pure unadulterated evil through and through. And for humanity, I wept.

www.ingramcontent.com/pod-product-compliance
Lightning Source LLC
Chambersburg PA
CBHW051518250626
47156CB00001B/135
9781735463605